THEIR TATTERED TRUTHS

THEIR TATTERED TRUTHS

TANGLED AND TRUE
DUOLOGY: BOOK 2

BRIELLA BREZZO

Developmental editing by Scribbling Crow, Ink, LLC
Copy editing by Ash Tree Editing

Book cover art & design by Julia Rohwedder
www.LunaryxDesign.com

ISBN 979-8-9939371-3-7 (paperback)

Published by Briella Brezzo
United States

First Edition 2026

Content Warnings

The *Tangled and True* duology references and portrays multiple forms of ongoing physical and emotional abuse, manipulation, and loss of personal agency. While no sexual violence occurs on page, rape is mentioned, threatened, and imagined.

Both books explore fantasy drug use and addiction. They include blood, violence, offensive/sexual language, and open-door spice.

In a gentle way, you can shake the world.

Mahatma Gandhi

Twenty-one years ago, the fae Queen Esyllt discovered her young son, Taran, was a powerful willbender, capable of compelling any who heard his words. Her attempt to kill him was foiled by her husband, who exiled her. Taran inherited the throne, but his father ruled in his stead, ending the millennia of war with humanity.

In the present, Eloise Detura arrived at the Arandur Academy, following her father into the Order of Incanters. She was partnered with Reid Vero, who introduced her to his best friend, Caeo Evers.

The two fell hard for one another, but whenever they were apart, they forgot each other entirely. With Reid's help, they worked around it, until Caeo's mother, the exiled Queen Esyllt, stole him away. She'd had her husband assassinated and was returning to reclaim her throne and reignite the war. She's the one who cursed Ellie and Caeo.

Taran kidnapped Ellie, planning to stop his mother and hoping Ellie would help Caeo see the truth. They were joined by his spy, Emlyn, and Reid, who were falling into a romance of their own.

Ellie latched onto Taran as the truth unraveled her world. Humans were once fae who betrayed the Land, the spirit the fae worship. The wars were the fae's attempt to restore the human realm, and incanting was humanity forcing magic out of the Land against Her wishes.

As Ellie fell for Taran, Caeo discovered he was a fae prince, engaged to the southern realm's Princess Owena. With her gift for curses, she broke Caeo's curse and restored his memories.

Reid rescued Caeo as Taran's plan to overthrow his mother failed, due to his fear of his own power. Ellie was forced to incant to save him and Emlyn, but Emlyn was badly wounded. Caeo insisted on bringing Owena with him as he and Reid escaped.

When the group reunited, Ellie finally remembered Caeo. Despite being overwhelmed by her guilt, there was no time for Owena to break her curse. The queen's soldiers were coming…

Prologue

Grace

My daughter is missing.

The news arrived days after it happened. A messenger, at our door. He rushed past the footman, barging into our sitting room. He spoke only to my husband. His superior.

The only one who matters.

I stood aside, my heart sinking deeper with every word, until I drowned in the silence that followed.

Hiram left immediately, sending word to every Order outpost. With no activity at the border in decades, he could afford to send his men looking for her. Before departing for the Academy, he pulled me into a warm embrace, swearing he'd find her. I pressed against him, hoping his solid presence would soothe my doubts.

It didn't.

How long has it been? Two weeks? Three? A spiraling tension twists tighter as the days drift past, blending together as I wait. For news, for his return. For her to show up at our door.

They said she'd run off, abandoning her studies for love. If that were true, then nothing would make me happier. She had never wanted her father's life, but I know my daughter; she hadn't yet found it in her to say no, and a few months at the Academy wouldn't have changed that.

And she would have written. She never wanted me to fret.

Had that been what happened, I would have reined Hiram in. Told him to leave her be, to allow her to live the life she wanted. Not to scour the countryside so he can lecture her about abandoning her responsibilities.

But it's not, so I don't, even though my throat constricts at what he'll say when he finds her.

If he finds her.

I'm being unfair. I saw it in his face—his love, his fear, fighting against his restraint. He's just as worried about her safety as I am. Perhaps part of him even blames himself. He only ever wanted what was best for her, and in his quietest moments, I know he's questioned what that was. We both did.

Now I stand on our balcony, numb to the sunlight hitting my skin and the serene twittering of songbirds. Ellie's easel sits to my left, awaiting her return. This was her favorite spot, overlooking the city's gardens. She never cared to paint the flowers, only the people strolling by.

Always longing for connection—the way she looked at those she drew, her eyes reaching for them. If I had fought for more freedom for her, maybe she would still be with us.

The door clicks behind me. A familiar hand, heavy and warm, wraps around my waist.

I turn to meet Hiram's gray eyes. For the first time since incanting drained away their ocean blue, they suit him. Worn and troubled.

"Any word?" I ask after he kisses my cheek.

"No," he sighs. "Her professors confirmed she attended her classes before the weekend. She could have disappeared at any point during the two-day break."

"Her roommates didn't notice her missing?"

"From what they said, they'd grown accustomed to her not being around. Always with that boy."

Who's also gone. All the evidence points to the same thing, but I don't believe it.

My chest tightens. "Is there anything else that could have happened? Any enemies you have, who might be using her for revenge?"

Hiram exhales. "None I can think of."

I glance back at the gardens, so peaceful and full of life. *Where could you be, Ellie?*

The door behind us flings open with a crash. A messenger, wearing the grays and violets of the Order, leans against its frame, panting. "News, sir."

Hiram stiffens, his fingers clenching against my waist. "Have they found her?"

The man shakes his head. "No, sir. It's the fae. They've crossed the border."

The world shifts, the pounding of my pulse the only thing anchoring me between the old and the new.

No. Not now.

My heart sinks, dragging with it all hope of finding my daughter. Hiram will recall the Order. He'll disappear again, to the border. Leaving me here—alone.

In a single breath, the search for Ellie has ended.

What does a mother's heart matter in the face of war?

Part 1

Tattered

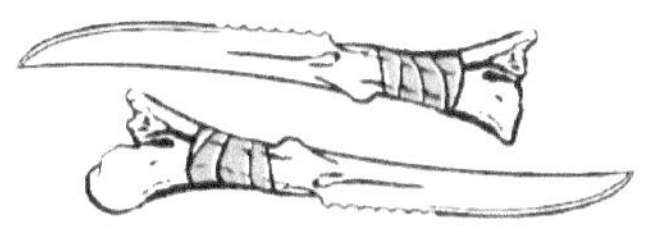

Chapter 1

Emlyn

I wake up in a poorly lit tent, still alive. Yay.

Unfortunately, in our attempt to kill Taran's mom and get his throne back, everything that could've gone wrong *did* go wrong; the most important of which being that I TOOK AN ARROW THROUGH MY FUCKING SHOULDER.

One moment, I was running away from the queen and her soldiers, arrows trained on us. The next, something pounded into me harder than anything's ever pounded into me before, followed by excruciating, mind-wiping pain as a bloody, broken arrowhead protruded from my chest.

I should've died on the walk back.

I know the exact moment it was supposed to happen. Everything began fading at the edges, my body growing cold and numb... but Taran fucking bent me, so instead of turning into a happy little wisp, every part of me erupted in flames of agony, burning everything to continue functioning when there was absolutely nothing left. The inferno lasted until I shattered and blacked out, my mind returning just in time for Taran to yank the arrow from my shoulder, and I immediately passed out again.

So here I am, waking up to Ellie—fucking Ellie—wrapping bandages around the right side of my chest and shoulder like she's punishing me for publicly cuckolding her father. Sure, I'd have no doubt died two more times if she hadn't abandoned Taran's stupid plan, but she had to save my life in the most painful way possible, outside of his willbending. She's the last person I want anywhere near me, other than Taran. Or his mother.

But of course, all I can manage to express my dissatisfaction is a groan that tears through me. *Where's Reid?*

"You need to relax, Emlyn. You've lost a lot of blood, but the shepherds' healer was here. She's optimistic you'll recover."

That must be why my mouth tastes like blood and dirt. The Land's medicines are great, but famously disgusting.

"Then why are you torturing me instead of her?" That was too many syllables. My body tenses with the effort, sweat dripping down my face. Fucking Taran. No way am I going along with his stupid plans ever again.

"They're trying to get out of here as soon as possible," Ellie says, her brown eyes darting to and fro. "They're worried the queen... or her soldiers... will be here soon."

Fuck.

The tent flap swings aside. Reid.

His face is stricken with worry, but the coil in my chest unwinds slightly. It tightens again as he stares at me, unmoving, every heartbeat stretching for an eternity. All my glamours have undoubtedly fallen, so he's seeing me—the real me, imperfections and all—for the first time.

Or maybe I'm just white as fresh snow from all the blood loss.

But then he scrambles beside me, kissing my cheek as he takes my left hand. The slight shift sends knives ripping through my right shoulder.

"What happened?" he asks.

"I was shot."

A hint of laughter breaks through his anxious expression. "Obviously. How?"

"With an arrow," I say through gritted teeth. Even on the verge of death, I can't resist needling him. It's a comfort to see the relief it gives him, his face softening.

"The plan failed," Ellie says. "I had to incant to get us out alive."

I have so many things I could say in response to that, but even thinking them reignites the burning stabs in my shoulder. *How the fuck am I supposed to relax?*

"Is there anything we can give you for the pain?" Reid asks.

"The healer gave me this." Ellie lifts a small clay jar from behind her. "Milk of… something."

"You've had that the whole fucking time?" My outburst costs me, and my jaw clenches as spasms ricochet through my neck. "What is wrong with you?"

"I didn't know how much to give you!"

"Dip your pinky in to the first knuckle," I say, grimacing.

Ellie pulls the stopper out and moves her finger toward it.

"Not you!" I instinctively try to smack her hand away, and my shoulder screams at the motion. So do I. But at least it still works. Small victories.

She quickly hands the jar to Reid, who dips his finger in then brings it to my mouth. I shamelessly suck it like a starving babe on its mother's teat.

A wave rolls over me, washing away the tension in my muscles, leaving me a puddle on the ground and dulling the pain, but only slightly. Normally, I'd be looping around the moon, but I've never taken it under this much duress before. Must be obliterating my high.

"Now… you suck… your finger." The words form like my mouth's full of jelly.

Reid's face goes stupid confused. "What? Why?"

"To share my pain." It has to go somewhere—balance in everything.

His eyes widen. "You should've told me that before."

"Would it've stopped you?" My heart skips a beat, and for a moment, I worry it won't start up again. Despite orbiting each other for months, we've only officially been together for a few days. The best of my life—that almost ended tonight.

A tender resolve warms Reid's expression. "No."

He sticks his finger in his mouth.

He grimaces as my agony recedes, coursing into him. It's not completely gone, but even half as much pain is bliss in comparison. I exhale, closing my eyes as my head sinks into the furry pillow I can finally feel beneath it.

A moment later, Reid settles next to me, the weight of his body warming my side as his fingers weave through my sweaty hair. There's a rustle of movement, followed by the sound of someone passing through the tent flap.

No more Ellie. Good. But that reminds me...

"I kissed Ellie," I mumble, and Reid's fingers still. "It was disgusting. I didn't want to, but there were guards—"

"Shhh." He renews his caresses. "You're not dying. You don't need to confess your sins."

"I just... wanted you to know." I open my eyes to meet his. "I felt bad."

"Don't worry about it. I'll just kiss Taran to make things even."

I let out a weak laugh, because that wouldn't tip the scales in the slightest, and Reid grunts as pain sears through me.

"Ancients, that hurts. No more jokes." He gently kisses my forehead, then continues his soft caresses until I drift away.

A few heartbeats later, he's patting my face.

I groan. *Just let me sleep.*

"We gotta get you ready to move." Reid's brow crinkles like furry little caterpillars, coming together for a kiss. Kind of creepy, really. They better not crawl on me.

Oh hey, there's the loopies. Hello, loopies.

"If you wanted me to move, you shouldn't have given me the milk." I barely form the words properly. "But don't forget it—I won't be able to move without it."

"That doesn't make any sense." Ellie's voice, though I can only see her shadow flickering against the leather tent. Fuck her.

"It would if you'd ever been impaled by an arrow."

"Can you sit up?" Reid asks.

"I'm giving you the finger right now." My hand may have flopped to the side; it's impossible for me to know.

"How are we supposed to be moving him?" Reid glances to where Ellie must be. My land-sense has gone all dizzy.

"Taran's getting a horse ready," she says.

"Fuck, I can't ride a horse right now." I think that was me. The loopies have left me a little unsure.

"I think the idea is to lay you across its back, and Reid and I will make sure you don't fall off."

Ancients, was killing me once not enough for Taran?

"We need to get you a coat or something, so you don't freeze," Ellie continues. "Maybe if you can sit him up, I can get his right arm in first?"

"No—Ancients, no." *Is she a moron?* Maybe she and Taran deserve each other. "Left arm, then drape it over the rest of me. And blankets. Lots of blankets."

Reid sidles closer. "I'm gonna sit you up now."

"Don't let her touch me."

"I heard that."

Of course she did. I wasn't trying to be quiet.

Reid scoots his arm under me and FUCK THAT HURTS. By his agonized grunt, he knows it, too. But I'm sitting upright now, my torso sagging like a dead weight against his chest, and Ellie's shoving my left arm into a coat sleeve. She awkwardly slides the rest of it between Reid and me, eliciting stilted gasps and groans from us both. As she tucks my right arm inside, my head droops down, to where more red's seeping through the bandage on my shoulder.

The last of my loopies slip away. "Just leave me here."

"We can't." The tent flap swishes as Taran's voice pours ice down my spine. "If we leave you, they'll kill you."

I can't bring myself to look at him. Because I physically can't lift my head, but also, I don't want to.

"At least they'll let me stay dead," I mutter.

"What's that supposed to mean?" Reid asks.

"I can't let you die, Emlyn," Taran says, his voice tight. "Not when this is all my fault."

"Then maybe you should bend people sooner next time."

Nobody says anything, and I'm still looking at my chest, so I can't see shit. I close my eyes. I just wanna go back to sleep.

"You'll be alright." Reid shifts from behind me, his breath tickling my face.

The hardest thing about loving a mortal is how easily they lie.

"Love?" His fingers press into me, his voice surprised.

Did I say that out loud?

"Yes, you did."

Fucking milk. This is not how I imagined telling him.

I strain, forcing my head to turn to his face. The movement drives a spike through me, its edges dulled by the milk. Reid grimaces as he feels it, too.

Dread floods my veins, replacing all the blood I've lost. He'll suffer just as much as I will.

"Don't let him bend me again," I whisper. "If this kills me, let me die."

Reid's eyes, a rich brown of the earth, search mine. His expression's unreadable—his lip twitches, but then he nods.

"Ellie, bring those blankets to the horse, then hold the tent open for us," Taran says. There's some rustling as he kneels next to my bad side. "Get one arm under his knee and the other around his back." He and Reid get into position, and my head falls to Reid's shoulder.

They stand, cradling me between them, then shuffle out of the tent. The cold has my teeth chattering after they lower my feet to the ground, and Reid hugs me upright while Taran adjusts the blankets on the horse's back.

And hey, there's Princess Owena! It's been a few years, but hers is a face that's impossible to forget. Her body, too, though it's currently out of sight, wrapped up in an oversized fur coat. She's not looking in our direction, which is probably a good thing; it's not a good time for her to recognize me. Her attention's focused on a dejected-looking Caeo, apparently the only member of our party whose skin hasn't been graced by my lips.

If I weren't half-conscious and beset with pain at every movement, I'd be laughing my ass off.

Now I'm being lifted onto the horse, mostly by Taran, with Reid helping guide my body. *FUCK.* Reid's grip tightens with every agonized stab. And someone's shoving blankets in the gaps between me and the horse because they've somehow convinced themselves that'll make this better.

"He's bleeding again," Ellie says. Hooray.

"Stop bleeding." Taran's voice echoes through what little blood I have left. I'm gonna murder him once I'm able to move.

"Did you just bend him?" Reid demands.

"Do you want him to live or not?"

"It doesn't matter what I want, he doesn't want you bending him!"

My hero.

At least I'm not moving while they argue. I'm sure once the horse starts walking, the fires of pain will blaze anew. But right now, I'm losing focus on their words, my eyelids are sinking shut, and it doesn't seem worth it to keep them open. I drift away, hoping that if anyone catches up with us, they at least kill me in my sleep.

Chapter 2

Ellie

The horse snorts, her breath a brush of warmth against the deathly chill of the night.

"You'll need to guide her toward the valley between those hills over there," Taran says, his voice strained as he points into the darkness. With the moon obscured by clouds, I can barely see the ground ten feet in front of me. The only reason I know there are hills ahead is because of the absence of stars in that section of sky.

I try to keep the nerves out of my voice. "I thought you were leading us." He knows my eyes aren't as good as his fae ones, and Emlyn's in bad enough shape as it is… I can't bear the thought of making things worse by stumbling blindly in the dark.

"I need to cover our tracks." He doesn't rest his hand on my shoulder like he would've yesterday; I shouldn't be making things about me right now, but it stings. Is he retreating into himself because I incanted? Or maybe it's shame, from his failure.

"Just go straight in that direction and don't look back. I'll return to take the lead soon." His hand shakes as he gives me the rope attached to the horse's bridle, then he disappears into the night.

He hasn't looked at me once.

My eyes meet Reid's, who's standing on the opposite side of the horse from me. His hands rest on Emlyn's back, steadying him.

"Are you ready?" I ask.

"Yeah, let's go."

I take a deep breath, then lead us blindly into the dark.

Only a few weeks ago, I wouldn't have had a problem with this. I'd have incanted a ball of fire and made it hover ten feet in front of me, guiding our way. Arandur's knickers, I could even have floated flames in twenty-foot increments between us and our destination, ensuring we stayed on course, puffing them out of existence one by one as we approached. But after seeing firsthand what happened to the Land when I incanted, the thought of ever doing it again fills me with dread from the pit of my stomach all the way up my throat.

Before we left, I wrapped my coat around the wool servant's dress I wore to the wedding, but the icy wind still bites through. We've been traveling through the darkness for at least a bell—uneventful, save for the occasional whiff of manure hitting my nose—and Taran still hasn't returned. Emlyn seems to be sleeping, but every so often Reid grunts, which I assume means the horse moved in a way that sent momentary pain through them.

The milk of... something... is unbelievable. A medicine that shares pain between people? I'll have to ask Taran about it when he returns.

That happens right as we reach the hills. I've only just realized my steps have slightly inclined when Taran's hand grabs the rope.

Not my hand.

"Not uphill," he says, his voice huffing with exertion.

I stop walking and try to make out his face in the dark. "Are you alright?"

"It's a significant effort to shape that much ground to hide our tracks." His emerald eyes, glowing faintly in the darkness, aren't looking at me. "I'll take the lead—you help Reid. I'll try to keep to a smooth path, but the terrain will be less even from here on out."

"Is anyone following us?"

"They've found the camp. Most are following Cadoc's people, which is unfortunate." He sighs, rubbing his neck.

His guilt likely feels similar to my own. It was his actions, his failure, that put the shepherds who harbored us at risk and got Emlyn hurt. I reach for his hand, but he flinches away the instant my skin brushes his.

"We need to hurry." He clicks his tongue at the horse and starts walking before there's a chance to respond. I catch up, my steps slowing once I rest my hand on Emlyn's back, steadying him as my thoughts swirl in a mix of heartache and annoyance.

None of this is right; my curse was supposed to be resolved by now. It would've been, if there'd been time for Owena to break it. The holes in my memory would've been filled, and I'd finally understand everything that's been going on.

Instead, Taran flinches at my every touch and tells me I can't look behind us, because that would trigger my curse and slow us down. I'm trying to accept that—he can't explain more without me forgetting what he said—but my frustration's coiling so tight I'm about to snap.

I have to put that aside. Keeping us moving is the best thing I can do right now, to protect him from his mother. My needs can wait.

"Can you tell me what happened?" Reid's voice breaks through my thoughts, his voice low.

"With Emlyn?"

"Yes, with Emlyn," he snaps. "What else would I be talking about?"

"Sorry, I was distracted—you don't need to get angry."

"You left, Ellie. You snuck away when I wasn't looking and almost ruined everything."

My fingers clench against Emlyn's back as heat rises to my face.

"I didn't ruin anything. Emlyn would've died if I hadn't been there."

Reid doesn't respond for a moment, and I can't make out his expression in the dark. Regret fills my chest, twisting like a knot. Even imagining what he's going through hurts too much.

The horse steps up, and Emlyn shifts with a wheezy groan. I adjust my hold on his side to steady him, then open my mouth to apologize.

"Just tell me what happened," Reid interrupts, minus the bite from before.

So I do. I tell him how Emlyn tried to get a shot at the queen, but the branch he was on cracked and she spotted him. How she bent us into falling multiple stories down, and I incanted the wind to cushion our landing. How the arrow hit him as we fled, and I created a wall of ice to block a volley from killing us all. I keep glancing Taran's way as I speak, but he gives no indication he's listening. He simply continues walking.

It must be that he's upset about my incanting. It hurt him so much, and he was so angry when Reid did it, even though that was also a matter of life-or-death. But he got past that. Maybe he needs some time to sort through everything?

When I finish recounting the details, I look back at Reid. He's tilted his head down, tracing his fingers along Emlyn's back.

"Thank you," he says, his voice thick. "Thank you for saving him."

"I'm sorry I didn't do more." While the idea sends my stomach churning, if I'd chosen to incant instead of simply reacting, I could've defeated the queen, saving the day. Same cost, but this would all be over.

I hesitantly move my hand to Reid's, gripping it tightly. He nods, then squeezes my fingers before pulling from my grasp.

For the first time, my thoughts drift past our current dilemma.

Wherever we're headed... will we be able to stay there? Or are we leaving Emlyn behind while we continue to flee? What will that mean for Reid?

"Taran?" I call, my voice catching on the wind. "Where are we going?"

"To Emlyn's mother. He'll be safe there."

He will. Not *we*. Not us.

My stomach sinks. Despite our recent quarrels, Reid's been a constant in my life for the past few months. Arguably my closest friend, which is depressing, given how disconnected we've been. I should've put in more effort. Perhaps then, we wouldn't have fought so much.

But it's too late now. I don't see him staying with us if we're leaving Emlyn behind. I wouldn't, if it were Taran.

"Reid..." *What words can I possibly say?* "I just want you to know—I appreciate everything you've done for me. I know it's been hard for you."

"Yeah?" He huffs a strained laugh. "Well, I hope everything works out for you. I certainly don't envy your position right now."

So much for being heartfelt. "You'd rather have Emlyn like this than be me?"

"Let's just say you should've listened to me. You'd understand if you looked behind us."

"Reid, stop. We don't have time for this," Taran says.

"Why? What's back there?" I was told Princess Owena could break my curse, but I don't remember what happened to her. Perhaps that's where she is?

Neither of them answers.

If that's how they're going to be...

I glance into the darkness behind us. The vague shapes of two people follow at the limits of my vision, shrouded in shadow.

"Is that Owena?" I ask. "Who's with her?"

"Ignore them. Keep your eyes ahead." Taran turns to look at me—finally. "Please." An emerald fire blazes in his irises.

I clamp down on my lower lip, then grumble, "Alright, I will."

And I do, despite the gnawing feeling in the back of my mind that something important's back there.

By the time we reach our destination, my body feels like it's made of lead, ready to sink into the ground. The sun has risen, and except for a couple brief breaks eating meager snacks from our packs, we walked through the entire night. A sharp pain's building behind my eyes, which I can barely keep open, the horse keeping me balanced as I trudge along beside it.

The home sits at the edge of a forest, built among a cluster of oaks, with warped wood and stone filling the gaps between the tree trunks. The lower level's larger than most of the fae homes I've seen, with a couple of rooms higher up, following the curves of thick branches. A handful of chickens and a goat wander nearby, without a fence in sight.

I let out a heavy exhale as Taran stops the horse a few feet from the door; a gnarly piece of wood covered in knots and whorls. It opens before he knocks, revealing a woman who I'd guess to be in her thirties if she were human, but that's meaningless for fae. Her sandy-blond hair matches Emlyn's, braids and all, and her face cinches with worry.

"Taran." She rests her hand on his face, then rushes past him, her eyes full of the terror only a mother can know.

"Emlyn?" Her voice quivers as she rests her hand on his back and stoops down to meet his eyes.

"Hi, Ma," he groans. I hadn't realized he'd woken up.

"What happened?" She looks between him and Taran.

Taran glances away. "I'll explain everything once we get him settled."

Emlyn's mother nods, squeezing her son's hand while tears glisten in her eyes. She lets go of him to prop the door open while Taran and Reid get him off the horse, and he howls in pain, sending Reid staggering to his knees—he'd given Emlyn that mysterious milk twice during the journey.

They all go inside, leaving me holding the horse's rope.

What am I supposed to do now?

I'm searching for something to tie it to when a hand lands on my shoulder.

It belongs to a fae woman, who, despite the shadows under her dark eyes, has to be the most stunning person I've ever seen. Unlike most fae, the sharp angles of her face blend into the soft elegance of full, rosy lips and gentle cheekbones, with her golden curls reflecting the early morning light as they trail down her back. She's swimming in a fur coat that's far too big, her fingers peeking out of the sleeves as she twists the rope from my grasp.

This must be Owena.

"I'll handle the horse," she says, her voice light but full of authority, like it'd never cross her mind that someone wouldn't agree with her. "You should go inside. I'll deal with your curse after we've rested."

"Um... thank you." I blink, searching her face, but there's nothing there besides a faint smile on her lips and eyes. She cocks her head toward the door, and I turn away, rubbing my temple as I drag myself into the home.

An overwhelming floral scent fills the irregularly shaped room, about the size of my dormitory's sitting room and bedrooms combined. Tree trunks break up the space like haphazardly placed columns, with planks spiraling around two of them, leading to holes in the wooden ceiling.

To my right is a kitchen, cluttered with clay pots, fresh fruit, and stacks of bowls. Shelves cover every inch of the walls, packed with cheese wheels, baskets of eggs, and assorted tools. My stomach tightens at all the food, but I hold myself back, forcing my gaze away.

Fur rugs cover the floor on the left, with mismatched pillows along the walls and a low wooden table sitting in front of the hearth. Shelves continue from the kitchen, broken up by colorful tapestries, while a simple loom and a basket of yarn rest against the far wall. Everything's so soft and inviting, my body sagging at the sight alone. The crisp morning air flows through open windows, lighting the room along with the dim glow of a pinkish-orange orb floating near the ceiling.

Taran descends one of the narrow staircases, his hand trailing along the trunk for balance. He pays me no mind, collapsing against a pillow and closing his eyes.

"Did Emlyn make it up alright?" I sit next to him, ignoring the call of the pillow as I rest my hand on his knee. I just want to melt into him and sleep.

He jerks away, eyes snapping open. Then he clears his throat, shifting his gaze from me to the floor. "Yes. Reid and Ceirios are getting him comfortable."

"What's wrong?" The words slip out, despite me wanting to give us a chance to rest. "Why won't you look at me? Why do you flinch whenever I touch you?"

"I don't mean to, I just..." He finally brings his eyes to mine, and the pain burning within them singes my heart.

But he's avoiding the question.

"Is it because I incanted? You have to realize we'd be dead if I hadn't."

"I know that," he says quickly. "*I'm* not angry with you. But I can't... I can't handle looking at you right now. I'm sorry."

What's that supposed to mean? If he's not angry with me... who is?

Taran pushes himself to his feet, then hesitates, looking around the room before his gaze lands on the door. His shoulders slump, and he brings his hands to his face, pressing his palms into his eyes.

Does he not want to go outside? What's stopping him from storming off like he always does?

I move in front of him, my voice wavering as I try to keep it calm. "You said everything would be figured out with my curse by now."

"I was wrong!" He drops his hands and looks at me, his face red and twisted. "Everything went wrong, and everything is worse now, because I failed. Because I can't do what I need to."

My frustration melts away. I reach for his hands, but he slinks out of my grasp, stumbling past me.

"Let me help you, Taran. We can still fix everything. We just need to think... to make a new plan."

He brushes me aside, staggering into the kitchen and burying his face in his hands against the counter.

"Just let me help you," I plead, rooted to the spot. "Please." I've already lost my family, the future I worked for my entire life—even *if* I can stomach crossing the border again, I can't go back to who I was. If I lose him, I won't have anything left.

When did I start tying everything to him?

Taran's voice comes out muffled by his hands. "You can't."

"I can if you'll let me. You don't have to carry everything alone."

The seconds pass, agonizingly slow, as he stews in place. I resist the urge to touch him again. If he needs space... a moment to himself... I need to give it to him.

He finally hauls himself up, rubbing his eyes. Not looking at me.

"I need to talk to Ceirios about getting some supplies. You should try to rest while we're here. We'll need to leave soon."

He goes back upstairs, leaving me alone as a numbness sinks through me. I force myself to stay calm, to think, but I only see three options: push, do as he asked, or demand Owena unravel my curse, hoping that will provide some answers.

But Owena warned that breaking the curse could break *me*, and I'm already beyond exhausted. I can't afford to cause any delays.

So I curl up against a wall pillow, closing my eyes and praying I'll wake with enough clarity to fix things.

Chapter 3

I squint against the rising sun as the endless tweeting of some bird drives a chisel into my skull. Owena said we should try to sleep, but neither of us are welcome in Taran's presence—she's his enemy and I'd remind him of what an asshole he is—so we're outside freezing with the chickens while everyone else gets to cozy up in whoever's house this is.

We're sitting back-to-back in the grass, propping each other up. I appreciate her warmth, but I'm screaming beneath the skin, trying to pretend she's just a rock that's been heated by the sun while cutting down all thoughts of the forced fucking we narrowly escaped.

There might as well be a stack of bricks pressing on my chest, every breath a struggle.

The wool robe of my wedding clothes provides a bit of insulation, as well as my stupid coat that's draped over Owena and as much of me as possible. I have the sleeves, which aren't helpful against the cold, but running my fingers through its soft fur is somewhat soothing.

If someone had asked me yesterday if my life could get any worse, I would've said no. Yet here I am.

While I'm overjoyed that I didn't have to suffer through my

wedding, that horror would at least be over by now. I'd be curled up in a warm, cozy bed, instead of acting as a backrest for my bride-to-be on a frigid morning after spending the entire night trudging behind my traitorous brother while trying to ignore the fact that Ellie was *right there,* loving him instead of me, because taking the time to resolve *anything* would've risked me falling back into my mother's clutches and Ellie probably being executed.

More than anything, it's my anger that's destroying any chance of sleep. Not just at Taran, but Owena, for refusing to break Ellie's curse. And Ellie, for siding with them instead of fighting for me. I'm fraying at the edges, a single tug of thread away from unraveling completely, and I don't know how many more times I can stitch myself back together. All I have is the hope that Ellie will still love me when all this is over.

"Hello," a voice says. A woman's. Pleasant, but unsure. I blink my eyes toward its source.

A fae in a simple woolen dress stands above us, her blond hair braided back behind her. She has a kind face, but more importantly, she carries a tray full of food and a pitcher. I tap Owena's shoulder, nudging her awake, and she lets out a soft murmur.

"Please tell me that's for us." I've only one proper meal in the last three days, thanks to imprisonment and some fucked-up plan to make me starving for Owena's blood.

My stomach heaves. *Don't think about that.*

The woman laughs gently. "I was told you might be hungry." She sets the tray down, and Owena jerks behind me as she wakes up enough to notice the food.

"Thank you very much," Owena says, pulling the fur coat on properly as the woman backs away. I avert my eyes at the flash of her skin beneath—her barely existent wedding dress still haunts me when I close my eyes.

Focusing on the food, I attack the bowl of boiled eggs, my tongue desperate for a flavor that's not the phantom tang of blood. Owena smacks my hand away before I take them all.

"What happened to all the etiquette I taught you? You're supposed to allow me first pick." She shoves an egg into her mouth like a hypocrite.

"Maybe if you'd removed Ellie's curse like you were supposed to." The words fail to deliver their bite due to my mouthful of food.

"I fully intend to do so. At the opportune moment."

I pause in my chewing. *That's a particular way of putting it...*

"Opportune for whom?"

Owena swallows before meeting my eyes. "There's more at stake than just you and Ellie, Caeo. We have an opportunity to broker peace—real peace—between all three of our realms. I didn't break Ellie's curse last night because I needed time. To sort through all the variables. To develop a plan."

Something she conveniently left out while insisting it would just take too long. Once again, she's more focused on the long game than my feelings. At least I can trust her to be pragmatic.

"And do you have that plan?" I ask warily.

The corner of her mouth curls up. "The beginning of it, yes. And releasing Ellie from her curse is an important early step—one I hope to do tonight."

My heart ignites, lighting up my face, but Owena holds up her hand, warning me down.

"But I will require certain favors from you in exchange."

A spike of indignation crushes my elation, plunging me into the cold, hard ground. "Are you seriously trying to negotiate breaking Ellie's curse?"

"No, Caeo." She tugs at her fluffy sleeves, her fingernails flecked with dirt. "I said I would, and I will. But I need your help dealing with Taran, and as unpleasant as it may be, it will benefit you and Ellie as much as it does me.”

I force some of my anger out with an exhale from my nose. “What do you need me to do?”

“Simply support me and follow my suggestions against Taran for as long as we’re traveling together.”

“You’re not gonna be more specific?”

“No. I’m afraid you wouldn’t agree if I were.”

Wonderful.

But vague outlines of her intent form in my mind. “Will it make Taran angry?”

“Very much so.” Owena’s face stretches into a mischievous grin as she pops a grape into her mouth.

“Fine. But *this*”—I wrest the apple she just grabbed from her hand—“is mine, and you’re breaking the curse tonight. Agreed?”

“Agreed.”

She smiles like someone who just got exactly what they wanted, because she did. And for now, all I got was an apple. Would’ve been nice if she’d been this motivated about getting out of our wedding.

Though, I can’t say I’m not looking forward to making Taran miserable. I just have to pray to Fortune that Ellie will realize what an asshole he is once the curse is broken and she has a chance to actually think.

I close my eyes, my hunger dissipating as my stomach sinks through the earth.

That’s what’ll happen, right?

She loves me. There’s no way she’d actually pick him.

My eyelids shut even tighter. I force myself to breathe.

Please.

Owena’s arm wraps around my shoulders. “Trust me, Caeo. I’ll make sure Taran doesn’t come between you two.”

"But you can't change Ellie's feelings. If she wants him, and not me..." My voice cracks with the words, and I can't bring myself to finish the thought. Without her, I have nothing.

"She still loves you, Caeo. I could see it in her eyes."

There's a hint of sadness in Owena's voice. I lift my face, forcing myself to look at her. She's smiling, but it doesn't reach her dark eyes.

"What's wrong?" I wipe the moisture on my cheek, then swat at an overly bold chicken investigating our food.

She shrugs, then looks away. "I had simply grown accustomed to the idea that I'd be marrying you—I could envision us having a happy life together. I doubt I'll be so fortunate with my next betrothal."

Ooof. What am I supposed to say to that?

There was maybe a moment, before I remembered Ellie, that I thought of Owena that way. That we could possibly be happy together. But she's mostly just been a friend.

"I'm sorry, Owena," I say, uncertain if I should rest my hand on hers. I should—she already knows my feelings. "I'm sure there's someone out there better for you than me. Someone who'll make you happy. Really happy, not just making-the-best-of-things happy."

She sighs, then rubs her thumb against my palm. "That's not how being a princess works. I'll marry whomever I must for the sake of my realm. Marrying someone who loves me, who actually wants to be with me... It's a fantasy. I've known this my entire life."

"Right..." I mumble. Which reminds me... "How long has that been, by the way?"

Owena blinks. "Did you just ask how old I am?"

"No one ever told me."

"Your mother never taught you any manners, did she?"

"She tried, but I've always been a terrible student." Despite the joke, there's a pain in my throat. Not my normal lying-pain, but something deeper. Back then, the worst she did was beat me.

I take a gulp straight from the pitcher as Owena rolls her eyes and says, "I'm thirty-two."

I sputter, water dripping down my chin. "You're twelve years older than me? Shit. You almost became a cradle-robber."

She smacks my shoulder. "We're fae. When your lifespan measures in centuries, twelve years is nothing."

Wait... Centuries?

My stomach tightens. "Will I really live that long?"

Owena presses her lips together. "It's hard to say. As far as I know, there's never been a half mortal, half fae before. My guess is that if you're able to shape, then you've inherited the Land's gifts, which should include a long life. But you likely won't know for another decade or two, when you either show signs of mortal aging or not."

"I thought you couldn't shape," I say, recalling one of our earlier conversations.

"I can't shape *well*," she stresses. "But all fae can do it."

Is that the 'pampered princess' bit that Taran was whining about? But doing it poorly is still better than nothing. "Can you teach me?"

She's just opened her mouth when the door to the house swings open.

Taran. Of course he had to show up. All my anger comes crashing back with him.

He clears his throat as he approaches, his gaze locked on the ground to his left. "We should leave soon. Ceirios wants to get a healer to look at Emlyn, and we need to be gone by then."

If he's not even gonna look at me, he doesn't deserve a response.

He glances our way, briefly meeting my eyes. "Reid's staying here. If you wanted to say goodbye…"

Shit.

I could kick myself for not realizing this sooner. I've been so caught up in my own misery that I forgot about what Reid's going through entirely. In the few weeks we've been apart—the longest I've ever gone without seeing him—our lives have veered in opposite directions: I'm a half fae prince, and he's abandoned his studies to fall for a fae who was almost killed during Taran's idiotic plan.

I grab a hunk of cheese from the tray and push myself to my feet, wobbling slightly before gaining my balance. I have no idea how my body's still going, but there's no way I'm leaving without saying goodbye. Taran stares at me for a second before stomping back inside.

The dwelling, while stylistically similar to what I've grown accustomed to, is significantly homier than any part of my mother's castle. Someone actually has a life here, someone with a personality outside of hatred for everything. The bright tapestries that decorate the walls match the floor pillows only in their rainbow of color and joy. The fae woman from earlier rummages through the kitchen, shoving food into a couple packs on the counter.

I stop mid-stride, my heart skipping a beat as I spot Ellie near the fireplace. Her beautiful face, perfectly relaxed as she sleeps curled into a pillow.

Maybe Owena was right to wait… I doubt Ellie could rest at all if she remembered everything. As irritated as I am, none of this is Ellie's fault.

It's Taran's.

My anger returns, sharpening into an arrow, nocked and ready to plunge into Taran as I turn back to him. He glances at me from the bottom of a simple staircase that curves around a tree trunk near the center of the room.

"They're up here," he says, then averts his eyes again.

Lucky for him, he doesn't look at Ellie, or I'd punch him in the face. Instead, I ram my shoulder into him as I pass, climbing up the narrow steps to the second story.

I enter through the floor of a small room that's almost like being inside a wooden egg wrapped diagonally around a massive tree branch, except the floor is level. A few round windows let in some sunlight, and despite most of its space being taken up by a bed— basically a mattress on the floor—what I assume is a small wardrobe, and a bedside table, it feels cozy instead of cramped. Emlyn's tucked under a mass of knitted blankets, while Reid sits against the wall nearby looking deader than I've ever seen him. His eyes light up when he glances my way.

"Hey, man," he mumbles.

I scooch past the bed to sit on the floor next to him. Emlyn looks asleep, but his eyelids twitch occasionally along with the random grimace. He's a lot paler than I remember, his forehead glistening with sweat.

"How's he doing?" I nod to Emlyn before meeting Reid's eyes.

"In and out of sleep. I think the fever's coming on. His mom's just waiting for the rest of you to leave before getting the healer from the nearby village."

That must be the fae woman downstairs. "So you're already moving into his mom's house? That's pretty fast, man."

He smirks and elbows my arm. "Shut up." But his smile fades as his gaze lands on Emlyn.

"And how are you doing?" I ask.

Reid exhales through his nose. "To be honest? Not great. From the day we found out about your curse, my life has been getting progressively worse. Except for Emlyn. And now..." His voice splinters, shards of his grief hurtling into me.

I pat my hand against his knee. "I'm sorry. This is all my fault, isn't it?"

Reid sniffs, then rubs his eye with his fist. "It's not. It's your mother's. But if it weren't for all of that, I wouldn't even know him, so I can't really be mad. I just…" He takes a deep breath before meeting my eyes. "I'm glad to be staying behind. Not just for Emlyn, but so I don't have to deal with any of that shit anymore."

I huff a harsh laugh. "Yeah, that's all on me now." It never should've been on Reid to begin with. I owe him more than I could ever possibly repay.

"I'm sorry I couldn't stop it, Cay. I tried, I really did. I think she was flailing, just grasping for anything—"

I raise my hand, cutting him off. "I don't want to talk about it. But I don't blame you."

"Not to interrupt such… heartfelt… conversation…" The blankets shift as Emlyn groans through gritted teeth. "But I'm in a lot of pain right now."

Reid sits up straight. "Right, sorry." He grabs a small clay jar from the bedside table and pulls the cork stopper out. He dips his pinky finger into the milky liquid up to the first knuckle, then leans forward to stick it in Emlyn's mouth.

All the tension in Emlyn's body unravels before my eyes, like he hit multiple puffs of red speckled long leaf all at once. My body twitches, aching for such relief.

Reid sets the jar on the floor between us, then sticks his finger into his own mouth. He shudders as his body stiffens, his face tightening. "Ancients."

Emlyn breathes out a deep sigh while I pick up the jar, examining it. "What is this stuff?"

"Milk of midnight star," he says, his voice droopy. "It's a special flower. Gives some cozy loopies on its own, but can share your pain with someone else if they're willing." His eyes go all lovey as they swim over to Reid.

"Can I try some?"

Reid gapes at me. "Fuck, Cay. I thought I wouldn't have to deal with your shit anymore."

Overreacting much? "What? You don't know what I've been through."

"Then maybe you should talk about it instead of getting high and ignoring everything."

Emlyn's words come out slurred. "You'll only want to put the teeniest bit on your finger, or else you won't be able to move. The cost of the loopies."

"Ancients' tilted toadstools, don't enable him!" Reid glares at Emlyn, who's too busy mouthing a 'b' and an 'l' shape over and over to notice, hardly making a sound. Balance, maybe?

I quickly dip the very tip of my pinky into the milk and stick it in my mouth.

The jar almost falls as everything horrible dissolves into nothing. "Fuck, that was fast." My hands fumble as I lower it to the ground, somehow not spilling it. I slouch against the wall behind me, staring at the ceiling.

"You should try this, Reid. It's like... I'm a cloud... sinking into the ocean..."

"Clouds float, stupid."

"Do they? What's fog, if not a sinking cloud?"

"But fog's heavy," Emlyn says. "I'm not heavy. Except I can't lift my hand... so maybe I'm fog? But fog doesn't have hands, either."

Reid sighs. "Can you walk, Cay? I think it's time for you to go."

I swing my head to look down at my body. My fingers wiggle, and I twirl my feet at the ankles. They might be a little slow, but that's probably fine.

"I think so."

Reid pats my shoulder. "Then I love you, I'll miss you, but get out of here."

"Can I take this with me?" I pick up the milk jar.

His face hardens. "You did not just ask if you could take the pain medicine away from the person who almost died."

"Should've died," Emlyn interjects, his voice still garbled. "Let's not diminish my suffering."

"Um... I did?" *I think I did. Is that bad?*

Reid brings his palm to his face, covering his eyes. "You have a serious problem, man."

Emlyn's gaze slowly focuses on me. "You can have it... if you kiss me."

Reid drops his hand as my head jerks back, hitting the wall. We both blurt out, "What?"

Emlyn grimaces as his shoulders barely twitch in what must be a shrug. "We can get more from the healer, and he's the only one I'm missing."

What does that mean? I feel like I should be able to figure it out, but my thoughts are like mud.

"What are you...?" Realization dawns on Reid's face, so at least someone knows what's happening. "Have you kissed Taran and Owena?"

"Uh... my lips have touched both of their bodies."

"What the fuck does that mean?"

As slow as my brain's moving right now, it's obvious it's time for me to go. I force myself to my knees and squeeze Reid's shoulder. "Best of luck, man. I'll see you around."

After a second's hesitation, I lean over and plant a kiss on Emlyn's soft lips. He slips me some tongue before I pull back.

I guess I've kissed a man now. I can see the appeal.

"Oh, fuck you." Reid grabs my robe and shoves me away. "Get out of here."

I snatch the jar of milk and stumble out of the room.

Chapter 4

Taran

The joyful rainbow of Ceirios's home mocks me; a cruel reminder of better days. Emlyn always hated his mother's taste, but as a child, I assumed it was an attempt to brighten my life. Until I visited her here and realized that's just who she is.

Children often think the world revolves around them. I wish it didn't.

She sets a cup of tea on the wooden table as she sits beside me, swirls of lavender wafting into the air, pulling me back to those days. She was my governess, practically my mother after mine was exiled.

The aroma stirs memories of Ellie, too. How it filled my every breath when we kissed.

I glance at her, sleeping peacefully near the hearth. A foreign rage flares within me, shoving my own feelings aside as it tries to burst free.

My nails scrape the table as my fingers curl into fists. The scent has been ruined for me, just like I've ruined everything.

Ceirios rests her hand on mine. "It's time you told me what happened."

I squeeze my eyes shut and pull away—I don't deserve her sympathy—but she grips me tightly.

"Emlyn may be my blood, but I raised you as my own." She presses her other hand against my cheek, turning my face to hers as my eyelids open. "You can tell me." Love I don't deserve pours out of her pale blue eyes. This could be the moment I lose it for good.

"It's my fault." My words choke on their way out. "If I had been willing to bend from the start, nobody would have been in any danger. I could have taken my throne, and my mother... I..."

What would I have done? Killed her?

She's barely been a mother to me. She tried to kill me; she had my father killed. But my chest fractures at the thought of ending her. I've never used willbending to murder someone, not even by accident. My father and Ceirios made sure of it, always sequestering me at the first glimpse of a tantrum.

They were right to. They knew what my mother was like, and I'm her son.

I swallow. "I don't want to be like her."

"You'll never be like her, Taran." Ceirios wrests my trembling hands apart, holding them tight. "You wouldn't struggle like this if that were a possibility."

She can say that because she doesn't know. Isolation worked back then, but I can't always do that now. People need me to be present. To stand up. Rule. She hasn't seen how easily I plummet in a rage, in desperation. How my principles unravel in a panic.

"I bent Emlyn," I whisper, unable to meet her eyes. "He lost too much blood—he would have died. But I forced him to live. It hurt him so much."

"And I forgive you." Ceirios's voice is soft as she squeezes my fingers. "I would've lost my son if you hadn't. He'll forgive you, too, eventually. You need to forgive yourself."

I can't; I don't deserve it. But she'll never see that. Never has.

So I nod, pulling my hands free to wipe the moisture from my eyes, wishing I could bend myself to make my limbs stop shaking. To let go of the weight of everything.

A series of thumps and bangs draws our attention to the stairs. Caeo stumbles to his feet at the bottom, his hand propped against the tree trunk for balance.

"Those are deadly." He points weakly at the stairs. "How did Emlyn even get up there?" He grabs the edge of a step at his eye level and attempts to wiggle it, but it doesn't budge.

My brow furrows, confusion interrupting my shame. I barely know my brother, but something's off. This is not the smoldering anger I anticipated upon his return.

Ellie shifts in the corner of my eye, and I bite back a groan—I'd rather not explain any more of my mistakes to Ceirios right now.

I grab Caeo's arm and pull him toward the door.

"Hey, let go of me!" He tries to tug himself free, but his movements are sluggish and uncoordinated. He probably needs sleep, but we don't have time for that.

"Tell Princess Briarwood we're leaving," I say, then shove him out the door.

Deep breaths.

Today is going to be miserable. None of us have slept, except for Ellie and her short nap. Caeo is a breath away from punching me, I can't look at Ellie without the Land's rage boiling through me, and the princess... I don't trust her. She's been the enemy for almost as long as I can remember. While Emlyn's said nice things about her, his standards of judgment differ greatly from mine.

But if I'd listened to him, he never would have gotten hurt.

"We're leaving so soon?" Ellie asks as I cross the room to the packs of food Ceirios prepared for us, careful to keep her out of my gaze.

"Emlyn needs a healer, and we can't be here for that. Both my mother and Ystyr's soldiers are undoubtedly looking for us, so we need to keep moving. Find someplace more hidden."

To do what, I have no idea. Try again? Fail again?

I'm rummaging through the packs just to have something to do, something to look at, when the door opens. Princess Briarwood peeks her head in, sending a throb of annoyance through my throat. *What could she possibly want?*

"Good morning." She steps inside, her midnight eyes absorbing the room. I lock onto her, wary of her intentions, but also to keep Ellie out of my field of vision.

The princess's gaze lands on Ceirios, still sitting at the table. "I was hoping you'd be willing to spare me some clothing, as I'm not particularly well dressed for travel." She unwraps herself from her oversized fur coat, dropping both it and my jaw to the floor.

She wears a traditional wedding dress—meaning, she's hardly covered at all. My eyes trace the thin strip of rose-colored silk that wraps around her neck and crosses her chest, barely covering her hardening nipples and goosebumps that reveal how cold it is, despite the heat in my face. The silk hugs her supple curves as it winds around her hips, barely covering her sex, where a few strips of fabric cascade down to the floor.

Muffled voices snap me out of my stupor, and I force my gaze back to the packs, unsure what I was doing with them. My irritation swells. *There was no reason for her to do that. What's her game?*

Footsteps thudding up the stairs match my land-sense, which I've been keeping focused on Ceirios to shut out everything else. The princess follows her. I look up, and Ellie's standing across the counter from me.

Ancients!

The shock of the Land's fury makes me jump. Even without her glamour, Ellie's still styled to look fae, with her braided hair and woolen dress. As beautiful as ever, but I can't keep my eyes on her.

I rummage through the packs as the temper flares within me—there's nothing else I can shove into them, but there's nowhere else for me to look.

"That was a little inappropriate," Ellie says.

I hold back a groan. *She caught me gawking.*

"It's alright. I was staring, too."

It's clear what she's doing. She wants to make me laugh. Lighten my load. To pull a smile from my lips, then kiss them, and make everything else go away for a while. Even after all the suffering I've put her through, she has the strength to keep going, and to lend it to me. I want nothing more than to let her do that. My body longs for it, yearning for release. I can barely stand it.

Which is how I ruined everything. All it took was a sympathetic face that wasn't afraid.

Until she was.

I saw it in the way she'd hesitate, as if she feared what pressuring me might bring. Yet her support never wavered. I wanted to be the person she saw.

I was too weak—to resist her, to be King. And I still am. I wish I could say that it's Caeo's presence that holds me back, my guilt giving me the strength to overcome my desire, but it's not. It's the murderous inferno of the Land's rage that's been blazing through me ever since she incanted last night.

But I can't tell her that. Can't burden her with that kind of pain. So I leave, like I always do.

"We should get on our way once the princess finishes dressing." I tie the packs shut before crossing the room, making sure not to spare a single glance at Ellie.

I pull the door open, letting it slam behind me as I step into the brisk morning air. With a deep breath, I try to calm myself. To focus on the clucks of chickens, the mix of the sun's warmth and the cool breeze on my skin, the feel of the soft earth beneath my feet. Everything that normally brings me peace.

But the Land's ire creeps through, despite me keeping my senses focused away from Ellie. There's been no indication of it letting up—if anything, it's getting worse.

The sharp bray of the goat draws my attention. He's only a few strides away from where Caeo lies spread-eagled on the grass, staring up at the sky.

My mouth goes dry. I really don't want to talk to him, but what option do I have? Wait around for Ellie to come talk to me? Have Ellie talk to him? Leave it to the Ystyrian princess?

Each possibility is worse than the last.

I take a deep breath and march over, dropping one of the packs next to him with a thud.

He blinks and tilts his head in my direction. "Hello, brother." His voice is full of venom, the word like a punch to the gut.

"Please don't call me that."

"I think I will, brother. What can I do for you, brother?"

Each repetition jolts my insides. This isn't how I wanted things to be. Ever since I first heard of his existence, I've wanted to know him. To have someone who might possibly understand.

But I ruined that.

"We're leaving. Can you carry this, or do I have to ask one of the girls?" I nudge the pack with my foot.

Caeo hauls himself into a seated position, wobbling and blinking upon arrival. My throat catches—he really does look like me. When I was younger, still soft with baby fat. The only difference is his eyes—blue instead of green—and his shorter hair.

I force a swallow. *No wonder Ellie found comfort in me.*

He clumsily swipes at the pack's straps, pulling it closer. He gets his arms through as if he's dressing with his eyes closed, then almost falls over as he gets to his feet.

"Are you alright?" I ask.

"No, I'm not alright. But I will be, because Owena's breaking the curse tonight. So let's get moving so nighttime gets here faster."

"That's not how time works," I mutter, trying to ignore the stabs of his words. I deserve to lose Ellie.

He stumbles off in the direction we came from.

"Caeo? Where's he going?" Ellie's voice, behind me, wavering on the edge of panic. I should've paid closer attention to her movements—we don't have time for the turmoil of her memories reemerging.

She rushes past me, and by instinct, I reach out, pulling her back.

My hands burn on contact, fire scorching up my arms, feeding the inferno blazing in my stomach. My fingers clench, wanting to tear her flesh apart, and my knees hit the earth as I force myself to release her, a roar of agony tearing its way out of my throat.

"Taran?" She turns back to me.

I avert my eyes, looking somewhere, anywhere but at her. "Just—don't touch me. Please."

"Tell me what's happening. I can't help you if you won't tell me what's going on."

I scramble to my feet, away from the sound of her voice. Trying to breathe, to quell the anger eating me up inside. My gaze lands on Princess Briarwood, her head cocked to the side as her evaluating eyes take in everything.

"Go get Caeo," I tell her, adjusting my pack and taking another breath. "Keep him behind Ellie."

She nods, her golden curls bouncing softly around her face, then strolls past me, calling Caeo's name.

"Taran?" Ellie's voice is close. I close my eyes, feeling her presence behind me, a blaze that sears my skin. "You need to talk to me."

"No. We have to go. Just follow behind me and don't look back."

I don't wait for a response.

I turn north, heading for the far-off hillside. Where it's cold and barren, with little risk of crossing paths with any other fae.

My land-sense tells me everyone eventually follows.

THE SUN TRUDGES across the sky as we drag ourselves over the treeless hills, breaking every so often for food and rest. While the others collapse in the tall grass, I backtrack along our path, shaping away any sign of our passage. It's draining, but necessary—my land-sense revealed a small group traveling from the capital arrived at Ceirios's home not long after we left.

They shouldn't make the connection; my mother barely acknowledged Ceirios's existence when I was a child, and Emlyn's put significant effort into distancing himself to protect her from any consequences of his work. Hopefully, they'll just treat them as witnesses and move on.

With the task complete, I wake the others before we continue. I lose track of how many times we repeat the process, my mind lost in a cloud of exhaustion. I'm the only one who can navigate the terrain. I'm the only one who can shape the earth to hide our tracks. It's a weight, but one I can manage. One that keeps my mind off everything else.

It's getting late, the sun hanging low in the sky, when I sense the princess catching up to me. My jaw flexes, and I pick up my pace.

"Taran, stop," her voice calls, light on the breeze.

I don't.

"We need to talk," she says, and I can picture her clambering up the hill behind me, practically nude in her wedding attire.

No—she changed her clothes.

My face burns as I force the image from my mind. "About what?"

"We need to find somewhere to camp." She grabs my arm.

I flinch, but nothing happens. No burning rage. So I stop, taking a breath. "We should keep going until dark. The further we get, the harder we'll be to find."

She releases my arm, stepping in front of me. The pinks and oranges of the setting sun reflect off her windswept curls and highlight the pink flush in her skin.

"You haven't said where you're leading us, and these hills are barren. Are you taking us to shelter, or are we simply walking until night falls? Any pursuers will see a fire." Her eyes come level with my chin, but she speaks as if she towers over me.

I don't have the energy to fight her, but her tone lights a spark of annoyance.

"Which is why we won't be making one," I say.

To my satisfaction, her eyes widen, her rosy lips parting before her expression hardens. "Some of us could freeze without a fire."

"Maybe a spoiled Ystyrian princess will, but I didn't want you here to begin with." If she never bothered to learn that the Land can keep her warm, that's on her.

Her gaze drifts behind me, and I belatedly realize Caeo and Ellie have caught up. My exhaustion must be getting to me.

"What's going on?" Caeo asks.

With a sigh, I turn so we're all standing in an awkward circle; Princess Briarwood glowering at me, Caeo looking at her, and Ellie beside me doing I don't know what because I can't focus on her.

"Tell Taran that we need to find somewhere to camp," the princess says. "Somewhere sheltered, since that's the only way we can have a fire without risking discovery."

Caeo turns to me. "Of course we need shelter. Are you stupid?" He gives me a harsh smile. "Wait, you don't need to answer that."

"Caeo, that's not helpful," Ellie says softly. She must have spent enough time looking at him while the princess and I argued to move past the hysteria of her memories coming back.

I throw my arms out to the sides. "Do you see any shelter?"

"So you were planning on us freezing?" Caeo asks.

"I didn't plan anything."

"Obviously. If you'd planned this, we'd probably have fallen into a ravine and died."

Anger boils within me, this time my own. I seize the front of Caeo's shirt, tugging him close. His eyebrows flick up in shock.

"Stop it, both of you!" Ellie grabs my arm.

It spasms at her touch, my fingers releasing Caeo before I wrest myself free of her grasp. The rage boils over, and I stagger away, kicking the hillside.

"Arrrgh!" Pain tears through me as I collapse to my knees, breathing heavily. My foot throbs, but I don't think it's broken.

Another deep breath. I squeeze my eyes shut.

A moment later, the princess speaks up. "You can shape us a shelter in the hillside. It should be enough to keep us warm, even without a fire."

I groan. Yes, that's a good suggestion, and normally I could do that without much issue. But I'm exhausted.

What other choice do I have?

Surveying the area with my land-sense, I search for a suitable location. There. With a sigh, I drag myself over to a steeper section of the hillside and place my hands against the earth.

Closing my eyes, I visualize what I need the Land to do—shape a cavern into the hillside, with an entrance small enough to be discreet. I'm vaguely aware of the others' voices, but they're meaningless now. My mind clears, my burdens fading away as I become one with the Land.

Time passes, but I have no idea how much. Only that it's dark now and I'm completely drained. I stumble back, eyeing my creation. All that's visible is a narrow cleft in the hillside and a small hole above to let in some moonlight.

Princess Briarwood hands Ellie one of our packs and guides her through.

The Land's rage spikes with just that glimpse of her. I should sleep outside, to have a break. Especially if Owena's breaking the curse, like Caeo said. Being trapped with Ellie and Caeo is probably the worst place I could possibly be.

But with everyone else in there—I can't keep watch for myself while I sleep, and I don't have it in me to make another shelter.

Resigned to just curl up against the wall and pretend I'm somewhere else, I step forward to go inside, but the Ystyrian princess blocks my way.

"No." Her dark eyes bore into me. "You and Caeo are camping elsewhere. Come back in two days."

I could yell. Rage. Demand an explanation. But "What?" is all I have the strength for.

"I'll be breaking Ellie's memory curse. She'll need time away from you both to sort through her emotions, and the two of you have your own issues to resolve." She holds up some strands of chestnut hair, and my stomach drops.

"You know my family's gift, what can be done with Ellie's hair. Do not return before two sunsets from now. Understood?"

Curses. The Briarwood gift is curses.

Did she already put one on Ellie? Freeing her from one just to trap her in another?

I frantically turn to Caeo, my palms sweating. I could bend her, forcing her to release any curses she may have placed and preventing any future ones, but she's Caeo's friend. Bending her could make things even worse between us. Maybe he can—

He grabs my arm. "Come on, we're going."

What?

I trip over my feet as he pulls me along the hillside, the princess's smug smile taunting me until I turn away.

Chapter 5

Caeo

I let go of Taran the instant I feel his steps willingly follow mine, but the shift throws off my balance, sending me stumbling into the hillside.

"Why are you so accepting of this?" Taran asks, his voice… grumpy? Is that the word? Spikey grumpy, maybe?

Long blades of grass tickle my face with the breeze. "Because I trust Owena and it annoys you."

We made a deal. She tricked Taran into thinking she cursed Ellie to get us to leave, and now all I have to do is hang around my shitty brother for two days. Not something I'm looking forward to, but compared to everything behind me, it should be doable. Especially with this milk helping me out.

I push myself back onto my feet. The hill's a little wobbly, but that's expected. Everyone knows hills roll.

I look around, trying to orient myself. I've always seemed to see better in the dark than everyone else, but now my eyes glow. Who needs light when it's inside your eyes? Not that there's much to see—these hills are naked. Assuming grass is their skin, of course.

Or is dirt their skin, and grass their hair? But if that's the case… what's Ellie sleeping against tonight? Is there a name for inside skin? The pink stuff that lines the inside of your mouth. I don't remember anyone ever talking about it.

Anyway—that's gross, but not important. It's blizzard cold out here, so we just need to find somewhere nice to snuggle up for the night. With the hill, I mean, not each other. That'd be warmer, but weird, since Taran's my brother. The only way I'm touching him again is to beat him to death.

Hmm. Maybe not to death. I don't think I want that hanging over me for the rest of my life. Maybe four-twelfths of the way there?

"Caeo, are you listening?"

I blink, and my face is inches from mine.

"Shit!" I jump back, the hill slipping out from under my feet. I grab my arm and pull myself back up, then realize that's bigger me saving me, not me.

Wait... There isn't a bigger me...

Oh yeah. Green eyes. That's Taran.

I punch him.

Blinding pain screams through my fist as his grip releases me.

"FUCK!" Did I even do that right? I've never punched anyone before. It was supposed to hurt him, not me.

"Ancients, what was that for?" Taran yells, his hand on his face.

"I said the only touching was to beat you, and you touched me." My throat constricts as I shake my hand out. It still looks like a hand, so it's probably not broken. Hurts like fuck, though. Which doesn't make sense. Fucking doesn't hurt.

"You never said anything like that!"

I didn't? I thought I did.

Taran rubs his cheek, stretching his jaw. "You didn't."

Huh.

"Either way, you deserved it, because you're an asshole." I suck my knuckles as I storm off—it feels appropriate. The storming, not the sucking. The sucking feels nice.

Taran's voice calls out from behind me. "Caeo, stop. That's the wrong way."

I turn back. "How is there a wrong way? There's nowhere we're going."

"That's where we came from. If anyone's following us, that's where they'll be coming from."

"Oh. Fine. We can go this way, then." I turn around and head in the opposite direction.

"That's the same way you were just going."

I spin on my heel and slip against the hillside before recovering into a graceful stride. "My mistake. This way."

MY HIGH'S STARTING TO DISSIPATE by the time we find somewhere to sleep that's out of the wind; my wedding clothes are decently warm, but the gusty breeze cuts through. At some point, Taran took the lead and found this stone outcropping. Probably through sheer luck, since he's a moron.

He drops his pack, collapses against a boulder, and closes his eyes.

"I still don't see why you can't just make another cave." I pull the pack to me, rummaging through it for some food. *Hey, nuts!*

"Why don't you try? See how exhausting it is for yourself."

"Fuck you. No one's told me how." Would've kept me from being a good little puppet.

I shove a handful of nuts into my mouth. They're surprisingly flavorful considering they aren't roasted or salted or anything. I guess all the food here is just better than home by default.

"You don't have a bond with the Land," Taran says. "You need to develop that first."

"No one's told me how to do that, either." They just sat me out in the woods and expected me to figure it out. Mother was probably laughing the whole time. Until I snapped, and she realized a broken puppet won't be of any use to her. Clawing at the grass, world spinning.

The mash of half-chewed nuts forms a dry lump in my throat. I swallow, forcing the jagged mass down. *Breathe.*

Taran sighs, tilting his head to the sky. "Even an infant in swaddling can do it," he mutters. "You might possibly be the worst fae ever."

That's it. My simmering annoyance bursts into full-blown anger, and I throw my remaining nuts at him.

"And you're most likely the worst brother ever."

The glowing green of Taran's eyes disappears as they sink shut. He drops his head, staring at his lap. "You're probably right."

I blink.

That's it?

No, he doesn't get off that easily.

"So why'd you do it? Huh? Why did you—" I choke on the words as images invade my mind. Him and Ellie, together. I close my eyes, shutting them out. "You knew, but you did it anyway."

"I…" Taran lifts his hands, staring at them for a moment. Then he buries his face in them.

Fuck this.

"No, you don't get to be the pathetic one. You're the asshole who fucked everything up."

He doesn't respond, and I'm not sitting around while he wallows in self-pity, making me feel like a jerk for not comforting him. He literally stole Ellie's heart away when she couldn't remember me. But he knew. It was the whole reason he kidnapped her to begin with. Because she loved me and he hoped I'd listen to her.

I dig through my pocket for the milk of whatever jar and stick my little finger about halfway in. Then I shove the jar back in my pocket and my finger into my mouth.

My muscles liquefy, and I fall backward with a thud. Long blades of grass fill the edges of my vision, slender stalks framing the cloudy night sky.

"That hurt," I croak. Pain radiates through my head, its edge dull. Like a knife made of lard.

Would that even work? Maybe if you froze it first?

"Caeo? What happened?" Taran asks. The fucker's voice sounds concerned, but I can't lift my head to see him beyond all this grass.

I try wiggling my toes.

Nope, not happening.

"I really can't move. Huh."

Taran's face appears above me, his eyes glowing amid the black hair hanging around it. Just like mine, but longer.

"Ancients. Did you take Emlyn's milk of midnight star?"

"He *let* me have it in exchange for kissing him. So that's one more person we've both kissed, you piece of shit."

"I've never kissed Emlyn."

I frown. Look at that—my throat *is* feeling tight.

Am I remembering this wrong?

"He said I was the only one he was missing. His..." *How did he put it?* "His lips touching bodies."

Taran groans and disappears from view, leaving empty darkness behind.

"Hey, where'd you go? What'd he mean?"

"That was ten years ago," Taran mutters. "We were young, and Emlyn was trying to figure himself out. He knew he liked women, but thought he was also interested in men. He asked if he could... try something... with me. I let him. But it was only the one time."

Try... something?

My mind's swimming through molasses trying to figure this out. It's right there, waving its hand at me. If it weren't for this stupid, wonderful milk...

"You let him suck your cock!" I exclaim. I did it!

"I didn't enjoy it—"

My eyebrows bunch up as I frown. "You didn't enjoy getting your cock sucked? Are you dead or something?" Personally, I think even my corpse would enjoy it.

"I didn't enjoy *him* doing it. Can we talk about something else, please?"

The image of a big, angry me with Emlyn's head between my legs blows up in my mind, and laughter tumbles out of me—oh man, laughing when you can't move is so weird. Like a rabbit hiccuping on my diaphragm while buried under a bunch of rocks.

"Fine, fine," I cough out. That actually hurts; my eyes are getting wet. "What about Owena? He said Owena, too."

The smallest chuckle spurts out of Taran. "I'd forgotten about that. It would have been two or three years ago? We sent him to infiltrate the Ystyrian court, and he decided the best way to do that was to get in the princess's bed. If I remember correctly, he ended up bedding her father, too."

"Shit, he's a bigger slut than I am." *Does Reid realize what he's gotten into?* Though, if he's Emlyn's Ellie, that shouldn't be a problem.

Wait a second... If I'm the only one he was missing... does that mean he kissed Ellie?

Taran clears his throat. "I wasn't aware of that happening."

Can Taran read my thoughts? Is that a fae thing? Can I do that?

"That's not a thing," Taran says. "Maybe you should ease off the milk."

"Maybe you should ease off stealing your brother's girlfriend." I get a decent amount of bite into the words, despite struggling to feel it with that bunny now snuggling sleepily into my chest. I swell with pride at my accomplishment.

Taran sighs. "I'm going to sleep. Try not to soil yourself."

Hmm... I suppose it would've been wise to take care of that earlier.

Chapter 6

Ellie

"Perhaps for tomorrow night we can find some firewood, assuming you know how to light one," Owena says. "No one would see the smoke in the dark."

She lowers herself to the ground next to me inside the cave Taran carved into the hillside. The space is maybe ten by five feet, with dirt walls and floor, but it's too dark for me to be sure. Moonlight trickles through a small hole overhead and the narrow entrance we squeezed through. Though it's warmer in here, out of the wind, the packed ground is still quite chilly.

While Taran was constructing this hovel, Owena informed me she would remove my curse once we were inside, under the condition that I follow her wishes and give her some strands of my hair. I agreed, desperate to finally fill the holes in my memory, and assuming those requests were related to the curse-breaking process.

They were not. She simply hadn't wanted me to fight her when she forced Taran to disappear for two days by making him think she had cursed me.

"Why did you trick me like that?" It's nearly impossible to see her in the darkness since her fae eyes don't glow like the others; I'm curious why that is, but it'd be rude to ask. I doubt it keeps her from reading me, though, so I press all my anger into my expression.

"I didn't know if Taran was listening to us," she replies with the tone of someone discussing the weather. "I could not risk him hearing my plan."

"And why should I trust you? For all I know, you could be removing my curse for your own personal gain."

"I am," she says, startling me with the confession. "But for the moment, unraveling your curse is in both of our best interests. Are you ready or not?"

My stomach leaps while simultaneously sinking through the floor. I've wanted this so much, but now that the moment's here… Can I really trust her?

"How is it in your best interest?" I'm reasonably confident it's in mine, but I don't see how it could benefit her. I rub my palms against my dress—they're clammy with sweat.

Owena sighs. "You don't know who I am, do you?"

The question surprises me. I hadn't put much thought into it, having barely seen her as we traveled. My worries about Taran and Reid kept me occupied.

"Just that you're a princess from Ystyr and here to break my curse. Are you what I was supposed to help Reid steal?"

"No. Taran did not intend for me to be here. He considers me his enemy."

"What?" While that makes sense—Taran said Ystyr and Aedys have been at war for decades—a lump travels slowly down my throat.

Owena runs her finger along the dirt floor. "As I'm sure you've noticed, Taran is struggling. If we want all our realms to be at peace, he needs to resolve his issues so he can take his throne. Breaking your curse will help unravel one of the many knots that keep him from being who he needs to be. That is why I am helping you. For my realm, and for my people."

I swallow. Owena's fae, so she can't lie. I don't see any holes in her words—Taran *is* struggling. I thought I was helping, but he's shut himself away again. It *will* be dangerous for him to face his mother as long as he's like this. And until he does, she'll be free to go to war against my home.

I take a deep breath and nod. "Alright. Break the curse."

Owena shifts in front of me, her shadowy form growing clearer as her face moves closer. Eyes as dark as a moonless night meet mine.

"This will not be pleasant for you," she warns, her voice soft. "I will help you as much as I can."

She rests her icy fingertips on each of my temples, her eyes closing as her breathing slows. I wait, my anticipation building by the second.

I cry out as a blade of fire slices through my mind, my eyes squeezing shut. It weaves up and down, in and out, through every slit and crack it finds. A burning, blinding light.

It dims as blood rushes through me, flooding me with images returning from the void.

It's Caeo. They're all Caeo.

His voice. His face.

His body joining with mine, making me whole.

A sob rips out of me as his gray eyes, full of devotion, flooded every inch of me with warm serenity when he promised never to break my heart. Those same eyes, now blue as the midday sky, shattering as I broke his. Over and over, an unending barrage of memories as the darkness presses against me. Every moment Taran pulled away. Not for himself—for me. For the love he knew I was destroying.

All while destroying him.

I fall forward, unable to hold myself up, my nails scraping the dirt. Owena catches me, my face burying into her shoulder. She wraps her arms around me in a hug I don't deserve as my body lurches with choked breaths.

"I-I—"

"Shhh." Owena's voice is gentle. "You don't need to speak yet. Just let it out."

I cry like I've never cried in my life. Until I run out of tears. Then I remember Caeo's skin against mine, his smile when he pulled away from our kiss, and I cry some more.

My lungs hitch long after the tears stop falling. Until I'm a husk of myself, with each ragged breath raking against my tattered heart.

SUNLIGHT SINKS INTO OUR HOVEL, my body aching from being curled up on the hard dirt. The weight of my memories crushes me, pressing down until tears leak out of my eyes. I try to breathe, but my lungs don't want to expand.

"Come on, sit up," Owena says, tugging my arm. "You're even worse than Caeo was. But at least you haven't vomited."

Of course I'm worse—Caeo never betrayed me. I blink, my head slowly lifting. Owena kneels nearby, casting me in shadow as the light spilling through the hole above frames her golden hair.

"You know Caeo?" It's a silly question. She was with him, helping him, when I chose to prioritize his safety over breaking the curse.

Nonetheless, my heart settles at the memory. I'm not simply a victim. I was able to make some rational decisions.

"Yes," Owena says. "Now sit and eat something, and I'll tell you about it."

I force myself up, wiping the tears from my cheeks with my dirty hands. Owena passes me an apple, but I have no desire to eat it.

She scoots in front of me. "Now, it may surprise you to hear this, but Caeo is my betrothed."

My stomach lurches into my throat. "What?! You're—you and Caeo—"

Owena holds up her hand, silencing me. "Eat the apple and I'll explain."

It crunches in my mouth as I take a bite, its juice dripping down my chin. I shoot her an impatient glare.

She starts with revealing how her father, King Dryfid of Ystyr, conspired with Queen Esyllt to kill the former king of Aedys. He had ended the war against my homeland, and since the Land values balance above all else, Ystyr couldn't attack us without Aedys joining in. Otherwise, Ystyr would've lost land to both Aedys and Llynos, the eastern realm. I'd heard pieces of this before, but it's difficult to sort through all these new memories—conversations that previously contained Caeo-shaped holes.

Owena adjusts her position, dirt clinging to her pants as she shifts out of the ray of light. "Ystyr and Aedys have been at war for twenty years, with my father attempting to motivate Aedys into attacking your people again. To explain our newfound peace, our parents arranged a marriage between Prince Caeo and myself."

"That was the wedding we interrupted," I mumble. Everything falls together. "I was supposed to rescue Caeo—I would've remembered when I saw him. But I left. I... I picked Taran instead."

"You did not," Owena says firmly. "You picked a known over an unknown."

"It doesn't feel that way." I sniff. Every chance I had to pick Caeo, I didn't: I didn't save him, and I chose to keep my curse instead of pushing to break it when he wanted.

I wipe the newly formed tears from my eyes. The well is

bottomless... I'll never cry enough to empty myself of the guilt for what I've done. Despite having the best intentions, I only made everything worse.

Why did I have to be so set on feeling helpful?

"Caeo doesn't blame you." Owena rests her hand on mine. "He knows it's not your fault. If you still love him, he'll forgive you."

"If...?"

The implication drives a knife through my heart.

Of course I still love him. He's everything. The only person to make me feel like being myself was enough. To fill my entire being with a sense of belonging I'd never known. That emptiness I was trying to fill—I was missing him.

I dive into my memories of his touch. The warmth of his lips against mine, his breath tickling my skin...

They're so far away. I squeeze my eyes shut, pressing my mind harder. But rather than becoming clearer, the memories bleed into ones of Taran, the fresher sensations staining the old, scabbing over until I can't make out the originals.

Owena brushes away my tears with her fingers.

"This will take you time to sort through, Ellie. That's why I sent them both away—and to force them to confront one another. We won't accomplish anything if they don't stop fighting." Her eyebrows knit together. "Though honestly, it would do you well not to have your happiness depend on either of them."

While my eyes narrow at that last comment, her words draw forth a memory from last night, while Taran was busy building this cave.

Caeo had snuck up behind me and taken my hand, pulling me away from watching Taran work. I had immediately fallen to pieces, mumbling apologies through my tears. He'd wiped them away, kissing my cheek, and told me Owena would remove the curse soon.

My heart swells, a warm glow illuminating within me the longer I focus on it.

"We can fix this," he'd said. And I'd believed him.

I SPEND MOST OF THE DAY on the floor, cycling between rivers of tears as I sort through my memories and a numb emptiness when they finally run dry. At least a bell's worth fell for Reid, for how I treated him after everything he'd done for me, everything he'd tried to do when I wouldn't listen. I have no idea how I'll ever make it up to him, or when—if I'll ever even see him again.

Owena leaves for bells at a time, never saying where she's going. When she's here, she doesn't force conversation outside of pushing me to eat. I don't want to, my stomach disinclined to fill the hollowness that I deserve, but she coaxes me into it by teasing stories of Caeo. I know she's trying to help, but each tale stings with the reminder that she was there for him when I wasn't.

She's been gone for a while now, and golden light drifts in from the skylight, forming a circle on the opposite wall from this morning. The next time she returns, she'll likely stay the rest of the night. Then it will be one more day until Taran and Caeo join us.

My stomach tightens.

What will I say to them?

There's no question what I want. What Caeo wants.

But Taran? I haven't the faintest idea.

I have to believe that our relationship brought him comfort. Why else would he have given in? He knew it would cost him whatever bond he hoped for with his brother.

I bite my lip as my heart twists. It didn't always bring him comfort—I was torturing him, too. He may very well have acquiesced only to get relief from the pressure I put on him. If only

I'd believed in myself enough to realize we didn't need to be romantically entangled for me to help.

I take a deep breath.

He cares about me. But does he love me like Caeo does?

Does it even matter? I should choose based on what I feel. Who I love.

Except... Owena said Taran needs to resolve his issues for there to be any hope of stopping this war. So it's not just about me and my emotions. My choice could determine the fate of all our realms.

He told me I inspired him to be stronger—what happens if I leave him to battle his demons on his own?

A brushing sound interrupts my thoughts as Owena sidles through the narrow entrance of our cave. She drops a pile of sticks on the ground next to me.

"It only took all day, but I finally found some wood for a fire. I do hope you know how to start one, so my effort wasn't in vain."

"Taran taught me, but I've never actually succeeded." My throat coils at the memory—when I'd asked him, I hadn't understood why he'd put all his efforts into teaching Reid instead of me. I burn with shame as the rest of that night runs through my mind.

"As it is, it really only affects you if you can't, so try not to pressure yourself." Owena sits next to me and starts untangling the braid in her hair, her windswept curls forming a messy halo around her head.

I clamp my jaw shut, trying to focus on Taran's instructions. Not the feelings.

"Can you shape this into a flat piece for me?" I hold up one of the thicker sticks. Taran told us how to make one without a base, but said this way was easier.

Owena frowns, but takes it from me. She squints, and it morphs excruciatingly slowly into a slightly thinner, blobby rectangle.

"Like that?" She hands it back to me, then returns to brushing her hair with her fingers.

"That... should work." I examine the piece. Taran's and Emlyn's were much smoother and only took seconds to make. It doesn't seem like I should ask her to make the divot. "Do we have a knife?"

"In the pack."

I find it in one of the side pockets, but my breath catches in my throat when I recognize the blade.

It's Taran's.

I swallow down my emotions as I grip the bone dagger tightly. "I assumed all fae knew how to start a fire." Taking a deep breath, I scrape a notch into the flat piece of wood.

Owena laughs. "I've never needed to. That's what servants are for."

"We had servants, too. But I often incanted fires to spare them the effort. My father wanted me to practice as much as possible." Back then, I'd never have imagined I'd be rubbing sticks together in a dirt cave. If Mom could see me now... The thought of her horrified expression sends a small smile tugging at my face.

"I see," Owena says, her taut voice snapping me back, and I wince—I might as well have just told her I kicked babies every day of my life.

This is what happens when I try to relate to people.

"I need to get some dry grass." I hurry outside.

Upon my return, I struggle to get the stick to light. Smoke wafts upward every so often, but no ember forms on the tip, and my arms are growing tired from spinning it. It's ridiculous how little my education focused on practical matters like this. As if everyone was fine with me having no use outside of incanting. I try to relax, forcing myself into a steady rhythm.

"Any other stories about Caeo?" I ask, bracing myself for the inevitable sting of self-flagellation they'll bring, but I don't know what else to talk to her about. I'm not sure I want her opinion on where I should go from here; as nice as she's been, she's admitted she's only helping me for her own benefit. That would likely color whatever advice she offered.

"Hmm?" She tilts her head, looking up from her fingers. She's long since finished rebraiding her hair and moved on to picking the dirt from her nails.

"Let's see." She taps her chin. "Much of our time was spent with me teaching him proper etiquette. There was the time we smoked long leaf together."

I almost drop the stick. "Smoked what?"

"Speckled long leaf," she repeats. "Orange, to be precise. He led me to believe mortals partake in that as well?"

Only degenerates, at least according to my parents. I've never actually encountered it myself. Father smoked tobacco occasionally when entertaining guests, but I've never understood why. It smells awful.

When I don't answer, Owena continues. "It isn't really appropriate for someone of my station, but Caeo asked me about it, so I sent my maid to obtain some."

I start spinning the stick again, hoping to appear nonchalant. "And you two smoked it together?"

Owena folds her hands over her knee as she focuses on me. "You seem surprised by this. He quite obviously partakes fairly regularly. With red, even."

"Red?"

"It's the stronger variety."

How did I not know any of this?

"What exactly does smoking it do?"

"The orange?" She glances at the spot of light on the wall, now just a faint crescent from the setting sun. "It typically loosens one's inhibitions, makes thoughts wander—much like imbibing too much alcohol."

"And red?"

Her lips tighten. "I haven't tried it myself, but I'm told it draws the mind into a state of oblivion."

My gaze drifts down to the stick resting in my hands. I don't know when I stopped rubbing it.

"Why does he do it?" I ask.

"He blamed his mother."

His mother. I met her twice in Haven, and then again at the palace. Nothing stood out at first—perhaps she was a bit overbearing—but I remember how she made Caeo feel. The urge to protect him that stirred within me.

If only I'd realized how dangerous she was. She attempted to murder her own child, did... atrocious things... to Taran's father, cursed Caeo and me, and now marches her people to war against my home. Of course being raised by a woman like that would drive Caeo to... this.

But why did he keep it from me? How did I not notice?

I inhale, trying to loosen the knot of betrayal and uncertainty in my stomach. An entire side of him that Owena's seen but was a complete mystery to me.

I push it down. "Well, he's free of her now, and he doesn't have any of that long leaf with him, right?"

"He does not," Owena says slowly.

"Then he can get past it."

I nod to myself. It has to be true. I've lost him too many times already. I won't lose him to this.

The knot tightens again.

But what if breaking Taran's heart dooms our realms to war?

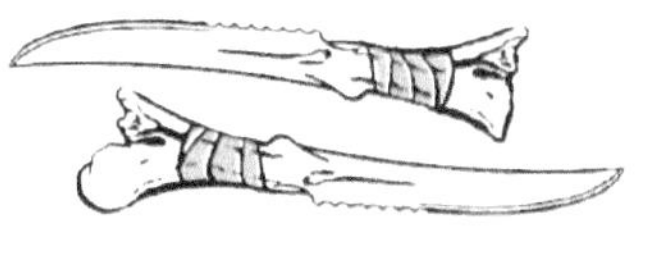

Chapter 7

Emlyn

"Taran and the others have left," Ma says, her head poking up into the room.

I blink at her through the haze blurring my vision. I'm propped up against some pillows in the bed she always hoped would be mine but never was, wrapped in woven blankets as I shiver against the cold no one else feels. My loopies were no match for the fever that overwhelmed them shortly after Caeo left, but at least they got me my kiss. Collection complete.

Ma sits next to me, a bowl of soup in hand—broth with swirled egg. "I brought you something to eat." She nods at Reid lying next to me, his hand resting on my stomach. "I had thought he could feed you while I went for the healer."

"Reid," I say, my eyes trailing his sleeping form. I long to curl up against him, but I can't move. "His name's Reid. I can wait for the healer. Let him rest."

Ma nods, bringing a warm spoonful to my mouth. *Ancients, I've missed her cooking.* But it doesn't make up for the rest of her momness—all her worries and opinions, wishing I'd live a quiet, boring life. She probably enjoys getting to feed me like I'm a barely weaned babe.

I grow more tired with every sip, the soup's heartiness pulling me down as it sinks into my belly, until I can barely keep my eyes open.

"I'll leave this here in case you get hungry while I'm gone." She sets the bowl on the bedside table.

My eyelids falter, and I drift away.

"Oh no." Ma's voice is shrill, panicked. My eyes crack open—she's at the window, peeking out.

"Soldiers." She turns to me. "What should we do?"

"Ugh… Fuck." I can barely focus. I'm not talking our way out of anything, and Ma's never deceived anyone in her life.

Think.

"Wake Reid."

Ma drops down beside him, shaking his shoulder. Reid startles up, his hand compressing my stomach—*OOF*—as he barely misses colliding with her.

"Fuck, that hurt," I say through gritted teeth. At least I'm more awake now. *Shit.*

Reid responds with a grimace of his own. "Sorry."

"Uh huh. Just glamour him, Ma."

"What's going on?" he asks as my mom sets her hand on his face, transforming his features. Not how I would've done it, making his nose and cheekbones far too sharp, but at least he looks fae.

"Soldiers are coming." I grunt. "You need to lie to them for us."

"Are you sure they won't see through this?" Reid's eyes dart nervously between my mom and me.

"You don't feel as different as the girl did," Ma says, taking a breath. Nodding to herself. Trying to believe this will work.

"What?" Reid asks. "How's that possible?"

"Maybe you've absorbed enough of my fluids," I offer.

Reid goes redder than I've ever seen him, and I love him for it.

"Ancients, Em," he mumbles, glancing at my mom.

"Don't worry. I know my son." Ma pulls him toward the stairs just as some loud bangs sound from below—the soldiers knocking on the door. How polite.

Halfway down the hole to the stairs, Reid pauses. "Wait—what do I tell them?"

"It doesn't matter," I say. "It shouldn't even occur to them that you're lying."

And then they're gone, along with the spike of energy the crisis gave me. I come crashing down, like an avalanche onto a flock of baby chickens. Darkness, with only the far-off, soothing sounds of Reid's voice.

I WAKE UP SCREAMING to someone unwrapping my bandages. The milk has completely worn off, and every move stabs a burning ember into my shoulder.

"FUCK!"

"They could have done a better job with this," my tormentor mutters. He must be the healer. Either that, or Ma finally decided to get revenge for all the times I never listened.

"No shit." My jaw clenches with another spike of pain.

"Who wants to give him some milk of midnight star?"

"I will," Reid says. He's sitting on the bed next to me, the healer on my other side with Ma hovering above. A moment later, his finger's in my mouth, and I turn to mush. The pain subsides a heartbeat after.

"How did this happen?" The healer inspects my wound, poking at it like a messed-up kid with a slug. Can't people just let the loopies take me somewhere nice for once?

"Hunting accident." Reid's voice catches with every prod. "I have terrible aim."

Is that what he told the soldiers?

"Hmm." The healer sits back, thank the Ancients, and pulls over his bag. He doles out instructions as he sets two small jars on the bedside table—to be taken three and four times a day—along with the milk and a sack of blood rose petals to layer against my wound.

Ma brings the first jar to my lips. It tastes like dirt, but I force it down. I gag on the contents of the second, and she has to clamp my jaw shut until I swallow. It's like drinking congealed blood.

"Can I die now? Please?"

"If I didn't know better, I'd say you already did," the healer says. "The arrow nicked an artery. I'm not sure how you survived the blood loss."

Fucking Ta—

Reid covers my mouth.

I must be thinking out loud again. The thought's muffled, like it's passing through someone's hand.

The healer wraps me up in fresh bandages, which is painful, but that's my life now: pain and poison and unable to do anything, not even keep my thoughts to myself.

Ma shows him out. I close my eyes, every breath haggard. Reid slides onto the bed, slipping his arm around me as I nuzzle into his chest. The movement sends a dull blade ripping through my arm and neck, but it's worth it.

I'm blanketed in his scent: a hint of nutmeg buried beneath musky sweat—who knows when the last time he bathed was—but it's him. It sends a wave of relief washing through me that rivals the milk.

My eyes burn behind their lids, tears trying to escape onto my cheeks. I let out a ragged breath and try to imagine it's two nights ago, when we slept at my house, pretending that was our future.

"Just sleep," Reid says, his voice soft. "Every time you wake up, it'll be a little better. And I'll be here, every time."

I fall asleep to the sound of his heart beating.

REID'S THERE, every time I wake, until the morning of the fourth day.

Pale light fills the room, and my mom sits against the wall, weaving one of her gaudy tapestries. My shoulder throbs, the milk having worn off sometime while I slept, and my whole body aches from lying in bed. The mattress was soft at first, but now it's just lumpy and uncomfortable.

But not as uncomfortable as Reid's absence. My heart sputters, making me sweat. "Ma? Where's Reid?"

"He hasn't left your side in three days." She lowers her project to look at me. "I made him take a break and go take care of himself. There was hair growing out of his face."

"I liked that," I grumble, exhaustion washing over me as my heart settles. Almost every morning when we were traveling, Reid had to spend time shaving. It's terrifying to watch; I can't imagine scraping a blade against such vital parts of my body just for appearance's sake. But he hadn't done it since the morning of the wedding, and dark hair collected like a handsome shadow along his jaw, scratching at my skin when we kissed.

"The healer's supposed to return today, and it'll be easier to glamour him without it." Ma feels my forehead with the back of her hand, then frowns—I guess I'm still hot enough to be considered feverish, but I can't tell anymore. *Like shit* has become my default feeling.

Her hand moves to the side of my neck, beneath my ear. "Your pulse is still weak." She sighs, then picks up the two jars of horrible medicine. "Which would you like first?"

"Fuck me," I groan.

"No, I'm your mother." She sets down the shorter jar and pulls the cork stopper out of the other. "But you better not be planning on doing that with Reid anytime soon, either. You don't need to tear open your wound."

"Ancients, Ma. Do you think I'm stupid?"

"Of course not. But you don't always think with your head."

I sigh. *That is true.* Or at least it used to be. But I need to be different now, so I can take care of Reid. "Did you at least bring anything to wash it down with?"

She nods toward a bowl of fruit and eggs on the floor. Solid food. *Yippee.*

I take the blood juice first, because it's the worst, by far, then chase it with the dirt. Ma sets the bowl in my lap, and I feed myself with my left hand. Progress!

Not really. I'm laboring through a shitload of pain to do so. But I can't eat on my own once I've taken the milk, and even having Reid feed me lost its fun after the first day. So I eat as much as I can until the pain becomes too much, then ask Ma to get Reid for the milk.

"He deserves a break from that, too." She opens the little jar and dips her pointer finger in, all the way to her last knuckle. Because she actually knows how the stuff works.

"Ma, that's too much."

"You're my son, no matter how big you are. I would take all your pain, all the time, if you let me."

That should probably make me feel cozy and loved, but it doesn't. Not when my suffering comes from living a life she doesn't approve of. But if it's this or nothing... I exhale slowly out my nose, then nod. She sticks her entire finger in my mouth, and then into hers.

For the first time in days, I'm completely pain-free. It's a good thing I can't move, because otherwise there's nothing stopping me from fleeing this cursed room to frolic in circles outside. Except for passing out. That would stop me. And lead to further injury.

Ma squeezes her eyes shut, grimacing.

"Your face is breaking," I say. "Is it too much?" Not that I can do anything about it. This was her idea. A stupid idea.

I laugh. Maybe that's mean, but it's funny.

"I'll be alright," she says, her voice tight. She shifts her position against the wall. "Just distract me. Tell me about Reid."

Uh... no? The last thing I want is her opinions on my love life. They've never been good.

"I'd rather not." It's annoyingly difficult to avoid looking at someone when you can't move, even though she's swimming through time and space right now. And it's annoyingly difficult to stay annoyed while on this much milk.

"I don't recall you ever having a relationship that's lasted longer than a few nights."

I can't stop blinking, my eyelids trying to catch her, to stop her wiggling.

"Emlyn?"

"Huh? Oh. It didn't really make much sense." That's a fun word. *Sensssse. Sen se.*

"Why not?"

"I can't really fuck people for information if someone's waiting for me at home, can I?" *I mean, I could, but it wouldn't be polite.*

"And Reid's fine with that?" Ma raises her brow through the pain contorting her face.

"Of course he isn't. But I'm not really running off to do Taran's bidding right now, am I?" *Why did I have to mention Taran?* Irritation wriggles its way through my loopies, grabbing hold.

"No, you aren't," Ma says. "But you've been with Reid for a while, haven't you?"

"What do you want me to say, Ma? What are you after?"

The light shifts, probably from clouds blotting out the sun. A shadow passes over Ma's face as she sighs, though it's more like a grimace with all my pain loaded on top. "I'm worried about you, Emlyn. Your entire adult life, you've used spying for Taran as an excuse to share a bed with as many people as possible. Now, you want nothing to do with him and have brought home a *mortal*."

More than spying. Extorting, killing... If she knew everything, Reid would be the least of her concerns. "He's more to me than just a mortal, Ma."

"I know, love, but our people are preparing for war against his as we speak. Are you planning to glamour him every day and hope no one notices? How will you survive without Taran's coin? I don't have the means to support the two of you much past your recovery."

"I don't know!" My heart strains, my vision blurring with every beat. "I haven't thought about it—this wasn't how things were supposed to go." Sweat drips down my forehead.

We were supposed to win. Taran was supposed to be King, and he could've let Reid stay, with no need to hide. I could've figured out another way to be useful—one that didn't make me drown myself in strangers' bodies to feel alive. But now, I can't even go back to that life.

Ma rests her hand on mine, meeting my eyes. There's tears in them, but I can't do anything about it, other than breathe. I inhale deeply, and Ma grimaces in response.

"I'm sorry, I didn't mean to upset you," she says, smoothing out my blankets. "There's time to figure everything out. And I'm glad you've found someone who makes you happy. Who clearly loves you."

He hasn't said he does.

"I wouldn't have had to force him away if he didn't." She leans in to kiss my forehead.

I flick my eyes away, wishing my head would follow. "I'm tired of talking."

Ma means well, but I hate everything right now. I hate all these thoughts, all these words. I even hate the pain being gone. Not being able to move made sense when it hurt. Now, I'm trapped in my body, in this suffocating room, with nothing but these stupid thoughts and words.

"Alright. I'll leave you be." Her voice is quiet, like her footsteps as she departs.

My eyes close as the first tear rolls down my cheek.

Eventually, my exhaustion takes hold, sending me into a mercifully deep sleep. When I wake, Reid's back, looking the cleanest he has since the day we left Haven—but different from back then.

His hair's grown just enough that his formerly pristine style, with its uniform edges that perfectly lined his cheekbones, no longer projects the aura of someone who cares too much about how the world sees them. He'll never get it looking like that again, unless he goes back to Lyndir. Our bone knives just don't have the precision for it.

But his razor must still be sharp, as he's clean-shaven, without a scratch. I should be able to keep that from going dull, since metal *does* come from the earth. He just won't be able to get a new one if he loses it. I suppose that's one of the many conveniences he's given up to stay with me, but he hasn't seemed bothered by it.

He kisses me shortly after my eyes open, cradling my head in his hand. I breathe in his scent, no longer the overpowering musk of sweat, but just him—nutmeg, with a hint of pine. Probably from the soap.

"You smell nice." I focus my attention entirely on him to keep out the radiating stabs in my shoulder. My face tightens with the effort.

"And you smell awful." He smiles. "I'm gonna give you a bath."

"That sounds simultaneously wonderful and horrible." I'm leaning more toward horrible, but I don't want to hurt his feelings. A week ago I would've jumped at the idea of him scrubbing me down, but now… I already can't piss or shit without his help. I don't relish the idea of him treating me even more like a newborn.

"You were gone a long time," I say, trying to change the subject.

Reid rubs the back of his neck as he leans into his pillow. "Your mom wouldn't let me back up here until the milk wore off. Didn't trust me being near you if neither of us was feeling your pain. You two don't really have normal boundaries, do you?"

"They're normal for fae. Sex isn't taboo for us the way it is for mortals." It couldn't be, thanks to our land-sense. Takes more than closed doors to have any privacy.

"Great. One more thing to get used to."

"I can tell her to leave you alone."

Reid raises an eyebrow as his lips curl into a smile. "Since when do you care about my comfort in conversations?"

"Making you squirm is a privilege I don't enjoy sharing."

He flushes, and my heart skips. It's almost like how we were before, except my shoulder's screams are becoming increasingly harder to ignore. My pulse quickens as I grab his hand, taking advantage of my mobility before the pain becomes unbearable.

"You'll have to tell that to the wisp downstairs." He tucks a lock of my hair behind my ear. "It was hovering uncomfortably close."

"That's my dad."

Reid's eyes widen. "Your dad?"

"Part of his spirit, at least. He died in the war, just after I was born." Ma always said I took after him. Hence all her worries.

I take a breath. "Maybe he was curious about the person his son said he loved."

Fuck. I really did just go out and say that, and I can't even blame the milk this time.

No. I blame my mom. For making me think all those stupid thoughts.

But the agony in my shoulder gives way to a tightness in my chest as Reid's cheeks redden, his lips pressing together. I don't know if I'm sweating from my fever or anticipation.

"You did say that, didn't you?"

"And you didn't."

Reid blinks as his smile falters. He brings his hand to my cheek, brushing my skin with his thumb. "Of course I do, Em. Why would I be here if I didn't?"

The room spins as my heart shivers against my ribs. "I don't know, because I'm a really good fuck?" Heat rushes through me, and my vision blurs. *Is this what love feels like?*

Reid laughs, squeezing my hand tighter. "You are, but no. I love you. Completely. Totally. Until you decide you're sick of me."

His words send the world spiraling.

"Oh, good," I breathe out. I want to assure him that won't happen, but I'm already drifting off. My eyelids flutter shut, and my hand goes limp, slipping from his grasp.

Not a problem. I don't need his hand. I have his heart.

Chapter 8

Taran

I don't remember the last time I slept through the night. Probably not since my father died.

Not died. Was murdered. By Ystyrian soldiers on behalf of my mother. I didn't even get to say goodbye. I fled, to the safety of Emlyn, like the coward I am.

Don't go there. That won't help me get through the day.

My dirt-crusted fingers rake along my face, a dull ache throbbing behind my eyes as I breathe in the cold, dark air. We're far enough north that it smells like winter rather than spring, and despite my exhaustion, I'm awake before dawn. With nothing to do.

I have no plan—not even an inkling. First, it was getting Emlyn to his mom. Then, to continue fleeing, to avoid discovery.

What now?

What can I do? The Ystyrian princess has trapped us here while she helps Ellie recover from her curse.

My jaw clenches, and my fingers press harder against my skull.

Of course she bound Ellie in another curse. I'd heard she was cunning, but Emlyn said nothing of such cruelty. How is Caeo so accepting of this?

The only explanation is that he knew. That the two of them conspired against me. That's to be anticipated from her, but Caeo?

He's...

He's the brother I betrayed before I ever met him.

I fall back with a painful thud against the cold, hard hillside.

Is it even possible to fix this?

I don't see how. He hates me, and I deserve it.

But don't I owe it to him to at least try? I don't want to be the brother who only existed to ruin his life.

My head rolls to the side to where Caeo's still sound asleep. He looks so peaceful, his face absent of the anger and grief that twist it every time he looks at me. Ever since he realized what I'd done.

Except for last night. For a brief moment, he forgot he hated me, even laughing at my words. Was that because there's hope for forgiveness, or because he was high on milk of midnight star?

I've used it before, when injured—nearly every fae has at some point. It's one of the many gifts of the Land to help maintain our long lives. But there's always those who abuse it, becoming addicted and wasting away because they can't handle facing their pain. Like the kind I brought him.

This is my fault too, isn't it?

I could fix it. Just bend him, tell him never to use it again. But then what happens if he ever needs it?

And why stop there? I should just tell Ellie to forget about me and choose him. Force him to forgive me. It would be so easy. With just a few words, all of Caeo's miseries would disappear.

He stirs. I push myself up, poking through our pack to have something to do other than meet his eyes—the eyes that filled with terror the last time I bent him.

A knot forms in my throat. *What am I thinking?*

I can't just bend people. That's how I become my mother. Twisting them into puppets, making them lose themselves to my command. My childhood's riddled with firsthand experiences of what it feels like.

But she never bends people to spare them their pain.

Caeo lets out a groan, rubbing his eyes. "What time is it?"

"Barely dawn."

"Shit. And I have to spend the whole day with you?"

"I can go."

He doesn't respond, so I risk a glance in his direction. He's pulling a small jar from his pocket.

The pack slips from my hands. "Caeo, don't."

"How else am I supposed to get through today without punching you?"

"That didn't stop you last night." I gingerly touch the swollen skin of my cheekbone, wincing as it stings on contact—I'll have to glamour that.

Which might just encourage him to punch me again.

A harsh laugh barks out with his words. "I suppose it didn't."

He pulls the stopper from the jar.

I sit up straighter, pulse quickening. "I can go somewhere else. Leave you alone."

Caeo sighs, then drops his gaze to the ground. "Not everything is about you, Taran. You're just the icing on top of a pile of horrible weeks."

Icing? Is that a mortal thing?

I shove my confusion aside. "Do you want to talk about it?"

He scoffs. "Not with you."

"Why not?" A pointless question that fell out before I could think. I wouldn't want to discuss it either—I'd just leave. It's strange that I'm the one pushing now.

"Because I hate you," he grumbles, picking at a long blade of grass. Then his jaw clenches with a grimace. "I mean, I very much don't like you right now." He exhales, his face relaxing slightly.

I suppose that's an improvement? I don't know why he corrected himself, but it encourages me to try again.

"Was it our mother?"

Caeo closes his eyes, his chest sagging. "Fuck."

"I know what she's like." I force myself to dig through memories long buried. Being bent for the simplest things—eating my supper, going for walks, picking up a toy. "I was young when she was banished. When she tried to kill me. I don't remember the details, just how it felt. She did it every day. To my father, too."

My throat goes dry, but I need to get it out. If not for me, then for Caeo, but I can't look at him right now.

"She was the world to me. I loved her unconditionally. And now, I don't know if it was because that's how all children see their mothers, or because she made me. But I remember the constant terror of not knowing what her next words would do."

I swallow, then glance at Caeo.

He takes a deep breath, looking at the jar cradled in his hands. "I don't understand how she just switched. She never bent me before we came here."

"My father cursed her." My words are slow. Quiet. "She couldn't willbend, and couldn't return, until his last breath." If he'd given it another loophole, then perhaps he would still be alive. But then the curse wouldn't have been powerful enough to contain her.

I asked him once why he didn't just kill her—he couldn't, because of their marriage bond. A lifetime of feeling her hatred, every moment of every day, was easier than killing a part of himself.

And made it too painful for him to even look at me.

"Why is she like this?" Caeo mutters, the dawn light slowly brightening his features.

I scratch my neck. "I don't know." It's a question that's haunted my entire life. "Rage, maybe? At the mortals, for killing her father?

At herself, for not being as strong as him? But I haven't spoken to her since I was a child, so I can only guess."

"It's like she became a different person." He lifts his head to look at me. "I'd never have said she was the greatest mother. Far from it. But I still thought she loved me, in her own messed-up way. Now…"

His eyes drift back to the ground, the grass unnaturally still compared to blades whipping erratically beyond our windbreak. "I was just a tool for her the whole time, wasn't I? Something to bring her comfort when she needed it. Once she got what she actually wanted… I didn't matter anymore."

I don't know how to respond. I close my eyes, bringing my hand to my face. There's a slight comfort in knowing I'm not the only one my mother's broken. And maybe this will help Caeo get past his anger with me. Maybe, when Ellie picks him, he can forgive me, and we can become the family we were supposed to be.

I look up just in time to see Caeo pulling his finger out of his mouth, the open jar of milk in his other hand.

Ancients.

IT TAKES HALF THE DAY for Caeo's high to come back down. Thankfully, he didn't paralyze himself this time.

I've been leading us along the hillsides, away from Ellie and Princess Briarwood. Even if our pursuers confirmed we stopped at Ceirios's house, these hills are too much for such a small group to search by themselves. They're likely waiting for reinforcements—otherwise I'd try to convince Caeo to go talk some sense into the princess. But every time I've attempted another conversation with him, even just to ask if he needs a break, he's snapped at me.

It was too much to hope that one conversation, no matter how much I opened up for it, could fix anything.

Other than the occasional dried-out shrubs, these hills are bare. My land-sense tells me a small stream runs through a nearby valley, so that's where I'm taking us—it'll keep us from using up all our water, and we can refill what's empty when we return to the others.

My stomach churns. I hate to admit it, but the Ystyrian princess sending us away has given me a measure of relief from the Land's rage burning me up inside. Instead, She's... discontent. Maybe because my mother's been tugging at our connection for weeks now, an intermittent prodding at the back of my mind, every day, morning through night.

I used to think it would be impossible for her to steal the bond from me, but every so often, a particularly violent heave makes me worry. There's been more of those today than ever before. Just one more thing threatening to undo me.

"I need a break." The words rumble under my breath. I shove off my pack and sit on the sloping hillside, pulling out some dried meat. Some gophers scurry around not too far away, but I don't have my bow, and my sword is useless against a rodent, so hunting would be a more gruesome process than I want to deal with at the moment. Another reason to get to that stream—fishing is much easier.

Caeo trips over my legs and stumbles to the ground, sending a spike of pain through my shin.

"Fuck!" he yells. "Why did you sit right where I was walking?"

"You had plenty of time to notice," I grumble, disentangling his legs from mine. He'd been trailing about twenty paces behind me— I knew this without even looking. Does he not have any land-sense at all?

Caeo pushes himself away from me, pulling the pack with him. He rummages through it until he pulls out a cloth bundle, untying it to reveal some cheese. Rather than look for a knife, he takes a large bite out of the side.

His eyebrows shoot up at the flavor, his eyelids twitching shut until he forces himself to chew.

He swallows. "That's... strong." He takes another, albeit smaller, bite. I can feel his every motion, even his jaw clicking, through my land-sense.

"Caeo, can you feel that I'm sitting here?"

"What are you talking about? I just wasn't looking. I know you're there now."

"No, not see me—sense me. Through the Land."

"What does that even mean?"

I sigh, then shove the last bite of my food into my mouth.

"Put that down." I scoot closer, gesturing at the cheese. His brow raises, but he complies.

"Lie down and dig your hands into the ground."

"What? Why?"

"To see if we can get your land-sense working."

His eyes narrow. "Owena's mentioned that, but I don't know what it is."

"All fae have it, but you've clearly never used it before."

He presses his lips together, then sighs. "You better not be playing some kind of trick on me." He flops onto his back.

His fingers strain against the ground, trying to dig into the cold, hard dirt beneath a layer of thick grass. I rest my hand nearby, loosening the earth with a shaping to make it easier for him.

"I'll have to touch you. Please don't punch me again."

He bites his lower lip, holding his tongue.

I rest my hand on top of his. "Try to clear your mind."

I gently tug on my bond with the Land until I feel Her steady pulse, my sole source of calm in life. It travels through Caeo, into my hand.

His fingers twitch.

"Do you feel that?" I ask.

He nods slowly, his mouth agape. "Y-yeah."

"That's the Land. Now, I'm going to focus on Princess Briarwood." She's been wandering around outside the shelter I made for some reason. She wouldn't be able to sense us from this distance, but this is my realm—it's impossible for me not to notice her.

"Can you feel her?"

Caeo's breath catches, then he nods again. "I can."

Owena's legs glide between tall blades of grass, her feet caressing the earth with every step. The Land pulses a warm glow in response to each footfall, stirring something deep within me.

My heart stutters. *I've never felt that before.*

Is it because she's Ystyr's heir? Do others feel something similar when they sense me?

No, they wouldn't. The Land doesn't reveal such things through normal land-sense. It's too dangerous. So what's going on?

Caeo's hand twitches beneath mine. "Can I sense Ellie?"

The warmth freezes over, and I clear my throat. "That... wouldn't be wise."

His eyes open. He blinks a few times, then glares at me. "Right. It'd be too weird. Like you kissing her or something."

"That's not what I meant," I mumble. "Ignoring... that... the Land is angry at her. It could be dangerous to focus the Land's attention on her."

"Wait, what?" He pushes himself up, and I pull my hand away, resting it on my knee. "Why is it angry with her?"

"She. Not it. If you want to do this on your own, you need to be respectful."

Caeo inhales deeply. "Sorry. Why is She angry with Ellie?"

"Because Ellie incanted here. Twice. To save our lives."

"And I assume the Land hates incanting just as much as our mother does?"

"Yes."

He closes his eyes. "Fuck." Then he falls back against the ground.

At least we agree on something. I shift my weight. It doesn't seem wise to let the conversation continue about Ellie, so I steer us back to safer ground.

"You should keep trying to connect to the Land yourself."

Caeo's gaze flicks to me. "Why? What's the point?"

Because it's better than wasting away while high on milk?

I sigh. "Because having a relationship with the Land is an integral part of being fae. Because you won't be able to shape until you do. Because if I die, I'd rather the realm pass to you than our mother."

He shoots back up. "What was that last one?"

Ancients. I shouldn't have said that. I've hurt him enough—he doesn't need my burdens as well. But I did, and I doubt he'll let it drop if I don't answer.

"I don't have an heir. If our mother kills me, the realm will likely pass to her. The only other option is you, but that won't happen unless you bond with the Land."

"But she's the queen."

A scoff bursts out of me. "That's what she wants everyone to believe. Aedys passed to me when she was exiled."

Caeo's eyebrows knit together. "Then why don't you just rally the people and overthrow her?"

My voice comes out louder than I intend. "Because she has the support of Ystyr and is willing to use my people as a shield to protect herself." Not to mention, no one's ever been enthusiastic about me ruling. Too young, too volatile.

"She can't willbend everyone at once." His volume matches

mine. "And if Ystyr's busy fighting the humans, they can't fight her own people, too."

The weight of it all presses down on my shoulders. He doesn't understand—I tried, and failed. I can't get near her without hurting, killing, or bending the very people I want to protect. Who already fear me for being the most powerful willbender in several millennia.

And even if I did, then I'd have to... My own mother...

I shove myself to my feet. "Just practice bonding with the Land."

I need to take a walk.

Chapter 9

I wrest my fingers out of the dirt and sit up, rubbing my temples as a slow exhale attempts to push out all my frustrations.

It doesn't.

I really am the worst fae ever, aren't I?

The sun has traveled a good distance across the sky since Taran stormed off. At the time, it was good riddance. But it's been gnawing at me as more bells pass without him returning, the air growing colder by the minute.

I can't say I hate my brother without my throat twisting at the lie, but I wish there was a word for 'temporarily having strong feelings of hatred toward' because saying 'I'm angry at him' doesn't do it justice. It's becoming more and more difficult to hold that anger, though; it's clear as glass that he's not *just* an asshole who stole his brother's girlfriend, even if she did push him.

He has some serious issues.

Our mother somehow messed him up more than she did me. Which is saying a lot, since the second my mind drifts back to any moment of the last week, my body goes cold and wants to curl up into itself as my lungs fill with rocks.

Like right now. The inescapable darkness pressing around me. Parched throat. Trapped with visions of what was coming, every heartbeat a ticking clock until the moment she'd… she'd…

Blood. Flesh. Everyone watching as she makes me thrust, thrust—

Breathe. Just breathe.

I dig my palms into my eye sockets, as if they can push the images away.

They can't.

But something else can.

My hands drop. The little jar of milk sits on the ground nearby.

I swallow.

Just a little bit, and everything will go away. Far away, where it won't bother me until nightfall. Then I can take it again. And again, and again, until the memories stop coming.

But I won't be able to figure anything out if I'm high as a cloud.

I shouldn't give a damn about Taran after what he did. The only thing that makes us brothers is sharing the same shitty mother.

Which makes him the only person who has any idea what I've been through.

Fuck. Of course that's how life works out.

I lie back down, close my eyes, and dig my fingers back into the dirt.

"Hello, Land."

Nothing. Just the whistling of the wind.

I haven't been able to feel that pulse a single time on my own. I've tried clearing my mind, talking—nope. It's like She doubts my sincerity.

Which… yeah, She probably should. Why am I doing this other than Taran telling me to? I don't want to be his heir, no thanks. It'd be nice to be able to shape, but that's a stupid reason, too. He said it was an important part of being fae…

It's like a mountain pressing into me, crushing the air out of my chest. I force a deep breath.

"I don't like what I am." The weight falls away as I say the words aloud.

Maybe if I'd known my whole life what I was, I would. I'd probably be proud to be the only half fae, half mortal to ever exist. It would've made me special, offsetting a lifetime of failure.

Instead, it's all wrapped up in the worst moments of my life. How can I be happy with what I am when I only exist because my mother essentially raped my father?

A tear rolls down my cheek.

Not essentially. She did. She forced herself upon him, just like she was gonna force me with Owen—

A blaze pulses through my fingers just as my heart cracks down the middle, surrounding the fracture in a sealing embrace.

My eyes shoot open, my breath hitching.

I'm a child again, wrapped in the warm hug I always wished my mother would give me but never did.

Her pulse beats in rhythm with mine as tears stream down my face, its heat flooding every inch of me. The only time I've ever felt anything remotely like this is lying in bed with Ellie, our limbs entangled and our bodies one.

The Land's pulse stutters, a seething rumble brewing beneath it.

My heart sinks. *You really do hate Ellie, don't you?*

I take another deep breath, forcing myself to push all thoughts of Ellie from my mind. I need to focus on my own relationship with the Land before I can fix things between Her and Ellie.

Her anger abates as my mind clears. I time my inhales to Her pulses, growing calmer with every exhale as they slow to a soothing pace.

I don't fall asleep, but time becomes meaningless. Just my breath and the Land.

All my turmoil washes away. I'm floating in an ocean of peace.

My eyes peek open. The sun has nearly set, and the Land still pulses through me. I'm hesitant to break the connection, but Taran still hasn't returned.

Maybe I can ask the Land where he is?

With a deep breath, I close my eyes again, picturing Taran in my mind. I push the image down, into the ground, and then—I don't know—bounce it around a bit? How do I ask where he is without words?

A few seconds later, I *feel* him, the same way I felt Owena before. Like there's a string coming out of my shoulder that connects us, buried in the Land. He's also lying on the ground, next to a stream.

He can feel me focusing on him. I don't know how I can tell that—it's like when someone's hovering over your shoulder, except I thought I was the one hovering.

"Let's see if I can get there." I pause, then pull my hands out of the dirt. Instead of disappearing, the pulse continues—faintly—in the air and where my butt meets the ground. I still feel the connection to Taran.

"This is so weird."

I grab my jar of milk from where I set it earlier, shove it into the pack, and follow the tether to Taran.

He's lying on his back amid the tall grass, gazing at the night sky as I approach. I go to the stream first, washing all the dirt from my hands and taking a drink. The icy water has the same bright, almost fruity taste that it did at the castle—so much better than back home.

I drop the pack and sit next to him.

"It took you long enough," Taran says, still looking at the stars.

"Tell me why you did it." The words come out all on their own. I swallow, then push the rest out. "Do you love her?"

Taran closes his eyes, then exhales slowly. My stomach tightens as I wait, my fingers clenching together as I fight the urge to press him.

"I... care for her," he says finally, his body tense. "She made everything feel lighter. And her determination, to keep pushing when things were difficult... It's a strength I wish I had. She made me believe I could."

My chest constricts. I could've said the exact same thing about her myself. What does that say about our love? Was it not enough? We knew each other for months, but thanks to our curse, she probably spent close to the same amount of time with him as she did with me.

Taran's eyes open, an eerie green light in the darkness. "I could tell she was drawn to me, and I tried to avoid her, but I couldn't. Everything was so heavy, and she wanted to share my burden. Pushing her away hurt her so much. So I gave in, because I couldn't bear causing her pain."

I've gone numb—my heart's cracked so many times that there's nothing more to break. It's just sinking slowly into nothingness. "It was all her, then. She fell for you."

"She doesn't love me."

I jolt upright as my heart thuds back to life. "What?" *He's not like me—he can't just say that if it's not true.*

Still on his back, Taran fidgets with a long blade of grass between his fingers. "I was just there—someone who reminded her of you, who she could latch onto as her world fell apart."

Confusion and concern spiral within me, and I scoot closer to better meet his eyes. "Why was her world falling apart?"

The grass whips through the air as Taran lets go of it, sighing. "I told her the truth about the enmity between our people—how mortals betrayed the Land, and how incanting desecrates Her. I had to, to convince her to help me."

"Why did you need her help to begin with?"

"I thought our mother would poison you against me. I knew she couldn't be exiled again. That I'd have to"—he swallows—"to kill her." Taran takes a breath, and his voice comes out a ragged whisper. "I didn't want to have to kill you, too. I hoped Ellie would get you to see the truth."

I groan, burying my face in my hands as everything sinks in. "So you're not an asshole, you're just completely fucked."

A huff escapes him. "I suppose that's one way of putting it."

Wonderful. And now that I know that, *I'm* the asshole if I keep hammering him. I need to be the bigger person, for Ellie's sake. And maybe my own.

Later, though.

"That's enough brotherly bonding for me right now." I lift my head and scooch further away from him, pulling the pack with me. Thankfully, Taran seems to agree and doesn't say anything else.

I dig through our supplies, and it's immediately apparent that we've gone through a decent amount of our food. I can't imagine Owena and Ellie are doing much better. At this rate, we'll probably be all out the day after tomorrow.

Just one more thing to worry about.

After eating as little as I can to keep from feeling hungry, I pack everything back up. Except for the little jar of midnight star milk.

A weight presses against my chest. I accomplished a fair amount today, having significantly improved my relationships with both the Land and Taran. So I shouldn't feel bad about having some now—it'll help me sleep. Otherwise, I'll spend half the night trying to plug the flood of memories leaching out of my brain.

My pinky trembles as it dips into the jar.

"HOW MUCH CAN YOU actually sense through the Land?" I ask, figuring it's the safest way to start a conversation. Unless Taran starts insulting my lack of ability again, but then our failure to get along is on him, not me.

It's shortly after dawn, because it's impossible to sleep in when you're sleeping outside. While my face is freezing from splashing it awake in the nearby creek, it wasn't as cold last night, the warmth of the Land radiating through me with every pulse. If that's what's normal for fae, no wonder Taran doesn't give two shits about finding shelter or making fires.

"It depends on the distance," he says, pushing himself upright. He runs his hand through his chin-length hair, moving it away from his eyes. "At the moment, I can only feel the princess if I focus on her, or if she makes sudden, large movements. But I can tell you exactly where every fish in this section of creek is, and where to find some berry bushes further downstream."

"That's... a lot." I glance back up the hill, then follow the trickling water as it flows into the valley where we sit. It continues beyond my sight, disappearing into the thick, gray fog.

Taran shrugs. "I'm used to it. Yours won't be anywhere near as strong, but you should be able to sense the fish and berries if you focus."

"How? Do I stick my fingers in the dirt again?"

He laughs, a weird break from his normally broody face. "No. We typically do that only when we want to speak with Her. It's like searching with your eyes, but with your spirit, I suppose?"

With my spirit? "What does that even mean?"

He sighs, then meets my gaze. "It means... Can you still feel me, like you did yesterday?"

"No."

"Try to feel that connection again."

"Alright." I shift so I'm sitting straighter, then shut my eyes.

"You shouldn't have to close your eyes."

"Shut up, I'm new at this."

Focus.

I try pushing myself—for lack of a better word—into the ground, searching for something that feels like the tether from yesterday. I already know where Taran is in relation to me, because I was just looking at him, but there *is* something there. A weight in that direction.

"I think I can feel you."

Taran doesn't respond, but the weight moves about ten feet to my right.

"You just moved."

"Good. Now, stop focusing on me. Feel past me."

I try to push past Taran, my eyes twitching beneath their lids as they attempt to help.

Then I sense it: the edge of the grass behind him, hanging over the babbling brook. A fish squirts away from another that swam too close.

My heart thuds in my chest. "I can feel the fish!"

"Now open your eyes and see if you can hold on to that."

I do, and I *can.*

I rush to the water's edge to see the fish with my own eyes. They're moving exactly as I expect them to, as if I'm seeing them twice.

"This is so weird." I can actually *feel* how the water flows between the rocks. Not in my body, but in the space around me. It's just... there.

I glance back at Taran. "We should try to catch one. We're running low on food."

The grass rustles as he kneels beside me. "I can show you how, but it won't help with our food shortage—it would spoil too quickly."

"I don't care. Show me how."

Taran rolls up his sleeve, then sticks his hand into the water upriver. The stream stops flowing. Like he dropped an invisible dam across the whole thing.

My eyes go as wide as tea saucers. "Whoa."

The fish flop around in the mud for a few seconds before Taran lifts his hand, and the water rushes forward.

"That's shaping?" I ask.

"Yes."

"And I should be able to do that?"

"Nothing has indicated otherwise."

A rush of excitement spurts through me, hopeful that I might actually be able to do something noteworthy for once. "How do I do it?"

"Focus on the water the same way you do with your land-sense, then imagine molding it into what you want."

I force an exhale, focusing on the water, just like he said. I can feel it flowing, as if it's a part of me, but not. Dropping my hand into the current, I imagine it splitting in two.

"Holy shit!" *The water actually listened to me!*

I move my hand up and down, watching the water join and split over and over again. I hover my other hand above the surface and imagine pulling the water up to my fingers, and it fucking works!

Laughter flits out of me like butterflies, my eyes wet with tears, but the happy kind. *This is so easy!* I struggled with incanting for months, convinced I was a failure, but really, I was just a fish flopping about in the mud when an entire ocean existed beyond the fog.

I abandon the water, turning my attention to the nearby ground.

Pressing my hand down, it shifts beneath my palm as if I pushed a bowl into a pile of clay. Then I pull my hand up, willing the earth to follow as I imagine it forming into the shape of a small person. The result's a little crude, but there's definitely a head and some indication of arms and legs. A closed-up flower bud sticks out of the figure's head, and I visualize it opening, and it does!

Taran's hand lands on my shoulder. "I know you're excited, but you don't want to annoy Her. We have our gifts by Her grace, and She'll take them away if you disrupt Her balance. Try to limit yourself to things you actually need to do."

It's like telling a child to ignore everything in a shop full of sweets. But I take a breath, forcing myself to calm down—I don't want to jeopardize my new relationship with Her.

Taran sits back. "Now we just have to work on getting your willbending under control."

My excitement falters. "I don't want to."

"I understand how you feel. But if you don't learn to control it, you risk hurting the people you care about."

The rest of my enthusiasm crumbles away. *He really knows how to kill the mood.*

"I know, I just... I don't want to think about it right now."

Taran lets out an exhale, brushing his hands on his pants. "Then maybe, for the time being, try not to speak when you're angry."

Because that's so easy. But I haven't accidentally done it since that night with Owena, despite being plenty irritated with him, so it's probably fine.

"We should head back soon," he continues, standing up. "Why don't you try to find those berry bushes? You should be able to make them sprout extra to bring with us."

That could be fun. I focus my attention downstream, searching the banks of the creek with my land-sense.

There.

I push myself to my feet and lead the way.

WITH A PACK STUFFED with an excessive amount of blueberries, I lead the way back to Ellie and Owena. Taran insists it's safe for me to search for Ellie, since the Land isn't the permanent presence within me that She is in him, but I don't dare risk it.

Instead, I focus my search on Owena's presence, but since my land-sense is nowhere near as strong as Taran's, I'm picking up nothing. So he gives me landmarks along the way to seek out—a cluster of rocks, a bush with a certain number of branches, a family of gophers burrowed underground. It takes a fair amount of effort, but I find them all.

It's just about sunset when I finally notice Owena. I stop, my heart thundering in my chest.

Taran comes to a halt behind me. "We're almost there."

"Yeah."

And what will happen then?

My mouth goes dry.

Ellie will pick me... right? I don't know what I'll do if she doesn't.

My hand twitches, itching toward the little jar in my pocket.

I sit on the steep hillside, digging the heels of my hands into my eyes. Taran's there, in the back of my mind, pacing with uneven steps.

If I believe everything he said, there's no way she wouldn't. She nearly fell apart the other night when we spoke, but her eyes shone through her tears with the same love as before. It was real. *Is* real.

Isn't it?

I could say it out loud. If it's not true, I'd know—my throat would twist into a painful knot.

But it's already twisting just thinking about it.

I exhale slowly, then push myself to my feet.

I have to believe in her. Believe in our love.

And when she tells me she still loves me, I don't want to be high.

I follow my land-sense toward Owena until I spot her in the distance, sitting outside the shelter Taran made. She lifts her head in our direction, but her features are too far away to make out. She must have sensed our approach.

Ellie should be inside, but I don't dare reach out to check.

Owena stands as we draw near. "I see you didn't kill one another."

My heart's racing in anticipation; I have no patience for pleasantries right now.

"How's Ellie?"

"I'm alright."

I spin toward her voice. Golden light softens her features as she stands at the narrow entrance to their cave, her hand resting on the grassy hillside. Nothing about her looks alright—streaks of dirt line her face where grimy hands wiped away tears, and her eyes glisten tragically with more waiting to fall. A weak smile quivers on her lips as she meets my eyes, but then her gaze shifts past me.

"Taran, we should talk."

Chapter 10

Ellie

Iknow what my heart wants, but I worry about the consequences of following through with it; we're only here because I plowed blindly ahead without having all the information. So I force myself away from Caeo's expectant face, blanketed in the warm glow of the setting sun.

I need answers from Taran. Only then will the turmoil twisting within me ease.

He hasn't been looking at me, his expression shadowed by his raven hair as he stares at the ground, hands on his hips. At my words, he closes his eyes, then lets out a slow exhale.

He marches away.

I waver, then steel myself to follow.

Just as I take a step, Caeo grabs my arm, driving a spike of doubt into my heart. If I meet his eyes, I'll lose my resolve. This choice is bigger than us. After all the damage I've done, I can't keep making decisions without considering the cost to others.

"Ellie—"

"I'm sorry, Caeo, but I need to talk to Taran first." Pulling myself free of his grasp, I hurry after Taran, my pulse racing.

A blinding, golden light outlines his dusky form against the reddening sky, his strides along the grassy hillside almost twice the length of mine. He isn't stopping.

"Taran, wait! I need to talk to you."

"You don't need anything from me," he says without a glance back. "Go pick Caeo and be done with it."

I stumble to a halt, as if he drove a lance through my chest. "Is that what you want?"

Have I misjudged his feelings for me?

He stops about twenty feet ahead, his voice so low I can barely hear him. "It doesn't matter what I want."

My hand twitches as my heart yearns to reach for him, then pulls back, unsure.

"Of course it does, Taran. Your feelings matter."

"Not in this instance."

I take a step toward him.

"Stop, Ellie. Don't come any closer. Forget about me and go be with Caeo."

"And you would be alright with that?" I take another step. His words... I can't trust that he truly means them without seeing his face.

"Please. Don't make me bend you."

I freeze, my heart trembling.

"Why, Taran? Why won't you even look at me?"

His shoulders sag as he wilts before my eyes. "You incanted in my realm," he says, his voice rough. "Every time I see you... touch you... the Land's rage burns through me."

A void forms in my throat, its gravity slowly sinking, pulling the rest of me with it.

My voice barely escapes. "I... B-but I had to. T-to save you! I didn't mean to hurt Her!"

"I know." His words are a whisper, hardly there.

Thoughts—excuses, solutions—scurry through my mind. "Isn't

there something... Can I make it up to Her? Reid incanted. Emlyn said She forgave him!"

"He incanted once. You did it twice. I can't guarantee She won't kill you."

My heart strikes against my ribs. The space between each beat is a vast emptiness, each thud hammering the finality of my fate. Everything I've done, all my attempts to help... I've ruined everything. Just like with Sophie.

It's worse than not mattering at all.

Following the angles of Taran's back, my gaze stops at the mess of his dark hair, his shoulders drooping from all the weight I've made him bear. I'd expected this conversation to be hard—I care about him too much to break his heart without nicking my own in the process—but this...

I lower my head in shame, closing my eyes against burning tears. "I'm sorry."

To him and the Land. I'd dreamed of helping him bear his burdens, of healing the rifts between our realms. To share what I'd learned so my people could repair the damage we'd done.

All those dreams, now shattered.

A hand lands on my arm, pulling me into a warm embrace. A familiar clove scent envelops me, calming my trembling heart.

Caeo.

"It'll be alright, Ellie. We'll figure it out." His voice is soft. Everything it needs to be, but words aren't enough.

"How?"

He pulls away just enough to tilt my tear-streaked face up to his eyes. Eyes so different from the ones I fell in love with. Where specks of cerulean once peeked through the gray, like a sunny sky behind a storm, they now glow like blue moonstones. Just as beautiful as the rest of him.

His thumb gently brushes the dampness from my cheek.

"Together. If... if you still want me."

The hesitancy, the doubt in his voice... My heart splinters.

I'll never be able to forgive myself for hurting him this much.

"Of course I do, Caeo. I'm yours." It was never a question. The way he challenges me not to try so hard. To be me, instead of losing myself beneath everyone's expectations. How he balances me in every way that matters.

The tension in his face melts away. He wraps his arms around me, squeezing me tightly as a tattered exhale escapes his throat. I wind my arms around him, breathing in time with his heartbeat. Absorbing his warmth. His love.

Despite everything that's happened, all the mistakes I've made... I'm home.

Caeo's hold on me relaxes. His fingers trace along my arm, prickling it with goosebumps while his eyes search my face. "Come on." He takes me by the hand, leading me toward our shelter.

I glance back at Taran. At some point, Owena must have passed us by, as she now approaches him, silhouetted against the oranges and reds of the setting sun. Her voice carries on the breeze as her hand rests on his arm, her words indecipherable. I swallow the lump in my throat.

I can't help him anymore, not if even the merest glimpse of me is torture. Hopefully, she can.

CAEO COLLAPSES against the dirt wall of the cavern Taran made, opening his arm so I can curl up next to him, tucking my legs across his lap. Neither of us speaks, caught between the familiar and the strange, like pieces of different puzzles that somehow fit perfectly together.

Now that I remember everything, it's apparent that whatever he went through during our time apart changed him, and I'm certain he feels the same way about me. His confidence, his carefree charm, has frayed, almost as if I stole some of it to fuel my reckless decisions. Thoughts race through my mind, searching for the best way to broach the subject, my heart sprinting to keep up as every idea seems worse than the last.

Caeo squeezes my leg. "Taran told me what happened. You don't have to explain."

My thoughts stutter to a halt.

"He did?" Hopefully he didn't share *everything*. I doubt Caeo'd be this calm if he'd heard every detail.

"Yeah. You could say we've... reached an understanding. He even taught me how to use my land-sense and shape."

My eyes widen.

Of course. Caeo's half fae.

Somehow, despite the changes to his eyes and ears being glaringly obvious every time I look at him, the reality that he's a half fae prince hasn't sunk in at all. Just one more truth about him I need to adjust to. I used to dread what my parents would think of a poverty-stricken future son-in-law on the verge of failing out of the Academy. Now *I* have the lower status and can't do anything special.

And he's one of the people my father's dedicated his life to fighting.

I rest my hand on top of Caeo's, shutting away those thoughts. "Can you show me?"

His smile, the one I've seen light up his face thousands of times, illuminates our shadowy cave. "Taran says I shouldn't do tricks because it'll annoy the Land, but..." His eyes sweep across the dark cavern to the pathetic pile of sticks leftover from my failed fire attempt. "...maybe I can make a fire?"

I glance away. "Making a fire is incanting." A knot twists in my stomach at the reminder of my sin.

"Yeah, but if we can get an ember glowing, maybe I can make it bigger."

Could that be how Emlyn and Taran always did it so quickly? Maybe I'm not as much of a failure as I thought.

Just human.

Caeo pats my legs, and I pull them off him. I crawl over to my discarded fire-making supplies.

"Owena made this." I show him the flattened piece of wood I spent forever spinning sticks into.

"Huh." He takes it from me, eyeing it skeptically. "She *did* say she was pretty bad at shaping." He shifts it into a more even, rectangular shape within seconds.

My heart skips a beat. Even an incantation wouldn't have done that so smoothly.

"You just—"

Caeo's eyes twinkle. "Yep."

After watching how he struggled to incant for months with no success, the grin that stretches across his face warms my heart more than a fire ever could. An overwhelming urge to kiss him surges through me, but I resist, not wanting to interrupt his success.

He grabs another stick, lining it up to the notch I'd made in the flattened piece. The divot reshapes to match the tip better, then he starts spinning the stick quickly between his hands.

I can't help the twinge of jealousy at how easy he's making this look. Though I try to smother it with my pride in his accomplishments, it doesn't quite go away, simmering quietly within.

"When did you learn how to start a fire?" I ask.

Caeo shrugs, briefly interrupting the stick's movement. "Sometime when I was a kid. Then Reid learned to incant, and I only ever had to do it for my mother. It's a lot easier with flint and steel."

Within a few minutes, a trail of smoke rises from where the two pieces of wood meet. He eyes the tip of the stick, meeting it with a clump of dried grass.

He drops it as it bursts into flame.

"Quick, get some wood on that!"

I grab a handful of sticks and toss them on top of the small fire.

"You want them to be more tent-like," he says.

My pulse spikes, and my voice comes out sharper than I intended. "You should've said that earlier!"

"Sorry, I wasn't really thinking this through." Caeo carefully brings his hands to the parts of the sticks that aren't ablaze, and they twist and bend upward into a more tent-like shape. Then he leans some other sticks against the structure, puffing the flame up to engulf them. A blast of heat warms my skin.

"At least you did it," I say, unable to keep the resentment from my voice as I lean against the cold dirt wall. "I barely got it to smoke. I'm useless without incanting."

"What?" Caeo looks my way, his face flickering orange in the firelight. "Why would you say that?"

I sigh. *Looks like we're doing me first.*

"I don't know how to do anything, and compared to the rest of you, I'm blind and deaf, bumbling around in the dark. I didn't even do what I was brought here to do—I abandoned you to help Taran."

Caeo settles next to me, taking my hand. "He said you saved his life."

"And now the Land wants me dead." The statement doesn't bring me to tears this time. It hurts, but without Taran around, it feels more distant. More abstract.

Or maybe the well's finally empty.

"We can work on that, Ellie. I connected with Her yesterday. She made it very clear She's angry with you, but She knows my feelings and still didn't break our bond. That means there's hope." He brings my hand to his lips, kissing it. "It may take time, but if we can find a way to balance things, I think She'll forgive you."

"Maybe." I exhale, his words bringing a hope I'm hesitant to accept. "You keep reminding me you're fae, now." *When will it stop surprising me?*

His voice softens. "I always was. I just didn't know it."

"But it's changed you." I reach my hand to his ear, my thumb tracing its pointed tip. "More than just your appearance."

"The last few weeks were... a lot. I'd rather not talk about it." His gaze drifts away as he takes my hand from his ear.

No, he doesn't get off that easily. We talked about me—it's his turn now.

"Please." I lean forward, trying to meet his blue eyes. They glow with an inner light that shimmers with the flames. "Let me help."

Caeo drops our hands to his lap. His eyelids sink down as he leans his head back against the wall.

"Owena said you were supposed to marry her," I press, squeezing his hand. "That your mother was willbending you. That"—I swallow—"you smoke speckled long leaf to escape."

He exhales slowly out of his nose. "I probably should've told you about that earlier."

"Why didn't you?"

He tilts his head toward me, his eyes opening. "I did it because I was miserable. It wasn't the sort of thing I wanted to bring up early on, and once we were seeing each other every day, I was happier, even when I couldn't remember you. I didn't feel the need for it. Not until..."

"Life became hard again." I scoot closer to him, wrapping my hands around his arm. If only he'd never been taken from me—he may have never used it again. One more way his mother wronged him.

"Yeah." Caeo's head rolls back along the wall, his gaze shifting to the floor. The sun must have set, and his features disappear into the darkness, turned away from the flickering light of the fire.

"You can tell me what happened, Caeo."

He shakes his head, so subtly it's more like a tremble. "Don't make me. Not today. Today was better. I don't want to ruin it."

My mouth tightens.

What am I supposed to do? Push him, or wait until he's ready?

If pressing him tonight is the wrong choice, I could ruin everything. Again. But if giving him time doesn't help, I'll still be able to push later.

"Alright." I lean against his shoulder. "Another time."

Please let that be the right choice.

Caeo relaxes, and I sink into him. A moment later, he shifts toward me, tilting my face to meet his.

"I love you," he whispers.

A warm, steady glow fills my chest. "I love you too."

He inches closer, more hesitant than ever before. I meet him halfway, pressing my lips softly against his, welcoming him back to me. My tongue brushes against his lower lip, seeking his familiar taste.

But he pulls away, and my breath catches in my throat. An exhausted smile forms on his lips as they part mine. He must be tired. We both are.

"We'll figure everything out," he says. "Together."

I take a breath, hoping to soothe my racing heart. "We will."

No matter how broken things may feel, I'm his, and he's mine.

While part of me still aches for hurting Taran, it's obvious now how wrong our relationship was. But Caeo and I, we'll find our way back to what we were, or discover something new. We always will.

Together.

Chapter 11

Taran

The warmth of the princess's hand seeps into my upper arm, exactly where expected if I were escorting her on a casual stroll. Not hiking along a precarious slope where tall, thick grass tangles our every step.

"Walk with me." Her voice is light, softer than the tone she typically uses when addressing me.

Fiery tendrils of apprehension blaze down my spine.

I grit my teeth. "What do you want?"

Keeping my gaze ahead, I focus the entirety of my land-sense on her to keep it off of Ellie and all the heartache between us, waiting for the murderous rage within me to cool down. But now I have my own irritation to contend with, and I'm unsure where the Land's ends and mine begins.

"It seemed prudent to intervene." She gives me a gentle tug. "As I don't wish to hover nearby as Caeo and Ellie reconnect any more than you do, we might as well take the opportunity to become better acquainted."

"Fine," I mutter, taking a step. "But I doubt there's anything you can say that will get me to trust you, Princess Briarwood."

"My name is Owena, and allow me to make my position clear: while I am not your enemy, I have no desire to be your friend, Prince

Evermoor."

I stop and face her. "Not my enemy? Your father had mine killed. We've been at war for twenty-one years. You're a curse-weaver!"

It's as if the flames of my anger reflect off her golden hair. Or perhaps it's the orange of the setting sun. I shift my gaze to her heartless black eyes.

They lock onto me.

"I have about as much influence on my father's rulings as you do on your mother's." Her grip on my arm tightens against my tensing muscles.

If that's the game she wants to play...

I march along the hillside, forcing her to either match my pace with her shorter strides or let go in surrender. To my surprise, she keeps up, her steps bouncing between a fast walk and jog as she traverses the uneven terrain.

"Why are you even here, Princess?"

"Caeo asked me to break Ellie's curse." Her voice comes out breathy. Despite her demeanor, she won't be able to keep up with me for long.

"And you've done that," I say. "So now you can leave."

"What good would it do me to wander these freezing hills by myself? I can't imagine any scenario where that would end well for me."

"At least I wouldn't have to suffer you."

"No, you would simply suffer the discomfort of traveling with Caeo and Ellie by yourself, while attempting to devise another plan for taking back your realm that will inevitably fail."

I stop so suddenly she stumbles, and I reach out on reflex, catching her arm. Once she straightens, I release her, pulling my other arm free of her grasp for good measure.

"Perhaps you shouldn't insult me if you don't want me to

abandon you out here."

The princess adjusts her coat, borrowed from Emlyn's mother. It's too big for her frame, obscuring the curves I know are underneath.

Heat burns in my face. She's infuriating.

"You're right. I apologize." Her dark eyes meet mine, and the fire sinks into my chest, waiting to flare up if this is some kind of trick.

"You do?"

"Yes, I do. I had hoped to improve our relationship to something better than outright hostility, but it would seem I've failed."

I bring my hand to my face, fingers rubbing my brow. As much as I loathe to admit it, with how things stand with everyone else in my life, I could use one less person to fight with. Even if that person is a Ystyrian princess.

"Fine. I'll try to be less hostile," I grumble, dropping my hand.

A smile curls on her lips. "Thank you. It would please me if you would refer to me by my given name."

She's insufferable.

I change the subject. "Will you need another shelter for the night?" My stomach twists, and I force the thoughts of what's likely occurring in the last shelter I made out of my mind.

"No. The Land will keep me warm."

My anger ignites again. "Then why did you demand I make the last one?"

"Two reasons." She holds up one finger. "First, the Land would not have kept Ellie warm. Second"—she uncurls another—"I needed you exhausted so you would put up less of a fight about leaving for two days."

"But you had already—" I can't complete the sentence. Realization hits me like a punch to the gut.

Her brow lifts as her lips purse. "I never said I cursed Ellie. You came to that conclusion on your own."

"You tricked me?" My arms tense, my fingers rubbing together to keep from forming fists.

She has the audacity to admit that after convincing me she wants to play nice?

A smile spreads across her face. "Have a good night, Taran." She lowers into a slight curtsy before turning away.

Eyes closed, I inhale the brisk air, trying to force calm upon myself. When I open them, she's strolling away along the path we took, my ire fading with every sway of her hips.

"Goodnight, Owena," I mumble, then reach out to find a comfortable spot to sleep.

Movement itches at the edge of my land-sense.

It was a struggle to sleep, my mind only succumbing to exhaustion as a faint light brightened the edge of the night sky. The mid-morning sun blinds my eyes as they open.

Twelve people, traveling as an organized group. Far away. If they somehow head directly toward us, it will be at least midday before they sense us, assuming we stay where we are.

So we should get moving.

I pick myself up and march back to the others. I can sense the three of them sitting outside the shelter I made, eating breakfast. A sharp pain slices through me as my land-sense passes over Ellie, so I force myself to focus on Princess Owena as she places a blueberry between her lips.

My stomach tightens, and my mouth goes dry.

I need to eat something. Then we'll leave.

And go... where?

My steps falter. I don't have a plan.

Where are we running to? Should we even be running?

I could handle these soldiers easily. For me, bending twelve is no different from bending one. I could send them away with no memory of where they've been. Or telling tales they saw us far away from here. Or with orders to kill my mother themselves.

Or we can run, so I don't have to bend anyone.

Coward.

Princess Owena and Caeo stiffen as they sense my approach. They stand, positioning themselves to hide Ellie from sight, sitting behind them.

Deep breaths.

I can do this. It's simply a matter of looking at either Caeo or Owena.

I keep my gaze on the ground. "We need to leave. There are soldiers approaching. Twelve of them."

"Where would you suggest we go?" Princess Owena asks.

"We need more food," Caeo adds.

"I know. We can follow that stream south toward the forest. That should provide us with enough food and water until we get there."

There. I made a plan. That wasn't so hard.

"And then what?" Owena sets her hands on her hips. "What is our ultimate goal? Do you expect us to run and hide while our realms go to war?"

My jaw clenches, and I can't keep myself from glaring at her. Of course she doesn't think that's enough. No matter what she said last night, she's going to make everything as difficult as possible.

"We can make a better plan once we've solved our current problems."

She steps forward, meeting my glare and pulling it with such intensity that I almost waver. I will myself to hold on.

"Or, we can go with my plan," she says.

My pulse blares a warning—danger. "I don't trust any plan of yours."

Caeo runs his hand through his hair. "Just hear her out. It's solid."

My eyes flick toward my brother's face. My brother who hated me two days ago. Is he once again following Owena's wishes, or does he actually agree with her? He doesn't seem to have the same limitations on lying as the rest of us.

"Fine," I sigh. "What's your plan, Princess?"

Owena weaves her fingers together. "Even if you were willing to face your mother and do what's necessary, that would only end the war with the mortals. If we want true peace between all the realms, we need to remove my father as well."

My heart slows with a heavy thud. That's not what I expected her to say.

"So, your plan is for us to kill King Dryfid? And my mother does whatever she wants with my realm in the meantime?"

Owena takes a deep breath. "Yes. When my father dies, Ystyr will pass to me. Then the two of us can marry, uniting our realms into a new one—one your mother has no claim to. She would lose whatever power Aedys gives her, as it would no longer exist, thus solving your problem without you ever needing to face her."

An eternity passes before my heart beats again. A sharp tug on my bond from my mother snaps me out of it.

"You want me to marry you?" Even during my four years with Aerona, it never crossed my mind to marry her. We're far too young to make that kind of commitment.

"I *want* to end these wars once and for all, and I'm willing to do what I must to ensure that happens."

I shake my head. "No, I'm not doing that. I refuse."

"We've talked about it all morning," Ellie says from beyond my sight. "I think you should consider it—you wouldn't have to carry everything yourself anymore."

A piercing crack splits my chest. *How can Ellie possibly think I want to hear her say that?*

"And Owena's not that bad once you get to know her," Caeo adds.

Owena narrows her eyes at him, and he shrugs.

"No." My feet have turned and pulled me away before I realize I'm moving.

This is insanity. How could everyone go ahead and decide this is what's best without me? When it's *my* life? *My* realm?

And Ellie... Did I mean so little to her that she has no qualms about passing me off to another woman so quickly?

It's like I've been stabbed in the heart.

She belongs with Caeo. She loves him. Even if the Land's fury didn't prevent us from being together, that would still be true.

But knowing all that doesn't keep it from hurting.

"Taran, wait."

It's Caeo. Better than Owena, at least.

"Is this your revenge?" I ask, keeping my pace as prickly blades of grass graze my legs. "I stole Ellie, so let's marry me off to my enemy to make sure that never happens again?"

"What? No. Will you stop?" He grabs my arm, halting me.

"Let go of me."

"No."

"I can make you," I say, burning into his eyes.

He meets my gaze, unflinching. "Then do it."

Several heartbeats pass, holding the cold air deep in my lungs. I exhale, releasing the coil within me.

Caeo lets go of my arm.

"Try to think about it objectively, Taran. Neither of us will have much success confronting our mother, and there's too much at stake to risk failing again. But if it works the way Owena says, we can take everything from her without ever having to see her again."

Him, too? It figures no one has any faith I can do this on my own—all I've done so far is make everything worse. Maybe I *should* let Owena make all the decisions. Let her carry the burden.

The soldiers itch at me, growing closer as we speak. We don't have time for this.

I groan, burying my face in my hands. "It will work as she says."

I hate saying it, but it's true.

"It won't be as bad as you imagine. I was supposed to marry her, remember? We didn't want to, but she ended up becoming a good friend. I wouldn't have survived without her."

"She doesn't want to be my friend. She told me so."

Caeo shrugs. "Maybe think of it more like an alliance."

I drop my hands, meeting his eyes, blue as the sky behind him. "You realize how long we live? I'll be stuck with her for centuries, if not millennia. Most fae don't marry young for that very reason."

"Then it'll give you plenty of time to learn to like one another. Or one of you can kill the other. The realms will have already combined, so it's not like they'd break apart again, right?"

I exhale. "No, they wouldn't." But he doesn't understand. The bond that marriage would form between us... It's supposed to be like becoming the same person. Bound in heart, mind, and spirit. Hating her would be hating myself. Like it was for my father, shackled to my mother. I could see it draining him, every day, until it seemed like he only kept going to further defy her.

I hated who that turned him into. Someone no more capable of love than she was.

It's a fate worse than death.

But Owena can't bend me. If anything, I'm my mother in this scenario. The one with all the power. And if Caeo trusts her, maybe we can learn to get along. If not, she can rule the south while I take the north. Emlyn would just tell me to establish such boundaries up front.

My throat constricts as the fight within me shrivels away. I'm in no position to criticize anyone else's plans.

Caeo pats my back. "Alright. So let's follow that stream south like you wanted, find some food, then go kill Owena's dad."

"You know that won't be easy, right? He's more powerful than our mother. His strength rivals mine, but we'd be facing him in *his* realm."

"I'm sure Owena has a plan. She always does."

That's not comforting.

But I follow Caeo back, locking my gaze and land-sense on Owena as I approach, stopping directly in front of her.

The morning sun reflects in her midnight eyes, resolve blazing out of their depths as she pulls herself up to her full height. For the briefest moment, she seems small, until her usual poise wraps around her, lifting her with a quiet, towering grace.

Not a hint of fear. She might be the only person who's ever looked at me without any.

I swallow, forcing myself to speak.

"I agree to your plan, to kill your father. If we succeed, I'll marry you and unite our realms."

A smile curls on Owena's lips, and something twinkles in the darkness of her eyes.

"Good. But to make matters clear: I will be killing my father myself."

Part 2

Twisted

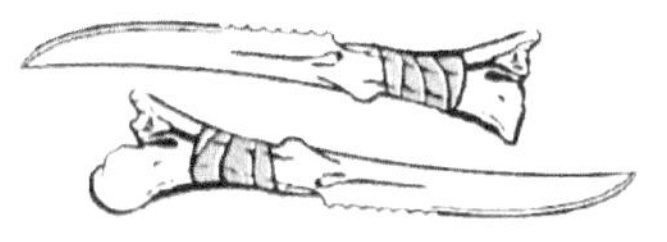

Chapter 12

Emlyn

Blinding sunlight streams through the window, making me squint as I drag my eyelids open. Another day in my shit life.

Well, it's not complete shit—I'm not bleeding anymore, my fever broke a few days ago, and my heart can once again race without me passing out. I can both stand *and* stumble downstairs, so no more disgusting medicine. Yay!

But now there's a different disgusting medicine. This bitter tea—Reid would love it—that I have to drink all day, every day. Something to do with restoring nutrients. Not even filling half the cup with honey can truly mask the flavor.

There's still a near-constant burn in my shoulder, but now I get to choose between dealing with it so I can move or taking the milk and just lying there for half the day. I honestly don't know which is worse at this point. I was so elated the first time I got to leave this fucking room that I nearly killed myself falling down the stairs, but that joy has long since abated.

It doesn't matter where I'm sitting around, I'm still just sitting there.

Rolling my face out of the light, my gaze lands on Reid, sleeping stretched out on his stomach next to me. Now that I've been moving around, he's been helping Ma more with the animals and chores, absorbing everything like a sunflower. Then every night, I fall asleep beside him after nothing but snuggles and light kisses. Still too delicate, too broken, to love him like I want to.

Even now, as my eyes trace the slopes and dips of his form, my heart longs to melt into him, but my body... is empty. Maybe the occasional ache or tingle, like at the moment, but nothing ever—

Hold on. Am I...?

My eyes snap downward.

I am. I'm actually hard.

A spark lights within me. "Reid, wake up." I frantically pat him with my left hand.

He yawns, blinking the sleep from his eyes. "Huh?"

"Ancients, wake up. I need you."

"What is it?" His eyes land on the tent pole that is my cock, then widen. "Oh." He glances back at my face. "What would you like me to do?"

"Whatever you want, just do it before it goes away."

"Alright, alright."

Reid nuzzles his face into my neck as his hand slips under the sheets, his lips brushing my skin while he trails his fingers down my chest, sending teasing tickles rippling through me. A groan rumbles out of me, and I clench in anticipation, kisses lacing my jaw.

His fingers inch closer and closer, tangling in the curls of hair before gently stroking up my shaft, tracing the tip just as his teeth scrape my earlobe. My muscles quiver...

A grunt bursts from me as my cock sneezes everything into the blankets. Reid freezes, then pulls away just enough to meet my eyes.

"Fuck," I groan, sinking into my pillow. I barely lasted a few heartbeats.

That's never happened before. Not to me.

"Hey, we have to start somewhere," Reid says. "It hasn't even been two weeks. I wasn't expecting anything for much longer."

"And that's supposed to make me feel better?"

"You're getting better every day. You'll be back to normal soon." He brushes my cheek with his fingers.

You can only say that because you can lie.

But I trap the thought, burying it as his lips meet mine, forcing myself to relax into his love. Failing, but he doesn't need to know that. For all he knows, the tears dampening his cheeks are from the release. As long as I don't say anything, he won't know: there's no normal to go back to.

Just a broken, useless me.

"I CAN CUT THAT for you."

"Huh?" I glance at Reid, once again glamoured to look fae.

At least I got to do it myself this time, instead of Ma obliterating all the cherished details of his face. Still, I didn't do as good a job as I would've liked, since it was rushed; some soldiers stopped by this morning, recruiting for the war. They immediately disregarded me, thanks to my injury, but Reid had to weave a lie about having already been recruited, saying he'll be heading west in a few days. There's been a somber air about him ever since they left.

"Your food," he says. "Should I cut it for you?"

My gaze drops to my untouched plate—some venison one of the hunters from the village brought over. I should probably eat it, but the bloody juices oozing out its sides make my stomach turn.

"No, I don't want it." I poke at the blackberries nestled against it instead.

"You need to eat," Ma says. She's over in the kitchen—I know that even without my land-sense—where she's been constantly preparing something for me, either my stupid tea or more food I don't feel like eating.

I'm tired of being here. This was never my home, and outside of my abandoned childhood stick collection, covered in dust on the shelves, there's nothing of me here. Just the discarded hopes of who Ma wished I'd be, and the floating spirit of my dead father.

Reid squeezes my hand, and I spare him a glance. Force a smile. What happened to the excitement that used to rush through me every time I looked at him? The urge to poke and prod him until I knew his heart pounded as frantically as mine?

"I love you," I whisper, mostly to confirm it's still true. It is, so why do I feel this way? Shouldn't being in love be enough?

"I love you too." Reid wraps his arm around me, careful not to bump my sling. My mom made it, and thank the Ancients it's not a garish rainbow like everything else she weaves. Just a deep, dark green.

I *should* talk to Reid. Share my worries. My fears. It's what I'd want him to do if things were reversed. But he has miseries of his own, and besides that—how could he hear those words and not come away fearing I resent him? Thinking he ruined my life?

The only other person I can talk to is Ma, but that's what made me feel this way to begin with.

Hmm.

I suppose I could talk to my *other* mom.

"Can you help me outside?" I ask Reid.

"Sure. You wanna try a walk?"

"No. I'm gonna seek guidance."

Something clatters in the kitchen.

"Emlyn, don't." Ma rushes over. Overreacting, as moms do. "She always takes something in payment, and you don't have much to give. It could set back your recovery."

"What are we talking about?" Reid asks.

"She'll take what's fair." It's never been too bad, just a day or two of exhaustion. Granted, I was in much better shape at the time.

Still—I push myself up with my hand against the table. Reid's on his feet, hands on my waist, steadying my wobbles.

I meet his gaze. "I'm doing this."

His eyes search mine for a heartbeat, then he nods. Ma reluctantly retreats, biting her lip with worry, as he hovers beside me all the way to the door.

"What exactly is 'seeking guidance?'" he asks once we're outside.

"Talking to the Land." I stumble past the goat to the nearest shady spot, already panting from the exertion. I check for goat and chicken shit before collapsing to the ground.

"Help me get this sling off."

"This won't hurt you, will it?" Reid unties the fabric from around my neck. I grimace as my arm slips out of it, even though he guides it as gently as he can.

"That likely depends on how the conversation goes." That's vague enough that I can say it. It's highly likely She'll take some life energy from me—it's how She keeps people from bugging Her all the time—but there's always a chance She'll decide we're even with only a minimal amount. She could even want a different payment entirely.

The goat sniffs at my toes, then nibbles at my wool pants; they're so loose I can pull them on and off with only one hand. I don't need them becoming even more unsightly, so I tell him to fuck off as nicely as possible in the Tongue.

"I've been wondering—what keeps him from wandering away?" Reid asks. Of course he would. Mortals fence their animals in.

"We ask them not to. Help me lie down."

Once I'm on my back, my shoulder throbbing from all the

unavoidable movement, I dig my left fingers in the dirt and grit my teeth as Reid helps my right hand do the same. I breathe deeply, trying to push aside the lingering aches. With luck, that'll be the worst of it.

"What now?" Reid sits beside me, leaning back into his hands.

"Now I just talk." I close my eyes and switch to speaking in the Tongue, the language of the Land.

"Honored Mother, I beg a moment of your time."

The Land pulses into my fingertips, Her warmth flowing into me. My remaining pain washes away.

Where do I begin?

"Thank you for all your healing gifts," I say, keeping to myself how She could've made them taste better. "I'd still be bedridden without them."

No change in the pulse, as if She knows that's not the reason I'm speaking with Her.

I take a deep breath. "Is Taran alright?"

The pulse thrums with cozy heat, and I sigh as a weight I hadn't realized was there crumbles away. Not that I care how he's doing, but him being alive is important for the sake of the realm.

"And the war? Has it started yet?"

A low rumble shakes the ground, Her anger reverberating through my bones. My jaw clenches as the vibrations perforate my shoulder.

Maybe talk about something else.

I inhale deeply, cold air filling my lungs. *Here I go...*

"I-I don't know what to do—who I am anymore. Everything I was is gone. All I have is Reid, but there's nowhere for us." I feel Reid perk up at his name, but there's no helping it.

The rumbling desists, the warm pulse returning. Soothing me, nudging me to keep going.

Tears stream down my face, and everything else follows.

"My entire life has been helping Taran, and I can't do that anymore. He left me behind. And even if he didn't, I can't be his spy. Because I love Reid. But he's stuck here, where he'll be killed if he's discovered. I don't know if I can live a life hiding away from the world."

My breath hitches, the words finally out. No longer pacing silently in my head, but heard.

A pulse courses through the ground from me to Reid.

"Um... what's happening?"

I open my eyes as the pulse drums harder. Reid's still sitting nearby, his hands hovering in the air as he looks at the grass.

"You think I should tell him?" I ask in the Tongue.

The pulse trills excitedly.

Shit. Ignoring Her would be a horrible mistake. A flat-out insult. So I close my eyes, take a breath, and repeat my words. In the common tongue, for Reid.

When I finish, it's quiet, except for my heart pounding in anticipation. Then Reid speaks, his voice low.

"It scares me, too."

I open my eyes as he lies on his side next to me, gently turning my face to his.

His deep brown eyes search mine. "I didn't say anything 'cause I could see you were struggling. I thought it was just the pain, the boredom... maybe your anger with Taran. I didn't want to add my worries to yours."

A warmth blooms in my chest at the confession, melting me into the ground. "I don't know what to do. Do you?"

"I don't." He moistens his lips, then swallows. "Maybe, once you're well enough to travel... I want to go back to the border. I need to see what's happening. I can't just ignore an attack on my home.

And I can't..." He takes a breath. "I can't let Alexis get pulled into it. Not when I know the truth."

My heart clenches with a pain deeper than my shoulder. I wish I knew how to fix this. I pull my hand out of the dirt to squeeze his.

"We can do that. It's easier to trick mortals with glamours than fae." Though, I'll have to glamour him, too, if we're going anywhere near the Academy—otherwise, he'll probably get arrested—so we'll need to bring a shitload of water. And the food's atrocious. Not looking forward to that.

Reid smiles, making his skin crinkle near his eyes. "Then we have a plan. We can figure out the rest after."

The Land's pulse prods impatiently at me, so I translate for Her. It starts beating like the skipping footfalls of eager children. Sounds like She agrees?

I shrug, sending a spike of pain through Her warmth, my fingers clenching in the dirt. "Alright," I say through gritted teeth. "Once my shoulder's better."

That'll only take, what? Another month? Hopefully I don't lose my mind before then.

Within Her pulsing heat, my shoulder tingles as if it's being kissed by thousands of ants, skittering beneath my skin. My eyes widen as nerves and tissue knit back together, tying off with a feverish blaze that jolts my body, leaving me breathless.

I jerk my shoulder again, and while it still stabs, the blade's dull compared to the sharp bite from earlier.

Did She just heal me?

"Whoa, hold on," I say in the Tongue. "I didn't agree to pay for that. I just wanted to talk." Seriously—I'm all for accelerated healing, but it doesn't seem like the sort of thing that comes cheap.

"What's going on?" Reid asks, gripping my hand tight.

"She healed me," I say, taking a deep breath. An overpowering scent of jasmine floods my nostrils, and an instant later, I'm alive again, the urge to spend the rest of the day kissing every speck of Reid's scrumptious body gushing through me.

I release his hand and grab his shirt, tugging him close until our lips meet.

The hunger within me roars to life as I press my tongue into his mouth. A muffled yelp bursts out of him before he matches my passion, and the lingering taste of berries adds its sweetness to his. His shirt twists as my fingers coil around it, his hand straining in the tangles of my hair.

Pain slices up my neck, the spasm breaking our kiss when a broken moan escapes me.

"Are you alright?" Reid asks, his lips glistening.

A sweltering heat boils in the pit of my stomach, radiating through my limbs. "It doesn't matter. Take your shirt off."

"Don't you have to settle a debt with the Land?" He pushes himself up, out of my reach.

My body twitches, desperate for him to return, and it hits me—something's off. I mean, I love sex. Would do nothing else if I could. But I usually have significantly more self-control about it.

I finally notice the tiny white buds unfurling their petals all around us.

Oh.

"Everyone knows the Land's a fucking voyeur," I say. "This *is* Her payment." With my next inhale, the flowers' sweet scent takes me, and I'm just gone, blood rushing to my cock so fast my vision blinks out for half a heartbeat.

I yank at my shirt, pulling the ties apart while Reid glances between me, the flowers, and the house, only ten paces away.

"Your mom's right there."

"I couldn't care less right now." There's a fire raging inside me, and I really need him to just—

"I'm not really comfortable with this..."

Fuck me.

"Ma!" I yell. "Go somewhere else, please! Now!"

A moment later, the door opens, and I feel her hurrying deeper into the forest.

"Alright, she's gone." I breathe heavily as my eyes land back on Reid, his gaze still focused on the tree line. "Can you fuck me already?"

He looks down at me, smirking as he rolls his eyes. If there were anything within reach I could throw at him, I would, taking his fucking time like this. I'm gonna bite him when he finally gets down here.

"Give me a second to find some oil."

Ancients. "Just use your spit."

"No, I don't wanna hurt you."

"I've done it before, I can take it." *And who knows? Maybe She'll heal my ass, too.*

"Two seconds," Reid says, then dashes back to the house.

"Liar!" My fingers clench against the dirt. I've never been this desperate in my life. The closest was waiting till we were far enough away from the charred remains of Reid's incanting when he finally gave in to wanting me. Before that... nothing. Everyone else was just there.

After the most excruciatingly long mortal seconds in history, Reid's back. He pulls his shirt off, his abdominal muscles rippling with the motion, then his skin meets mine, his warmth pressing into me as he encompasses me in another kiss. Despite the insatiable need racing through me, I can't let go of him, can't stop devouring him as I grip his pecs tight. Before I follow through with biting him, he pulls his lips away—but instead of removing his pants, he kisses down my neck until they dance across the bare part of my chest, sending goosebumps quivering along my flesh.

I moan, my eyes rolling up into my head. "We can foreplay another time, but I need you inside me *right now.*"

"Yes, love." The words almost have me bursting by themselves.

Reid tugs my pants off, then pours some oil into his hand. His lips return to mine as my legs curl up, then he circles the rim before stretching me open. A groan rolls from me into him as he works, filling me with his fingers. One. Two. Then three. So fucking full, so tender, just like he's always been. Why did I need to hear him say he loved me? It's been obvious with his every touch, every time. Had I just forgotten in my misery?

"You doing alright?" he asks.

"Yep." A grunt escapes. "Anytime now."

I whimper as he retreats, finally pulling himself free of his pants. His magnificent cock, thick and dripping and ready to go. Then he leans back over me, lining himself up with my hole.

I cling to his back as he enters, my head tilting up as he slides in, pushing a gasp out of me.

"Is that it?" he asks.

"A little—"

Reid shifts my hips and thrusts again, slow and deep, exactly how I taught him.

"Oh fuck, that's it." My lips graze his cheek as his breath presses heavy against me.

We stay like that, his weight on my chest for a pounding heartbeat until our eyes meet. A deep, beautiful brown. Warm, like his nutmeg scent overwhelming my every inhale. This closeness... I can't even... Nothing else compares.

"I love you," I whisper, my breath steadying as the desperation fades away. Now, it's just him. Wanting me. Needing me. Making me whole.

His voice comes low and thick as he runs his fingers gently through my hair. "I love you, too."

The thrusts begin, Reid slowly rolling his hips into me as he perfects his angle, our bodies synchronizing until each one is a wave of pleasure unlike anything I experienced before him. Tears leak from my eyes like a fucking fool. I had three nights of this. Three nights of finally comprehending what was always missing, that I almost lost forever.

And now it's back.

"Oh fuck, Reid. Fuck."

A laugh huffs out of him, interrupting our rhythm. Then he picks up his pace, our breath coming faster as my body coils around his, my fingers digging into him.

Overwhelming heat. Hot. Slick. I can't kiss him, my lips just rubbing his cheek, his jaw, trying to grasp him in every way possible but failing horribly. Pleasure pulses through me from the pressure building low in my belly, my mind flashing with every slap against me.

"Reid." I claw at his back as I start shaking uncontrollably.

"Emlyn." He groans into my neck as I clench around him, my body throbbing from the flood of tingles within. With a final, sharp thrust, he shudders, then grunts as he empties into me.

He collapses into the mess of my own release, and I absorb his warmth, still trembling as we catch our breath. My fingers find his hair, weaving among the sweaty strands as I pull him close, spattering him with kisses as his own lips peck lazily along my skin.

This is it. All that matters. And I'll die before I let anyone take him away from me.

Chapter 13

Owena

So far, everything is going according to plan.

Ellie's love triangle with Caeo and Taran is over and done with, and the two of them have taken their first steps down the path of brotherhood. As I hoped, Caeo's been helpful in managing Taran—he only agreed to my plan because Caeo convinced him.

Since then, our marching order has changed; Taran leads the way, followed by me, acting as a buffer between him and Ellie, which works in my favor. My land-sense won't be anywhere near as strong as his until we reach Ystyr, but I can still feel his focus—a faint warmth simmering the air around me as we tromp along these frigid hills.

If only the Land weren't tormenting him over Her issues with Ellie. Then I would be more confident about everything pulling together in time to face my father. But the longer Ellie remains with us, the more volatile I fear Taran will become. If she doesn't realize she should part ways with us soon, I may need to take matters into my own hands.

What I'd really appreciate is for Taran to be capable of ruling competently on his own. Then I wouldn't have to clean everything up myself. As it is, there's no room for unpredictability. I have one chance, and everything must line up perfectly.

Ideally, Caeo would trail behind me to further separate Ellie from Taran, but he spends a significant amount of time at the back, covering our tracks. Taran would be better at it, but then he'd be at greater risk of laying eyes on Ellie. Thus, I've spent half the day watching his tight leather pants cling to the curves of his well-defined backside with every step he takes. Since I'm marrying him, there's no shame in enjoying the view.

Except now he's stopped walking, his gaze focused on storm clouds gathering in the east.

"Is that something we need to worry about?" I ask as I approach. My land-sense tells me Caeo and Ellie have stopped farther behind us.

"It will hurt our pursuers more than us, but we'll need to find shelter. Something sturdier than the forest canopy."

"Can you make another cave?"

Taran glares at me. "Will you be helping this time?"

My mouth tightens to keep my cheeks from flushing. As far as I know, he's unaware of my limitations when it comes to shaping, and I'd prefer to keep it that way.

"Of course not. This is your realm, so you can do significantly more than I can. I would get in your way."

"So you admit to being a burden?"

Heat rises in my chest, making it even more difficult to keep it from my face. If I actually could contribute, I would be the first to volunteer. He has no idea what it's like to be dependent on others for everything. "I admit when I am out of my depth, which is perhaps something you should learn from."

His nostrils flare. "What's that supposed to mean?"

"Which part didn't you understand? I didn't use any overly complex words."

Caeo clamps his hands on both of our shoulders, having clearly caught up during our discussion. "Come on, you two. Why don't you try acting like people who are getting married soon?"

At least Taran and I agree about the glares we burn him with.

"Fine, maybe not." Caeo lifts his palms in surrender. "But arguing won't help anything."

"No, it won't," I concede. "So tell us, Taran—where is the best place to seek shelter from the storm?"

He sighs, eyeing the barren landscape. "Probably further up that hill," he says, pointing. "On the leeward side. I can make another cavern." He glances at Caeo. "You can help."

"What about more food and water?" I ask. "We haven't reached the stream yet."

"You can take Ellie to collect that." Taran tosses his pack into my chest.

I step back as it collides with me, barely keeping it in my arms. "What?" My face burns as my irritation boils over. This will make concealing my deficiency impossible.

"You should be able to make it to the stream with your land-sense. It's that way." He gestures in the direction we were heading. "There's fish and berries, which even a toddler should be able to gather with minimal shaping. And don't forget firewood."

I purse my lips, quelling the anger within me. He is trying to get under my skin, and I won't let him.

He thinks I'm nothing but a spoiled princess. At least that means he'll underestimate me.

"If you insist." I pull the pack on. "Come along, Ellie."

"ARE YOU SURE we'll make it back before it rains?" Ellie asks.

She's carrying the pack as we trudge back up the hill to the shelter Taran and Caeo have been making. From what I've gathered, she spent the last week gallivanting across the realm with Taran, so it's only logical that her stamina outpaces mine, especially when most of my exertions come in short bursts in my bed or on the dance floor. She also didn't have to do much other than fill waterskins and break branches off the shrubs and bushes we passed.

"Just go ahead." I sit on the grass while I recover my breath. "They're not far. I'd like a moment to rest—by myself."

"Are you sure?"

"Yes. Please, go." I appreciate her concern, but prefer to recover from my failures alone.

How will I maintain my dignity once Taran discovers the scant amount of food I could procure?

I rub my fingers against my temples, trying to ease the pain leaking out of my bottled-up frustrations. I've been unable to properly shape since my father shackled my magic as a child—the same binding that limits who I'm able to curse.

A sap on your magic...

There's only so much 'spoiled princess' I can play. For any of this to work, I need Taran to at least respect me. More than that, eventually. But respect is the first step.

Everything would be so much easier if Caeo were still the prince I had to marry. He wasn't perfect, but...

I wrap my arms tightly around myself and shake those thoughts away. It's pointless to consider that anymore. I lost him the moment I broke his curse, if I ever even had him to begin with. But he appreciated me for who I am, which is about the best one can hope for in an arranged marriage. Taran likely hopes he can get away with ignoring my existence after we're bound together.

A miserable way to live, but I already have experience being half of what I should be.

Rain splatters against my clothes. Lightly at first, but quickly turns into a freezing downpour, soaking my coat and threatening to chill my skin. Pushing myself to my feet, I clamber up the hill, my face turned downward as I shield my eyes from the deluge.

I should have paid closer attention to the storm.

I curse as my feet slip on the rain-soaked ground, then reach out with my land-sense to ensure I'm still heading in the proper direction.

Pausing, I lift my gaze up ahead.

Taran.

He gracefully moves down the hillside, not slipping once while still maintaining a steady, quick pace. His right hand hovers palm up above his head, shaping the torrential rain away and keeping him perfectly dry.

Within a breath, he's grasping my arm and I'm in his bubble, raindrops no longer pelleting my skin.

"Are you trying to freeze to death? How did you not sense the rain coming?"

"I w-was d-d-distracted," I say, my teeth chattering.

"Give me your coat." He lets go of my arm, and I shrug it off. He catches it before awkwardly removing his own. Rain breaks through and onto his back as he pulls his arm free from the sleeve, keeping his hand above me. Shielding me.

He wraps his coat around my shoulders, blanketing me against the cold. His musky pine scent rises to my nostrils, sparking a flame within me.

"Come on." His warm hand encompasses my frigid fingers.

Taran guides me through the rain and into a toasty cavern, similar to the last one he made but slightly more spacious, with Caeo and Ellie sitting beside a fire. At our arrival, Ellie scoots back into an alcove made by a wall of dirt that effectively hides her from sight, for Taran's sake, while keeping her close to the flames' heat.

With his hands on my shoulders, Taran sits me in front of the blaze, and a rush of heat floods through me. My fingers tingle as the cold retreats, and torrid air presses against my skin, heavy with the weight of his focus.

"Perhaps you can back off your land-sense a smidge?" I ask as his hands release me. "It's a tad overwhelming."

"I wish I could." His eyes flick over to the barrier Ellie hides behind. He retreats, sitting against the wall as far away from her as he can without rain landing on him. Which isn't very far.

I turn my attention back to the crackling fire, attempting to ignore the oppressive force clinging to me. Small pieces of skewered meat hang roasting above it, their gamey scent filling the cave.

"Where did the meat come from?" Not my first choice for a meal, but my mouth's already salivating for it. How quickly one's standards fall in the face of hunger.

Taran huffs. "I figured you wouldn't be successful, so I caught some gophers."

My cheeks pinch inward, holding back a retort that won't help anything.

"How exactly?" Ellie asks from beyond her wall. "You don't have your bow."

"I collapsed their burrow and smothered them until they stopped breathing."

My eyes widen. "That's ghastly."

He shrugs. "We needed food, and it was the best I could do with what was nearby. Wouldn't have had to if you were capable enough to catch a fish."

"Owena's very capable," Caeo says, and I thank him with a smile. "Just not with shaping."

My face falls. *I need to redirect this conversation.*

Pushing myself to my feet, I peel my wet pants down my legs.

From a young age, I learned that even Father's most tightly bound attendants would bend at a properly timed glimpse of skin. Perhaps someday, I'll be treated with the respect everyone deserves, but until then, I have to rely on the tools I have.

"What are you doing?" Taran's voice pitches higher than normal. His face isn't visible as I struggle with my pant legs bunching at the knees, but my imagination steps in, heat building in my chest as I contain a chuckle.

"They'll dry faster if I set them by the fire." I keep my small clothes on for Caeo's sake and angle my backside toward Taran as I spread my pants out next to the fire—it's not as if they'd be spared from the dirt with me wearing them. Then I sit, pulling my knees in front of my chest to keep my legs fully on display.

"When will the meat be done?" I glance back at Taran.

His eyes trail along my skin, the weight of his focus dragging along with his gaze.

"Taran?"

He blinks, then clears his throat. "It's probably fine now." He locks onto the meat as he moves over to it.

He ends up giving me the smallest piece.

Caeo joins Ellie in her alcove, leaving Taran and me eating to the sound of their hushed whispers, which I have to spend effort to ignore; I have no desire to listen to their sweet nothings, reminding me of the love I'll never have. I occasionally glance Taran's way, but he keeps his eyes on the entrance, watching the rain.

After I finish, I clean my hands and get started on my hair—it will be a frizzy mess when it dries if I don't get it under control now. Untangling the old braid, I run my fingers through my damp curls, searching for any hints of knotting. They stick in a few spots, and I busy myself working out the tangles.

Taran's watching me again.

Beneath the weight, something flutters in my core. Plenty have eyed me in the past—both men and women alike—but never with such intensity. A hopeful spark lights within me.

Ellie's voice interrupts the rising heat. "Maybe we should play a game?"

Blinking, I glance her way as Taran's weight withdraws slightly. Caeo scoots back out where I can see him.

I swallow, then knit my brows together, forcing my attention beyond the pressure so I can form a response. "A game? What for?"

Caeo shrugs, then rests his back against the far wall. "It's better than sitting around awkwardly."

"We should sleep," Taran grumbles.

"It's not even dark yet," Caeo scoffs. "It doesn't matter how tired I am, I'll be up at midnight if I fall asleep now."

"Please?" Ellie's voice adds. "I know a few, but I've never gotten to play any. I've only ever watched others."

My mouth tightens. While she's dallying with being pathetic, I can understand the longing for connection. And maybe I can turn this in my favor.

"How about *Never Ever*?" I offer, wiping a smudge of dirt off my knee. It's always been a popular choice at revels, with fairly simple rules compared to others, and has never failed to spice up an otherwise dull affair.

Taran groans.

"What's that?" Ellie asks.

I straighten up. "You admit something you've never done, and anyone who has raises their hand. We could say something instead, so you can play. I'll start: I've never ever had a female lover."

Taran raises his hand apathetically, and Caeo follows with slightly more enthusiasm.

"You need to speak so Ellie feels included," I remind them.

"Fine. I have," Taran mumbles.

"Same," Caeo says, "but she already knew that."

"Just to clarify, my silence means I have not," Ellie says from behind the wall.

"Taran's turn." I give him my most expectant smile. I doubt he'll offer anything I can use, but one never knows. Even the smallest nugget of information could be used to relate to him if necessary.

His brow furrows, then he rolls his eyes and looks away. "I've never ever eaten squid."

"Really? That's such a boring one." But I commit it to memory, nonetheless. I raise my hand. "Me. I've eaten squid."

Caeo's face blanches. "That's disgusting."

"It's a delicacy in the south!"

Ellie's hand slips out from behind her wall to tap Caeo's arm. "I have, too. It's not bad once you get used to the texture."

"Thank you," I say, then nod to Caeo as he shudders. "Your turn."

"Uh..."

"Something interesting, please." It's likely up to him and myself to pull anything worthwhile from Taran.

"I've never..." Mischief twinkles in his eyes. "I've never ever had my cock sucked by a guy."

Taran's head falls into his hands. "Do you want me to hate you?"

My eyebrows perk up. "Is that a yes?"

He groans. "Yes. Move on, please."

I look him over, sitting with his knees tucked up, feet spread apart. I'm not sure this tidbit will be of any use, but heat billows in my chest as my mind wanders through tantalizing imagery.

"Ellie is next," I say, forcing my gaze to her wall.

"Um. I've never... hmm, there are a lot of things I've never done."

"Try to come up with something better than Taran's, at least,"

Caeo says.

"Alright." The fire pops while I assume she thinks. "I've never... I don't know—I've never ever been intimate with more than one person."

"Do you mean in general, or at the same time?" I ask.

"I don't... The second one, why not?"

With a shrug, I raise my hand. "Me." The answer would have been the same either way.

"Fuck," Caeo says under his breath. His hand lifts slightly, but there's no doubt Ellie can see him from her angle.

"What?" she exclaims.

"I told you I had experience!"

"You never said anything about multiple women at the same time!"

Heat presses into my side as Taran moves into my space, inciting my heart to beat mercilessly against my ribs. *Why is he so close?*

"Have you used milk of midnight star?" he whispers in my ear.

My eyes widen, and when I tilt my head to meet his gaze, his face is barely a kiss away. Those eyes... I could get utterly lost in those malachite depths.

Then a twisting knot forms in my throat, pulling me to my senses. Caeo's use of the substance was quite obvious during our travels—surely Ellie will notice on her own at some point. And with how she reacted to his long leaf use... "Do you really wish to be confined to this cave when she finds out?" I ask, keeping my voice hushed.

Taran's lips twitch. "The sooner she does, the better. We can leave for the worst of it."

"What are you two whispering about?" Caeo's voice breaks out of the background.

Taran pulls away, and I glance between the two of them. My

mind races, unsure.

If I play this perfectly, this could be the opening I need with Taran. A moment he'll remember as a time I listened to him, that will allow for some time with only the two of us.

But Caeo may never forgive me. I'd like to believe that after everything else, their love is strong enough to get through this, but there's no way to know.

I paint a casual smile on my face. "It's my turn," I announce. "I've never ever used milk of midnight star."

Chapter 14

Caeo

Fuck.

My fingernails dig into my palms as the cave shrinks, the fire's heat twisting into a cold, empty lie.

"Milk of midnight star?" Ellie asks. "That sounds familiar."

"It's a milky substance drawn from the midnight star flower," Owena explains, her gaze fixed on the wall that separates Ellie from her and Taran. "We mainly use it for pain relief, but it's also highly euphoric—more so than speckled long leaf."

"It's what Reid gave Emlyn," Taran adds, then he raises his hand. "I've taken it." His eyes turn to me, piercing through the shadows.

That's what they were whispering about. *Is this because I made him admit to getting sucked off by Emlyn?*

I'm gonna kill him.

I shoot a glare at Owena. Why'd she go along with this? I thought she was my friend—that she understood.

She tilts her head at me, raising her brow as if confused.

Damn it.

"So... is it Taran's turn now?" Ellie asks.

"No, not everyone has admitted yet," he says.

I can feel Ellie's eyes land on me. The weight of her gaze. There's no one else left to say anything.

I close my eyes and push an exhale out through my nose.

"Caeo?" Her voice is soft.

I swallow, then force out another breath.

"Me. I've used it."

I open my eyes. Not to Ellie. To Taran. He doesn't look smug or satisfied. Just... grim.

"When?" Ellie asks.

I bite my lip, hoping to temper the storm brewing in my chest, pounding against my ribs.

She won't understand. She's from high society, with their fancy, forgivable drugs, hidden behind closed doors. Pretending they're better than the rest of us. I know that's not her, but still.

"He started the morning we left Emlyn," Taran says.

"Why are you doing this?" The words blurt out. They probably aren't helpful.

Nothing's helpful right now.

Taran keeps his gaze locked on me. "Because you need to stop, and as long as she doesn't know, you aren't going to."

"It's barely been four days. That's hardly a problem." My throat betrays me, twisting at my words. An icy chill coats my insides, but I shudder free. *Who even decides what's true, anyway?*

"You took it from someone who actually needed it."

"He said I could!"

Taran raises his voice. "He made you kiss him for it!"

"Wait—what?" Ellie grabs my arm, her eyes wide.

"Don't act like it's a big deal," I snap, wresting my arm away. "You've kissed him, too."

Why am I snapping at Ellie?

"Not by choice!" she exclaims.

I blink a few times. "Hold on... what?" I'd assumed it was just another memory-related fuck-up.

"Don't make this about me." Ellie's ears are turning red—I've never seen that happen before. "How much of this milk have you been using?"

"Almost the entire first day, half the second, and I'm guessing every night," Taran says, because he can't mind his own business.

"That's not that much!" My fist clenches, knuckles still sore from the last time I punched him.

"It is for someone who doesn't need it."

"I *do* need it!"

Taran's jaw snaps shut.

Every beat of my heart echoes through me. This cave might as well be collapsing, its walls pressing in. I brace my head against my hands, my fingers scraping through my hair.

"It's highly addictive, Caeo," Owena says. "You need to stop before you can't."

There's nothing but the sharp pain of my fingers clenching clumps of hair. Then Ellie's arm slinks gently around me. A soft, warm anchor.

"Why, Caeo? Why do you need it?"

My eyes squeeze shut. "I don't want to talk about it."

"You won't get past it until you do."

Breathe. Breathe.

I can sense Taran and Owena sneaking outside—being out in a storm must be better than being here. It is for me, too, but what happens if I run? Will Ellie still look at me the same?

I lift my head. Her cinnamon eyes search my face, full of fear. Of worry.

With an exhale, my gaze drifts back to the floor.

"My mother never loved me, Ellie. She forced some unwilling man to father me, so she could have someone who loved her. Once we came here, I became just another tool."

Her fingers jerk tight around my shirt. "I'm so sorry, Caeo. I can only imagine how that must feel."

My body shakes with a harsh laugh. "That's only the beginning."

Ellie loosens her grip, then caresses my back. "You can tell me what happened. I love you, and nothing you say will ever change that."

The heel of my hand presses into my forehead, my nails digging into my scalp. My mouth twists along with the knot in my chest. "I don't want to..."

"Was it her willbending?"

She already knows the answer. That doesn't make this any easier.

I exhale, then barely manage a whisper. "Yeah." A weight sinks down my throat, dragging the rest of the words with it, but I push them out. "It was every day. Almost every conversation. I didn't realize it until Owena told me. I just did what she said. She told me to accept my new home, and *I just did.*"

My mouth is dry. Ellie's hand keeps rubbing my back. I swallow.

"Then Owena broke my curse, and I remembered you, and I couldn't... I couldn't get married." Tears burn behind my eyes. "But I couldn't get away. I was trapped."

A sliver of light, erased.

Fingers straining against the floor. Body of lead.

My breath is hitching, catching in my throat. Ellie squeezes my hand.

"Th-the wedding." My eyes squeeze shut. "They... I had to... They wanted me to..."

I force myself to swallow the nausea.

"I-I didn't want to, but she was gonna willbend me. To force me. I tried to escape. She trapped me in the dark. And then, in my own body. I couldn't move. Just stuck with my thoughts, knowing at any moment she could come back, and force me, to..."

A black dagger. Blood. Thirst.

Owena.

My palms dig into my eyes, burying the visions of our writhing, naked bodies in darkness. I exhale, shuddering.

There's a pain in my stomach, but everything else is numb. Hollow. The pressure of Ellie's arm wraps around me, her body pressing against my side, but it's distant.

I take another breath, and my throat sticks to itself. I choke halfway through the inhale.

Ellie's fingers brush against my cheek, gently tugging, turning me to her. The firelight flickers against the tears in her eyes.

"I love you, Caeo. And I'm here for you. I'm not going anywhere."

My heart cracks.

"I can't… That's not enough, Ellie. I want it to be, but I can't keep my mind away. It keeps going back. But the milk—the milk keeps it away." Just thinking about it, my body yearns for its release.

"You can't keep depending on that. I'll be here helping you, but you have to try."

There's nothing to say. I want to try, for her. She's my everything. I can't lose her.

But I don't know if I'm strong enough.

I close my eyes and sink into her. Breathing in her lavender scent. Her warmth.

My heart spasms as I remember lying in the grass, wishing her arms were around me as my sanity slipped away.

She squeezes me tighter, because this time, she's real.

IT DOESN'T MATTER how real she is. In my exhaustion, I fall asleep quickly, but it doesn't hold me for long.

I lie curled up on the cold dirt, next to Ellie as she sleeps. Her beautiful face breathes easily, relaxed and peaceful, completely oblivious to the torments barreling through my mind. It's not as dark as that night. That day. The eternity that stretched between them. Nothing ever could be, but it still presses around me.

My head throbs with every thought, reliving moments of panic and dread—but now, they're joined by Ellie's fearful eyes. By my guilt and shame.

I sit up, rubbing my face and forcing myself to breathe. The storm still rages outside, but it's barely a breeze compared to what's within.

I know what I'm doing before I do it. I quietly dig out the little jar of milk, careful not to wake anyone. Acceptance sinks through me, and with it, a momentary peace.

No one has to know.

Chapter 15

Standing outside our cave, it occurs to me that I should have thought this through more.

The idea of forcing Caeo to admit something uncomfortable began as petty revenge, but I barely know my brother, so there wasn't much to choose from. Revealing his milk use seemed too cruel at first, but the more I thought about it, the more necessary it became; for his own sake, as well as for his relationship with Ellie. Hopefully someday he'll realize that.

I did not take into account how bad the storm had gotten.

It slipped my mind. I couldn't see Ellie in the cavern with us, but the space was cramped enough that the only way I wouldn't sense her was if I focused the entirety of my land-sense on someone else. Caeo was too close to her—not to mention it's uncomfortable to focus on my brother like that—so Owena was the only other option.

Then she had to make everything more difficult by removing her pants. Which she's still not wearing. She didn't bother putting them on when coming out into this raging tempest so that Caeo and Ellie could have some privacy.

She presses against my side, wrapped in *my* coat, while I hold the torrential rains and howling winds at bay. Freezing gusts pierce my shirt.

At least the amount of effort it takes blocks everything else out. But it's too much. I won't be able to hold it back for long.

"You could help," I say, loud enough for Owena to hear over the storm.

"I really can't," she yells into my chest.

Of course not. Spoiled princess. "Then we need to move somewhere more protected."

Owena clings to me as I search the hillside for any formations that might easily shape into something useful. I don't have the energy to make another cavern.

There. The ground makes a steep drop where part of the hill crumbled away. With some extra shaping, I should only have to protect one side of us.

Owena slips, her nails scraping along my back and stomach as she keeps herself upright. I can't offer her a hand since both of mine are occupied holding back the storm, so I grimace through the pain, a fire burning where her fingers dig into my skin.

"Try not to do that again," I say as her grip slackens.

"I'm doing my best."

Your best at what? Scarring my flesh?

"I'm going to shape the hillside, so unless you want to get soaked, you need to move between me and the earth."

Owena scrambles against the wall of dirt, stone, and grass, tucking her legs up against her chest. Her bare legs, long and slick with rain, the elegant lines of her calves meeting those of her thighs, down to—

Why did I think this was a good idea?

Keeping one hand above us to shield Owena from the downpour, I press the other into the hillside, closing my eyes as I focus on the shape it needs to take. Concave curves, bending into the ground, with a ledge overhead. I shift forward, pressing deeper, as icy rain pelts my back.

I can feel the shape of the hill with my land-sense, how the rain trickles down its sides. This should work, as long as we press in tight and I shape the air to our front.

I open my eyes to Owena's face, only a breath away. Her dark eyes dart across my face, her full lips slightly agape.

A rush of heat accentuates the chill soaking into my shirt. I scoot into our alcove, shoving my back against the dirt, ignoring the pounding in my chest as I focus my attention on pushing the wind away. Since we're no longer moving and there's only one direction I need to worry about, I shouldn't need to use my hands.

I'm mostly successful until Owena slips her leg against my knee and presses into my side.

"What are you doing?" My body tenses, fighting to move in every possible direction—back into the storm, deeper into the earth, and tighter against her.

"It's freezing!"

"Get your warmth from the Land, not me."

"Where do you expect me to go? You didn't make enough room to spread out."

"I'm not an endless spring of shaping. If you want more space, make it yourself."

"I told you, I can't."

My eyes flick to her face. Her cheeks have flushed rose, matching her lips—pressed tightly together, slightly pursed.

"What do you mean, you can't? All fae can shape."

"My father cursed me when I was a child." Her voice softens. "I've barely been able to shape ever since."

That's... I can't imagine going a single day without shaping. It'd be like binding my wrists.

I shift my gaze back to the rain. That's where my focus needs to be. But something gnaws at the bottom of the throat. I mocked her earlier. She may be irritating, but she doesn't deserve that.

"I'm sorry. I didn't know."

"Of course you didn't. It's not something I typically share."

I glance at her out of the corner of my eye. "Is that why you want to kill him? To break the curse?"

"He needs to die for the sake of peace. I'm willing to do it because I must."

My stomach twists as the wind picks up, whistling wildly. *What does that say about me?* I couldn't kill my mother, even after everything she's done.

I meet Owena's eyes—they don't look like those of a killer. But what do a killer's eyes look like? Hollow voids?

Peering into those midnight depths, I almost see a flicker of light.

"And you're certain you'll be able to do it?" I ask.

"As long as everything goes according to plan."

My shoulders tense. "What plan?"

Owena's brow raises slightly. "I'm not telling you."

"Why not?"

"Because then you might believe we're becoming friends, which is something I have no desire to be."

Rain pelts my shoulder as I push away from her. "Then why do you insist I marry you?"

"I told you. For peace." She shifts to better face me, her legs pressing into my thigh.

"Wouldn't our marriage be more peaceful if we were friends?"

"I don't need a *peaceful* marriage, Taran." Her eyes burn into me, flames surging through my chest. Then deeper, until they meet the heat of her legs against mine.

Thoughts scatter. Her face is so close. Eyes that could swallow me whole. A mouth that could...

My lips stick together, unsure what to do as a coil winds within me. My mind pushes through, forcing a swallow. "What do you need?"

"What I *need*"—her tongue flicks out to moisten her lips, and the coil twists tighter, ready to launch me into her—"is for you to stop feeling sorry for yourself and do what needs to be done."

Everything stalls. The coil unwinds, sinking down. Icy rain seeps into my skin.

"What?"

Her gaze holds tight. "You heard me."

My chest burns with a different flame than before. "Why would you say that?"

"Someone has to. You are the single most powerful fae in all the realms, but you can't hold on to your kingdom because you fear your own strength."

Her words hit with a crash, shattering in my head. Whatever I thought I saw in her eyes—it was an illusion. Gone. Nothing but a heartless void.

"If that's what you think of me, you can stay out here by yourself." I push myself to my feet, back into the storm, taking my protection with me.

I don't look back.

By the time I stumble into the cavern, Caeo and Ellie are asleep, as best I can tell. I don't dare check; they're curled up together, which is good enough. I focus my land-sense on whatever I can— blades of grass drowning in the storm, worms digging through the dirt—anything to keep it away from the bonfire of Ellie, blazing in the back of my mind thanks to this cursedly tight space.

If I had anything left in me, I would have shaped myself another shelter somewhere far away. But even my bond with the Land won't keep me warm overnight in this kind of weather.

My stomach tightens. I shouldn't have left Owena out there by herself. Especially since she only spoke the truth. But my anger boils away my shame. She knew what she was doing. Does she want me to hate her?

But then, why did she keep drawing me closer? Flaunting her skin, pressing against me.

So many emotions warring within, threatening to tear me apart. I can't let her do this. Owena's proven herself both calculating and shrewd. Her every move, every word, every touch... They're all intentional. She's playing some kind of game, and she thinks I'm a pawn in it.

She's moving.

When did my focus shift to her?

I lie down as far away from Ellie and Caeo as I can, facing the wall, and focus all my attention on a colony of ants about sixteen paces into the hill.

It's not enough to miss her return. Her sigh as she sits by the dying fire. The motion of her body as she pulls off my drenched coat and wrings the water out of her hair.

Ants. Focus on the ants.

I lose track of how many implode under the weight of my attention as my mother starts tugging at my bond again.

I ERUPT OUT OF OUR SHELTER as the last of the rain passes, shortly before dawn. Without my coat, the frigid air pierces my shirt, but it doesn't matter; I'm wound up inside, ready to burst. I need to get away, from Ellie and from Owena.

My head pounds as I march toward the stream, my boots already soaked from the remains of the storm. The others should be smart enough to figure out where I've gone once they wake up. If not, I'll find them once everything inside me settles down.

I've never hated my connection to the Land—in the past, She's always been a source of comfort. But now, She's consuming me from the inside, Her rage increasing by the day, burning away everything I ever felt for Ellie. I don't know how much longer I can bear being around her until the pressure becomes too much and I break.

My haggard breath crumbles out.

There's no escape for me. If I leave, I'll be abandoning my people, my kingdom, to my mother. If I stay... what happens when I finally cave?

The exact same thing, except the Land will have killed Ellie using my hands, and my mother will steal my bond from whatever remains of me.

I fall to my knees, and the icy grass soaks through my pants. I savor the chill, something to feel other than the devastation within.

Why did Owena have to make everything worse?

If I had asked a different question—if she had given a different answer—last night could have gone differently. Would everything be easier now, if it had? Would that flame have been enough?

It flickers back to life at the memory of her pressed against me, her lips a hair away from mine. I wrap my arms tight against my chest, holding on to that warmth. If I just focus on that... nothing before, nothing after...

I swallow, trying to breathe.

I have to pull myself together. Do what needs to be done. If Ellie was able to do that every day after I unraveled her world, then I can, too. I just need to channel her strength. Focus.

My breath scrapes through my lungs.

Today. Today, we need food.

I can do that.

The storm will have washed away any trace of us, save for our shelter. By the time our pursuers find it, there could be days between us. As long as I stay at the edge of Caeo's land-sense, he should be able to follow me. They'll figure it out.

By the time the sun rises, I have a fire going beside the stream, cooking skewers of fish as I disperse its smoke by shaping the wind. I've already eaten my fill, and this round is for the others. I can sense them moving in our shelter, and as long as they don't tarry, it shouldn't spoil by the time they get here. Just to be sure, I wait until I sense Caeo heading in this direction before moving on.

I concentrate on what's ahead, occasionally checking on the others' progress behind me. I take a break when they stop to eat the fish, then start again once they finish. If I reach even further back, I can pick up our pursuers wandering the hills. They've split into smaller groups, and while I can't sense all of them, so far none are heading toward the cave we left behind.

Our destination is a village we should arrive at tomorrow. There, we'll be able to resupply before continuing south to Ystyr. That's the last place my mother should expect us to go, so it should be easy going from here. It won't be difficult to avoid anyone who would report us—I'm the only one who's recognizable, and my land-sense is wider than everyone else's. I can always glamour myself if I need to, though I've never been the best at it. Emlyn usually did it for me.

A hollow pain digs into the back of my throat. The Land confirmed the soldiers spared him and Ceirios. Now I just have to hope he recovers.

I plan our route to stop at every food source I can sense without deviating too far off course, eating my share before ensuring there's plenty for the others to eat and add to their packs. As evening approaches, the stream leaves the barren valley and flows into a birch forest. The village is further in, and now I have no choice but to wait for the others to catch up.

It was nice while it lasted.

Under the shelter of the thin white and black trees, I get another fire started and catch some more fish while I wait, my insides coiling tighter as they approach. I focus all my attention on the fire, its flames blazing bright to match the growing inferno within me.

"You finally decided to wait for us?" Caeo asks once they're close. I shift my land-sense to him, ignoring everyone else.

"Only to teach you how to glamour—Ellie will need one since we're near a village. Come on." I don't wait for him to follow, heading deeper into the woods.

He grabs my arm as he catches up. "What's going on, Taran? You're not even gonna talk to me about what you pulled last night?"

I don't need this right now. I wrest free and continue walking. "I was trying to help. If you weren't going to listen to me, I thought maybe you'd listen to Ellie."

"It's not…" Caeo's steps slow, so I stop, despite the rage still simmering within me. He exhales. "You know what your weddings are like. I wasn't—I can't…"

What does that have to do with anything? But he's twitching, his head jerking away from my gaze.

My stomach lurches as it becomes clear.

His reaction to my willbending. The need to empty his mind. What our mother did to my father, forcing him into her bed.

To plan to do the same thing to her own son, with Owena…

Ancients.

I plant my hands on his shoulders. "You're safe now, Caeo. You have Ellie. Me. And our mother has no reason to suspect where we're headed." My ribs constrict—if anything, this reinforces the need to keep to Owena's plan, so we can defeat our mother without risking him going anywhere near her.

He nods shakily, and several heartbeats pass before he meets my eyes. "Yeah... I know... I just—"

"Stop. You don't need to explain. I'm sorry, I should have handled that better." I squeeze him with my fingers, then release him. I'd like to do more, but my arms are on the verge of trembling from all the Land's anger. "We need to keep moving. We're not far enough away."

I turn to go.

Caeo's voice catches as he follows. "What are you talking about?"

"Last night was too much—I can't be anywhere near Ellie anymore. Keeping my land-sense focused on something else... it's not working. I'm either going to burn up inside, or..."

Caeo steps in front of me, forcing me to stop. "Or what?"

I sigh. "You know what the Land wants, Caeo. Just let me stay away and it won't be a problem."

"That isn't how it works, Taran. It might keep you from hurting her, but that's not a solution. How do we get the Land to forgive her?"

I rub my fingers against my temples. "She needs to balance the scales, but I don't know how to do that without paying with her life." While She forgave Reid, Her anger with him—short-lived due to his quick apology—was significantly less.

"You can talk to Her, right? Can't you ask?"

"It doesn't work that way. She doesn't answer in the Tongue. She answers in raw emotion."

"Then try convincing Her to forgive her!"

I throw my hands up. "Do you think I haven't? It's only made things worse!"

Caeo bites his lower lip as he watches me, then brings his hand to his face. "Fuck."

I flinch at another violent tug from my mother. It's almost like she can tell when I'm struggling and waits until then to strike. I take a long, slow breath, then glance ahead. "We're still not far enough." The undergrowth brushes my feet as I press onward. After a moment, Caeo follows.

We finally reach a spot where I can focus, so I turn to face him. "Alright. Try to see yourself through the Land."

"What?"

I groan. While I've enjoyed helping Caeo learn to be fae, I've never had the patience for teaching. It's a good thing he's been picking things up quickly. "Just how you see everything else with your land-sense, but focus it on yourself."

"Fine." He closes his eyes.

"You don't need to—"

"Shut up."

I wait as Caeo scrunches his face.

"I think I'm doing it?"

Moving my hand in front of his nose, I shape a glamour, giving it a sharper dip. "Do you feel anything different? Like a veil against your skin?"

"No."

My shoulders sink.

This is going to take a while.

Chapter 16

Ellie

Caeo's been gone for at least a bell, and the sky has long since darkened. I jump to my feet at the sound of his approach, his feet brushing against the ferns and fallen leaves of the forest floor.

"How'd it go?" Even though Caeo assured me he wasn't angry with Taran, after how things went last night, I couldn't help worrying they'd erupt into another fight.

He plops down in front of the fire, next to where I'd been sitting. "I managed to glamour myself, but he wouldn't let me practice on him. You'll have to be my first test."

I join him on the damp ground. "It's alright. I trust you."

Owena laughs from where she sits across the flames, and Caeo's eyes snap to her. "What?"

"I don't doubt you'll be able to do it, but it's highly unlikely you'll make her look convincingly fae. You simply don't know our faces well enough."

"Perfect," he mutters. "Then why don't you do it?"

Owena's brow furrows. "Did Taran not tell you?"

"Tell me what?"

She shrugs, her smile returning, though she looks away. "I can't cast glamours. If I could, he probably wouldn't have bothered teaching you."

My eyes widen. "You naturally look like that?"

It makes sense now that she says it; her hair and skin are as dirty as mine, while Taran and Emlyn have never looked anything short of immaculate. But despite that, she's still the most beautiful person I've ever seen, with radiant skin, graceful curves, and eyes like a moonless night. I thought it had to be a glamour.

That is not fair.

But I should draw her sometime.

"Typically much cleaner, but yes. This is me." She sighs. "Perhaps I should take the opportunity to bathe while Caeo… fusses with your face. I'll let you know how successful he is when I return."

She disappears among the birch trees to where the stream flows nearby.

Caeo turns to me, taking a deep breath. "I'm not feeling as confident about this now."

I take his hand. "Don't worry about it. Just try not to make me too ugly."

He laughs. "I could never make you ugly."

"Not even with a pig nose?"

"Why would I give you a pig nose? I don't want to fuck a pig."

The words deliver a burning heat deep in my core. He's rarely spoken to me like that, mostly saving it for my bedroom, when it's sent a thrill rippling through me every time.

"Oh?" I lift my eyebrows as the blaze rises to my cheeks. With all the difficult conversations and exhaustion, we haven't had a chance for anything past tender kisses and cuddling since being reunited. But today's been better, *and* we're alone now. "Does that mean you want to…?"

Caeo's mouth goes slack, then he swallows. "I mean, yeah, I guess we could."

My heart ceases its flutters. "You don't seem very excited about it."

"I'm... I don't know, Ellie." He rakes his hand through his hair. "I *want* to want to. But..." He takes a deep breath, letting out a slow exhale. "I used the milk again. Last night, after you fell asleep."

All the heat disperses, leaving a chilling cold behind.

"Why?" I thought, after we talked... I thought I'd helped.

"I woke up, and all the thoughts—they're still there." Caeo pauses, then brings his eyes to mine. "I knew it'd disappoint you, but I couldn't get them to go away. I just... I need more time."

"And what if you get addicted during that time?" *What if he already is?*

No—Emlyn must have used it more than Caeo by now. It has to take longer to take hold, or it'd be foolish to risk it for any injury at all. We should still be safe.

He sighs. "I don't know. I'll use as little as I can, and only if I really need to, but I don't know what else to do. I know what'll happen if I get lost in those thoughts, and I can't go through that again. I can't." The light in his eyes quivers, pleading.

My body grows heavy as disappointment sinks through me. I take a deep breath, forcing it back.

He told me this time. He's talking about it. This is still progress.

My tongue is thick in my mouth, dry as sand. I swallow, trying to restore some moisture. Caeo's eyes flicker, his brows upturned as he waits for me to say something.

I reach my hand to his face, nuzzling my fingers into the warmth of his hair as my thumb grazes his cheek. "Alright. But you're not doing this alone. You need to keep talking to me."

Caeo nods, giving me a weak smile, but it's enough to warm my heart. He closes his eyes and exhales. Then they open again, with a hint of their old spark returning.

The corner of his mouth curls up, and he wraps his hand behind my head, his fingers tangling in the mess my hair has become. "I'm gonna kiss you now."

My heart squeezes into my throat. "Good."

He tugs me forward, and I pull him close, our lips meeting as the space between us shrinks to nothing. I let him in, his tongue dancing with mine, the cold disappearing as his warmth presses into me. Bringing my other hand to his face, I brush my fingers against his cheek as I melt deeper into him.

We separate only to renew our kiss again, a fire blazing with every graze of his lips, every flick of his tongue. He keeps his hand buried in my hair, but the other moves along my side, arching me into him. The second we part for air, I'm going to pull my shirt off and drag him on top of me. Steamy memories of our moments in my room flash by, my core throbbing in anticipation.

A spike of alarm blares in my mind.

We're not at the Academy!

I pull away, breathing heavily. Caeo's lips shine with the wetness of our kiss, and he blinks against the heaviness in his eyelids.

"What's wrong?" he asks, his voice breathless.

My face flushes. "I couldn't get pregnant at the Academy. Alexis said it was something about incanting draining the life away." My core aches as the fire within me sputters out. I've always wanted children, but now's the worst possible time to risk it—we've only just gotten back together, a war's breaking out, the Land wants to kill me, and Caeo's fighting addiction.

He shrugs. "It's probably fine. I've never gotten anyone pregnant before."

It's like a clack of billiard balls knocking together in my mind. "Exactly how often were you sleeping around?"

"I wasn't always sleeping around—I courted a fair amount of them for at least a month."

I sigh, forcing my insecurities down. Not once have I caught him looking at anyone else, no matter how gorgeous they are. Part of me is even a little jealous of all his experience. "It doesn't matter. But I don't want to risk it. I need to talk to Owena."

Caeo's fingers flinch against me, his shoulders stiffening. Then he drops his hands, swallowing. "Yeah, sure." He nods quickly. "Do what you need to do."

"I'll be right back." I give him a quick kiss, then scramble toward the stream.

I find her sitting at the water's edge, her back to me. Completely nude, scrubbing her wet hands against skin that practically glows in the moonlight. I avert my eyes, looking at the grass.

"Owena? I don't mean to intrude, but I was hoping to ask you something?"

"You wish to know if there's anything that can prevent you from becoming with child," she says.

My gaze darts toward her. "How did you know?"

"Even ignoring my land-sense, fae hearing is better than yours."

She heard everything? My cheeks burn, and I look back at the ground.

"Right. So... is there?"

"Fae men rarely become fertile before their third or fourth century, and even then, birthrates are low—our population would be unsustainable if we multiplied like mortals. I don't know if Caeo takes after his mother or father in that regard, but based on his history and the other fae traits he's shown, it's likely you have nothing to worry about."

My heart settles, but it's still on edge.

"Is there anything I could use to be sure? A tea, maybe?"

Owena sighs. "It's possible a healer in the nearby village may have something, though any of us asking would lead to questions. We're all too young to need it."

I mumble some thanks, then weave my way back through the trees, their white bark shining in the moonlight between harsh black scars. Caeo sits by our flickering campfire, its warmth fading as it slowly dies. I drop a few more branches on the blaze, then turn to him.

He's staring at a small jar in his hand. My ribs go tight.

"Caeo?"

He jolts, fingers clenching around the jar as his hand twitches to his side.

"Is that the milk?" My temperature rises, the cold air burning away. "After everything we just said, you were about to use it again?"

"I wasn't—I was just looking at it!"

"How is that any better? You wouldn't be looking at it if you weren't planning to use it!" My body coils, then snaps forward. "Give that to me, now."

He doesn't resist as I snatch it from his hand, but a second later, he's on his feet. "What are you doing?"

I march away, nearly tripping over a fern. "We need to get rid of it." I stop after a few steps, realizing I can just empty it onto the ground. He can't get addicted if he doesn't have any.

His hands grab mine just as I tug at the cork, stopping me. "You can't—please. I still need it."

"No, you don't. You need—you're stronger than this. I know it. I won't sit by and watch you destroy yourself."

Caeo's arm trembles as his grip tightens. "Ellie, please. I won't use it tonight, I promise." His breath catches, coming out erratically between words. "You can't—you can't get rid of it. You don't know. You don't..."

His eyes widen as his inhales pick up, cutting off his speech. He gags, then brings his hand to his chest, his body jerking in what seems like dry heaves. Folding forward, he releases me as he tumbles to his knees, body shaking and gasping for air.

"Caeo!"

I abandon the jar in the grass as he lets out a strangled groan, his eyes squeezed shut. I take him in my arms, my heart pounding in time with his tremors. Is this addiction, or memories of whatever his mother did to him?

No, not whatever. I know what she did—she willbent him. Took his choices away. Trapped him with everything he wanted to escape.

Just like I was about to.

I let out a slow exhale as I run my fingers through his sweaty hair. He clings to my arm, face tight between breaths.

A hollowness takes over my chest. As much as it hurts, and as wrong as it feels to step aside, it's not up to me to protect him from himself. I'll only make things worse.

"I'm sorry, Caeo. I shouldn't have done that. I just... I didn't know what to do. Please forgive me."

His grip on my arm tightens, and I pull him closer, squeezing him with everything I have.

"I'm here. I love you. I won't take it again."

He doesn't speak, his ragged breaths accompanied only by the sounds of insects chirping in the night. Eventually, he steadies, with the occasional sharp inhale or shudder breaking his calm.

I caress him gently until he falls asleep.

THE NEXT DAY, Caeo seems to be back to his old self, though the occasional tremor or far-off stare keeps me from breathing easily. He and Owena go to the fae village for supplies, since Taran's more likely to be recognized—Caeo even made himself blond to hide his resemblance. But Owena took one look at the glamour he placed on me and claimed it wouldn't fool anyone.

So I'm spending the afternoon by myself, mostly sketching some flowers that don't exist back home. At the warmest part of the day, I take a freezing bath in the creek, then occupy the rest of the time sorting through my thoughts while my teeth chatter.

Before I get very far, an eerie stillness presses in around me. I take a deep breath, the woody scent of the forest filling my lungs, but the unease persists. I stand up, turning around—

A fae. Heavyset, male, and with hair so light it almost matches the bark of the birch trees. His head's cocked to the side as his eyes roam over me.

"You look funny," he says slowly. "Feel funny, too."

My pulse races, and I take a step back. The village should be behind me—he must be on his way there.

"I-I don't know what you mean." My fingers clench into fists, my ankles brushing against the undergrowth as my feet continue pulling me away. It's probably not helping, only making me more suspicious, but I can't stop myself.

The fae's eyes narrow. He starts to open his mouth, but it snaps shut, his gaze darting behind me. Leaves rustle, then his expression transforms from distrust to surprise.

I peek around...

Taran.

He strides toward me, eyes locked on the fae, until he comes to a stop between us. The fae takes a step back, then folds into a hurried bow.

"Your Highness." He glances up before quickly dropping his gaze back to the ground.

"This is my business," Taran says, his back to me. "Be gone from here."

"Of course, Your Highness." After a shaky nod, he turns and bolts between the trees.

My entire body relaxes with my exhale, but coils again as my mind digests what just happened.

"You didn't bend him," I say, slowly approaching Taran. "What if he tells someone about me? About us?"

His voice comes out tight. "Caeo and Owena are almost back. We'll be well on our way before anyone he tells would return here."

That's not entirely comforting. But I can't do anything about it. I'm only safe because Taran showed up. This is his realm. His people, his decisions.

I hate feeling so helpless.

Coming to a stop next to him, I glance up at his strained expression.

His arm jerks toward me.

Taran's fingers dig into my wrist like knives, pain shooting through my elbow as his grip tightens. Horror flashes across his face, an emerald fire blazing in his eyes. I shriek as he yanks, my knees buckling beneath me.

"Get away from her!" Caeo's voice slams against my eardrums.

Taran's grip on my arm releases as he throws himself free of me, colliding with the tree behind us. His head knocks back, hitting the wood with a hard thump.

Soft arms catch me, guiding me down to the ground. Owena.

"Are you alright?" she whispers.

I nod, my lungs seizing as they struggle to breathe and form words. "I-I'm fine. There was a fae. He made him leave, and then—"

"It's the Land," Taran groans, rubbing his head. "I can't..." His flaming eyes dart to Caeo, who's standing between us like a barrier, his body so tense he looks ready to snap. "I told you I can't be around her anymore."

Taran pushes himself off the tree, then stumbles away, leaving us no choice but to eventually follow.

DROPS OF WATER sprinkle against my coat, and I pull my hood up. It's been raining intermittently throughout this third day of hiking, but never strong enough to warrant seeking shelter. The worst part is the moisture that collects on the meadow's tall grass, seeping into my pants with every step. It's a good thing extra clothes were part of our resupply back at the village, or we'd never be fully dry.

It's slightly less cold now, with the landscape varying between lush forests of deep greens and browns and rolling hills speckled with wildflowers and sheep. There's not a single moment where the sights are anything short of picturesque, but I can hardly appreciate the splendor thanks to our pace, Owena's increasing irritation, and the knowledge that all this beauty wants to tear me apart.

I catch up to Caeo, a few feet ahead of me. "How much longer do you think it'll be till he stops?"

"No idea. But if you want, we can take a break. I'm sure he'll notice and wait." Despite his anger as he fussed over the bruises on my arm after the Land's attack, he and Taran smoothed things over later that night. Neither of them was at fault, and while he didn't intend to bend Taran, I don't want to consider what would've happened if he hadn't.

I sigh, glancing back at Owena. She trails about twenty feet behind us, her arms wrapped tightly around herself as she tromps through the field. Coupled with her scowling countenance, I'd say her mood hasn't improved since our last respite, when she snapped at me every time I attempted conversation. I don't know what I could've done to upset her, so I keep telling myself it must be something else, but it stings—I'd hoped we could be friends. I've settled on silently sketching her, hoping she'll appreciate the drawing when I'm done.

"No, we can keep going," I say.

Caeo slides his hand around my waist and plants a quick kiss on my lips, pausing before he squeezes my side. While we haven't gotten anywhere closer to the intimacy we once had, he *did* get some herbs from the village healer that should prevent any accidental pregnancies. From what he said, he almost doubled over in pain as he lied to the man, saying they were for his mother, but the healer just assumed he was feeling unwell and gave him a constipation remedy, too.

Yet every night, when the two of us finally have a chance to be alone, he hasn't been interested. He only wants to cuddle and talk. I'm trying my best to be patient, but I miss being close to him, our bodies melding into one as ecstasy courses through us. My core aches, yearning to be filled by him again.

There's something he still hasn't told me. Words he hasn't been able to form. I could ask Owena if she knows, but that'd just be taking another choice away from him. So I resist the urge, as tempting as it is. All I can do is wait—to be there for him until he's ready. As such, I push those thoughts from my mind and focus on something I *can* try to solve.

How to get the Land to stop hating me.

According to Caeo, Taran insists that whatever Reid did won't work. She's too angry and would kill me instead of hurting me. They both refuse to help me attempt it.

Caeo has occasionally tried reaching the Land, lying down and digging his hands into the dirt. His face will relax into tranquility for a few minutes, then contort in pain after he thinks of me and ends up breaking the connection. While Taran can actually speak to Her, he claims he hasn't had any more success.

So I need to find a way to restore balance on my own, and I have no reason to believe that continuing on this journey with Taran and Owena will help me accomplish that.

First off, it's torturing Taran. Making him suffer every day can't be helping my case.

Secondly, I have no role in their plan. I'm just excess baggage while they do all the work. Even if they succeed, it won't balance anything for me, because I won't have done anything.

If I ignore all potential hindrances, the best thing I can do for the Land is to return home and convince my father of the truth about incanting. As High Marshal of the Order of Incanters, he has more power than anyone to end its use, outside of the king. As his daughter, there's a chance I might actually persuade him.

I hope. I've never actually convinced him of anything before, simply following along his path every day of my life. But maybe standing up for once will get his attention.

If that doesn't balance things with the Land, I don't know what will. The problem is returning home.

My veins freeze at the thought of crossing the border again. It was a shattering experience, and after the first time, I feared I'd never be able to return home because I didn't know if I could go through it again. And that was before the Land wanted to kill me.

But it's also the only way I'll have a chance to face Her myself, since Caeo and Taran won't do it. Maybe She'll be able to feel my intentions. Maybe I can convince Her to let me pass, so I can get my people to stop hurting Her.

Please don't let that be a fool's hope.

A grim acceptance settles in my stomach, its weight like a boulder. It may be a silly dream, and it may fail horribly, but I don't see what else I can do. I can't hide from this for the rest of my life. I need to fix it.

As the sun begins to set, a brisk chill gusts into me, and we spot a campfire ahead. Taran sits beside it, roasting some kind of meat over the flames. He stands as he senses our approach, turning his back to us.

To me.

"Plan to leave at first light," he says as Caeo drops our pack, sitting down by the fire. Owena trails behind, lowering herself gracefully on the opposite side of the flames. Taran makes to move away.

"Wait!" I call, and his feet hesitate. "There's something I need to say."

His shoulders tense. "Then hurry up."

Caeo and Owena look up at me, their eyes expectant.

I take a deep breath, clasping my hands behind my back to keep them from wringing; I can't have anyone questioning my decision. Straightening myself to be as tall as possible, I speak, willing my voice to remain steady.

"I want to leave. To go back to Landore. For you to continue south without me."

Chapter 17

Owena

Things with Taran haven't been progressing the way I'd hoped. My moment with him in the monsoon went perfectly. Fiery. Intimate. Even though he stormed off in an anger that matched that of the tempest battering the hillside, leaving me to freeze in its downpour, the heat of his focus—burning into me through my land-sense—kept me warm until I grew tired of being thrashed by the wind.

Since then, however, I've hardly seen him. For the past four days, I haven't had the faintest idea where he's at, mentally, outside of knowing that he's still thinking of me. Not all day, but in random spurts throughout. The air around me will grow heavy and warm as a fire blazes through my nerves from the Land beneath my feet. It happens so often at night that I barely need to rely on Her for warmth. Does he even realize he's doing it?

And now Ellie's announced her intention to part ways with us.

I expected it to happen eventually. In fact, if she hadn't suggested it, I would have given her a nudge in that direction myself—it would be impossible to confront my father with her and Caeo present. But I worry I won't be able to get Taran where he needs to be by myself. His trauma runs too deep, and Caeo and Ellie both have roles to play in healing it. Until then, he won't be able to be a proper king, let alone someone I can depend on.

Which leaves me no choice but to take a monumental risk.

As anticipated, Taran departs our camp, heading deeper into the woods shortly after Ellie's proclamation. This time, I follow.

"Taran, wait," I call, once I'm certain we're far enough from Ellie for his head to be reasonably clear. Not that he's been unaware of my pursuit this entire time.

He stops, his reluctance palpable as he slowly turns to face me. "You're not going to stop following me, are you?"

I pick up my pace, weaving through the tangled thickets of the forest floor. As I draw near, I deliberately trip on a root obscured by an overgrown fern. He's shown an instinct for catching me that would be foolish to ignore.

And he does, his hands seizing my waist as I wrap my fingers around his arms.

He lets go almost instantly, wresting himself from my grasp. "You did that on purpose, didn't you?"

"Why would you suggest that?" I ask as I regain my balance.

Taran rubs his face. "I'm not in the mood for games, Owena. Even a child would have sensed that root."

My lips press together, clamping down on my rising ire. I'd hoped that after he apologized for belittling my shaping ability, he'd be done with being condescending to me. Apparently not.

"I thought it might do you some good to discuss Ellie's decision," I say, changing the subject.

"Why would I want to do that?"

"Because avoidance isn't a healthy way to cope, but it's clearly a strategy you rely on far too much."

Taran glares at me, then turns away.

"If you leave, you're only proving my point."

He groans as he looks back at me, his eyes bleeding impatience.

"Fine. What do you want me to say?"

If only there were somewhere to sit that wasn't a knot of brambles. Since there isn't, I straighten myself up and meet his gaze. "Why don't you start with your feelings toward Ellie?"

His eyes narrow. "Why do you care?"

"I think I deserve to know if the person I'm marrying is in love with someone else."

He blinks, his mouth twitching like that was the last thing he expected me to say. Then he recovers with a frown. "Does it matter? From everything you've said, you're not after my heart."

His words pierce, and it's only decades of practice masking my emotions that keeps my face from betraying me. I want nothing more than to marry someone who loves me, but he's not yet capable of that. You can't truly love someone if you don't love yourself.

So I try a different angle. "I deserve to know what scars I'll be living with for the rest of my life."

Taran exhales, turning his gaze to the ground. He grinds his jaw, as if debating whether to speak. "They aren't your burden, Owena," he says at last. "They're mine."

My heart melts at his somber tone—I know all too well what it's like to carry everything yourself—but I keep my voice firm. "When we marry, they'll become mine. As mine will you."

His malachite eyes flick back to me, his thoughts whispering within them. He may not have considered it before, but he should understand the weight of our marriage. The bond that will form between us, binding us just as deeply as the one he currently shares with the Land. Perhaps more.

When he speaks, his words are a soft rumble. "What scars could you possibly have?"

"Did you forget my father uses curses to control people just as liberally as your mother willbends? Not to belittle your experience, but your mother left when you were five. I've spent thirty-two years under his rule."

Taran straightens, his gaze focused, as if he never noticed me before. A moment passes, and his voice drops low, edging into vulnerable. "Yet you seem so untouched. How do you bear it?"

I shrug, looking away. I bear it with a fire fueled by anger, resentment... and hope. It needs only to last a little while longer, keeping him close for a couple more weeks, and then I'll be free of it forever. "It either burns you alive or turns you into a flame yourself."

"I have no desire to become anything like my mother."

A sharp laugh huffs out my nostrils. "Becoming a force to be reckoned with doesn't automatically turn us into our parents."

I glance back at him. Our eyes meet, and a lump forms in my throat at the recognition in them, his defenses lowered.

Too close—I can't have him seeing me as a confidante. Not yet.

It would ruin everything.

Though it hurts, I have no choice but to sever the connection. So with a heavy heart and an icy glare, I slip my mask back on and force myself to continue.

"You need to stop being weak."

Taran's face flinches, then the softness hardens into ire. "Back to this again?"

My own words dig into me. "You let your inadequacies rule you."

His gaze lingers for a moment, unreadable. Then he turns away. "I should have anticipated this."

Unfortunately, there's still more to push, so I give chase as he storms off. "You're afraid of doing what you need to do. What you want to do."

Taran spins around, his shoulders tense as he towers over me. His face twists with anger. "What do you know of my wants?"

I push back against his stare. "I know you want me—the weight of your focus is impossible to ignore. So toughen up and take it."

His lips press together, and for a ragged heartbeat it almost seems like he might. But his jaw tightens, and he retreats.

"Leave me alone."

"Back to avoiding me, then?" I call as he marches away. It will do me no good to follow him any longer. "You can't keep running forever."

He ignores me, and my heart thunders as he disappears among the trees.

I let out a heavy breath, hoping to calm myself as I review the words we exchanged. With luck, Taran will spend the night stewing over everything and emerge with newfound resolve. If not... then perhaps a day of brotherly bonding with Caeo will bring him some clarity.

My stomach wrings uncomfortably. If only there were an easier way to depose of my father. To ensure peace between realms. I've spent decades searching for a solution, and this is the best opportunity I've ever had. Yet it hurts so terribly.

I'm not my father. While I learned to manipulate others to survive his court, it's not a skill I pride myself on. Curses, betrayals—that's him, not me. But there's only one way to get close enough to him to free my people from his cruelty. If the suffering it took were mine alone, I wouldn't hesitate. But Taran's...

What I need is guidance, and there's only one way to get any.

I wander through the woods, tangling my feet in the occasional bramble, until I find a clear enough patch of undergrowth to lie down. While I've sought counsel from the Land before with little issue, it's foolhardy under these circumstances—though Her payment can vary based on Her mood, She typically demands some life energy. Otherwise, the world would tip out of balance, with everyone demanding Her direction all the time. Amid weeks of physical exertion, I can hardly afford to make my travels even more exhausting, but it's a price I'm willing to pay for assurances that I'm on the right path.

It's a struggle to loosen the frigid soil enough to dig my fingers in without shaping, but I eventually get my hands buried deep enough. I breathe deeply, focusing on my bond with the Land.

Her pulse radiates through me, from the tips of my fingers down to my toes, filling me with a warm glow that tingles against the chill of my skin. My heart calms, beating in rhythm with Her. If all I wanted was comfort, this would be enough. She already senses my torment, likely feeling it with every step I take. With our connection now amplified, Her compassion flows through me.

I open my mouth and speak in the Tongue.

"Glorious Mother, I beg your guidance. I've always assumed you wanted peace between all realms. Is that true?"

Her pulse drums with steady affirmation.

I swallow. "And if I can get that? No matter the cost? The suffering?"

The pulse beats stronger, its heat permeating my entire body like a lover's embrace. Tears stream down my cheeks. In relief, that my torment is not in vain. And dread, that I must continue down this path of misery.

Her pulse continues as my tears fall, my breath tattered between moments of calm. Until they finally stop, the river dry.

"Thank you," I whisper, and my heart tenses in apprehension. "You may take your payment."

But all I feel is Her continued pulse, warm and comforting. After a momentary confusion, the skies clear.

Of course. If this is what She wants, then my success will be payment enough. A moment of comfort is nothing compared to the price of getting there.

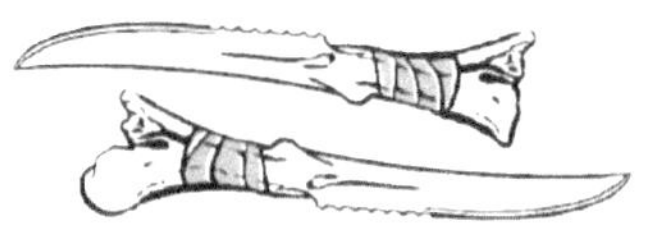

Chapter 18

Emlyn

I roll off the satisfied puddle that is Reid, panting as I dissolve into the ground. The moment I hit the dirt, the pulsing heat I've grown accustomed to floods my right shoulder. I close my eyes as tiny tingles pepper the area, restoring my muscles.

Apparently, I've discovered the secret to miraculous healing that no one else in our seven thousand years of remembered history has uncovered—letting the Land watch you fornicate. *A lot.*

Well, there's probably more to it than that. Maybe She really supports our decision to go to Lyndir? Not that I know why. Or we're just particularly fun to watch? Whatever it is, I'm not complaining. All that matters is that every time we finish, a wave of warmth washes through me from the Land, drawing away the pain. After only a few days, almost full mobility's returned to my arm. While the scar's hideous, I can easily cover that with a glamour.

"That was a good one," I let out between breaths. The Land clearly agrees.

"They're all good ones." Reid groans as he pushes himself up beside me, a sweaty, beautiful mess.

I lazily tap his leg. "Just give me a bit and we can go again. It's your turn to top."

"Uh uh. We've already gone twice, and you said we'd leave today."

I peek his direction. He's pulling his shirt on, the dappled forest light dotting his deep olive skin.

"I did say that, didn't I?" Kinda wishing I didn't, with all the danger our journey will bring.

Ever since we realized how quickly I was healing, Reid's been antsy to get out of here. I want to leave too, because I'm completely over living with my mom, but he's motivated by worries about his home. I'd do anything to calm his mind, even if it means putting a hold on our copulation marathon so we can risk our lives, returning to the world beyond the two of us.

We *should* get going. Reid can only see well enough to travel by day, and we have all night to get back to this.

He leans over to give me a quick kiss, but slinks away before I can grab him and hold him down, the bastard. That's not an insult—he literally is one. And I say it with all the love in my heart.

"I'll go finish packing," he says. "You get the horses?"

"Sure, but try not to make a thing about leaving with Ma. I'd rather avoid a big goodbye."

Reid pauses, frowning. "Why are you such an asshole to your mom? You're lucky you have one that cares so much."

Ouch. Of course he'd see it that way; his has neglected him his whole life. But even Taran's never asked me that before—though, if he actually understands or just considers me heartless, I don't know.

I scratch at the grass itching my side as I close my eyes. "She doesn't know the extent of what I do. Have done, for Taran. If she did... Well, she'd probably blame herself, because I'd never have known him if she hadn't been his governess. And he needs her love more than I do, so..."

Reid sits next to me, rubbing my shoulder as I trail off. "That doesn't mean you can't be nicer."

A few heartbeats pass before I open my eyes to the pine needles above, then shrug. "It's easier to disappoint her by being distant than by being who I am. Besides—if everyone thinks I don't give a shit, it's less likely anyone will go after her as payback for something I did."

Reid brushes my cheek with his thumb, turning my face to his for a kiss on my nose. "I don't think she'd ever be disappointed in who you are. But hurting her for her sake? That's just fucked."

I laugh, despite the gnawing in my stomach, then give him a gentle shove away. "Fine. I'll say goodbye. Now go get packing."

He gives me one last smile before disappearing among the trees.

I keep my land-sense on him as he heads toward the house. He cares about privacy, so we've been going well past what Ma could see or hear, until I can no longer sense her. We've been out here enough times that he shouldn't have a problem finding his way back on his own, but I like to make sure.

Once he's within sight of the house, I pull on my clothes so I can head to the village. We've been gathering supplies these last few days, and all that's really left are horses and empty jugs to hold the obscene amount of water we'll have to bring. I have no idea how long we'll be in the mortal realm, but I'll need to drink some every day to maintain a glamour.

I told Reid I'd go to Lyndir like it wasn't much of an issue. At the time, I didn't think it was. But with every passing day, the reality of what we're doing sinks deeper, bringing anxiety with it. Just crossing the border is a risk in itself; I meant it when I said I never wanted to drag Reid through that again. If this goes poorly, hopefully I can pull him back before he gets killed, but what'll it do to him if we discover he can never go home?

Maybe I'm worrying too much. The Land clearly likes something about us. Yet despite constantly telling myself that, my apprehension lingers like a stain that won't wash out.

If we do make it through, I'll be a lone fae wandering a realm at war with mine. It wasn't as worrisome before, when the fighting had been over for two decades, but now, everyone'll be on edge. Will they be content to believe their armies have stopped all fae at the border, or will they be suspicious of anything out of the ordinary?

Hopefully I don't have to cut my hair.

But first I need some horses. The village skirts the edge of the forest not too far from Ma's house, and some frolic in a nearby meadow. I move close enough that they can all see me, so I don't startle them when I bring my hand to the side of my mouth and yell in the Tongue.

"I need two horses to get to the mortal realm. Anyone interested?"

A couple of mares trot over, a chestnut and a buckskin. Perfect— we'll have an even number of each kind of genitalia. Balance in everything. I give each of them an appreciative scratch behind the ears before leading them to the nearby tack shop.

My stomach tightens. This is where things get tricky.

I don't have very much money. Worse comes to worst, I can ride bareback, though it'll slow us down because it'll be harder on the horse. But Reid will need a full set of tack—we aren't going anywhere otherwise. Normally, I'd offer sexual favors as payment, but I can't really do that anymore.

While the horses wait outside, I stick my head into the shop: a mostly open-air space among a grove of pine trees with a thatched roof above. It smells strongly of oiled leather.

"Hello?"

A mass of curly red hair pops up from behind a stack of saddles. My tension eases slightly.

She's not the type who'd go for that kind of negotiation anyway.

"Can I help you?" she asks.

I glance at her wares, stacked on tables, filling baskets, and hanging from poles. "How much for two sets of tack?"

She thinks for a moment, her brow scrunching up, then gives me a number slightly more than what I have.

Stealing it is!

I lean against the saddle next to her. "Is there any way we can get that number down? What if we drop one of the saddles and stirrups?"

"That would save you some money, sure."

I meet her eyes and smile, tracing my finger along the stitching in the leather. "Is there anything else you think I could go without? I'm a little tight on funds."

She chews her lip, then lists what she thinks I could skip, which matches what I already knew. But she insists on stirrups and reins, claiming most people wouldn't be comfortable without them.

"I'm sorry, I didn't catch your name," I say.

Her eyelids flutter in surprise. "Oh, I didn't—sorry, I'm Rhian."

"Well, Rhian, it's a good thing I'm comfortable with a lot of things." I lean a little closer, and a blush creeps into her cheeks.

"I'll just—I'll go get everything for you." She bumps into the saddle as she scampers away.

One by one, she brings pieces of gear over to the horses, and I make sure to *accidentally* brush my fingers against hers each time I take something from her, until the horses are ready to go. The buckskin's more willing to have me go bareback, which works out—the chestnut will match Reid's hair nicely.

When it comes time to pay, I hold her hand while I meet her gaze, thanking her for all her help. She doesn't notice that I only put half the number of coins we agreed was fair into her hand.

I close her fingers around the money, then give them a kiss, before hopping onto the buckskin and riding away.

That was surprisingly easy. Maybe I don't need to sleep with everyone to get shit done.

After one more stop for water jugs, I head back to Ma's. Reid sits against the wall outside, surrounded by clucking chickens, waiting for me.

"I don't have any food for you," he mutters in the Tongue to a pushy hen pecking at his leg. He's been learning more every day while helping Ma with chores, and I've been teaching him the less appropriate words since the Land seems to appreciate dirty talk.

I tell the bird to skedaddle before lowering myself beside him, then clap my hand on his leg. "You ready to go?"

"We're not leaving without saying goodbye."

"I know, but I kinda had to steal some things, so we should get moving."

"So you weren't planning on sneaking off this time?" Ma stands in the doorway, eyeing me with that motherly look of hers.

I bite my tongue. While I've had my fill of heartfelt conversations with her for this decade, I *do* see Reid's point. With a grunt, I push myself to my feet and offer him my hand, pulling him up.

"Bye, Ma. I'll see you... sometime."

She steps over and smacks my arm. "Don't give me that. You don't get to show up at my door for the first time in years, practically dead, then leave like you'll see me next solstice." My head jerks as she pulls me into a tight hug.

I grumble as her warmth envelops me, then bring my arms up to hug her in return. Against my instinct, I give her a squeeze before she pulls away, her eyes glistening as they search my face.

"I love you, Ma. You know that, right?"

Her lips press together, and she nods.

Alright, that's enough. I pick up one of our bags and start fastening it to the chestnut's saddle, making sure the load's balanced with all the empty jugs.

Ma puts her hand on Reid's shoulder. "Take care of him."

"I will."

I bury the smile tugging at me by rolling my eyes as I finish tying my knots, then give the chestnut a pat on the shoulder. "Come on, Reid." I cup my hands together and give him a leg up, then pinch his thigh for good measure once he's settled.

"Stop that." He doesn't mean it at all, because he's smiling.

"You know you like it."

I pull on my pack and move over to the buckskin, giving her a few scratches on her chin. I grab a handful of her mane with my left hand and press my right into her withers. With a forceful push off the ground, I jump, swinging my leg over her back.

"Let's go."

IT'S ABOUT A FOUR-DAY RIDE to the border, trying to balance speed with not exhausting the horses. Or Reid. Despite the workout I've been giving him lately, it's entirely different to spend four whole days on a horse. It's rough on me, too, but at least I have two decades of riding experience to make up for the last few weeks of being almost dead.

As it is, neither of us has the energy for more than one round of passionate, mind-blowing sex each night, but the Land continues healing my shoulder afterward, anyway. Hooray!

I suppose that'll stop once we cross the border. I've been purposely avoiding thinking about that.

Even last time, I already had feelings for Reid. I wasn't entirely sure what they were, but they were there, poking around like a fox seeking a cozy burrow. Realizing that the Land might kill him forced me to acknowledge how much I actually cared. Afterward, I joked that I'd never drag him through there again, partially because it was so miserable, but also because I wanted him to stay.

I'd like to believe that since the Land's excited about us going there, She won't kill him. But who knows? She can be feisty like that.

For now, we're stopping at the last decently sized village for a quick resupply before shifting north, where there's nothing worth taking from the mortals and the terrain's easy on the horses; from what I've gathered during our previous stops, troops have been marshaling further south, to better coordinate with Ystyr.

Supposedly, the queen's traveling with the bulk of the force—my guess is to keep as many people between her and Taran as possible. I have no idea what the upper limit of how many people he can willbend at once is, if he were even willing to do it, but it's probably not enough to turn the entire army against her.

But that's not my problem anymore.

I kiss Reid's nose after I pull my hand from his face, glamouring him for what will hopefully be the last time until we get near Haven. I get that keeping Alexis out of the war is important to him, but I don't think he appreciates how risky that will be. Nor have we worked out what we'll do after that. But improvising has generally worked out for me, more so than following Taran's plans, at least, so hopefully that luck continues.

"How much money do we have left?" he asks, pulling his hood up. Sure, it's cold, but it's mostly that he still struggles to trust the glamour.

"Hardly any. I'll probably have to cheat someone, so you'll need to play the distraction. Just be confident, like no one should question what you're doing."

"Easier said than done," he mutters. I guess he's less confident about stealing when he isn't incanting.

I pull my pack on, then rest my hands on his shoulders. "I believe in you."

Reid's lips twitch into a smile, then he nods.

We can't bring the horses with us, since the ridiculous amount of water jugs would make it abundantly clear we're going to Lyndir, so they stay behind while we huff the rest of the way on foot. Like most of our villages, this one's built among an ancient pine forest, with public spaces shaped between the tree trunks and homes wrapping around the canopy.

But as we make our approach, something feels off. A sizeable group of people gathers on the south side, spread out among the trees. I keep it to myself since I don't need Reid's nerves spiking, but my fingers drift to the daggers strapped to my thighs.

Two men stand stationed right where the forest path enters the village proper. Too late to turn back—it'd be suspicious if we suddenly turned around. So I lean into Reid, whispering in his ear, "Remember to be confident."

"What?" he hisses. But by now, they can see us, so I just kiss his cheek and pull away.

"State your business," the older one says, forcing us to stop. I'd guess he's in his four hundreds.

"Just hoping to get some supplies," I say.

His partner, a scraggly man with long black hair, leans against a nearby tree. "Where're ya headed?"

Oooh, secret weapon time. "Was it Brightwater?" I ask Reid, my chest constricting with the hope that he gets the ruse. I'd rather avoid having to kill anyone today.

He blinks, then realization smacks him in the face. "Yeah, Brightwater."

The older one steps forward. "We have orders to recruit all able-bodied men for the war."

"Why?" I ask. "We already have an army."

"Yeah, but most of the Fallen are practically children who've never seen battle," Scraggles says, picking at his fingernails. "We're hoping to overwhelm 'em with a big push."

Fuck. "Well, you'll have to look elsewhere. We already have a mission." To save Alexis.

"Yeah... We're delivering an important message for the queen," Reid adds, then swallows.

The two soldiers look at each other, eyes narrowing.

Scraggles's boot scrapes the tree as he pushes off it. "We've also been ordered to keep an eye out for any Fallen infiltrating our realm. Ya seen any?"

I resist the pull of my fingers toward my daggers. If Reid doesn't answer soon, this could get bloody fast.

"No, we haven't," he says, his voice firm.

Scraggles looks to me, his eyes widening.

"You trying to say something?" I ask, crossing my arms. "He already told you we haven't. You really can't tell I'm fae?" Need to keep their suspicion on me, the one we can prove is fae.

"A Fallen couldn't get here without help. You could be glamoured and lying."

I let out an over-exaggerated sigh, then switch to the Tongue. "How many Fallen can speak the language of the Land?"

They glance at each other again, then at Reid.

"I'm fae, ass," he says in the Tongue. Short and sweet, his accent perfect. I would kiss him, but now's not the time.

The older soldier sighs, then steps aside. "Fine, you're fae. Go about your business, then get on your way."

"Going." I grab Reid's hand, then pull him the rest of the way to town.

We need to get out of here as quickly as possible.

Chapter 19

Caeo

"Right now, we want to go south by southeast," Taran says. "Can you tell which direction that is?"

I look up, searching for the sun, but the forest canopy's too thick. "Uh... no?"

"Use your land-sense." He gestures at a patch of dark green on the oak he's leaning against. "In Aedys, trees tend to have moss on the north side of their trunks, and more leaves on the southern side. The hills are usually drier on the southern side, with more plants on the north. None of that's reliable by itself, but if you search the full scope of your land-sense, you should be able to find some patterns."

That sounds like a lot of work. "Can't you just draw us a map in Ellie's sketchbook?"

"A map is useless if you can't identify the landmarks or tell which direction you're going."

I press the palms of my hands against my temples as my fingers dig into my scalp, rubbing in circles. I groan, but none of my balled-up tension escapes with it.

It started building as Ellie announced her intentions to leave last night, winding tighter with every word. Obviously, I'm going with her, but I wish she'd talked to me about it first. Her reasoning makes sense; while I'd be falling apart without her, I can appreciate how that isn't enough for her to feel useful, and *if* she can convince her dad to put an end to incanting, that's just about the best thing she could do for the Land—but I would've liked to have had some say in the matter. While I'm not feeling great about escorting her to her doom, I've already disappointed her enough. I need to be strong, for her.

Owena's helping her write some words in the Tongue, an apology and explanation, that she's hoping to memorize by the time we reach the border, and Taran says he'll continue trying to convince the Land to show mercy. All I can do is be supportive and try not to shit myself every time I think of the suicidal risk Ellie's taking.

And, of course, everything else.

Not only will I have to navigate, I'll have to gather all our food, find us shelter, and keep us out of sight and safe from all the fae along the way. Everything Taran's been doing, except I've only known how to use my land-sense and shape for barely a week, *and* he's significantly more powerful. That shelter we made in the hills? That was at least seventy percent him, and I was completely spent after my meager contribution.

I'm beginning to understand why he's so grumpy all the time.

With a final squeeze against my skull, I drop my hands and sit on the forest floor. I take a deep breath, holding it for a few seconds before slowly exhaling. Then, I close my eyes and reach out with my land-sense.

The forest is a mix of evergreens, maples, and some others whose names I never learned. The evergreens have significantly more moss on them, wrapping their trunks in all directions, so I focus more of my search on the others. But it's hopeless. There's moss all over the place.

Think. Taran wouldn't say I could do this if I couldn't.

I open my eyes. "Maybe I need to look where the trees are less dense? Where more sunlight breaks through?"

Taran looks down at me, arms folded. "Can you figure out what direction that would be?"

I quickly check my land-sense again. "Um... that way?"

He nods. "Good. But only go as far as you need to—you don't want to get off course. Try to remember how this spot feels so you can find your way back."

This is gonna take forever. Taran's acting like we have time for this, but apparently we only just missed a group of soldiers recruiting at the village we stopped at. They'll probably arrive at the border a few days before Ellie and me, which means the war will likely be well underway by the time we do. Because more danger is exactly what we need.

I push myself to my feet and start walking.

"So, when do you think we should start heading west?" I ask as we hike toward the sparser stretch of forest. Owena should be keeping track of us today, making sure she and Ellie stay close enough to not get separated.

Taran matches my pace beside me. "I wouldn't wait more than a day or two. We can try to go mostly south today, but Owena and I need to head slightly eastward to make the best time. The longer you stay, the further you'll have to travel."

Wonderful. A day or two to master everything.

Taran exhales slowly, rubbing his neck. "Once you leave, I don't know if I'll ever see you again."

My steps slow to a halt. That honestly hadn't occurred to me.

"Yeah, I dunno." I scratch behind my head. *Why'd he have to say that? Now everything's awkward.* It's not like I'll miss him much—in the scope of my life, the time I've spent with him is hardly a hiccup. But I guess it felt like the beginning of something more.

I glance over at him, and he's stopped, too. He shrugs and looks away.

"Anyways, we can talk about that after you teach me how to willbend." It was pure luck that it worked back when the Land had him grabbing Ellie—and if I add how I accidentally hurt him, the whole thing really hammered home how much I need to learn to do it properly. I don't think I can take a Land-possessed Taran in a fight.

I take another few steps before he speaks: "I'm not teaching you to willbend."

Stopping short, I nearly trip on a bulgy root as I spin to face him. "But it was your idea! You said I need to learn to control it."

"So you don't accidentally bend people. That's not teaching you to use it."

My pulse quickens. "How else am I supposed to protect Ellie if we run into trouble? Punching you is the extent of my fighting experience."

He glances away. "I don't know? Avoid running into anyone?" Then he marches past, leaving me hurrying to catch up.

"My land-sense isn't like yours. By the time I sense someone, they'll have sensed us, too. And they'll be better than me at everything. Willbending's the only advantage I have."

"You couldn't successfully bend Owena, and I already wanted to get away from Ellie when you bent me, so I barely needed a nudge." He rubs the back of his head. "Would have preferred it to be less painful, though."

"Would you stop?" I grab his shoulder, and while he shrugs me off, he does. "I bent the guards at the castle. It was almost enough for me to escape. I would've, if our mother hadn't shown up."

Taran exhales, balling his fists before pinching his brow. "That's different. They probably weren't trying to kill you, and I doubt you bent more than one at a time."

"Maybe I could do better if I actually knew what I was doing!"

"What would you tell them to do, Caeo? If two soldiers—two of *my* people, who think they're only following orders—if they find you, how would you bend them, if you can only bend one? How would that help you?"

I throw my arms up. "I don't know? Maybe tell one of them to fight the other so we can get away?"

Taran grabs my shoulders. "And you should understand more than anyone what that actually means, Caeo. To force someone to attack their comrade, helpless to stop themselves."

A boulder tumbles down my throat and slams into my stomach. *Fuck.*

I swallow, and Taran's grip on my shoulders slackens. I nod my head, understanding, but it doesn't stop nodding. Just like my feet, jerking after my mother. No choice. No. Can't move.

I'm shaking. Sinking. Ground.

Breathe.

I squeeze my eyes shut, trying to stem the panic racing through my veins. Taran's hands press against the back of my shoulders, keeping me from falling over.

Breathe.

"I didn't, I wasn't—"

"It's fine, Caeo." His voice is steady. "I'm sorry. I only wanted you to see."

I take another chilly inhale, holding it as long as I can, then release it. Again, and again. Until my heart stops slamming against my ribs.

"I-I wasn't thinking—I just wanted to protect Ellie." I close my eyes, trying to hold off the memories banging around behind them. When will they stop coming?

The milk... Where is it?

Taran's hands leave my shoulders, and his back pushes into mine, propping me up as he sits behind me. Sturdy. Warm. My fingers twitch away from my pocket. *Breathe.*

He exhales. "I think that's a good sign. You could see it as something useful, not just a curse. I'm not even there yet."

My head falls forward, and I open my eyes. My hand rests slack among blades of soft grass. I glance at my other one, on the opposite side of me. As if drawn by something deep within, I inch my fingers into the grass, digging into the dirt.

A warm pulse rolls through me, each wave eroding the tension in my muscles, the panic crumbling in its wake. Like the milk, but different. As if oblivion cared.

Heartbeats pass, each thumping softer than the last, the silence between them lingering longer and longer with every beat.

With the comforting presence of the Land quieting my heart and mind, I can speak.

"You still willbend, when you need to. I need that option, too. I can sort out what it does to me later."

Taran sighs, the weight of his exhale pressing into my back.

"I'll think about it."

If I've learned anything from my own brain, that's the best I'm gonna get for now, and I shouldn't push. Instead, I close my eyes and press my fingers deeper into the earth, relaxing into Her serenity. Nothing but my breath, the thump-thumps of my heart, and peace.

Time becomes meaningless. I could spend minutes or days here, and it'd feel the same.

Then Taran interrupts my calm, because that's what he does.

"There is something else I could do to help you."

My right eye pops open. "What's that?"

"I can name you my heir. It would increase your land-sense and the power behind your gifts. Nowhere near where I'm at, but you'd be stronger than average."

A lump forms in my throat. "But then if you die, Aedys would pass to me."

"Let's hope that doesn't happen, but yes. As it is now, it would go to our mother. I'd rather it went to you."

Not really the kind of responsibility I want, but what does that matter?

It'd be stupid not to take more power, and stupid not to do everything I can to keep that power from falling to my mother. Even that it means that someday, I could be…

Nope. Not going there. The now is what matters. Keeping Ellie safe.

I force an exhale. "Fine. How do we do this?"

There's a pause before Taran speaks. "Give me your hand."

I pull my left hand from the dirt and stick it out to my side. Taran grabs it, then starts speaking words I can't understand.

For a moment, nothing happens.

Then the Land's pulse increases rapidly, tingling through me from both my right hand buried in the ground and my left hand held by Taran. It grows in speed and intensity, my mind throbbing with every beat. My muscles tense, my fingers clenching against Taran's. The pounding inside me builds to a crescendo, overloading me with sensation, until it suddenly releases with a climactic beat that trembles through me, washing away the tension.

A curse escapes with my next exhale. That was something I never wanted to experience while holding my brother's hand. It's genuinely shocking I didn't spill in my pants.

Taran lets go of me, and my hand drops to the ground. "It's done. You're my heir now." A hint of relief softens his voice, probably because he just dropped one of his many weights onto me: a model of stability. He really does make a lot of well-intentioned, horrible decisions.

"Wonderful." Now I just have to hope he lives forever.

The Land pulses through my right hand, stronger than before. I stretch out through my land-sense, and its edges reach further. It's easier to catch things—the movements of animals, the wind rustling leaves—and everything's more... detailed. As if I were looking through a dirty window, but now it's clear.

Taran shifts behind me and pats my arm. "We should go. You still haven't figured out which direction is south, and more power won't help with that."

Of course it won't. That would've been too much to hope for.

He pushes himself to his feet and offers me his hand. I pull mine out of the ground, breaking my connection to the warm pulse, though its ghost continues to drum in my senses. After grabbing his arm, he yanks me up.

I glance at a nearby tree. "Back to checking for moss."

"And leaves," Taran adds, and I grumble at the reminder.

Someday, I might be able to do this without standing around like an idiot with my eyes closed, but for now it's still easier for me to focus when I shut out my vision, even with my increased strength. At least Taran's stopped commenting on it.

My fingers twitch, straightening at various angles as I try to keep track of which directions the moss and leaves are favoring on all the nearby trees, and my lips flick with the occasional whispered note. Eventually, I *think* a pattern has emerged.

"I want to say south is... that way?" I point my finger in what I hope is the right direction.

Taran smacks my back. "Good job. So south by southeast is...?"

"This way." I start walking.

Taran grabs the back of my shirt. "Wait."

"What?" My weight swings back toward him.

"Reach out in the direction you want to go and find two landmarks in a straight line. Once we reach the first one, you'll want to find another directly past the second. That will keep you on course."

"Alright." I find a young maple tree near the edge of my land-sense, and a broken, moss-laden stump about halfway there. "Let's go."

We walk for a few minutes, the crunching of our feet against dead leaves the only sound, until Taran speaks again.

"Do you sense anyone following us?"

Seriously?

My shoulders sag. "I've been trying to keep my focus on my landmarks."

"You still need to pay attention to your surroundings," he says, his voice firm. "Watch for large movements."

"Yeah, alright." I try to stretch my awareness all around, while still staying locked on the tree and stump. It's like I'm made of dough, rolling myself out in all directions.

"Ellie and Owena are following us," I say. "We should probably slow down so they don't lose us? Or is Owena's sense as strong as mine?"

"Not here, but it will be once she returns to Ystyr. Stop focusing on them. Let go, until their movements are just an itch in the back of your mind. Then extend that everywhere."

I try, but all my attempts to 'let go' result in me locking on tighter. I instinctively close my eyes, but that only makes me trip, as I'm focusing so much on not focusing that I've lost the ground in front of me.

This is exhausting.

I rub my temple. "Is this what all fae do, all the time?"

"No, but if you do it long enough, it will become second nature."

"As long as my brain doesn't break first," I grumble.

By the time we reach the stump, I think I've finally gotten the hang of it and am ready for a break. I sit on its broken surface and massage my head—it hurts all over. My arm twitches, wanting to go for the milk in my pocket, but I hold back. I can't afford to lose half a day to being high.

Instead, I squeeze my temples, shooting a sharp, relieving pain through my skull.

Taran grabs a stick and places it pointing toward the maple tree. "Whenever you take a break, mark your direction so you can easily find it again."

"Uh huh." I appreciate everything he's doing, but the constant lessons are grating. I need him to shut up for a while.

An idea pops up.

"So how do you feel about traveling with just Owena?"

Taran stiffens, then clears his throat. "I've been trying not to think about it."

"She's been grumpy these last few days. Like she thinks you're avoiding her, too, not just Ellie."

"That might be true," he says slowly, then sits against the base of a nearby hickory tree. "Don't eat these, by the way." He points to some nearby mushrooms. "They're poisonous, and not the fun kind."

He just can't help it, can he?

I raise an eyebrow while glancing over at him.

And I just can't help poking at him.

"Are you worried you'll end up fucking her before your wedding?"

Taran's head snaps in my direction, his cheeks flushing. His eyes dart away. "Why would you think that?"

That's not a denial. "You couldn't stop staring at her the night of the storm."

He actually squirms against the tree trunk. I curl my lips in to keep from grinning, and then, since he isn't saying anything, take the opportunity to continue pressing him.

"From everything I know about her, I'm sure she's fine with tumbling in the grass beforehand."

Taran closes his eyes and squeezes his brow between his pointer finger and thumb. "Please stop."

"You're not afraid she'd be disappointed and call off the wedding, are you?"

The glare he shoots me would probably send most people running. But he's my brother, so it only sends me falling off the stump, laughing. He buries his face in his hands, but his body hiccups with a suppressed chuckle.

After a minute, he lifts his head, a serious expression plastered over his face as he rises to his feet. "Come on, Caeo. That's enough of a break."

I cough away the rest of my laughter and get up, bringing my focus back onto my maple tree landmark and finding a new one. Taran shoves my shoulder lightly as I pass, then falls into step beside me while I lead the way.

Chapter 20

Owena

The air, still far too cold, carries the faint scent of damp soil and blooming wildflowers as I sit on a log, scratching specks of dirt out of my pants. A futile endeavor. The soft rustle of pages interrupts the sounds of the forest—twittering songbirds and the occasional patter of squirrels cavorting in the branches above.

With an affirmation from the Land that I'm on the right path, I set out this morning with my heart hardened by resolve. Taran's been spending the day with Caeo, teaching him how to navigate back to Lyndir. It must go well. Parting with his brother on good terms is paramount to easing Taran's inner turmoil, surpassed only by getting Ellie as far away from him as possible. With the latter happening any day now, my nerves are twisting with worry that Caeo's spent the entire day tormenting him.

He'll never stop fearing himself—never be able to rule, to love—if he can't stop drowning beneath his burdens.

I've been traveling with Ellie, keeping her far enough from Taran to give him some peace, but close enough that I don't lose track of them. My land-sense has remained trained on Taran the entire time, and while I doubt he feels it as strongly as I do his, I'm certain he's aware of it.

Ellie's kept quiet most of the time, no longer attempting

conversation, and I fear that perhaps I've been too cross with her these past few days. After all, should the waters favor us, we could very well end up being family someday—a thought that warms my heart after a life with only my father. My frustration with Taran's absence is partly to blame for my distance, but it's mainly that I don't enjoy being an appendage to her and Caeo. Outside of my brief conversation with Taran last night, it's been five entire days around only the two of them, with their constant doe-eyed gazes, hand-holding, and lingering embraces. Everything I'll never have. It would send anyone into a quagmire of misery.

On our breaks, she's kept her head buried in her sketchbook, working hard to memorize the words of apology I helped her prepare. She occasionally asks for clarification on how to pronounce something, and she'll scratch some lines with a piece of charcoal after. I must admit, the process has clarified the benefits of having a written language, something I'd never even considered before. Perhaps when I'm Queen, I could devise a way to use such a thing without being wasteful. If it looked elegant enough, we could potentially shape words into our walls. Though I'm sure the mere suggestion would outrage the Keepers of Memories.

"Why don't you read the whole thing aloud again?" I say, growing bored with tracking the boys' movements. Taran's currently teaching Caeo how to crush an animal to death as a hunting tactic. It's unsettling, but there's only so many ways one can hunt through shaping.

Ellie looks up from her spot in the grass, meeting my eyes. "Are you sure? I don't want to be a bother."

Too cross, indeed.

I give her one of my friendliest smiles. "You aren't. And I would feel terrible if your plan failed because I didn't ensure you pronounced your words correctly." She deserves to succeed, for how much care she's putting in.

Ellie swallows. "Do you actually think I have a chance?"

My lips tighten. Her plan rivals my own in its risk, so I understand her worries all too well. She's entitled to some comfort, but there's only so much I can twist my words to offer it.

"I know two things about the Land: She demands balance, and is completely infatuated with love. It's impossible to predict how She'll respond to your promise, but Caeo loves you, so She may be moved to show mercy."

Ellie inhales slowly, then nods with her exhale. She's an intelligent woman, well aware that I'm incapable of lying. There's little doubt she understands my choice of words.

"Alright." She straightens her posture as she lifts her book in front of her. "Ready?"

I nod my head, and she begins speaking the words in the Tongue that I told her earlier. It's an odd thing, listening to someone *read* out loud. Her diction is entirely off, her voice inflecting the wrong words. I have her repeat the entire thing, interrupting to tell her which words to stress and which to breeze through. She makes some more scratches each time, and on the third attempt, the short speech sounds a bit more natural.

A spark of heat in my legs reminds me to check on the boys again. It's growing late, and Caeo has finally ended the poor rabbit's suffering. I doubt we'll be traveling any further tonight.

I get to my feet. "Let us continue. They should have supper cooking soon."

And I have no intention of letting Taran run off tonight without speaking to me.

We've been keeping to the edges of the forests, which provide enough cover for the nightly fire Taran's been allowing. He and Caeo have finished building one and are halfway through skinning the animal when I arrive. Neither looks up to greet me, fully occupied with their task. Caeo's struggling with the bone knife Taran gave him; it clearly lacks the edge of the obsidian blades servants use when preparing my meals.

"Ellie was more than happy to wait until you finished with this part," I say, sitting next to Taran.

He doesn't spare me a glance. "And you couldn't be bothered to keep her company?"

"I've been keeping her company all day. I need some variety. Someone broody, who scowls at me."

Caeo chuckles as Taran stiffens, then he rubs his forehead with the back of his wrist. His eyes flick to Taran's face. "Hey, don't glare at me—glare at her. She's the one who wants it."

Taran sighs, then stands. "I think you have a handle on this. Come find me when you're ready to leave in the morning." He grabs his pack and stomps away, deeper into the forest.

Not this again.

Caeo gives me an amused look before I scamper after Taran.

"Have a good night," he calls after us.

"Why are you following me?" Taran asks as he marches, not deigning to look my way.

It's difficult to match his pace, and my face already flushes from the effort. "Aren't you hungry?"

His jaw clenches. "Leave me alone."

"Why? Do you not like my effect on you?"

He whirls to a stop, finally facing me. His nostrils flare, anger accentuating the sharp angles of his face.

My breath stills.

"What is your game, Owena?" Despite his ire, my pulse quickens at the sound of my name on his lips. "You've made it clear you want my attention, but then you insult me when you get it. I don't enjoy being played with."

I consider my words carefully, my heart fluttering with nerves. I need him to break—to bend to his lust, while still holding onto his anger with me.

"We all have flaws. We don't have to like one another to enjoy each other's company."

Taran's eyes widen, darting across my face. Then his gaze narrows. "That's not the kind of relationship I want."

I step closer. "At the moment, I'm not interested in what *you* want. I'm interested in what I *need*."

"Which is for me to stop feeling sorry for myself, right? To stop being weak?"

"And to do what needs to be done." To claim what he desires.

Taran presses his lips together. "I *am* doing that. I'm marrying you, because despite your provocations, it *is* the best thing I can do. For everyone."

With a measured breath, I move into his space. He stands his ground, his shoulders tensing as his chin dips, his eyes locked on mine. His dark hair hangs forward, framing his face in shadow.

"You find me provocative, then?" I curl my lips into a sultry smile that I hope hides the pounding of my heart.

He exhales from his nose with enough force that it brushes against my face.

"Exceedingly," he says through gritted teeth.

His piercing green eyes linger on mine for a moment longer as my heart rages. My weight teeters, pressing me closer to him. I couldn't have hoped for a better response.

Then he steps back. "Goodnight, Owena." He turns away and starts walking.

"Stop following me," he shouts, keeping his gaze ahead. "I'll bend you if I have to."

Heat rushes through me.

That's a tantalizing threat, indeed.

"WERE YOU PLANNING on having Taran draw you a map before you depart?" I ask, the cold air drying my throat with every breath. I've grown more accustomed to our day-long hikes, but doubt I'll ever adjust to the chill.

Today's path follows a river that carves along a hillside, making the terrain rougher than I prefer. I'm suspicious of our route— Taran's land-sense ranges far wider than mine, so while there may be a reason he chose this path that I cannot discern, part of me suspects he may have encouraged Caeo to go this way simply to irritate me.

"Caeo asked him to, and he said he would," Ellie replies from where she trails behind me, her breath catching slightly less than mine. "I'm hoping he will tonight, and that we can leave tomorrow."

"Has he taught Caeo to willbend yet?"

She lets out a deeper exhale. "No. Caeo said he'd ask again today, but he's not optimistic."

"That's a shame." I don't *need* Taran to willbend, but there would be no better sign that he's capable of achieving inner balance than him doing so without unraveling. If he can't even bring himself to teach Caeo, then he still has a long way to go.

"Are you sure you want to marry him?"

My footing slips as I come to a halt, turning to face Ellie. She startles, pressing her hand into the hillside to maintain her balance.

I raise an eyebrow. "Why do you ask?"

Ellie takes on the aura of a frightened rabbit. "I just... Obviously, I haven't seen you two together much, because I haven't seen Taran in almost a week, but it doesn't seem like you like each other. Otherwise, you could've kept him company instead of sticking with me and Caeo."

My eyes must have narrowed, because she quickly adds, "Sorry if it's not my place, but I'm a little worried about how things will go once we leave. I still care about Taran, and I want him to be happy. You, too."

While my heart warms at her concern for my well-being, her implication digs uncomfortably into me. With a sigh, I turn and continue my trek along the hillside.

"Worry not, Ellie. There are few things I wish for more than for Taran and me to someday find happiness together."

No matter how miserable I must make him to get there.

I shift my focus, momentarily broken by Ellie's words, back to the boys. They've stopped walking. Which is unfortunate, because sitting on this slope would not be my first choice, but the entire reason we've been following behind is to keep Ellie as far away as possible. Moving to a more comfortable spot would negate that.

I'm weighing whether adding that stress to Taran would be beneficial or detrimental to my cause when Caeo begins walking back.

Not walking. Jogging. And Taran climbs further uphill.

"Is something wrong?" Ellie steps slightly down-slope from me so she can meet my eyes.

I hadn't realized I'd stopped walking.

"There must be. Caeo's coming back to us." With renewed vigor, I pick up my pace, intent on meeting him halfway. We lost our pursuers long ago, and no one should be looking for us here, not without guessing my plan.

"What's happening?" I ask as soon as I'm close enough to not have to yell.

"Taran senses soldiers heading west," Caeo says, panting as he comes to a stop.

Waters sheathe me. "How many?"

"Two platoons? Not that I know what that means. He thinks they must be recruits gathered from villages east of here."

I press my fingertips into my temples. "I assume Taran is content to have us wait until they pass?"

Caeo's jaw ticks. "He didn't say. But what other option do we have? If we get too close, they'll sense us."

"He could solve an entire slew of problems by bending them," I mumble, then march past him, up the hillside.

It quickly becomes steep enough that I need to use my hands to maintain stability. After a moment, Caeo and Ellie follow, and by the time the three of us reach Taran, we're all huffing and puffing.

From our high vantage point, peeking over the crest of the hill, we can easily see the troops marching into the pale green valley below, well out of my land-sense. If any of us moved a few paces over the summit, they would undoubtedly spot us. For the most part, they march single file; a long line of ants that will eventually split the basin in two.

Taran watches them beside me, his jaw clenched tight.

Grass pricks through my coat as I angle myself as best as I can in front of his eyes without moving into a position where I could be glimpsed from below. "You need to bend them."

"We can wait for them to pass."

I bite back a surge of annoyance and force my voice to remain calm. "Think rationally, Taran. We could lose the entire rest of the day waiting for the last of them to pass where they can no longer see or sense us."

"A single day doesn't matter—we've lost more than that already."

My mouth tightens. To him, perhaps, but how many of our people will die every day once the fighting begins? There's no time to waste.

"They're moving in the same direction Ellie and Caeo will. Their journey will be significantly more difficult if they're traveling alongside an entire company of soldiers."

I hadn't thought it possible for Taran's jaw to clench tighter, but it does.

"If you bend them, you can simply tell them to return to their homes, where they will no longer be at risk of giving their lives for a foolish war."

He closes his eyes, a sharp breath pushing out of his nostrils.

"She has a point," Caeo says from where he lies on his stomach next to Ellie, with a significant gap between him and Taran to keep her safe. "A lot of points, actually."

"Can you even do it?" Ellie asks, and Taran flinches at the sound of her voice. "Can you bend that many people at once?"

He knows he can. His earliest ancestors were famous for it, and it's long been touted that he's the first to have such strength in millennia. He just needs to stop believing that doing so will destroy him.

Instead, he pushes himself to his feet and storms back down the hill. Leaving, like he always does.

I charge after him.

Chapter 21

Taran

"You can't keep running away from who you are," Owena says as she slips down the slope behind me. She recovers, scraping her hand through the grass.

"I'm not." It would be reckless to run down this hill.

I'm heading to a grove of trees in the valley ahead. Waiting in the shade will be better than baking in the sun all day. Better than stripping anyone of their autonomy, like my mother does.

Caeo and Ellie aren't following. That's fine. I could barely handle Ellie being as close as she was. It's already becoming easier to think with the distance I've put between us. If Owena could've stayed put, too, then maybe the inferno blazing inside me would cool down.

"Being a king means being able to put yourself aside and do what's best for your people." Her voice is uneven with the effort to keep up with me. "In this instance, willbending is what's best for your people. There isn't a single good reason not to."

"Other than forcing my will upon them."

"You think they're all marching to war by choice? Your mother is forcing her will upon them, whether she bends them or not."

I slide to a halt. I hadn't thought about it that way.

Owena stumbles past me, having lost her footing. I catch her as she goes by, wrapping my arms around her waist. Her warmth

219

presses into me. The moment she recovers her balance, I release her and back away.

"Bending is different," I grumble as I continue downhill, cursing the flames rippling in my chest. "It's a violation."

"I wouldn't know. But I'm certain a good number of those men would be relieved you forced them to return home to their families, even if the method is as defiling as you believe."

My anger surges as I spin back to her. "It's not a matter of opinion. You've seen what it's done to Caeo. To me."

For once, her dark eyes are level with mine, due to the slope of the hill. They burn into me.

"You were both abused by a power-hungry despot who doesn't understand the meaning of love," she says, her voice firm. "You are not her, and you never will be. You can use your willbending to save people instead of ruining them."

The confidence in her tone. The certainty. But it's unfounded.

"Like I saved Emlyn?" I bite back. "He wants nothing to do with me after what I did."

"What exactly did you do?"

I could answer. Let the thunder rumbling inside me out. But Owena's twisted every moment of genuine connection into a game of insults. So I let it rage, storming toward the trees. I don't deserve peace. I push the winds to whip harder and faster, stoking them with my guilt.

Instead, the gusts slow, unable to maintain the force they once had.

I swing my pack off my shoulders and drop it to the ground, the loss of its weight barely noticeable with everything I still carry inside. My face falls into my arm against the trunk of a tree, and my fist clenches, grasping for the storm.

It slips away.

I can't hold on to it anymore—it's too heavy, and I'm exhausted. My fingers slacken with my exhale, their tension moving to my jaw. I want to let it go, but what happens then? How many people will I hurt if I can't restrain myself?

With effort, I roll off my arm, my back hitting the tree trunk. I slide to the ground, scraping against the rough bark. My sword, hanging from my hip, catches on the grass, and I toss it aside. Propping my elbows on my knees, I bury my face in my hands.

"What did you do, Taran?" Owena's voice drifts down from above, a few paces away.

I take a haggard breath. Why did this conversation have to be with her? Anyone else would have been better. I can't trust that she won't hold on to everything I say to exploit me later.

But no one else is here, and I'm so tired of dragging this weight around.

I take another breath. "I forced him to live when he should have died." My voice drops. "His pain was unbearable."

For a moment, there's silence. Then, "Could you have spared him that pain if you had bent someone else first?"

My face cinches tight. "I would have had to bend everyone at your wedding." It seemed unconscionable at the time. But now...

"To do what?" Owena's tone is gentle. "Go home?"

All the weight I've been carrying settles into my stomach.

She makes it sound so easy. Irresponsible, in hindsight.

Owena steps closer, lowering herself next to me. "You need to accept that sometimes, willbending *is* the best option. It's not always bad. And people won't always hate you for doing it to them."

Her hand comes to rest on my knee.

The weight in my stomach flips over with a thud. I lift my head, peeking above my hands. Owena's leaning into the tree trunk beside me, her legs tucked beneath her. She tilts her head to meet my eyes, her golden curls tumbling down with the motion.

"Please don't touch me," I mutter, trying to ignore the warmth radiating from her touch, despite spending every night imagining it.

I glance away.

Brushing aside my request, she instead trails her fingers down the inside of my thigh. My body comes to life with every twist and curl in their path, my leg twitching as heat gathers in my chest.

I push myself back, knocking against the hardwood behind me while my lower half protests, digging in against my retreat.

"What are you doing?" My cheeks burn as heat creeps up my neck—from anger or panic, I don't know. I could swat her away, but my hands stay put.

"What do you think?" Owena moves closer, wrapping her hand tenderly around my leg. Her eyes lock onto mine with such intensity that I could drown in their depths. My fingers clench against the ground, tearing at the grass, to keep me from tumbling into the abyss.

"If you want me to stop, bend me."

My heart stutters.

She wants me to bend her?

The deluge of heat seeps into my veins. I dig my fingers deeper into the ground, and an enthusiastic pulse emanates from the Land, splintering my shield.

I swallow.

I summon the power in my blood, infusing my words with all my authority. My insurmountable dominance.

"Don't stop."

My mind reels at my mouth's betrayal, but it's over the instant Owena's lips curl into a smile. Her fingers trickle lower. My legs fall further apart as blood rushes downward, an ache building between them with every stroke of her fingers.

"Tell me what to do," she whispers, the heat of her breath skimming my ear, her soft skin pressing against my cheek. "But I'll only do it if you bend me."

I groan, biting my lip as a knot twists in my chest and another coils below. I would call her cruel. Evil. Twisted. Yet none of the words escape my lips.

I should have run.

"Mount me," I rasp, hating myself for bending the words that lift a weight with each syllable.

Owena braces her hands on my shoulders, pushing me against the tree, and straddles my lap, slowly lowering herself along the hard length straining inside my pants.

"What now?" Her cheeks have gone a luscious pink from the heat coursing through her, burning out of her eyes and into mine.

The word rips its way out.

"Grind."

Owena's eyes widen as her hips roll into me, excruciatingly slowly. My hands squeeze her waist as my head tilts back, a moan rumbling out of me. Her breath picks up, light wails flowing out of her as she strokes her sex along mine. My eyes roll back in my head as sensation takes me, everything else disappearing into nothing.

"Faster."

Her pace increases as she bucks her hips, pressing into my chest, and her hair falls around my face, blanketing me in her sweet, citrus scent. Flames writhe through me in waves, pulling me to the edge. My body demands I speak, to make her remove our clothing so I can take her, fill her, give her my all, but the floundering, rational part of my mind desperately shatters each thought before it can escape me.

"I'm so wet," she moans, and the undulation of her voice sends me over.

The coil within me bursts. I curl my fingers around her backside, pressing her into me as my entire body shudders. A half-sob escapes my throat, and everything spills out, emptying into my pants. Heat washes over me, pooling in my face.

I exhale, my breath ragged.

"I can't—stop," Owena gasps, her eyelids fluttering.

"Stop. You can stop."

Her body breaks against me like a wave on the shore, exhaling into my neck. Sinking into me as we catch our breath.

After several heartbeats pulsing through us, Owena lifts her head. A smug smile curls her lips. With exhausted eyes, she pats my cheek. "Good job."

Then she pulls herself off me and strolls away.

Just like that.

I watch her leave, trying to form thoughts on what just happened, but they slip away like I'm grasping at clouds. My body's completely relaxed, my head clear, for the first time since my father's death. Even my mother's incessant tugging at my bond has ceased.

I lean back against the tree, tilting my head up to the afternoon sky, and breathe. My eyelids sink shut, and I disappear into the peaceful darkness.

When I open them, the sun has barely moved in the sky. I could close them again, but anxiety is creeping into me. There are still the soldiers to deal with.

Thoughts of Owena flit through my mind. I don't want to think about her. What we just did.

What I did.

I willbent for personal gain. For pleasure.

And she was happy about it.

Why? Did I fall victim to her games? Give her power over me?

Prove her right? Or did she actually enjoy it?

Does it matter?

The one thing I can say for sure is Owena's not a fool. She has a better grasp of what it means to rule than I ever will.

And she knows what it's like for a king to abuse their power.

Bending everyone at the wedding wouldn't have been a violation, not if I just sent them home. And it would have spared Emlyn. Prevented Ellie from incanting. Kept my people from being forced into war.

I failed them all.

A slow exhale escapes, my heart heavy.

I can't change my past mistakes, but I can save those soldiers' lives if I bend them today. It won't turn me into my mother. It will free them from her.

And I'm done letting the people I care about suffer because I won't step up.

But before I can do that, I need to change my pants. I reach for my pack—

Little white flowers speckle the ground.

Those weren't there before.

That pulse. The flowers. Is the Land just being Her voyeuristic self, or is this something more? Does She want this union between us?

Then She better tell Owena to stop playing games.

I drag my pack over and dig through it for my spare clothes, eating some berries with the hope they'll settle my stomach.

They don't.

By the time I'm cleaned up and heading back up the hill, the weight has crept back. Lighter than before, but still there. The others sit near the summit, and with every step toward them, the burden grows heavier. I avert my eyes, not needing to add their expectations to what I already carry. Especially not Owena's. My heart spikes at the mere thought.

No one speaks as I march past, over the crest of the hill, and down into the valley below. At any moment, one of the soldiers, one speck in the long line ahead of me, will glance this way and spot my approach.

There's no turning back now.

The breeze picks up. The terrain isn't as steep on this side, my footfalls heavy but smooth as I descend. My heart thuds against my ribs with every step.

I'm about a third of the way down when someone cries out. The line of troops stops moving, with nearly eighty sets of eyes turning toward me.

I swallow. *I can do this.*

Voices carry on the wind as someone shouts orders. The line compresses as they fumble into a ragged formation. New recruits, mostly untrained, save for a few officers. Their arrows will most likely miss if I get within range.

But I shouldn't have to.

I shape the wind to my favor, unleashing a steady, relentless gale that surges from behind me toward them. Battered by the wind, they struggle with their bows. Some try to press back, but their shapings falter under the onslaught. Their bond with the Land pales compared to mine, and their movements sharpen with fear as the realization sets in.

That bond won't matter if they build up the courage to rush me.

It's time. No more hesitation.

Power courses through my veins, my heart thundering. I've never bent this many people at once before, but there's not a drip of doubt that I can. I need only the will.

I force that will upon them, the wind carrying my words.

"Do not fight me. You have a new destination. Return home."

They lower their weapons, and I ease up the wind, returning it to a gentle breeze.

They turn eastward and start marching.

I let out my breath and collapse to the ground, running my hand through my hair as I watch them go. A few glance back, but they keep a steady pace out of the valley. I can't make out their faces, can't see if they're full of fear or relief. But it doesn't matter. They're going home, away from a needless war, to be with their families.

The weight is still there, settled deep in my chest, but it's not digging as sharply as before.

Caeo plops down beside me. He came alone, the others waiting at the top of the hill. *Thank the Ancients.* I can't handle seeing Owena's face right now. Just imagining that smug smile of hers sends a tremble from my chest down to my—

Stop.

I close my eyes and force another exhale.

"I can't believe you just did that," Caeo says. "That was... You have to teach me how."

"You'll never be able to do that," I mumble.

Caeo elbows me in the side. "You know what I mean. I don't need to willbend entire armies. Just enough to keep anyone from killing us."

I sigh, then look at my brother. His eyes widen, awaiting my answer.

Emlyn suffered because I refused to willbend. I can still spare Caeo and Ellie that pain—I just have to trust that my brother won't abuse it. After what he's gone through, I don't think he will.

And if he does, I'm stronger.

"Figure out our heading, and I'll teach you as we go."

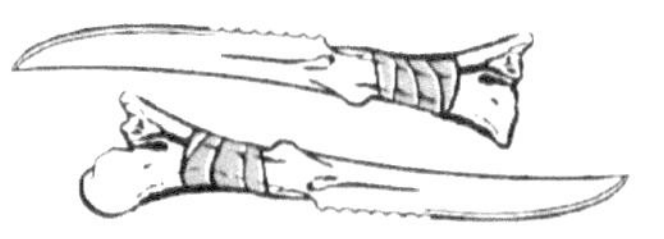

Chapter 22

Emlyn

I t's a chilly morning. Northern Aedys is like that—just a boring stretch of tundra until you reach the far-off mountains. We camped overnight near a small branch of Anwen's Tears and should reach the border by midday.

"Do you really need this much water?" Reid asks. He's filling our fourth jug while I try to seal the other three as securely as I can.

"I can't begin to guess how long I'll be stuck over there," I reply. "If all I have to do is glamour myself, this will probably last me about four months." Much less if I have to glamour Reid. It's a lot harder to maintain them away from your own body.

"You can't use a charm like Caeo's?"

I force the stopper into the third jug. "That sort of thing costs more than I'm willing to pay. Besides, I have a feeling I'll need to shape and use my land-sense, and that wouldn't help with that."

"You won't be able to use your land-sense?"

"Not without drinking more water. I'll be spiritually as blind as you." I splash him as I fill our waterskins. *Fuck that's cold.* "But I'll still be able to see in the dark."

Reid splashes back. "I can see in the dark just fine."

"Keep telling yourself that. It won't make it true."

"You don't get to decide what's true."

"If I say it, it has to be true."

"Then say it. Say, 'Reid can't see in the dark.'"

My eyes narrow. *I think he got me there.*

"Reid can't see in the dark," I say, then mumble quickly, "very well compared to me."

The smug grin that stretches across Reid's face is worth my misstep.

"Just give me that." A shiny stone, speckled with blue, catches my eye as I take the final water jug from him. It'd be nice to add to my collection, except I have no idea when we'll go back to my house again. "Are you ready to go?"

Reid looks around the mossy riverbank for his pack. "I need a few minutes to shave first."

I glance up, my eyes tracing the angle of his jaw. "Could you maybe not? Since I don't have to glamour you anymore?"

Reid raises an eyebrow. "You want me to grow a beard?"

"Maybe not a beard beard, but just skip a couple days." Heat fills my chest. "I liked it."

"I'll look like a mess."

I give him a quick kiss on the lips. "An irresistible mess."

Reid's jaw juts out and his eyes narrow like he's thinking, but a smile peeks out and betrays him. "Only if you stop hiding your freckles."

I cringe. I'd forgotten he'd seen them when I was too weak to glamour myself. But outside of him, it's not like I'm gonna see anyone whose opinion I care about anytime soon.

"Fine." I drop my glamour. "But don't get used to it."

"Same to you. I don't need to look homeless around people I actually know."

"You *are* homeless. We both are."

Reid's smile turns wistful. It's the sad reality of our situation. At least for now, one of us will always be hiding in a realm where everyone wants us dead.

I nuzzle into him, kissing what's left of his smooth jawline goodbye, then pull away. It's not the time for heartfelt discussions or anything more; we have a lot of distance to cover if we're gonna cross the border and find somewhere in the mortal realm bearable enough to sleep before nightfall.

"Time to go."

Before I stand, I snatch the pretty rock from the freezing water. It can be the start of a new collection.

WITH THE ABSENCE OF TREES, we spot the border long before we reach it—a thick, bluish-purple fog that hangs over the horizon like an impending storm, defiant against the chilly northern wind. In the past, the sight of it didn't bother me at all, but my pulse quickens with worry. I tell my horse, who I've been calling Daylily, to stop, letting Reid pull up beside us.

"How're you feeling?" I ask.

"It doesn't feel as ominous," he says slowly, "but that could just be from the distance? Last time, the trees kept us from seeing it until we were right next to it."

I chew on my lip, thinking. Back then, the aura of the fog made it so that he could hardly move. It'd be very bad if that suddenly kicked in while riding. "Maybe we should ride abreast from here on out? Just so I can keep an eye on you."

I click my tongue to Daylily, and we're off again. My nerves twist as we approach, and I keep glancing between the fog and Reid, waiting for some sign it's affecting him, the tension winding tighter with every heartbeat.

But there's nothing.

What's going on? The Land clearly approves of us coming here, but I wouldn't think She'd be able to single him out of all the rage mortals feel just looking at the border.

"You're still not feeling anything?" I ask.

"Nope." He looks about as comfortable as he always does on a horse—mostly relaxed, but with a skittish energy waiting to burst the instant the animal does something unexpected. It's clear from his tight grip on the reins.

An exhale presses out my nostrils. *I can't take this anymore.*

"Canter," I say in the Tongue. Icy wind slaps my face as Daylily takes off, Reid and his chestnut following behind.

The fog looms before us, towering higher and higher the closer we get. I ask Daylily to stop about twenty paces from the base, about how far away we were last time when Reid and Ellie lost the ability to move.

He pulls up next to me, face flushed from the cold, but otherwise fine.

"It's still not bothering you?" I ask.

"No, it's not." Reid's gaze travels up and down the wall of cloud in front of us, his brow furrowed. "It doesn't feel like anything. Just fog."

My teeth dig into my lower lip. I don't like this at all. It'd be nice if the Land could speak in something other than pulses. I'm tempted to just try saying out loud that he'll be fine, but we generally avoid trying to predict the unknown that way—it doesn't always confirm things the way you'd expect.

"Time to dismount," I say. Having Reid ride while being crushed to death would just be cruel to the horse.

I grab his hand and pull him toward the border.

Only a few paces away now.

"Still nothing?"

"How about you stop asking and I'll tell you if I feel something."

I bite back a snide response, instead yelling to the horses to join us. My stomach eats at my insides during the eternity they take trotting over. Once they arrive, I have Reid take the reins of his while I rest my left hand on Daylily's shoulder. Squeezing Reid's hand tightly, I dig deep, preparing myself to pull him back the instant something goes wrong.

"Alright. Let's go."

We step into the fog.

It's just like it's been every time, at least for me. Cold and slightly damp.

The air's heavy, so thick that I can't see Reid, but I can feel him, his hand clutching mine. Step by step we go, every footfall muffled, accompanied by the horses' snorts and rhythmic jangles of our belongings.

Reid stays quiet, no complaints. If anything, his fingers relax the further we go, a steady warmth against my palm.

We keep moving forward... and then we're out.

I barely keep from doubling over as a hollowness crashes into me. It's so quiet. So gray.

So dead.

My stomach lurches into my throat. *I forgot how horrible it is here.*

Reid glances behind us, his brow furrowed. "It still feels fine."

At least something does. I take my hand off Daylily and press it against my chest, trying to hold back from vomiting.

Reid drops my other hand and steps back into the fog by himself.

"Reid!" A spike of panic shatters my nausea. I dive after him, wresting him back into the horrible emptiness of the mortal realm. "Ancients, are you trying to kill me?"

"Calm down, I'm fine." His eyes search the fog, bottom to top. "She must be letting me pass because She wanted us to come here?"

I'm about to agree, but I can't—the words won't come out.

So that's not the answer.

My gaze follows his, up into the sky. "I don't... This doesn't..."

I try again. Nope.

I can't form complete sentences. Which means that somewhere in my mind, I know the reason. I just need to figure out what it is.

Taking a deep breath that fills my nostrils with the stench of rot, I push down my rising nausea so I can think. A stabbing headache's already forming at my temples.

Stupid mortal realm, always making me feel like shit.

Anyway—the fog is part of the Land. The Land doesn't want mortals entering Aedys, so the fog scares them away and tries to crush them if they try to pass through—we saw that with both Reid and Ellie.

But She's not trying to crush Reid anymore.

You don't feel as different as the girl did.

Ma said that to Reid. Weeks ago.

Is it possible...?

"I don't think the Land considers you mortal anymore," I say slowly.

Reid frowns. "What?"

"The Land doesn't consider you mortal anymore." Saying it confirms the truth. My heart flutters like a flock of geese ready to burst out of my chest, and a smile stretches across my face.

"What does that even mean?" Reid asks, looking down at himself. "I'm clearly still mortal."

"By your definition, not Hers. And it's Hers that matters!"

I grab Reid's face and kiss him. He accepts my lips, my tongue, but pulls back a heartbeat later.

"My definition matters, too," he says, a smirk slipping through the grumpy crinkles he's forcing onto his face. He's just arguing for the sake of it—it's practically foreplay at this point.

"Just shut up and let me be happy about this." I shove him back into the fog, yelling at the horses to give us some privacy, so I can show him *exactly* how happy I am.

UNFORTUNATELY, expressing the full extent of my joy would take far longer than we have, so I have to cut Reid's orgasm short at about twenty mortal minutes. We're in the middle of nowhere, and we need to find an inn before nightfall. It's not up for negotiation—the ground is far too disgusting for me to sleep on. Even the horses seem to take light, tentative steps, not wanting their hooves to press into the corpse beneath us.

Reid takes the lead as we ride along the fog, with me trying not to fall off Daylily from all the head-spinning nausea. We'll need to head west soon, but I'm reluctant to head deeper into this wasteland.

The range of my land-sense is already shrinking.

Reid pulls his horse to a stop. Daylily halts, too, 'cause that's what horses do.

"That's an Order outpost ahead," he says.

I bring my eyes up. Off in the distance, buried in the haze—the normal, gray haze, not the border fog—looms a tall, stone rectangle. The Order of Incanters, who have dedicated their lives to killing fae.

If we can see them, they can see us. And no mortals would ever be this close to the fog.

Sure enough, a few heartbeats later, a horn's deep bellow carries through the air.

My tongue presses against the roof of my mouth as I try to keep my stomach down. "Go west. Now." If we go back across the border, they'll just increase patrols in the whole area, delaying us for days. We need to outrun them.

Reid doesn't hesitate; he knows better than anyone the danger of encountering fully trained incanters, especially if he's still hoping to avoid doing it himself. He turns his horse, kicking her into a gallop.

I can be proud of his skill later. Right now, there's some movement at the base of the tower, so we need to get the fuck out of here. I tighten my grip on Daylily's mane, the wind whipping through my hair as we soar across the plains.

I chance a look back. Four riders, charging toward us.

At least the rush has killed my nausea.

Chapter 23

Ellie

"Are you sure you're ready for us to leave?" Caeo asks.

Nervous energy surges through me. It's a cold morning, with a heavy mist blanketing the forest floor. I'm teetering on my tiptoes, fighting the urge to get moving—not only to heat up from exertion, but to finally release the tension that's built in anticipation of our journey. Until then, Caeo has me wrapped in his arms, keeping me warm against the chilly air. My cheek rests against his chest.

"Not until Taran gets here with our map."

Caeo adjusts his hold on me, his arms tightening as his chin presses into my hair. "I'm still not sure this is the best idea, Ellie. I want to support you, but even if I get us to the border, I'll never forgive myself if the Land kills you when we arrive."

I squeeze my eyes shut, and all my anxiety twists into a knot. I hadn't looked at it that way.

Maybe we shouldn't go. That'd be the easier choice. Caeo would get to stay with his brother, and we could live a simple life, avoiding everything and everyone that wants me dead.

The knot tightens, then releases.

No. While the idea lights a warm glow in my chest, I can't live the rest of my life trapped by fear. I have to believe that the Land will see my truth. That I want to help Her. To make up for my offenses, and those of my people. That She'll understand that I can only do that if She lets me live.

"It'll be alright." I look up and meet Caeo's eyes, a more brilliant blue than the pale morning sky.

His eyebrows draw together in a wistful furrow. "You're the only one here who can say that. What does that tell you?"

"Only that fae can't predict the future." I bring my lips to his, pressing against them. My hands slide up from their warm spot between us to wind behind his neck, into his raven hair that now hangs past his ears, and my lips part as I pull him deeper into me. His tongue slips in, and—

"Enough, you two." Owena's voice interrupts our kiss, and I drop from my tiptoes as Caeo shoots her a glare. She's sitting on the ground by the smoking remains of our campfire, her arms folded around her knees. "Taran's on his way, and I'm certain he'd appreciate it if you made this as easy on him as possible. Which means not making him stand around and wait while you explore the depths of each other's mouths."

"You're just grouchy because you're not exploring the depths of *his* mouth," Caeo says, and my lips curl inward as I suppress a giggle.

Yesterday, after Taran stormed off and Owena went after him, we eventually followed—until we got close enough that Caeo could hear their argument. He stopped me as he listened, his land-sense picking up everything they were doing. I'll never forget how wide his eyes went when he realized what was happening. While my heart initially squealed with relief that the two of them might find happiness together after all, an ache tugged from beneath: a reminder that Caeo and I haven't gotten back to that point yet.

We agreed to pretend we didn't know, curious to see what they'd do next, but as best as we can tell, they haven't spoken to each other since. I suppose with our departure imminent, Caeo decided there was no point in pretending anymore. It's a bit rude, but every glimpse of his playful spark returning lightens the weight in my chest.

Owena simply glowers and turns away.

"Be nice, Caeo." I kiss his lips and lower my voice, not that it matters—fae have frustratingly good hearing. "We don't know if we'll ever see them again. You don't want to leave on bad terms."

His cheeks pucker as he stifles an exhale. "You're right."

He pats my hip before letting go of me, then heads over to Owena, pinching her arm as he sits next to her. She smacks his hand away and mumbles something that, thanks to my regular human hearing, I don't quite catch.

Not wanting to eavesdrop, I wander over to our pack, rifling through it to occupy myself until Taran arrives. Caeo's told me more about his relationship with Owena during our nightly talks where I try to help him fall asleep without using the milk of midnight star, which we're only successful with about half the time. But he swears he hasn't used it at all during the day, so it seems like we're making progress. If only he were in a place where I could exhaust him with something more passionate, rather than boring him with the intricacies of incantation theory.

Nonetheless, I have to fight back the envy curling within me. It's clear he and Owena have a special bond, despite not having known one another for very long. It stings, knowing she was there for him when I wasn't—couldn't—but it's mostly that Caeo's leaving behind a good friend and his brother, who he may never see again. Which is tragic. Not the sort of thing I should covet, at all. But I'm leaving behind someone indifferent to me, and someone whose life will monumentally improve with my absence. Is it wrong to wish they'll miss me when I'm gone?

If this entire venture ends with my death, will anyone miss me other than Caeo?

Mom would, though she'd likely never learn what happened; only that her daughter went missing and never returned. Perhaps Caeo could find her and explain things someday, or at least send a letter. And my father... He'd mostly be disappointed that all his efforts to mold me into his successor amounted to nothing.

Before my thoughts can spiral too deep, I perk up at the sound of the grass and dead leaves crunching beneath feet.

Taran. His gaze drifts over Caeo and Owena as he walks, and his jaw tightens. Then his eyes focus on me, their inner light twisting with a raging fire.

He's actually approaching *me*.

I slowly rise to my feet. My hand travels to the bruises throbbing beneath my coat sleeve, recalling the last time he came near.

He averts his eyes at the last second, looking at the ground, and his body's as tense as I've ever seen him. Caeo stands warily, watching us from Owena's side.

Taran digs through his pack and pulls out my sketchbook, offering it to me. "Here. I drew multiple maps, as best I could." His hand jerks, shaking it, reminding me to take it from him.

I quickly grab it and pull it to my chest. "Thank you. I really appreciate it." As I trace the angles of his face, latching on to his emerald eyes, an echo of what was once between us aches in my heart.

His fist clenches as his arm drops, his jaw tightening. "I'm sorry about how everything worked out, and that I can't give you a proper farewell. I'll do my best to convince the Land to forgive you. When this is all over, I hope our realms will be at peace, and that I'll see you again."

My heart's ready to burst, tears stinging my eyes. He still cares about me, despite all the misery I've brought him. It takes all my willpower not to throw my arms around him in a tight embrace. I squeeze my fingers around my sketchbook instead.

"I'm not sorry I saved your life, even if it ends up costing me mine." My voice catches in my throat. "I hope to see you again, too."

Taran's eyes cinch shut, and he nods. Then he turns and marches away.

Caeo rushes over, resting one hand on my arm while the other brushes against my cheek. "Are you alright?"

I wipe away my tears, then bob my head. "I am. You should go say goodbye before he gets too far."

His eyes briefly flick away. "Yeah. I'll be right back." He kisses my forehead before going after Taran.

I take a deep breath, pushing the air through the coil in my chest, hoping to loosen it. My body shudders with the effort. I tighten my grip on my sketchbook.

My sketchbook. The maps.

I flip through the pages, eager for something to distract me. I find them about halfway through, right after my notes on the words I want to say in the Tongue.

The lines are shaky, obviously drawn by an unpracticed hand. Which makes sense—fae don't write, and if they draw at all, it certainly isn't in small books with delicate pieces of charcoal. If I ever do return, perhaps I can see some examples of fae artistic expression.

The first map appears to be the entirety of Aedys. Mountains and hills are represented by upturned angles and bumpy curves, respectively. Forests consist of clusters of roughly drawn trees, with blank circles speckled throughout. While most of the circles are buried within the forests, there's a handful scattered on the open areas of the map.

Those must be villages.

A long, thick line carves through the map, splitting the east and west. It must be Anwen's Tears, the river we crossed on our journey to the capital. Using that as my guide, and my recollection of what villages we visited, I'm able to roughly trace the path we traveled along these past few weeks. Comparing that to the distance we need to travel from where we are now, the location indicated by a starburst of lines in the middle eastern part of the map, I estimate we're about nine or ten days from the border.

It's like a cold, hard stamp of finality on my heart.

"A moment, Ellie?"

I blink, lifting my head from my sketchbook. Owena stands before me, her hands tucked behind her back with all the poise of a princess. She tilts her head to the side, curiously looking at the map with her dark eyes.

"Yes, of course," I stammer, shutting the book and pulling it back to my chest. *Why does she make me so nervous?*

Owena's lips purse slightly before she speaks. "I wanted to wish you farewell, and good luck. I regret not having formed a better friendship with you. I've been occupied with concerns of my own, and as a result, I may have been more aloof with you than I intended. But I do wish you well and hope to see you and Caeo again." The corner of her mouth curls upward. "Should all our plans come to fruition, I imagine we'll be sisters someday."

Sisters? Of course. If they succeed in killing her father, then she'll marry Taran. So if I survive... if Caeo and I ever marry... she would be my sister-in-law.

There's so many ifs, but they can't hold back the excitement whirling within me.

A smile stretches across my face as I bounce onto my toes. "That would be—" *Don't make a fool of yourself!* "I-I hope to see that day." Unsure what to do next, I throw my arms around her in a hug.

She startles backward. "Oh!" Seconds later, she pats me gently on the back. "I suppose we're hugging?"

I let go of her and hastily step away. Owena straightens her clothes and clears her throat.

"Sorry, I shouldn't have—"

She holds up her hand, interrupting me. Then she smiles. "Not to worry. It was simply unexpected." She glances over her shoulder, to where Caeo and Taran stand, separating from a hug of their own.

My heart swells at the sight. With where they started, I had feared the chasm between them was insurmountable. It means everything that I was wrong.

"I should go before he storms off without me," Owena says, turning back.

"Just a minute—I almost forgot!" I flip through my sketchbook, scanning for the drawing I did of her. Upon finding it, I carefully tear the page out and hand it to her. "I took some liberties with your eyes—not that they aren't beautiful, but I've been struggling with getting my subjects to feel alive. I think adding some specks of light helps."

Owena slowly takes the paper, her gaze locked on her depiction. A smile forms on her lips, and she blinks several times before her glistening eyes shift to me. "Thank you, Ellie." She exhales as she pulls it closer to her chest. "You don't know what this means. I will treasure it always." She nods, then her face returns to its usual poise. "May the waters favor you."

"And you," I say, then belatedly realize she said 'waters,' not 'Fortune.' That must be the fae version of the phrase. Though now that I think of it—how does Fortune relate to everything I've learned about the Land?

After one last smile and dip of her head, she saunters briskly over to Taran and Caeo, as if holding herself back from running. Caeo passes her on the way and gives her another hug, then her pace quickens as she hurries after Taran.

Hopefully they can find happiness together. Taran certainly deserves it.

I shove my sketchbook into our pack, then hoist the whole thing onto my shoulders. Taran told Caeo to take most of the food, so it's stuffed to the gills with various types of berries and what remains of our resupply at the village, along with extra clothes and waterskins. With everything else on Caeo's shoulders, the least I can do is carry our things.

He takes both my hands as he stops in front of me, forcing out a deep exhale. His palms are clammy with sweat.

"You're nervous." I pull his hands up between our chests as I step closer to him.

"Uh, yeah. I've failed at almost everything I've ever done, and now I have to get us through weeks of surviving in the wilderness without getting lost or discovered by people who want to kill you. What could possibly go wrong?"

A bundle of heat unwraps in my chest, longing to pull him in. I squeeze his fingers and press closer to him.

"You failed at almost everything you ever did *before*. As a human. From what I've seen, and the stories Owena's told me, you're actually pretty good at being fae." I latch onto the blue sky of his eyes. "I have faith in you. You can do this."

Caeo's face softens, and he lets go of my hand to brush his thumb against my cheek. "Thank you for believing in me. In this, and everything." He closes his eyes, then exhales, pressing his forehead against mine. His eyes twinkle when they open.

"Alright. Let's get going."

Chapter 24

Owena

Taran doesn't speak to me, doesn't look at me, our entire first day together.

He marches through the wilderness at a pace I can't match, only slowing when I fall behind, and only enough that he stays within sight as I plod along behind him. Our only breaks are motivated entirely by me, when I collapse to the ground in exhaustion.

The first time, he circled back to drop our pack at my feet before bolting away. He never came back for it, and I've been bearing the burden of our food and water ever since.

This last time, he's been wandering around ahead, presumably hunting, while I rest with my back against a tree trunk. The sun will set soon, and that's been his routine every evening since the storm: hunt, make camp, then disappear, finding somewhere to sleep by his lonesome while sporadically smothering me with the intensity of his land-sense. There's no reason to think it will change now.

I'm at a loss as to whether it would be better to allow that to continue, or to force my presence upon him. No doubt I would fail— he may very well march through the night to avoid me.

Despite my experience navigating the politics of Ystyr's court, Taran's an enigma. He bears his emotions for all to see, which may be part of the reason he isolates himself—it would be impossible for him to survive otherwise. As it is, he clearly absorbed my words, having found the strength to bend the soldiers. My heart swelled as I watched, yet he's avoided me ever since.

I'm unsure as to why. Shame, perhaps? It's good that he's conflicted, but it hurts.

All of this hurts.

After tracing my finger one last time along the wondrous eyes Ellie gave me in her drawing, I carefully tuck it into our pack. She may never realize the hope, the strength, it provides. A reminder of why this is all worth it.

Time to make Taran come to me.

Wrapping myself tightly in my coat, as these northern forests are still quite brisk in the evenings, I push myself to my tired, aching feet and continue walking. Not toward Taran, but around him.

He picks up on my movement immediately, the heat of his attention igniting in the soles of my feet and blazing up my legs. I shut away my sense of him, focusing entirely on the path in front of me, littered with scattered pine needles and clumps of decaying leaves. He should notice the absence of my gaze. It takes all my resolve not to peek back at him, but doing so would ruin everything. He would decide this is some kind of game and let me go.

It's not a game, not for me. It's life or death.

With my land-sense focused ahead, there's no need to look where I'm going. I close my eyes, hoping the darkness will bring me calm. The distant chirrups of crickets fill my ears, with the crunching of my footfalls providing a steady rhythm to their song.

A discordant beat rustles behind me. Louder thuds, kicking up the debris as they grow nearer.

"Where are you going?" Taran asks.

My stride doesn't break. *Let him see what it feels like, for once.*

"South. Toward Ystyr."

"Do you intend to walk all the way there tonight?"

I whirl to a halt, and he barely stops in time to avoid colliding with me. As he steps back, I follow, occupying his space. "No. I *intend* to spend tonight in your company. But if you force me to spend another moment in solitude, then perhaps I shall."

Taran's jaw clenches as his eyes lock with mine. My heart races as I match their burning intensity.

Air puffs from his nostrils before he speaks. "Fine. But no games. I still don't trust you."

He tears his gaze away, marching back the way we came. I allow the smallest sigh of relief to escape before following.

Taran abandons his hunting efforts, and we eat a scant supper of leftovers in silence as a fire crackles between us. For now, this is enough. From this point on, it's only the two of us, so I can allow him the night to become comfortable with my presence.

Perhaps comfortable is the wrong word.

I am certainly *not* comfortable, and if his thoughts wander down similar paths as mine, I doubt he is, either.

I'm no stranger to physical intimacy—plenty of lovers have warmed my bed over the years. But nothing has ever exhilarated me more than the moment we shared yesterday. Breaking beneath the force of his domination nearly sent me to the edge all by itself. Losing control of my body, completely succumbing to his will, unable to stop grinding against him well beyond my point of climax... Heat engulfs the deepest parts of me, flooding up to my face at the recollection alone.

The memory refuses to retreat, and a near-constant ache pulses in my core every time I look at him. His soulful eyes, blazing bright, softly shadowed by his midnight hair.

The yearning spikes. Sharp. Unfettered. I shift my position every so often, hoping for relief as I try to turn my thoughts elsewhere, but there's nowhere for them to go.

"Why don't you trust me?" The question blurts out as my mind grasps for something to latch onto. My cheeks flush at the eruption, and more words spill out. "I've answered every question you've asked."

I can't afford to behave like this. I need to control myself. To ensure every word draws him where he needs to go.

Taran tilts his head up, glaring at me from beyond the fire. The flames flicker in his eyes, their light dancing across the angles of his cheekbones.

"We both know that answering them isn't the same as speaking the whole truth," he says. "I'm certain you're hiding something."

At least his intuition is strong—a good ruler needs that. But sharing my secrets before he's bound would alter his perception of me, ruining everything. So I steady my gaze, putting on my thickest mask.

"Why? What would I have to hide?"

He shifts his position. "You tell me. You're the one opposed to having a real relationship. Do you think this"—he gestures between us—"is what I want for our marriage?"

My mouth twists, working its way through possible responses. It's a risk, but perhaps it's time for some vulnerability on my part. My lips loosen with an exhale.

"It's safer this way." I drop my gaze to the sputtering flames as my voice lowers. "Our marriage is one of necessity—it will solve so many problems, for so many people. It'd be easier to bear if I kept my heart out of it."

That may have been *too* revealing. I can't bring myself to look at his face, not even when the silence lingers, punctuated only by the pops and cracks of the fire. All the heat within me has died, blinking out like its blaze, replaced by a twisting knob in my throat as the cold air settles in around me.

"I think it's best if I go to sleep now." I push myself to my feet, leaving behind the dying campfire to find a comfortable spot of grass to settle into.

"Owena…"

My steps pause. "Stop. I don't want your pity, and I don't want you to pretend you care. We're not friends—we have an alliance. That's all."

No matter how much I dream of something more.

I SPEND MOST of the next morning's hike silently cursing all my decisions. Figuratively, of course. Decisions have no physicality and therefore cannot be cursed. If they could, I would doom them to loop back upon themselves until they managed a satisfactory outcome.

At least Taran's done with avoiding me. As such, I've finally recovered my view of his exquisite backside as he marches ahead of me. Every step exhibits the sensual perfection of the male form, his strong shoulders tapering smoothly down to his lean waist and snug rear end, while his sword bounces at his side. I only have a few days to enjoy the sight: once we reach Ystyr, I'll have reason to take the lead in our trek.

Then he'll be watching me.

The closer we get to the border between our realms, the smoother the terrain becomes, and the warmer the air grows. I only require my wool coat in the early mornings and evenings now, though the occasional gust of crisp wind reminds me we're still in the north. The flora shifts as well, with bright, broad leaves now outnumbering the pines of Aedys's evergreens, while hardy mountain blooms give way to the lush flowers of my home.

Anticipation thrums through my chest, my body soothed by the familiarity but wary of what our arrival in Ystyr will bring.

It's around midday when we stop near a creek to break for food. According to Taran, we'll pass a village soon—the last one before we reach the border. He sits on a low outcrop, about knee-high, with our pack between his feet, taking stock of what we have to determine if it's worth stopping for more supplies.

I take the opportunity to rinse the sweat from my hair and face in the frigid waters of the stream. This entire journey has been a nightmare for my curls, and the further south we travel, the more likely they'll poof into a frizzy mess. I need to get them under control if I want Taran to look at me without being repulsed.

I'm pulling my tresses into tight braids when he speaks up.

"I don't have much coin left, but I think it would be wise for you to get some more food at the village. I don't know what to expect from foraging in Ystyr, and if my abilities diminish as I predict, I may not be able to gather as much. Unless you plan on picking up the slack."

I look over my shoulder and raise an eyebrow at him.

He rolls his eyes. "As expected," he mumbles, then starts shoving our supplies into the pack.

I return to my braids, my fingers twisting the locks as securely as possible.

Just as I'm finishing, Taran speaks again, his voice softer.

"We should talk, Owena."

The sound of my name on his lips melts some of the tension in me. When did he stop calling me 'Princess Briarwood?'

But talking would send us down the wrong path. Or, the right path, but too soon. Such a twisted tangle to navigate. As of now, he's barely within the limits my father imposed, and I must keep him there.

Knotting the end of the final braid, I turn to face him, still sitting on that rock. His green eyes gleam as I meet them, reflecting the warm tones of the forest.

"I don't want to *talk,* Taran. I'd prefer to delve deeper into our intimacies from before."

His eyes narrow, staying locked on mine, but his legs shift oh so slightly further apart.

"I told you, that's not the kind of relationship I want."

"But it's the only kind I'm willing to give you at the moment." As I approach, his gaze burns me with every step. My skin simmers between my nerves and the heat of his focus.

He flinches as I shove the pack aside and kneel in front of him.

"Let me show you what it could be." I trace my fingers along the curves of his thigh muscles, firm beneath the supple leather of his pants, from his knees all the way to the bulge between his legs.

He trembles at my touch but doesn't pull away. Doesn't resist.

His voice comes out deep and gravelly. "Do you want me to bend you?"

I flick my eyes up to him, my hands resting on his hips. What a far cry from where he was mere days ago. A warm glow brings a smile to my lips. Solace, that I haven't only been hurting him.

"I want to do this on my own. But perhaps..." Heat surges through me, and my core tightens in anticipation. "Perhaps you can satisfy *me* with words alone."

Taran swallows and nods, and I liberate him from his pants.

My eyes widen at his erect form. I could tell from before, when I stroked my clit along its hidden length, that it was... extensive... but seeing it is an entirely different matter. Desire blazes between my legs—a longing, a need, to be filled completely by him.

A quivering breath escapes me. "Tell me I can feel you entering me."

A bead seeps out his tip as my fingers trail along the length of him, stroking the soft, silky flesh, gloriously hard underneath. Taran trembles, his hands pressed against the rock he sits on, and just as my tongue licks the salty, sweet droplet off him, he speaks.

"You can feel me," he says, the words echoing as they break out of a groan. "Stroking against you, sliding into you. Deep."

And waters sheathe me, I do.

My eyes nearly pop out of their sockets as my body buckles and my legs spread, my knees digging into the grass beneath them. A phantom pressure glides in, stretching me as a whimper falls from my lips. My underclothes are already soaked, my back arching as the sensation pushes deeper, filling me to the brim.

I bring my fingers to his cock, wrapping them around, and he shudders as I stroke along his shaft, pumping again and again as I draw my lips to its head, teasingly sucking the tip.

"Owena," he moans, arching into me.

"Tell me more," I whisper, then take the entirety of him into my mouth.

He lets out a groan, and his words echo again. Frantic, between breaths. "I'm thrusting into you. Over and over."

My body convulses as a force pounds into me from below, and his cock presses deeper into my throat, suffocating the wails that attempt to escape with every plunge. Pleasure cascades through me with each one. I need him to feel it. To share it. To unravel along with me, more than I've ever needed anything before.

"Harder. Deeper. Rubbing against you."

I press my hands against his hips, taking him all the way, in unison with the thrusts reverberating through me. Friction builds against my clit as Taran's hands wrap around my braids, his fingers tangling in their weave, undoing all my efforts, but I couldn't care less. Holding my head, he slams into me, again and again. My body is jelly as he fucks me—fills me—from both ends simultaneously.

This is beyond anything I've ever imagined. My mind is gone, completely overrun by the pleasure of his use. His power over me. My cries are muffled as my fingers clench against his sides, everything building to an apex.

I'm cresting my climax, and it crashes into me, my body shuddering in magnificent relief, when Taran grunts, spilling everything into me. His grip loosens as my body continues quaking with the unyielding thrusts of his will. My mouth slides off him, swallowing his release, then I collapse into his lap, whimpering as my hips jerk beneath me.

"I'm done," Taran gasps, panting heavily. "You feel me withdraw."

I melt into the ground, unable to hold myself up, already aching at the loss of the pressure of him buried deep within me, despite him never being there. I would give anything to experience that again. He's completely wrecked me.

This isn't how it was supposed to go. I was supposed to be ruining him. But I can barely think, let alone plan where to go from here.

So I breathe into his thigh, and our breaths calm together, the fire dying and settling into a warm ember. Eventually, his fingers caress the tops of my braids, and if I could dissolve any deeper into him, I would.

"I'm sorry I ruined your hair," he says, his voice low.

It doesn't matter.

It was worth it.

Don't worry about it.

All things I could say. All things I *want* to say.

But I can't. It'd bring us too close.

I lift my head. His face is softer than ever, the shadows of his hair from the warm afternoon sun blurring its sharp edges. His jade eyes glint as they meet mine.

"Next time, let me know you're in the mood before I expend the effort." I trail my finger along his exposed skin before I stand, forcing a casual smile, then return to my spot by the stream. I keep my eyes on its waters as I untangle my tresses, wishing it were so easy to untangle the knot twisting in my heart.

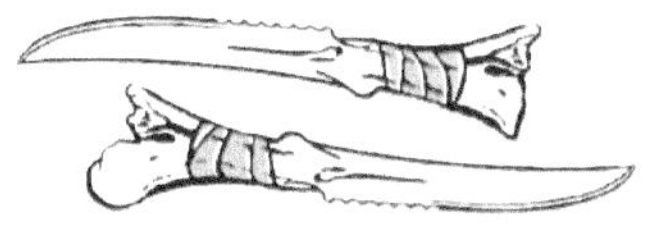

Chapter 25

Emlyn

"You're not looking too good," Reid says, glancing up at me as he refills our empty waterskins at the edge of the nearby creek. Not that I'll be drinking any of it—it tastes like ash.

We're only taking a break for the horses' sake. The sun's about halfway through its descent into night, and we pressed them hard, barely outrunning our pursuers by the time I spotted this spruce and birch forest. With my land-sense having completely faded away, every rustle and snap has my insides lurching, expecting incanted flames to shoot between the trees at any moment.

"I'd forgotten how horrible it is here," I mutter, standing on my toes to avoid touching the wretchedness beneath me as much as possible until I get back on Daylily. I've already vomited twice.

While I know from experience that things will get better, the first few days in the mortal realm are always the worst. Their entire world is completely, utterly dead. Even the clear, sunny sky is gray, hanging above a dull, decaying earth. It takes everything I have not to chug all the water we brought with us.

Reid's lips press together as he looks me up and down. "You weren't like this before."

"I'd been here a couple weeks before I met you. I'd gotten used to it."

"Is there anything that would help?" He grimaces as he sips a handful of water—clearly, he can taste the difference, too.

"Alcohol. Lots of alcohol." Hopefully we can get some at whatever inn we find. Which we need to do before nightfall, since there's no way I'm sleeping on this blighted dirt.

"Seriously?"

"Why do you think I spent so much time at that tavern?"

"I'd hoped it was because I did."

Nope, not at all. But I'm not gonna say that. I groan, rubbing my temples instead.

I practically jump when I open my eyes. Reid's standing right there, his gaze boring into me. Without my land-sense, I missed him moving.

"You're avoiding answering," he says.

Ancients. He's gotten too good at this.

I glance at a nearby tree, crawling with bugs like the carcass it is. "You were a benefit of spending time at the tavern, but not the reason I was there."

"So what was?"

"I was spying on Caeo."

"You were there a lot of times when Caeo wasn't."

I look back, placing both my hands on Reid's shoulders. "Look. I love you, but don't ask me about things I did before I kissed you. You won't like any of those answers, and they don't matter, because they're in the past."

His eyes widen. "Fuck, Em. I wasn't *that* worried about your answer, but now I am."

I let out a grumbled sigh. This conversation was always gonna happen, I just wish it could've been when my stomach didn't feel like a horse trampled all over it.

"Do you accept that I've been with a lot of people?"

Reid's brow raises. "How many are we talking about?"

"A lot. I stopped counting years ago." Normally I'd laugh at how his face quirks with a mix of confusion and shock, but it doesn't feel appropriate, and my head hurts too much.

"How many years ago?"

Ugh. Don't make me think.

But his eyes are burning me, so I try. "I'm twenty-four now? So maybe… four years ago?"

"And what was the number back then?" he presses.

"Please don't make me answer that. It's not important right now. What's important is that I love *you*, and you're the only person I ever want to be with ever again. Which, if anything, you should take as a compliment—I picked *you* over everyone else."

"You know this will bother me until you tell me."

"If you insist." I close my eyes, dropping my head. "I stopped counting at a hundred and six."

"WHAT?"

I wince.

"And that was four years ago?" He pushes my hands off his shoulders. "So you're probably at, what? Two hundred by now?"

I keep my mouth shut.

"Fuck." Reid sits forcefully down on the dank, mossy ground.

Hopefully he's forgotten his original question, at least.

He doesn't need to know that I was doing it for money, too. Not that I see much difference between that and information, favors, general espionage… but I feel like he would. He's mortal, after all, and some prejudices are too ingrained.

I cringe as I lower myself next to him, trying to ignore the silence of the festering earth.

This is disgusting.

I swallow, forcing myself to breathe as I focus on his face.

"You've had an idea of what I was for a while now. The specific details don't change that."

"It changes the scope." His eyes shift to mine. "How do I know you won't get bored with me? I can't compare to hundreds of people."

"No, it's the hundreds of people that can't compare to you." I bring my hand to his cheek, stroking its prickly hair with my thumb. "All of them—they were just fun. Or work." I exhale. "Or a way to cope with what it required of me. But with you... I've never fucked you, Reid. I may have said I would, intended to... but it's never worked out that way. What we have, it's more. And I wouldn't trade a single touch from you for all the sex in the world." It's weird to say that out loud. I knew it was true, but the confirmation stirs a warm glow in my chest.

Reid breathes out his nose, and a heartbeat later a smile starts to form on his lips.

It's great. Adorable. But I can't stand being this close to the ground any longer. He leans in right as I shoot to my feet.

"Sorry. I love you, but I can't kiss you while sitting on the corpse of the Land. I'm getting on that horse right now because my feet can't take touching this pestilence any longer."

He chuckles. "I love you too."

His words send a rush of heat through me as I pull myself onto Daylily's back. The grotesque air's still seeping through my pores, but at least I'm off the ground.

I wait for Reid to mount the chestnut, then we continue riding southwest, which I assume is the direction of the Academy and where we should find Alexis. Neither of us has ever been this far north in the mortal realm, and with my land-sense not working, we'll need to get directions soon.

I have no doubt we'll come across a town at some point, since

Lyndir's more densely populated than any of the fae realms; it's just a matter of if the horses can make it that long. But there's one more problem we need to solve before we can get anywhere near a human population.

Mortals don't dress anything like fae—they have this ridiculous obsession with hiding their necks. Wearing a comfortable shirt is tantamount to walking around with your cock flapping in the breeze. I'm so glad Reid got over that quickly. But it unfortunately means we can't let anyone see us till we get new clothes; all of Reid's old ones ended up getting used as bandages at some point. Without mortal money, we need to steal them.

Which, by *we*, I mean *me*.

After spotting a farm near the edge of a small forest that stinks of death from all the trees it's lost to mortal axes, I chug half of a waterskin to get my land-sense functioning again. More importantly, it'll give me enough strength to glamour my clothing in case I get caught.

Reid's staying behind. We both agree that him incanting is a last resort, and he's not much of a thief without it. At least drinking all that water has the added benefit of making my headache go away. Yay.

So here I am, creeping along the side of a barn in the evening light, on my way to steal some farmer's smelly clothes. And any money I can find while I'm at it. And some food. The farmer's busy fixing his plow out in the fields, but someone's in the house— probably his wife.

Time to negotiate with a horse.

I slip inside, getting slapped in the face with the stink of dead grass and shit, then push open the stall for a hefty bay, probably around sixteen hands high. He tilts his head so he can stare at me.

"You're a big one, aren't you?" I give him a pat on his shoulder.

His coat's uneven against my hand, rough with dust and dried sweat—the mortals haven't done the best job brushing him. "Any chance I could get you to stick your head in the window of the house over there, then run off when whoever's inside sees you?"

He whinnies.

"Are you more of a fruit or vegetable kind of horse?"

A snort huffs out his nostrils. He's not *actually* answering me, but I've been around enough horses that I get the gist of what he means.

"Fruit? Yeah, I can do that. And your freedom, of course. You don't have to come back."

The bay sniffs at my clothes.

"You're welcome to come along, but I'm fairly certain Daylily's heart belongs to her lady friend. No harm in asking, as long as you promise to behave if she says no."

He neighs in agreement.

"Alright. I'll open the door, you do your thing, and we'll meet in the woods over there with whatever fruit I find."

The plan works perfectly, with me recovering two shirts, a satchel of coins, and some apples. Unfortunately for my new friend, I was right about Daylily's tastes. He opts to part ways with us, searching for greener pastures. Or more willing lady horses.

I wish him the best. With luck, he'll find his way to Aedys, where the grass actually tastes decent. It's unfortunate we can't join him.

A COUPLE DAYS IN, and I'm going through our water far too quickly.

The problem is money. I still can't sit on the ground for too long without being smothered by all the death and decay, so sleeping outside is out of the question. But I can't just warm some stranger's bed like last time I was here, nor can I sell myself for the coin we need.

Which means I have to steal everything. I'm generally fine with that, but I've usually relied on seduction as a pretense—pickpocketing's never been a strength of mine. Since getting caught would end very poorly for me, I need to use my land-sense and glamours. As a result, I've already gone through half of the first jug we brought.

At least Reid understands our situation enough that he's fine with me flirting my way to free drinks.

Long wooden tables fill the crowded tavern on the first level of the inn we're staying at, with benches to sit on, bumping shoulders with strangers. The air—thick with an unpleasant mix of mortal sweat, roasted meat, and spilled ale—buzzes with overlapping voices. Chalk screeches against slate as a barmaid crosses 'chicken pot pie' off their list of offerings on the far wall.

I gotta admit, reading and writing *does* make communication easier, and it wasn't *that* hard to learn. At home, they'd have to repeat their menu all day long.

"That didn't take very long," Reid says as I squeeze in next to him with my tankard. I dropped his off a bit ago.

"You just have to pique their interest till they buy you a drink, then get out quickly by detailing some of the more unorthodox fetishes." I tilt my eyebrows up at him as I take a bite of our honey chips—those are cheap, thankfully. Like all the food here, they taste horrible. Sweet, with an aftertaste of death that clings to every surface of my mouth. Alcohol's one of the few things strong enough to hide it.

"I'm not gonna ask."

"Good, you're learning." I down a mouthful of my ale, grimacing as I swallow. "Ancients, that's terrible." Far too bitter.

Reid bumps his shoulder into me. "Watch what you're saying—people can hear you."

"Relax. The nonsense you spew draws more attention than anything I'll say." Especially when he's overwhelmed by pleasure; whoever's in the room next to ours is likely very confused. And jealous. "Besides, it's too loud in here. Even I can barely understand the people next to us."

I pause to listen, just to prove my point.

Something, something... war... something... the Academy...

I slip off the bench and then squeeze back in on the other side of Reid.

"Did I hear you say something about The Academy?" I prop my head against my hand as I lean into the table. "I was close to a girl there."

"Oh. Um, yes, you did," the woman says, startling back at my proximity. "I was just telling my friend that I heard they've sent the students to help support the war."

"What?" Reid pipes up from behind me.

I stroke his leg with my foot under the table. "The war? Has it really started again?"

"You don't know? The fae have been pushing at the border about a day's ride south of here. They called for reinforcements from the Academy because the Order's spread too thin. We were thinking of leaving in case they can't hold them there."

"That'd probably be wise," I say, my mouth tightening.

The woman's face softens. "I'm sorry about your friend. I'm sure she'll be fine."

I shrug. "It's what she signed up for. Killing fae." I genuinely hope she gets over that someday. It'd be nice if Reid's friends didn't want me dead.

"Thank you for the information." I give the woman a smile before turning back to Reid.

"I guess we're not going to the Academy anymore."

Chapter 26

Caeo

"Let me see the map again." I glance over at Ellie, her beige coat several shades darker than normal from all the rain. I'd almost stopped noticing it after the days of near-constant drizzle we've trudged through since leaving Taran and Owena.

She digs her sketchbook out of our pack, and I flip through it to Taran's drawing of central Aedys. I've checked it so much that the charcoal lines have blurred thanks to my clumsy fingers, but it's still legible, despite looking like a four-year-old drew it.

We've long since left the eastern hills and entered a large, bowl-like valley, where scattered forests break up the grassy plains. It's been difficult to avoid other fae here—almost every sizable chunk of trees hides a village somewhere within, and what seems to be some kind of nomadic groups follow behind the grasslands' herds. All the animals are completely unfamiliar to me, like the deer-looking things grazing up ahead. Their straight, pointy antlers twist at the very tips, and dark brown stripes their bellies. They have surprisingly large hooves.

"Alright." I snap the sketchbook shut before too many droplets splatter its pages, then hand it to Ellie. I'd tried, back when the rain first started, to shape it around us to keep us dry. But I couldn't keep it up for long, which makes it pointless outside of the occasional downpour or gusty wind.

"I have an idea," I say. "It may be stupid, but I don't really want to take the time to go around them, and walking through the herd seems like a good way to end up smooshed. Or stabbed."

Ellie tucks the book close to her chest as her mouth presses into a smirk. "What's your stupid idea?"

"Scare them into running north. With luck, it'll also distract the fae that are following them and send them off course."

She glances from me to the herd. "That sounds risky. What exactly do you plan on doing?"

I crouch down and press my hand against the grass, testing my reach. A mound of dirt pushes up about thirty feet away.

"Hmm. Guess I'll need to get closer." I look at Ellie. "Wait here."

"What? Where are you going?"

"Just stay there. I'll be right back," I call over my shoulder, then walk as non-threateningly as I can toward the deer-things.

As I draw near, some of the closer ones take a break from munching grass to eye me suspiciously, but I guess they're used to fae following them around, and I'm fae enough for them, so they turn back to their meal. I bring my hand to the ground again and visualize what I want to happen.

I never would've been able to do this before Taran made me his heir.

A pillar of earth shoots up from the ground, mud flying with the force of its ascent. The nearby deer-things startle away, leaping into the herd just as it drops back beneath the surface.

Rushing forward, I make another one erupt even closer.

Hooves thunder against the ground as the animals explode into motion, rippling through the herd until they're all running.

I chase them with pillars for a few seconds more, until I stumble to my knees, exhausted.

Maybe I overdid it. But they're stampeding northward now, so... victory?

My land-sense picks up Ellie running toward me well before her hand lands on my shoulder. "That was completely ridiculous," she says, kneeling next to me. A smile brightens her face. "But it worked."

"Yep." I push myself to my feet. "Now we have a straight shot until we get to those trees." I nod at the western horizon. "Should get there within a few bells."

"Hopefully the rain lets up by then." Ellie's face looks mostly dry, but water's dripping from the hood of her coat. I never would've thought she'd be so comfortable on a journey like this back when we first met. It's not surprising that she is—it's that same strength I always saw peeking out. But now it's there, all the time, for everyone to see. I wish I could match even half of it and be the person she deserves.

"Yeah, hopefully," I mutter. Off in the distance, a clear blue sky has teased us all day, staying ahead, never nearing, while rain clouds hover above. I take Ellie's hand, and we set off, grass and mud squishing beneath our feet with every step.

The rain finally stops pestering us well after we reach those trees and have marked a new destination.

Around late afternoon, we come across another small grove of oaks that, judging by the map, is the best spot we'll find to camp for a while. Decently protected, and far away from any fae settlements. And by stopping early, I might actually get us warm and dry before nightfall.

The first thing to do is dry out some of the earth so we don't have to sleep in muddy puddles. I find a spot that's slightly more elevated, and pressing my hands against the grass nearby, I pull the water from the higher ground to the lower ground, forming a miniature lake. It's a lot of work, but the good kind of tiring. The kind I always imagined farmers feel when they harvest their fields, getting to finally enjoy the fruits of their labor.

I end up needing multiple breaks, but we eventually have a nice, dry patch of grass, big enough for us to lie down next to a fire. Which I have to suck all the moisture out of some broken branches and grass to create.

At least Ellie's gotten better at the rubbing sticks together part. Once she gets some smoke going, I puff the ember into a hungry blaze, just as the sun's setting. I collapse on my back as Ellie gets the fire settled, feeding it a decent portion of the dehydrated sticks.

Shit. I'll have to make more.

And I still have to dry out all our clothes.

I groan as my eyes sink shut, my head starting to throb. It's not from exhaustion, but the beginning of something far more worrisome—I know because it's been happening every night, and instead of just dulling when I take the milk, it disappears entirely.

"I shouldn't have chased those deer-things as long as I did."

"It's alright, Caeo. You can rest. The ground's dry, and we have a fire. We can let our things air-dry for a while."

Through my land-sense, I can feel her pulling off her wet clothes. My heart thuds as she moves over to the tree to hang them from its lower branches.

I peek my eyes open.

Yep.

I follow along the outline of her legs until they reach where her small clothes cling to the crisp curves of her ass. The fabric tightens and catches against her skin as she lifts herself onto her toes, tossing her shirt over a thick branch.

I could watch her all day.

She turns around, her belly button peeking out from under the hem of her chemisette, leading my eyes up to the soft mounds of her breasts, where thin white cotton drapes from the peaks of her nipples.

Fuck, I've missed them. Nothing made her wet faster than when I played with those rosy buds, whimpers fluttering out of her as I took them between my lips, tugging with my teeth just enough to make her beg for more.

"You look hungry."

I blink, my eyes shifting up to Ellie's. Her hair, clumped into thick, twisted locks from the rain, frames the amused smile lighting up her face.

Maybe I do—there's a bit of a lustful ache building in my cock. But it's grown accustomed to disappointment, my brain inevitably slamming the door in its excited face as all those memories claw their way up from the darkness, so it's kind of wary about everything right now.

What I'm really feeling is a coziness spreading out from my heart all the way to my fingers and toes. I love her with all my soul, and I don't spend enough time truly savoring that.

I tuck my hands behind my head. "It's been a while since I've just looked at you."

Ellie's cheeks flush a bright pink. "But your eyes won't keep me warm, so get your wet clothes off and come snuggle with me."

"Yes, ma'am."

I pull off my boots and strip down to my drawers, hanging my wet clothes next to Ellie's. Then I settle on the prickly grass a comfortably warm distance from the fire. Ellie cuddles into my side, her legs tucked in my lap, the heat of her soft skin pressing into me. I wrap an arm around her, tracing the graceful curves of her arm with my fingers, and she lets out a soft sigh as we melt into one another.

My heart beats in a peaceful rhythm alongside the crackling fire as we watch the flames. I wish we could stay in this moment forever.

"How do you think things are going with Taran and Owena?" Ellie asks, nuzzling deeper into me.

I huff a laugh. "They're either fucking or fighting right now. Or both."

"There's no need to be crude." She playfully smacks my shoulder.

"What do you want me to say? That they're bedding each other? There aren't any beds out here. Besides, I doubt it's anything that tame. I've never met anyone as pent-up as Taran."

Despite the lightness in my voice, an unease creeps within me. This subject... It's too close. My fingers twitch, itching for the jar in my pocket, but my clothes are hanging in the tree.

Ellie's lips press into a smile that tugs at her dimple. "It would've been nice to see them get married."

My stomach drops with a thud.

I try to swallow, but can only gag, my arm leaving Ellie to smack my fist against my chest.

"Caeo? What's wrong?"

Ellie rests her hand on my leg, her big brown eyes full of concern.

I wave her away, moisture blurring my vision.

"It's nothing. I'm fine." My throat spasms with a violent twist. *Fucking fae limitations on what's true.* "Fine," I grunt. "I'm not fine."

Breathe.

Breathe.

"What is it?" Ellie's fingers clench, digging into me.

I close my eyes and push an exhale out my nose. When I look back at her, she's biting her lip, her gaze darting across my face.

The air slowly leaves my lungs. "You don't want to see a fae wedding. Trust me."

"Why not?"

I can't bring myself to answer. Instead, visions rise out of the darkest corners of my mind. Blood, dripping down my arm. The metallic tang, filling my mouth.

Ellie traces a winding, tender path along the tensing muscles of my back. "You can tell me, Caeo."

My gaze drifts down to the ground. Dry, because of me. Something I could do.

Stop holding it in. Just say it.

Taking her other hand from my leg, I interlace our fingers, squeezing tightly as my eyelids press shut. I take another deep breath, and the words come out calmer than I expect.

"You don't get to eat anything for two days before. You're supposed to spend the entire time in isolation. Most fae probably spend it bonding with the Land, but I couldn't do that at the time." A sharp exhale. "Trapped in the dark, without any water. In the end, I couldn't even move. All I could do was worry about what was coming."

Ellie squeezes my hand.

"For the ceremony, they have an obsidian blade, that you're supposed to use to..."

I swallow.

"...to slice open each other's arms and drink their blood."

Ellie's fingernails jerk into my skin. "That's—that's horrifying." She pauses, then her voice comes out softer. "They were going to make you do that? With Owena?"

The weight of the memory pushes all my air out.

"My mother was gonna bend me. I'd have done it, without any control of my own body. But that... that wasn't the worst part."

Ellie's thumb strokes against me. Soft. There. "You don't have to tell me if it's too hard."

I meet her eyes. So beautiful, so troubled, but bleeding her love.

If I can't tell her now, I never will.

"After that, the couple..." My mouth's gone dry. I swallow, but it's like forcing down sand. "They have to... to consummate the marriage. In front of everyone."

Her eyes widen.

"She was gonna make me, Ellie." My eyes burn. "My own mother was gonna take control of my body and force me to do it." More images flash by, the same that haunted me that day. Owena pressed beneath me, my body thrusting uncontrollably. My mother's eyes locked on me. Smiling.

My voice cracks. "All I could do was lie there, helpless, just waiting for it to happen. I know it never did, but my mind... it keeps going back."

A weight drops.

I said it.

I finally said it.

Ellie wraps me in her arms, my tears leaking onto her shoulder. I squeeze my eyes tight as I force a deep breath through my nose.

Lavender.

Calming lavender, and her.

The images fade as Ellie takes my face in her hands, her eyes pouring out a steady warmth despite the tears glistening within them. "It'll be alright, Caeo. I'm here, and I love you. I'm not going anywhere."

She brushes her fingers against my cheek, and my heart thuds a heavy, tranquil beat.

"We'll make sure you never have to worry about her again."

Chapter 27

Taran

I add one last moss-covered stick to my collection, my foot snagging on a gnarled root as I turn away. Rough bark scrapes against my hand, my pulse quickening as I catch myself on the tree trunk, barely keeping everything in my arms.

That's never happened before.

My mind's in chaos, my rational thoughts tangled with muddled emotions and carnal desires. I've traded one knot of torments for another, and it's all Owena's fault. She guided me toward peace, snuck past my defenses, and now she's destroying me.

Amid the turmoil, my mother's continued her strikes, clawing relentlessly at my bond. I can't tell if my land-sense is shrinking or I'm being paranoid. What will happen when we finally enter Ystyr? I should have thought of that before agreeing to any of this; will my absence make it easier for her to claim Aedys for herself?

I wish I could talk to Owena about it, but she spurns my every attempt at conversation, walking away if I press. Half of my mind screams that I've fallen into her game, warning me to get out. The other half begs me to reach for her, until she lets me past her walls—if she does, maybe everything could work out.

I can picture her as Queen. A good queen. I've heard the wisdom in her words, witnessed her willingness to put her people's needs ahead of her own. She could guide our realms to a peaceful prosperity we haven't known in nearly a millennium, and I could give her my all, supporting her. We could be happy. But every time she teases open the depths of her mind, she shoves me back into the cold before I get a single foot inside.

It's infuriating, but the fire within me twists into raging flames of raw, aching desire the instant her devouring eyes lock onto mine, and whatever resistance I built burns away.

She's doing it again.

After yesterday's... escapade... she's been cold and distant. She went to the village for supplies and has barely said a word to me since. But now, as I settle to the ground to build a campfire in the darkening forest, she kneels next to me and rests her hand on mine.

My body ignites as my mind groans in exhaustion. "What do you want?"

"To hear what you want."

I meet her midnight eyes, clamping down on the anticipation they send rumbling within me. "I've told you what I want, Owena. A real relationship. Not... *this*."

I stiffen as she leans closer, bringing her lips to my ear.

"Besides that," she whispers, her breath warm against my skin. "What do *you* want to do to *me*?"

Her face is a breath from mine, her mouth right there. My mind holds my body back by a thread, and as my eyes trace the curve of her pink, inviting lips, it snaps. My head jerks forward, desperate to claim her mouth with my own, but she pulls away.

"Tell me what you want to do to me."

My mouth has gone dry. I'm so tired of fighting with myself. With her. The words stick as they tumble out. "I want to taste you."

I close my eyes, hating myself for once again giving in.

When I open them, those teasing lips curl into a smile. She

stands, watching me as goosebumps scatter across my skin. I'm burning up inside, wary of her intent, but invigorated with apprehension like never before.

Owena's fingers grasp the bottom of her shirt. "You can taste me anywhere"—she pulls it over her head—"except my lips."

My eyes widen.

She tugs down the waist of her pants.

My cock throbs as I take in every detail of her pale skin and supple curves. She pulls her hair out of its braids, her golden curls tumbling down, caressing the peaks of her nipples on perfectly ample breasts. My gaze trails downward, along the crescent of her belly, until it lands on her sex, right at my eye level.

Where do I even begin?

I should say no. To refuse to play this game. That's what I should have done yesterday, instead of giving in.

But I'm weak, and my body's starving for her.

"Get down here." It comes out as a bending, without even trying. My mind bleats a warning at being so reckless, but it's lost the instant she's on the ground. Then I'm on top of her, pressing her back into the earth as her eyes widen, lips parting with shaky breaths.

"Spread your legs."

Owena gasps as her legs follow my command, and I lean down, bringing my mouth to her breast.

My tongue circles the hardened bud of her nipple, and she whimpers as I take it in my mouth. Her fingers clench against the ground, and she cries out as I let it scrape against my teeth on release. The scent of her sex overwhelms my next inhale, pulling me between her legs, where she glistens on full display.

I breathe in her sweet scent, filling my lungs, and all other thoughts drift out of my head. I pull my tongue right along her center, and she moans as her taste sends my mind reeling.

My fingers press against her hips, and she writhes beneath me as I devour her with stroke after stroke of my tongue, lapping and sucking against the bud of her pleasure. Owena's wailing, her fingers twisting in my hair. I slide my tongue into her, and she bucks her hips into me.

When I pull back for air, I find her face. Panting and flushed, desperate for more.

"Is this what you wanted?"

Her eyes pierce into me.

"I want you to take me. Use me. To pound into me so hard that I'm screaming and then go even deeper."

My heart stutters beneath the roar of desire urging me to do exactly as she said. That's not what it wants. It yearns for us to hold one another's gaze as we meld together, laid bare as we entwine into one.

But she's not there yet. Maybe someday, if I keep giving her everything she wants, she will be.

I swallow, and the bending falls out. "Flip over."

Owena scrambles to her hands and knees, presenting her sex to me, ready and waiting. I free myself from my clothes, then embrace her from behind, one hand gripping her breast as I guide the tip of my erection to her slick entrance. I stroke myself between her folds until I'm glistening wet, then press in, slowly, submerging myself in her warmth. The guttural moan she lets out as she stretches around my girth unravels me completely.

I pull back, this time thrusting sharper, deeper, all the way in. A cry rips out of her. I retreat, then plunge a third time.

"Faster, Taran."

I pick up the pace, thrusting again and again, slamming into her. Her screams resonate within me, reverberating in my mind, as sensation tightens its grip. She clenches around me, and the twisting coil of pleasure almost bursts. My hands move to her hips, and I pound myself deeper and deeper, over and over, my roars joining with hers, intermingling in a cacophony of raw, primal ecstasy.

With a final, balls-deep plunge, she releases the resounding wail of her climax. Mine chases hers, my body shuddering as I empty myself into her.

Owena collapses to the ground, a panting, messy heap, my seed dripping down her thighs. My breath almost comes out as a laugh, the wreckage of her such a contrast to the poised perfection she typically embodies. I crumble onto the grass next to her, rolling onto my back.

"That was..." The words escape between breaths, but I have nothing to follow them with. My mind is blank.

Owena pushes herself up, meeting my eyes. There's a flicker of softness within them, a warmth, before they harden into cold, black stone. "The key to a tolerable marriage, one might say."

Not me. That's not what I would've said at all.

My heart sinks to the ground with my next exhale.

I LIE AMIDST THE SOFT FERNS of the forest floor, staring up at the starry sky between gaps in the leaves. A cool breeze caresses my skin, still burning within. Owena rests beside me, panting, the only sound beside the occasional hoot of an owl and rustling leaves.

How did this become my life?

I set out to reclaim my kingdom from my twisted mother. Instead, I've spent the last two weeks marching through endless wilderness toward an enemy kingdom with a woman I promised to marry, who, despite the whole thing being her idea, wants nothing to do with me if it doesn't involve being dominated by my will or my cock.

We've full-on rutted, what, five times now? Including the first, two nights ago. Without a single kiss between us. I wouldn't have believed it was possible to be so close to someone, yet so distant, but here I am. I keep telling myself each time will be the last, that it won't happen again until she lowers her guard and opens her heart to me, but then the moment comes... and I can't say no.

Despite my hopes that physical intimacy will lead to a deeper, emotional one, it hasn't. At least not for her, and I don't think I can keep this up. Her dismissals cut deeper every time.

Why can't she just open up to me?

I want her to be the person I can share my life with, more than I've wanted anything ever before. I never thought such a thing was even possible—to find someone brave enough to challenge me, to go out of their way to irritate me, without any fear. Even Aerona, as aggressive as she can be, still retreated before my temper.

I have to try something else. If she won't talk about us, maybe she'll talk about herself? I need to know more about her plan to eliminate her father, so perhaps I can use that to coax something out of her.

If I can't, I don't know how I'll survive this any longer.

The moonlight kisses her pale skin as she gathers her clothes, her thighs still damp with the remnants of our passion. I watch, jealous of the celestial body. My arms tense with the urge to pull her back to me, but I know she'd only slip away. An ache pierces my heart just thinking about it.

I prop myself up, my elbows pressing into the prickly grass, and take a deep breath.

Here goes nothing.

"Tell me about your curse. The one your father put on you."

Owena stills, her eyes flicking briefly to mine. "What?" She gives a curt shake of her head. "No."

"Why not?"

"It's personal."

Looking her up and down, I raise my eyebrows. "We're about to enter Ystyr, where I'll lose a significant amount of my power. You claim you want to kill your father yourself, but you said your magic's bound by a curse. So how exactly do you plan on doing that?"

She pulls her shirt on. "With a blade, I suppose."

Of course. How foolish of me. "I need more than that, Owena. How do you plan on getting close enough to stab him?"

She doesn't meet my eyes. Instead, she gathers her curls in her hands, smoothing them with her fingers. "With you. Willbending is a bloodline trait—being in Ystyr should have no effect on its power."

Time slows as realization bites into my chest. "Is that why you pushed me to willbend?"

Owena shrugs, then finally looks at me. "I pushed you to bend for many reasons, including my desire to experience the exhilaration of being under your control."

What? But she...

Her words were so wise. Supportive. They made me see, gave me strength. Yet now she diminishes them to nothing more than a fetish?

I grab my clothes, yanking them on as my indignation roars into anger. By the time I'm done, we're both standing, fully clothed, glowering at one another.

"Tell me about your curse, or I'm not going any further."

Her eyes narrow, burning into me. For a heartbeat, my pulse slows from a worry that I've pushed her too far. Then her gaze cools, though her mouth remains tight.

"A sap on your magic,
    to lose all worth;
    half by half by half.
    You may still curse,
    but are unable to bind
    either friend or foe,
    commoner or king."

She rips her eyes away from me as the words cycle through my mind.

Her magic—that's her shaping, her ability to glamour. The rest, those conditions...

My voice comes out quieter, some of my anger dissipating. "So you truly are bound? You can't curse anyone?"

Owena sighs. "That's the loophole, which all curses must have. There are a limited number of people who would fall outside of those bounds, but my father is not one of them, as he is both my enemy and a king."

I step toward her, then stop, quelling the instinct to take her hand. "Why couldn't you just tell me? Why do you have to make everything so difficult?"

She turns back to me, her face hard as stone. "Because I don't want your pity or your friendship. Such things would only hinder what I actually need from you."

Her words hit like a slap. I'd hoped she was past that, now that we'd...

My confusion's blown away as a thundering fury blasts through me. "Which is what? For me to bend at your beck and call?"

"No, I simply enjoy that." Her smile is unnerving, sickly sweet.

The storm rages, thrashing against my ribs, my heart floundering beneath the waves.

Her lips twitch as they press together, then she glances away, picking up her coat and tugging it on. As if the chilly air could bother someone with a heart of ice.

Why did I ever think there could be more between us?

I force an exhale, trying to calm myself, but failing miserably. "No more of this, Owena. I'll get you to your father, and if you manage to kill him, I'll marry you, as promised. But I'm done being your plaything."

I walk away from her, all my hopes for the future crumbling in my wake.

Chapter 28

Ellie

Caeo scratches the back of his head. "That's... wider than I expected."

We stand on the grassy banks of Anwen's Tears, its deep blue waters flowing like rippled glass. Guessing the distance to its far-off shore is nearly impossible, though I remember it being a long way away. But Caeo has his land-sense now, so he can probably count all the fish swimming in its depths.

A spark lights within as I watch him, his brow furrowed as he considers the river. He was so nervous about guiding us to the border all on his own, but he's taken to it well, his confidence growing every day.

His gaze shifts to me. "How did you and Taran cross it before?"

"He..." My mouth tightens as heat seeps into my cheeks. "He held back the water while we walked across it." *With his arm wrapped around me as he told me a love story, my heart pounding the entire time.*

Caeo doesn't need to know that part.

"I don't think I'll be able to do that." He looks back at the river, his jaw clenching. "Did the maps show any bridges?"

I pull out my sketchbook, searching its pages for the one focused on this region. "There's one south of here, I think?" I point to the bridge, marked by a narrow curve over the line of the river. "But

Taran avoided it because it'd be impossible to escape notice."

A while back, Caeo stopped at a small village for news, and apparently the war starting up again has been blamed on me incanting at the capital and stealing Aedys's and Ystyr's heirs—I'm trying not to let it bother me. If I weren't the scapegoat, something else would've been. It does, however, significantly increase the danger of someone discovering us. Caeo's still not confident he can glamour me well enough to trick fae eyes, and we'd still have their land-sense to worry about. In my earlier travels, most of the fae we passed brushed off whatever oddities they picked up because they had no reason to ever suspect a human had entered their realm. Now, anyone focusing on me long enough to discern those differences will most certainly sound an alarm. Then we'd be done for.

Caeo leans over my shoulder to scan the map, his warmth radiating into me. "He was in a hurry then, yeah? If we wait till nightfall, maybe it'll be less busy?"

I bite my lip. "Maybe." With how well fae see in the dark, I wouldn't expect them to limit their travel to daytime as much as humans do. We may find ourselves waiting quite late for them all to go to sleep. The only other solution I can think of is Caeo shaping a boat—but harvesting that much wood might anger the Land.

He slips his arms around my waist, his bright eyes capturing the clear midday sky. "Don't worry. I'll get us across somehow."

And I believe him, my heart pressing against my ribs as it swells with a bundle of emotions. Pride, in how far he's come. Desire, stirred by his confidence. And apprehension, at what will happen at the end of our journey.

I bury that last one deep down. I've done everything I can to prepare for the border. Worrying won't help anything.

Letting my sketchbook fall, I wind my hands behind Caeo's neck, my fingers sliding into the tangles of his ebony hair. "I suppose we have some time to kill, then."

He blinks, then a cheeky grin tugs at his lips. "I suppose we do."

An ember flares in my chest, its blaze pulsing down to my core.

It's been so long, and though I've been yearning for the passion we once shared, we've settled into a different sort of intimacy these past few weeks. One where I've seen the darkest corners of his mind and become his warm, comforting light, nourished by his own love for me. It almost makes the love I confessed the night of the ball feel like a lie—a naive wish, before I understood what it actually was. But now I do, and it can't even compare.

A few days ago, he finally revealed the entirety of what happened to him, and my heart fell to pieces. Suddenly, everything made sense—why he turned away every time a moment between us became too heated. If only I'd known sooner, but I understand why it was so difficult for him to tell me.

I'll never forgive his mother for what she's done to him. Taran and Owena stealing everything from her won't be enough. She deserves a long, drawn-out suffering.

Since then, I've been mindful of Caeo's pain, keeping my touch soft and serene. Yet, despite being closer than we've ever been, I miss the physical part of our relationship. The raw desire, melding into one. Only when we find our way back to that will we truly be whole.

"We don't have to," I say, my voice quivering. "I mean, I don't want to push you."

How things have changed since we first met, when I was the one holding us back. I bite back the grin tugging its way free, curling my lips inward.

Caeo chuckles, probably having a similar thought, but a familiar spark lights his eyes. "You're not pushing me. You've been amazingly patient."

His lips brush my cheek, light kisses burning a path to my ear. His breath is heavy against my skin as he whispers, "I want to."

Heat courses through me as elation stretches across my face. I twist my fingers through his hair, gripping him tightly as my anticipation builds.

Then I glance around us.

It's the middle of the day, and other than the river ahead, we're in a big, empty meadow, the sun beaming down on us.

"Maybe we should find somewhere less exposed?"

Caeo wraps his arms firmly around me. "We're more likely to be noticed if we go near the trees."

"I suppose that's true." Though it's hard to ignore a lifetime of believing the opposite. The idea of being so open in our lust, free for the world to see... My heart rate picks up as I pull myself close to his face, where his breath sends shivers across my skin.

"If you're sure," I whisper.

Hesitation flickers in his eyes, and my breath catches. Maybe it's still too soon.

But then he swallows, and the shadow retreats. "I am. I don't want to let my mother keep me from you anymore."

He leans in, his lips gently brushing mine. I melt into him, into our love. A smile presses between us, breaking our kiss. Even that was enough.

His eyes gleam, then he kisses me again. Demanding me, savoring me. I meet him in kind, encircling my arms around his neck as I devour him. My back arches as I push into him, his fingers trailing down my hips until they wrap around my backside, teasingly close to my most sensitive flesh.

My exhale bursts out at his touch, and I press my forehead against his.

"Take your clothes off," he says, his voice thick with desire.

"Only if you do."

He grins mischievously, and his arms release me. I stumble with the sudden shift in balance, the tall blades of grass brushing my legs, but then he's pulling my hands off his shoulders, as well as his shirt. His toned muscles flex as he tosses the garment aside.

His fingers land on the waist of his pants, tugging them down slightly, then he pauses, right before revealing the length that strains beneath them.

"Are you just gonna watch?"

My eyes flick up to his face. "Maybe?"

Caeo's lips quirk up in the corner, and he gestures me toward him with a tug on an invisible thread. "Come here."

The second I'm within arm's reach, he wraps his fingers around the hem of my shirt and tugs it up. I lift my arms, my breasts perking up with the motion, and my chemisette clings to the fabric as it slides over my head.

He discards my clothing without a glance, his eyes locked on my chest as he steps closer. Sunlight warms my skin as he scoops my breasts in his hands, the rough skin of his thumbs brushing against my nipples. I dissolve into his grasp.

A moan rolls out of me as my face tilts up to the sky, and Caeo's chuckle has my heart thumping with joy. With a quick motion, he pulls me close, spinning me so my back lands against his firm chest.

He buries his face in my neck, painting it with kisses. One hand grips my breast, kneading it with his fingers, and the other slides downward along my belly, pressing me into him as it moves lower and lower. His hard length digs into me, right where my thighs meet the curve of my backside. My hips tilt toward him and my legs shift apart, aching for him to enter despite the layers of cloth between us.

"What are you doing?" I gasp between breaths.

Caeo's lips take a break to whisper in my ear.

"I think I owe you a few before I get any."

Then his fingers slip under the waist of my pants.

A sigh quivers out of me as he takes me in his hand, claiming me as his touch glides between my slick folds. I lift onto my toes, my body begging his fingers to find their way into me, all while his lips continue to feast on the sensitive skin of my neck and his other hand twists and pulls at my breast. He's overloading my senses, my mind spinning wildly between his every caress.

Then he strokes the knot of nerves between my legs, and a spike of pure pleasure drowns out everything else.

"Caeo."

His fingers rub faster and faster, stoking the fire burning within me, until my legs can't hold my weight anymore. A stream of vocalizations flutters out of me, my muscles clenching as everything builds, coiling tight.

With a final twist of ecstasy, I cry out as my body releases all its tension. I melt into his grasp, his sweet kisses lingering on my neck.

I'm panting, dazed, as Caeo lowers me to the soft grass, speckled with wildflowers. His face appears over me, a halo of sunlight framing his tousled hair.

His eyes brighten with his smile. "Ready for round two?"

My breath catches. "What?" In the past, we've almost always reached completion together, then had to wait for him to be ready again. "I don't think I can."

"But we've barely gotten started." He moves between my legs and yanks down my pants. A second later, his tongue glides across the center of me, drawing out a moan that follows along his teasingly slow journey.

I force myself up, my legs trembling as I reach for him, interrupting his second swipe to pull him close.

"I want you," I whisper.

His eyes find mine, and he traces his fingers along the edge of my face, stopping on my chin to tilt my mouth to his. He kisses me slowly, and the taste of me on his tongue ignites a pulsing desire.

Caeo pulls away, and his blue eyes pour out a love as infinite as the sky. "I'm yours."

"Good. Now get in me before I lose patience."

His jaw drops, then a laugh lights up his face. "Have I told you how sexy it is when you get bold?"

"Not in a while." Despite trying to keep my face coy, my own laughter breaks free.

"So sexy." He sneaks in a kiss. "Hot, and sexy…" He brushes my nipple with his thumb, then flicks it hard before pulling away, sending a rush straight through me. "And absolutely perfect."

A cool breeze tickles my skin as he shifts, removing his pants, then frees my feet from the bunched-up fabric at my ankles. I lie back down, my core aching in anticipation as he settles between my legs.

The moment I've been longing for.

He adjusts my hips, and my legs spread further apart as his firm length slides against my entrance.

Then the tip enters, a slow glide, stretching me around him.

With a sharp thrust, he's in. Filling me fully, completely. A part of me, now and forever.

"I love you."

Caeo presses into me, skin against skin, as close as he could possibly be. "I love you, too." Then his lips envelop me in an all-consuming kiss.

My legs wrap around him as his thrusts begin. Slow. Deep. I rock my hips, moans trickling out of our kiss as our pace increases. It's not the desperate, spiraling pleasure from before. Every motion builds upon the last, the tingling coil tightening within, complementing the fire burning between us. The flames of our love—of our oneness.

Our breathing picks up, as one.

Our hearts race, as one.

And when we crest our climax, we cry out as our bodies shudder, ecstasy pulsing through us.

My love. My life.

My everything.

Chapter 29

Caeo

Ellie and I spend most of the afternoon wrapped up in one another, rolling around in the grassy meadow. It's everything I needed. In all my darkest moments, it was easy to forget how much she completes me.

Golden light warms her skin as she cries out my name, clenching around my cock, breaking as I empty whatever I have left inside her. A couple more thrusts to make sure she's satisfied, then I dissolve into her warm embrace.

It's almost as if the last few weeks never happened.

But they did, and in some ways, we're better for it. The love that fills her every touch... She's been with me through my worst. Put up with my weakness, my shame, and still loves me. More than ever.

"I don't know what I did to deserve you," I say, brushing her hair away from her flushed cheek.

She runs her fingers behind my head, pulling me into a kiss. Her muscles tighten as my cock throbs within her.

"You saw me," she whispers, only inches away.

Just like she saw me.

A few slow grinds eventually turn into another round, until the sun sinks low enough that we can't delay anymore—not if we want to reach the bridge with enough time to sleep before dawn. The wind picks up, rustling the tall grass as we pull our clothes back on, then we follow the river south hand in hand.

It'd be nice if we could've stayed like that forever. Savoring our love, forgetting everything else. Once we cross Anwen's Tears, it'll be just a couple days till we reach the border.

A couple days till the Land decides if Ellie lives or dies. Every step we take along the river's banks drags us further from our bliss and into that reality.

A similar dread builds on Ellie's face, with her chewing her lip as we walk. I squeeze her hand tightly as the setting sun bathes the sky with orange, deep pink, and violet. The colors reflect off the river's waves.

"I'll miss the beauty of this place when we go home," she says, her steps slowing to a stop. "It's like I didn't know what color was until we came here. Everything's so rich, so alive."

I look around at the wildflowers dotting the meadow, to the far-off trees in the east. Back where we left Taran and Owena. Sure, it's pretty here, but that's the least of what I'll miss. Outside of Ellie, everyone I care about—Reid, Taran and Owena, even the Land—they're all here.

"Caeo? Is something wrong?"

I snap back to Ellie, then force a smile. "Just thinking."

She rubs her fingers against mine. "About what?"

I take a deep breath, trying to figure out how to respond without adding to her worries. "About home. I don't really know where that is anymore."

She stiffens, her arm flinching closer to her body.

Shit. Messed that up. "I didn't mean—it's wherever you are, of course."

"No, it's fine." Ellie takes my other hand, gripping them both tightly. "I'm just realizing I don't really, either. I hadn't thought that far." She inhales. "Even if everything goes well, I'm not going back to the Academy. And I don't want to live with my parents in Durnam, either. Not with you."

I lean in, kissing her forehead. "We'll figure it out. After we figure out how to convince everyone to stop incanting."

If the Land even lets her live.

I shove the thought away and pull Ellie back into a walk. I can't let myself fall back into the darkness, not after finally breaking free. There's gotta be something more pleasant we can talk about.

"Taran told me the story of this river's name. Anwen's Tears," Ellie says.

I sigh in relief, glancing over at the deep blue water. "Sounds like it has a sad ending."

"It does. Anwen was a princess in Aedys, who fell in love with a prince of Ystyr. I guess if they'd married, they'd have done what Taran and Owena are trying to do, but their parents wouldn't let them. Anwen's father had the prince killed, and supposedly, the Land was so moved by Anwen's grief that She cracked the earth in half, creating a river filled with her tears."

I hold back a snort. "That doesn't sound true at all." *No one can cry that much.*

"That's what I thought, but Taran could tell the story, so it has to be, right? And Owena *did* say something about the Land being completely infatuated with love." Ellie's brow furrows. "In that case, maybe She really could've been devastated by watching Anwen lose her lover."

I stop walking. "Something's bothering you."

"Hmm?"

"Your face is all pinched."

She lets out a small laugh. "No, I'm just thinking. If people in love really do move the Land that much, then maybe there's hope She'll forgive me."

An icy breeze chills my entire body, despite the sun still warming my skin. For the first time this entire afternoon, my fingers twitch toward my pocket. I squeeze them into a fist, my nails digging into my palms, then take a floral-scented breath.

"Maybe."

Ellie's face falls. "You don't think so, do you?"

I force another inhale, trying to stay calm. For her. But she wouldn't want me to hide my feelings—I don't want to, either—so I make myself speak. "I want to believe that, Ellie, I really do. But I'm terrified that if I say anything too optimistic, my body will tell me I'm lying, and then I won't be able to bring you anywhere."

My chest feels lighter, but the weight creeps back as I take in Ellie's expression. Her lips curl inward, and she seems to be holding her breath. But then she nods and steps closer, wrapping her arms around me.

"I understand," she whispers, closing her eyes as I fold her into a tight hug. Cozy lavender fills my lungs as I nuzzle into the soft, tangled mess of her hair.

She'll be fine. She has to be.

Our pace slows for the rest of the journey south, the lapping sounds of the river accompanying our footsteps in the tall grass. Once the sun sets, I draw Ellie closer to better guide her way; the moonlight's plenty for me to see by, but she keeps stumbling on the uneven terrain. It reminds me of when I had to guide her up the stairs of the clock tower—how she pretended to see the face I added to a flower, choking on an oversized cock. Twelve-year-old me thought it was hilarious.

So is imagining Ellie's face if she ever sees it for real.

Something itches at the edge of my land-sense. I squeeze Ellie's hand, then gesture for her to stop with my other.

"What is it?" she asks, her brow tight with concern.

"I sense the bridge. There's three people standing there, like they're guarding it." My mother must've assumed I'd try to go home. Or maybe they're expecting Taran, not that it matters either way. What matters is that I've only ever bent one person at a time. While they haven't sensed us yet, they definitely will, and long before I'm close enough to bend them. I can't assume they won't notice Ellie's human.

I sigh. "One of them will probably run off as soon as they sense us, to warn someone else. I don't think I'll be able to do anything to stop that."

"So that would leave two guards?" Ellie's lips press together. "Can you handle that?"

"I can try." Taran said I probably could, as long as I believed in myself. Didn't waver. Didn't let my own fears get the best of me.

Another deep exhale. I have to succeed. For Ellie.

"Stay behind me. I doubt my mother would've ordered anyone to kill me, but who knows what she said about you."

With a quick squeeze of Ellie's hand, I pull her along, dashing the rest of the way. I position myself between her and the river, steering her away from all the bumps and ditches that would trip her up.

I can feel the moment we enter the range of their land-sense, all three of them stiffening. Two turn in our direction, while the other starts running across the bridge. Just as I expected.

Soon, their dark forms appear in the distance, right at the water's edge.

"Halt! Who approaches?" one of them calls.

My steps slow. I gather my power, just like I practiced, but my throat goes tight. My body jerks, recalling the feeling of losing control. The panic. My grip on Ellie's hand tightens, my palm slick with sweat.

"Halt, or we'll be forced to attack!"

I can see them clearly now, drawing their bows. Ellie ducks behind me. I have to protect her—it's now or never. I pick up my pace as power builds in my lungs, ready to explode.

An arrow flies toward us.

"Get down!" My voice echoes through the night.

Ellie yelps as she slams to the ground. Something slices my arm. My hand shoots up, grabbing my bicep. It comes away bloody.

Fuck! I bent Ellie instead of them.

I focus my gaze back on the guards, sliding new arrows along their bowstrings. Summoning the power again, I shout, "Stop!"

They freeze, going completely still. My heart catches, my body seizing as if I bent myself.

But I didn't.

Taking a deep breath of chilly air, I help Ellie up, tugging her behind me. "Are you alright? I didn't mean to—"

"I'm fine," she says, nodding shakily. She squeezes my hand as we creep toward the fae, waiting for any hint of movement.

Nothing. It's as if they're carved from stone. They aren't even breathing, just like when my mother did it to me.

I swallow back the nausea rising in my throat. I'm not her. She's the reason I had to do this.

"You can breathe." The words echo. Loud exhales burst from the guards' lungs, but they otherwise don't move. It won't last forever—even my mother's bendings eventually wore off. If I did it right, they should be free in a few minutes.

Which means I need to do one more to keep us safe. It's either that or kill them.

"Forget everything about us."

I don't wait to see what happens. I guide Ellie across the bridge, into the darkness on the other side.

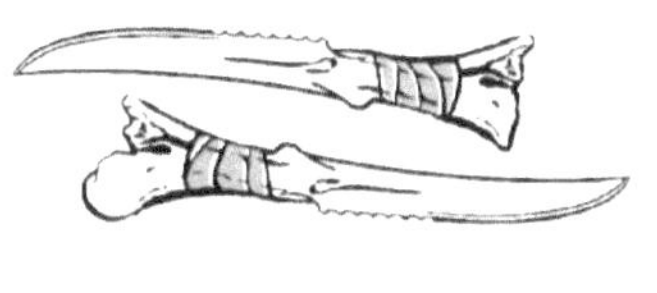

Chapter 30

Emlyn

"This is one of the stupidest things I've ever considered doing," I mutter, looking at the encampment in the valley below. I'm on my belly in the tall grass to keep from being seen, but it's getting late and mortals can't see shit in the dark, so maybe I'm worrying too much.

I'm not. This is a terrible idea. But at least my stomach's stopped heaving when I touch the ground. Yippee.

We're mostly here because it's what Reid wanted, but I haven't forgotten that the Land supported the whole thing. How could I? I'd still be stuck healing at my mom's house if She didn't. My best guess is that She doesn't like the war and thinks that maybe we can do something about it?

Not that walking down there and saying, "Look, mortals and fae can love each other," will accomplish anything other than getting me killed. Outside of that, my best skill is fucking, which isn't particularly helpful in this scenario. And while I love him, Reid's not exactly overflowing with useful abilities, either.

"Are you sure Alexis is worth risking our lives for?" I ask. "We don't even know if she'll want to leave."

Reid's lying on his stomach next to me, pretending he can see anything other than the hundreds of flames from torches and campfires. He's clean-shaven again, having done so this morning before we left the inn. Whatever. He's still handsome, and I take a beat to brush my knuckles against the smooth skin of his jaw. At least I don't have to walk around with freckles anymore.

"Of course she is," he says. "I don't want her to die fighting an enemy we shouldn't be fighting."

"They should absolutely be fighting. Everyone in your realm will likely end up dead if they don't."

"And I don't want her to be one of them."

I groan, dropping my head.

"You realize you're a former student who disappeared weeks ago along with the High Marshal's daughter, right?" I lift my head back up to face him. "They'll want to question you—and that's the best-case scenario. Worst-case, Alexis and Sophie talked, and everyone knows exactly where you've been all this time."

"Very few people down there will actually know who I am."

"It doesn't matter. Even with a glamour—which I'd probably have to chug the rest of our water to maintain—they aren't gonna let a couple civilians meander into an army camp. Telling them who you are is the only way they'd let you in, and only so they can interrogate you."

"So what do you think we should do, then?"

A weight settles in my chest, and my head falls forward again.

"You're gonna stay here and pray to whoever it is you mortals pray to"—I think that's Fortune, which is hilarious—"and I'll go look for Alexis."

The things I do for him...

Reid stiffens, propping himself higher on his elbow as he turns to me. "What? You can't go down there by yourself. It's too dangerous."

"It's less dangerous than bringing you." I push myself off the repulsive ground, then head down the opposite side of the hill to where the horses munch on grass, ignoring our nearby piles of stuff.

"Emlyn, wait!"

"I'm going alone, or we're not going at all." Digging through our packs, I pull out all of our waterskins. I grab the second jug of water, our first one having been abandoned when emptied, and begin filling them.

"I'm gonna end up hiding in the woods in just a few days at this rate," I grumble.

Reid puts his hand on mine, stopping me mid-pour. "It's not worth risking your life."

I look up at his earthy eyes, and my heart aches at the worry within them. "Yes, it is, Reid. You won't be able to leave and pretend none of this matters to you."

"I can." His hand squeezes tightly around mine.

I close my eyes and breathe out a soft exhale. "Don't lie to me."

"It's not a lie, Em!" Reid turns my face to his, and my eyes open at his touch. "If it's a choice between you and pretending, I'll choose you every time. Yeah, it might make me miserable, but nowhere near as much as losing you!"

My heart folds in on itself, and I rest my hand on his cheek. "I can't live that way. Not when I can do something about it. I'm sorry, but you need to let me do this for you."

His eyes glisten, darting back and forth as they search mine, probably hoping to find a chink in my resolve. He won't. He swallows, then gives the smallest of nods.

I empty one of the packs of all our food and other supplies, then fill it with the waterskins. I pull off my shirt and change into the stupidly uncomfortable mortal one—I've been trying to wear it as little as possible. By the time I finish, it's completely dark out; the one saving grace of this idiotic pursuit.

I take a deep breath, bouncing on my toes as I shake out my hands. "Alright. Time to do this."

Reid grabs my arm and pulls me to his lips, and all my nervous energy flies into kissing him. Shoving my fingers into his hair, I deepen our kiss as his tongue sweeps through my mouth. Mine presses back, then I scrape his lower lip between my teeth as I pull my lips and my heart away.

"You're trying to get me to stay, aren't you?"

"Was it that obvious?"

My mouth tightens as I muss his hair with my fingers. "I love you. I'll try to be back soon."

Then I slip out of his grasp and clamber down the hill toward the several hundred incanters who want me dead.

I take a swig from one of the waterskins and cloak myself in a glamour of night while making my way down the hill as quickly as possible; the more time this takes, the more water I'll have to use. My steps slide through the grass and dirt, occasionally needing the balance of my hands in the steeper sections. But I'm not really worried about the sounds of my footfalls or small rocks tumbling down the hill, since mortals are practically deaf.

Thanks to my glamour and useless mortal eyes, I can take a pretty straightforward path to the encampment, but it helps that they don't expect anyone to sneak up from this direction. Crouching down, I get near enough that the guards will see me by their torchlight if I move any closer.

Here goes nothing.

I take another drink of water and shape the wind, gusting it toward the nearest guard. Not enough to put out his torch, but enough for him not to immediately assume he's being attacked when it does go out.

Right now.

He plunges into darkness, and I rush forward, grabbing the back of his neck with my left hand while clamping my right on his jaw. A twist and snap before he makes a peep, and his body falls to the ground. There was no way around it—if I left him alive, he'd wake up before I got out and sound an alarm.

Breathing heavily, I replace my glamour of darkness with one that looks as much like him as possible with the time I have, which isn't much.

"Jefferies?" someone calls out.

"The torch went out!" I yell. "There was a sudden gust of wind!"

Not a lie.

Ignoring the lump formerly known as Jefferies, I force my attention on reigniting the torch using the ember I intentionally left glowing. Dark spots dance in my vision, and my stomach rises to my throat. I finish the rest of the first waterskin and drop it to the ground just as a wave of dizziness crashes between my ears.

That was a lot.

I stumble over to the guard who called for Jefferies, keeping the torch in front of my face in case I messed up on the details.

"I'm not feeling too good," I mumble, making my voice thick. "I think I might hurl."

"Ugh. Go back and tell Hunter to get out here."

I pull out my second waterskin and down half of it on my way into camp, which does nothing for my nausea. Large encampments of anyone gathered in one place for long periods of time always smell horrible, but mortals are especially bad. Even if I could ignore the stink of so much body odor mingled with shit and smoke, the putrid stench of incanting saturates the air, as if someone shoved rotting entrails up my nostrils. It's an effort not to retch.

But the water steadies my steps, and I weave through the city of tents, packed with soldiers passing the time before they tuck in for the night. It's easy to pick out the Academy students—while they wear the standard uniforms I'm currently glamouring over my clothes, a simple gray shirt and trousers, their faces are taut with the nerves of a gerbil cornered by a honey badger.

Starting on my third waterskin gets me feeling slightly better, but keeping this glamour up will drain me fast. Usually, there's some civilians with an army: cooks, whores, and tradesmen. If I can just get—

There.

My land-sense picks up Alexis. It's a blessing that I know her so intimately, or I might have missed her.

Though, the last time I saw her, that was also the reason she tried to kill me, so it might not be a blessing after all. One of the bigger mistakes I've made, if I'm being honest.

I did not think this through.

She's inside a large tent with at least two dozen other people, spread out in even rows. Some lying down, others, including Alexis, sitting. It must be one of the women's barracks.

Fuck.

I *can* glamour myself to look like a woman, though it'll be significantly more effort than anything I've done so far because of the size difference. Even back home, it'd be exhausting, so I won't be able to hold it very long. But I won't *sound* different. The instant I open my mouth, it's all over. I'll somehow have to get Alexis to follow me out of there without saying a word.

There's only one option, and I hate it.

I duck behind a tent and double-check no one can see me. I drink the rest of the third waterskin, as well as my fourth, then focus on my transformation.

Into Ellie.

I eye myself as best I can. Small hands, uniform similar to what the women I've spotted wandering the camp are wearing. I tug at the now-brown hair hanging from my head. Good enough.

By mortal standards, it's fairly dark inside the women's tent, lit by a scattering of flickering candles. Alexis is easy to spot because I never took my land-sense off her, so I make a beeline in her direction, my legs already cramping from walking in a half crouch to match Ellie's height. She's sitting on her bedroll, braiding her hair with deft fingers.

Those were fun braids. And fingers.

I kneel in front of her, and she glances at me, then does a double take. Her eyes go wide, and her fingers drop from her hair.

"Ellie? You're back—"

Bringing my finger to my lips, I gesture for her to follow me. I don't wait for her to follow, trusting that curiosity will get the better of her. I can't afford to take any longer than necessary.

"Where are we—"

Shushing her again, I desperately scan the area with both my land-sense and my eyes, trying to find a tent with no one inside. There!

My heart thunders in my chest as I grab Alexis's hand and pull her along with me, past a group of soldiers casually sharing stories by a campfire. I drop her hand as soon as we're in the tent and pray that I'm not about to be murdered.

"Ellie, what's going on? What happened? Where's Reid and Caeo?"

My glamour's already falling as the tent flap closes behind her. I take a deep breath and turn around.

"I'm not Ellie, I'm Emlyn. Reid wants to see you, please don't kill me."

My insides freeze as Alexis's eyes turn to ice.

This was definitely a bad idea.

Chapter 31

Owena

We've abandoned our coats amid the marshy wetlands of southern Aedys, where the scent of decaying vegetation and the constant drone of unseen insects thicken the air. Despite my best efforts to follow Taran along the drier ridges, my pants are drenched from all my accidental stumbles into the bog.

He hasn't spoken to me since I revealed the entirety of my curse last night. While I do not believe that will hinder my plans in the short term—he was more focused on his feelings than the specifics of my curse—it's left a constant ache in my heart. I wish he hadn't pushed me. Then the next few days could have been speckled with at least some momentary bliss.

Instead, we approach Ystyr's border with heavy hearts. It was never going to be a joyous occasion, not with what it will do to Taran, but I had hoped to experience a modicum of relief at finally returning to my homeland. Instead, each step reminds me how close I'm teetering on the edge of becoming my father. How I must use his own means to end him. I can only hope it doesn't ruin us.

Borders between fae realms are barely a thing, unlike the one between us and Lyndir. That one, you can see blanketing the horizon from a day's walk away. The one between Aedys and Ystyr, you don't so much *see* as *feel*.

Taran still marches ahead, his shoulders rigid, his movements tensing with every step. Meanwhile, a nostalgic warmth seeps through my veins, calling me home. I soon outpace him, my strides quickening, my gait lighter, while he practically sinks into the dirt.

I hesitate as I pass him. "This seems more difficult for you than most."

He grits his teeth. "My connection to Aedys is deeper than anyone else's. She doesn't like it when I leave." He wipes his brow with the back of his hand. "We'll need to move faster once we cross. I fear what my mother will gain in my absence."

That hadn't occurred to me. All my planning, and that single, important detail slipped through. How long will it take for her bond with the Land to surpass Taran's as monarch?

But it's too late to reconsider—we'll simply have to hurry. I reach for his hand, but he whips it away.

"Let me help you, Taran."

His eyes are hard, untrusting. A splinter pierces my heart.

I deserve that.

"Please," I press, extending my hand again.

After a tense moment, he surrenders. I interlace my fingers with his, pouring Ystyr's warmth from me into him. His grip relaxes as his shoulders dip, then he grasps my hand with renewed vigor. I turn my gaze away from him, looking ahead, and pull us forward.

My hand smolders in his, our palms growing sweaty. My heart begs me to stop, to tell him I'm sorry, that we can find another way to end the constant wars between realms. But that would be selfish—abandoning my people in favor of my wants, my needs. I couldn't live with myself if I did that. I can only hope Taran will understand and forgive me.

A breath away from the border, my resolve wavers. For a single, heavy heartbeat.

He falls to his knees the moment I pull him into Ystyr.

Releasing my grip on his hand, I scramble in front of him. "Taran? Are you alright?" I wasn't with my father when we traveled to Aedys for my wedding. He kept only his most tightly bound guards by his side, sending all others away, so no one could witness his moment of vulnerability and exploit it. I had no idea what to expect for Taran.

He nods shakily. "I'm fine. I just... It feels empty. More than when I went to Lyndir."

"There's nothing in Lyndir to contest your bond. You should still feel it here, as I did in Aedys. The difference is simply greater for you, since I'm not yet a monarch."

My land-sense is already expanding as I speak. In Aedys, my bond was weaker than the average native fae, but here, I have the strength of an heir. It pales compared to what Taran and my father know, but it's stronger than most.

And it picks up soldiers patrolling nearby.

Too soon.

"We need to move. My land-sense is stronger, but my abilities are otherwise unchanged. Our only defense is your willbending, and we're already at risk of being discovered."

"That's unfortunate," Taran mutters as he pushes himself to his feet, leaning against my shoulder. I press my hand against his chest, steadying him. For a heartbeat, our faces are a breath apart, his eyes meeting mine.

I swallow the urge to bring my lips to his, then step back. "Think of what you want to say to them if we cross their path. I'll do my best to keep us out of their senses."

Taran nods, straightening.

"Lead the way."

THREE DAYS INTO YSTYR, and the landscape has transformed into the world I'm accustomed to. The sultry heat permeates my bones, and I'm finally warm for the first time in over a month, save for the precious moments spent engulfed in Taran's blaze. The thick canopy blocks the sun's rays, and the scent of decaying leaves and wild cinnamon floods my every breath. Our steps are more measured here, weaving between dense ferns and low shrubs, with a rainbow of flowers blooming on their branches.

I pause to inhale the sweet perfume of a hibiscus, one of my favorites, hoping it will ease my heart.

It does not.

Nor do the melodic sounds of whistling birds and chirping insects, the peaceful songs that lulled me to sleep every night of my life, until I traveled north.

But while my misery stews within me, Taran's seeps out of him.

He's tied his hair up in a knot in a vain attempt to keep cool, his skin dripping with sweat. Even if I hadn't upset him, hadn't driven him to shut himself away from me, I doubt he'd be able to partake in any passionate exertions. Adding the heat of my body to his would likely melt him into a puddle, but a significant part of me longs to do just that—to dissolve into him and let that be enough.

"What do you think of my homeland so far?"

Taran exhales heavily as I glance back at him, trudging behind me. "It's sweltering."

I wipe away a trickle of moisture from my brow. "I suppose you'll want to live in the north, then, once we marry?"

"Yes, please."

"Perhaps we should establish a new capital somewhere central. One that's tolerable for both our tastes."

"Uh huh."

This is the most conversation I've gotten out of him in days.

Perhaps time has cooled his temper, though in this heat, I doubt it. More likely, he's too distracted by his suffering to continue spurning me.

That doesn't bring me any joy. My nerves have been tightening all day, twisting into a knot that threatens to pull me apart at the seams.

My father would have sensed Taran the moment he stepped foot in his realm—there was no way to avoid that. And if he's currently residing where I suspect, any forces he sent for us would likely meet us today. It's only a matter of time.

It may seem like a waste of lives to send mere soldiers after as powerful a willbender as Taran, even one with his reputation for restraint. But my father's liberal use of curses on his own people easily negates that threat. It will require perfect timing, perfect positioning, to keep us from being overwhelmed and killed. I have no doubt I can do it; the only question is whether I'll destroy my own heart in the process.

The sun's rays struggle to pierce the leaves above, so it's impossible to know the time of day by its position. By the sweltering heat and my inner timekeeping, I would say it's late afternoon when a familiar presence crosses the edge of my land-sense, along with a dozen others.

My exhale of relief drowns under the thundering of my heart.

They won't have sensed me yet, but once they do, they'll head straight for us. Then Taran will sense them, too. It's time to act.

"Let's take a break," I announce, coming to a halt.

Taran collapses against the trunk of a tree, his head tilted up to the forest canopy as he closes his eyes and takes several deep breaths.

The soldiers move closer.

I brush aside a fern's bristly leaves and lower myself next to

Taran. "Can we talk?"

His head rolls in my direction, then he opens his exhausted eyes. Their green feels brighter here, no longer absorbing the depth of pine trees, but the vibrant saturation of the rain forest. It's like seeing home in them.

"What do you want?"

I force a mischievous smile. "Are you certain you wish to ask me that?"

Taran sighs, and his eyelids sink shut. "I'm done with games, Owena. If you have something to say, say it, or else leave me alone."

"I'm sorry, Taran."

His eyes flutter open. "For what?"

I scoot closer, my knees pressing against his outstretched leg.

"I have... reasons... for everything I've done. Ones I hope you'll understand someday. I wish things could be simpler between us. That we could give each other what we want."

Taran's face softens, and he sits up, tilting closer to me. "I only wanted you to let me in."

My eyes sting. I won't be able to contain the tears that threaten to escape, not for long, not with my heart crumpling beneath the weight of what I must do. It's the only way to save the Land from war. My people from my father's rule. Myself, from this half-life he doomed me to.

Ellie's drawing flashes through my mind. The wonderful light in my eyes.

"I can't do that," I whisper, my resolve hardening. "Not yet. I've tried to think of another way, but there is none. I'm... I'm sorry."

He takes my hand, and my heart cracks in half. "What are you talking about?"

The soldiers approach. Taran hasn't noticed, all of his attention on me. I'm running out of time.

I force myself to gaze into his eyes.

"I'm sorry."

A flicker of hesitation, then I kiss him.

It's everything I ever dreamed it would be. I climb into his lap as I bring my fingers into his damp hair, and his musky scent—sweat, mingling with pine—swirls around me. His lips part and our tongues meet, savoring the flavors they've longed to taste. He brings his hands to my face, pulling me closer as our kiss deepens.

But the heat rushing down from my lips dies in my chest, unable to fill the bottomless pit in my heart.

I untangle my fingers from his hair, tracing them down along the curves of his face, his neck, until they rest between us. On his chest, right above his heart. Pressing my palm against him, it thunders for me.

I break our kiss.

His eyes meet mine, and my blurry tears aren't enough to hide the concern that seeps out of them.

My voice trembles. "Forgive me."

Confusion flits across his face, then I whisper the words that ruin me.

"Not a sound, nor utterance,
    will escape your lips,
    Until you speak the words
    that will save me."

The light goes out of Taran's eyes.

My body goes cold, every bit of warmth abandoning me, as understanding washes over his face. His lips move, trying to form words, but nothing escapes.

"I'm sorry, Taran. I'm so sorry. It was the only way."

His features contort, outraged at my betrayal, and he pushes me off him. I land hard on my backside as he silently yells at me. I turn away, unable to face him.

A rustle of leaves.

They're here.

I scramble up, throwing myself in front of Taran, my back to his chest. A dozen soldiers step out of the surrounding trees. Bows drawn and ready, trained on us.

"Stop!" I shriek, my desperation thwarting any attempt at royal dignity. "I have him cursed. He cannot willbend. I'm bringing him to my father."

My pulse pounds in my ears, waiting for a response.

Then Barri, sweet Barri, my former guard, steps forward, lowering his bow. The others remain still. I have no idea what Taran is doing behind me, but he isn't a fool. They would kill him in an instant if he tried anything.

"Your Highness? We're under orders to kill the prince and return you to your father."

"I'm asking you to disregard that order and escort me home. The bound Prince of Aedys is more valuable alive than dead, and I'm certain my father would agree."

Barri's eyes narrow, darting between me and Taran as he considers.

"Let us prove he cannot speak." Barri nods to two of the others, who lower their bows and approach. They wait for me to move aside.

With the resignation of one facing their own execution, I force myself into my regal bearing and step away. I swallow the anguish clawing its way up my throat as I meet Taran's dark eyes.

It takes all my resolve not to crumble at the hurt within them.

His gaze turns to the ground.

He barely resists as one of the soldiers locks his arms behind his back.

He silently doubles over as the other punches him hard in the stomach.

Again.

And again.

Each hit shatters me.

"That's enough!" I glare at Barri. "You've proven he can't make a sound. Unless you plan on carrying him, he needs to be able to walk."

Barri nods at his men. The one punching Taran backs away.

"Bind his wrists. We'll see what the king wants to do with him." Barri offers me his arm as the others follow his command. I take it.

It's too late to turn back. Taran will die if I do.

Chapter 32

Caeo

I'm an idiot for not seeing this coming.

According to Taran's map, the bridge we used to cross Anwen's Tears is in the southernmost part of Aedys. Which means, if Aedys and Ystyr wanted to gather a large number of forces for a unified push against Landore, it's in the ideal location.

That's apparently what they decided to do.

We've left the basin of central Aedys, heading into rolling hills near the border. Thousands of fae block our path, gathered in a large valley that angles southwest into Landore. The only bright side is that I can sense them before they can sense us.

Thank you, Taran.

I release my fingers from pressing firmly against my brow. "We're just gonna have to go north until we get around them." Beyond the hills, if we want to avoid notice. It's an unfortunate example of when fae vision's the problem instead of their land-sense.

"How long do you think it will take?" Ellie asks.

I step out from under the two trees we've been hiding beneath to check the position of the sun—somewhere near the middle of the sky—then shrug. "I think we would've arrived later today if we could walk straight there. So, tomorrow, maybe?"

Ellie unfolds her arms, then her fingers tap idly against her legs. "If there's this many fae gathered here, it's likely my father's set up on the other side. So we shouldn't have much further to travel, if that's the case."

Perfect. "We'll just cross the border right where an army's waiting to kill me."

I have no idea what to expect once I'm back in Landore. While I lived there my entire life without anyone suspecting I was anything more than a regular human, I have no idea if that's because of the charm my mother had me wearing, or if my mortal half somehow lets me blend in there. I definitely didn't have any fae abilities back then like I do now, so who knows if I'll still be able to use any of them?

Taran warned me to fill all our waterskins before we cross, just in case it works the same for me as it does full-blooded fae. If so, I'll need to drink water from here every day in order to use my land-sense or glamour myself. We already did that, but according to the map, there aren't any more water sources between us and the border. Adding an extra day to our journey already hurts our plans.

Ellie squeezes my arm. "I doubt that—if we're going around this army, we should be crossing north of Landore's forces, too."

"They'd be stupid not to have people patrolling the border."

"So you'll glamour yourself to look human before we cross and then let me do all the talking. At worst, you can return to Aedys, and we'll find our way back to each other after Taran's King and orders a withdrawal."

That's not the worst that could happen.

It's pointless to say that out loud. We've come all this way so that Ellie can beg the Land's forgiveness or die trying, and she'd spend the rest of her life completely miserable if I stopped her now. She seems confident that everything will work out, but maybe she's just projecting her hopes because someone has to.

I'm still full of doubt. I haven't been able to bring myself to bond with the Land for several days now, because I know that if I felt even a tinge of anger toward Ellie, I'd be dragging her as far away from the border as possible. It's made resisting the milk harder, especially when I wake up in the middle of the night worrying. I should get rid of it, like Ellie wanted, but I can't keep her safe if I'm not sleeping.

And I can't be the cause of her misery, so onward we go.

Herds of sheep dot the hills, each with a small group of fae shepherds tending them. I can't imagine they'll be a problem for us; unless we get close enough for them to sense Ellie's humanity, they have no reason to abandon their flocks to attack or report us. And even if they did... I can just bend anyone who comes close, and if they send word to the army, we'll hopefully be across the border before someone catches up.

Just to be safe, we don't make a fire when we find a nice spot in a cluster of trees, out of the wind, to camp for the night. We don't really need one, as the heat of our bodies joining is more than enough to have us sweating. The hard part's getting Ellie to stifle her cries so they don't echo through the hills. It's like her years of bottling herself up in silence come pouring out in those moments, and she just can't put a cork in it. I fucking love that I do that to her, but it'd be nice if it didn't risk our safety. Once this is over, I look forward to plowing her till her vocal cords give out.

For now, I pull my coat over us as Ellie snuggles into my chest, completely spent and already dozing off. I close my eyes, hoping to join her.

But sleep doesn't come.

A tightness builds in my chest until I can't take it anymore. I tuck my coat around Ellie as I slip away, pulling my clothes on to make up for losing her warmth.

I purposefully kept us low on the hillside to obscure our view of the border. Ellie told me it looks like a thick, purple fog, heavy with murderous intent—at least for her and Reid. According to her, Taran and Emlyn just saw it as fog, so it should be the same for me.

The hill's steep, but I'm too wound up to find a gentler slope, so I hike straight to the top. Breathing heavily, I turn my gaze westward. Even with my fae eyes, I can't make out the color in the darkness, but a thick haze hangs on the horizon. I sit down, staring at it, while a chilly breeze sends shivers down my spine.

Other than the cold, I feel nothing. It's just fog.

How could this thing be such a threat to Ellie but not give a shit about me? If the Land hates her so much, why doesn't She hate me for loving her?

Ellie told me that the rage was so heavy, she couldn't move when she felt it. Will I be forced to drag her to her doom?

I bury my face in my hands and exhale slowly. *How am I possibly gonna do this?*

With a deep breath, I dig my fingers into the cold, hard soil.

The Land's pulse thumps through me, warm and steady as it's always been. Comforting. Like being wrapped in the embrace of someone who loves you, except the heat radiates from within.

I focus my thoughts on Ellie, and the pulse seethes at a slow boil. My heart splinters as tears leak from my eyes.

Please. Please forgive her.

But I don't speak the Tongue, so She can't understand. I should've asked Taran to teach me, even just a little, but I was already drowning under everything else. It didn't even occur to me.

So I pour my heart out through my fingers, into my connection with the Land.

All my heartbreak.

All my love.

Please don't take her from me.

I pour everything out, until there's nothing left, just a throbbing pain in my head.

I pull my hands free of the earth and curl up, sobbing, on top of the frigid hill.

AFTER WHO KNOWS HOW LONG, I return to Ellie, tossing and turning until the dark sky glows at the edges. At that point, I only manage to fall asleep using the milk of midnight star.

When Ellie shakes me awake not long after dawn, I'm still high as a cloud. The good kind. Not the evil kind that wants to kill her.

Why are we going there?

"Caeo? Are you alright?"

I groan, my eyes wandering from the swaying leaves above to Ellie's concerned face. She's sitting beside me, dressed and ready to go.

"No." I shake my head slowly. "No, I'm not alright. Can we go home now?"

A wistful smile washes over her face as she tucks my hair behind my ear. "That's the plan." She swallows. "I was hoping you could go over the words with me before we leave? Make sure I'm saying them right?"

I blink a few times, trying to focus. "Yeah, sure."

Ellie lifts her sketchbook out of her lap so I can see it. A bunch of meaningless letters with illegible notes scribbled next to them.

"I don't think I'm gonna be much help."

"Don't worry about the notes, just follow along and let me know if I leave anything out."

With a yawn, I sit up and take the book from her, shivering as the cold air wraps around me. "Whenever you're ready."

Ellie takes a deep breath, then speaks a bunch of gibberish I can't understand.

I trace my finger under the letters on the page as I think she says them, trying my best to stay focused. I don't *think* I miss anything, and I don't *think* she does, either.

"I think you got it," I say once she finishes.

Ellie lets out a sigh of relief, then nods her head. "Can we go through it one more time?"

"Yeah, in a minute. Let me... wake up more, first."

I push myself to my feet, stumbling a few steps before catching myself against a hardy trunk that's happy to lend me a branch. I nod my thanks to the tree and continue a ways away to relieve myself. It'd be rude otherwise.

I stagger back and pull out one of the waterskins to swallow some down.

"We need to conserve that, remember?" Ellie says, her voice pitching up.

Oh. Right.

She takes the water from me and rests her hand on my shoulder. "You took the milk again, didn't you?" Her voice is gentle, but the words still prick.

My eyelids sink shut, trapping me in the darkness with my shame. "I couldn't sleep."

Her fingers twitch where they press into me. Disappointment, or fear? A sharp breath, then she squeezes me tight. "I understand. Today's a hard day."

I open my eyes and look at her. Her beautiful face, lips trembling. Scared for me, or herself?

My brain's gone tight, trying to come up with something to say. Something to... *Fuck.* It's right there, but I can't focus. Why do I have to keep disappointing her?

With a deep breath, I force a smile. "Let's just get it done with."

She nods, as if reassuring herself. "Are you sure you can find the way like this?"

A harsh laugh slips out of me. "It's hard to miss." I glance at the hillside, its long grass waving at me. Hello or goodbye? I'm not sure.

Ellie's fingers brush my face, turning me back to her. "We have to believe it'll be alright. That She'll see my intentions—that She has more to gain by letting me live."

Her words are already floating away. I wrap my arms around her before she does, too.

"I'll try."

We eat a bit of food, neither of us very hungry, before setting out. It's not as cold as it was overnight, with only the occasional, annoying blast of cool air. I keep us traveling northwest along the slopes for as long as possible, until it becomes clear that if we don't scale the hills soon, we'll end up turning north and never reaching the border.

Which is fine by me, but not for Ellie.

She trails behind, muttering her speech over and over, while my mind wanders between everything from Ellie's upcoming death, to my potential immortality, and whether or not dirt is the Land's poop. All things of equal importance.

I mean, all living things poop, right? And the only thing it makes sense for Her to eat is corpses, which turn to dirt after. Ergo, dirt must be Her poop.

So the Academy is actually surrounded by shit.

Yeah, let's never go back there.

My high slowly dissipates as we hike uphill, its final vapors lost to a gust of wind as we trudge over the summit and lay eyes on the border—a thick purple cloud sinking into the valley below.

Ellie freezes in her tracks.

"Ellie?" I take her hand and move my face directly in front of hers.

"It's... it's as bad as before." Her brown eyes quiver as she looks *through* me, like I'm not even there.

"Maybe that's a good sign?" I squeeze her fingers. "If it's not worse?"

How did I suddenly become the optimistic one?

Ellie takes a deep breath, and her eyes shift, focusing on mine. "Maybe? But I can't move my feet."

"What if you close your eyes?"

Ellie inhales through her nose and nods quickly. She closes her eyes, and with her exhale, she takes a step.

I take both her hands in mine, and walking backward with my land-sense as my sight, I slowly guide her down the hill.

My insides knot up completely, twisting tighter with every step I take. Ellie trembles, her eyes squeezed shut and her breath ragged.

"I'm scared, Caeo."

My voice catches in my throat. "Me too. But you came all this way. You won't be able to live with yourself if you don't try."

"But at least I'll live."

I stop walking and bring my hands to her face.

"No, you won't. You'll torture yourself until you build up the courage to try again. And you'll keep doing that, over and over, until the misery takes you or you finally step through."

Ellie's eyes open, focusing on mine through the moisture pooling within them. "I love you, Caeo. I want to spend the rest of my life with you. I don't want to die."

My heart constricts, begging me to take her as far away from here as I possibly can.

But she gave me her strength when mine was lost. It's my turn to do the same for her.

"I won't let you." I wipe her tears away. "After everything you've done, if the Land can't see your heart, if She doesn't think you're worth forgiving, then She deserves all the suffering we're trying to end."

And She better kill me, too, because I'll never forgive Her.

I scoop Ellie into my arms, and before the rational part of my brain has a chance to stop me, I march us the rest of the way down the hill, into the fog.

Part 3

True

Chapter 33

Ellie

Caeo staggers to the ground, almost dropping me, within seconds of entering the fog.

It's impossible to see him through the thick purple haze, even with my face buried against his chest. His fingers strain against me, pinpricks of warmth against the seething cold fury.

A force presses down on us—on me. So much stronger than last time, so much worse.

The sound of a torrential wind fills my ears, drowning out everything else, but there's no breeze on my skin. Only pressure. Crushing, relentless pressure.

Caeo releases me to the ground. Boiling rage sears through me on contact.

I whip my hands back, screaming.

"Ellie!"

Caeo's hands pat desperately against me, pulling me close, his warmth breaking me away from the frigid cold. Then his hand finds mine.

"I'm gonna bond through you to the Land." His words barely break through the roar. He shoves my hand into the ground, and it softens, my fingers sliding in like it's a bowl of jelly.

Boiling hot jelly.

I scream as a pulse shatters my bones.

It resonates through my heart, consuming it. With a hard yank, it drags everything within me toward my fingers, ripping away at the inside of my skin.

A warm blaze travels from my hand up through my arm, interrupting the Land's pull. Blocking it.

Caeo's love, gushing into the Land, through me.

The searing pain where my skin touches the earth diminishes.

"Say your words, Ellie." Caeo's voice, right next to my ear, breaks. His hand digs into mine, pressing it deeper into the earth, his other arm around my torso, holding the rest of me up.

My voice quakes as I force out the foreign words I've practiced countless times, so many that I've forgotten their meaning.

Not good. She needs to *feel* them.

The shrieking wind intensifies, slamming against my eardrums.

I repeat the words, sending along my guilt.

And again, with my sorrow.

And again, my voice growing stronger, with my determination to make things right.

My eyes squeeze shut as She pulls relentlessly, tugging against Caeo's barrier. Every time it cracks, he pours more of his love into it.

Into me.

Into the Land.

My bones creak under Her pressure. I repeat the words again, thinking of Taran, and how all I ever wanted was to help him.

And again, thinking of Owena, knowing her dreams of peace won't truly come to fruition until someone makes my people see the truth.

Of Reid and Emlyn, who won't have a home where they can live happily together until there's peace between our realms.

Of my father, who's unknowingly spent his life violating the

Land, who I have to find a way to reach. To save him from himself.

Of Caeo, who doesn't deserve the pain of losing me.

And of myself.

My purpose.

To make things right.

My heart thuds against my ribs just as a pulse reverberates through Caeo's barrier.

The tugging ceases, withdrawing.

The roar of the wind diminishes. Still there, but not quite as wrathful.

And the soil no longer burns my skin.

The pressure still pushes against me, as it did when I passed through with Taran. But compared to what it was, it's barely noticeable.

"Ellie?"

I open my eyes. The fog's still too thick to see Caeo's face, but his breath's warm against my cheek.

"I think She forgave me!" I yell.

He flinches. "Why are you yelling?"

Right. This is just fog to him.

I lower my voice. "It's really loud for me. We should go."

"Alright. Can you stand?" He tries to pull me up with him, but I don't go anywhere. The pressure's still quite strong.

"I don't think so."

"One second." Caeo's arm unwraps from around my waist, and he shifts in front of me, grabbing my arms and winding them around him. Soft hair brushes against my face.

"Climb on."

I pull myself close, winding my arms around his shoulders and holding on tight. Caeo wobbles as he pushes into a stand and hooks his arms under my legs to support me.

With slow steps, he carries me through the fog.

I close my eyes and snuggle into him, breathing in the scent of his hair. Based on his gait, I'm fairly certain the border's just as intense as it was the first time, but it doesn't feel that way. The Land may still hate what I am, but She's forgiven me. She's given me a chance to fix things. So even though the fog weighs down on me, I feel lighter than air.

"Remember when you carried me to your house?" It was so long ago.

"You were nowhere near as heavy then." Caeo's voice is tight between breaths.

"It's not me—it's the Land."

"Uh huh. I'm bringing a cart next time."

Next time.

My heart lights up with a warm glow. Not only did She let me live, but I can come back, with Caeo. I'll be able to see Taran and Owena again.

I breathe in deep, peaceful breaths. There's still so much for me to do, and I'm under no illusions about how difficult it'll be to convince everyone to stop incanting for good, but in this moment, everything is right.

Caeo stumbles, and my eyes snap open as his grip on my legs tightens.

We're out of the fog.

"You're getting down now," he says quickly, his voice strained. He crouches down, and I slide off his back. He keeps going until he's kneeling on the ground.

He immediately throws himself back onto his feet, retreating into the fog. "Fuck!"

"Caeo? What's wrong?"

His voice is near, but I can't see him at all through the fog, and my body paralyzes the moment I look at it. I squeeze my eyes shut, and with effort, force my hand back through, reaching for him. It lands on his chest.

He wraps his fingers around it. "Everything feels wrong."

"What do you mean? How's it wrong?" A knot twists in my throat. We can't have gone through all that just for Caeo to be unable to come here with me.

"It's all... dead. Like I'm walking on a rotting corpse and breathing its stench."

"But you didn't have any problems here before." Of course, that was before he ever bonded with the Land. But Emlyn lived here for months, and Taran was alright when he kidnapped me. "Maybe you'll get used to it?"

Caeo groans, then my arm bends as he steps forward. The second he breaks through the fog, I pull him close.

"Don't hug me. I don't want to throw up on you."

I squeeze him tighter.

"You think I'm joking, but I'm not." He frees himself from my grasp and moves away. "Fuck."

I rub my hand along his back, then turn from both him and the fog so I can open my eyes.

The first thing that strikes me is the color. Despite this being the world I spent my entire life in, the last month in the faelands has left it a pale imitation of what life's supposed to be. As dull as the Academy when I first laid eyes on it.

My heart constricts as I take in the view. The bland greens, the dirty browns. How will I ever paint again? Every shade feels so... empty.

But I can't dwell on that. Not now.

The valley we stand in continues westward into a forest, with hills to the north and south. If the Order of Incanters set up anywhere to fight the fae army, it would be beyond the southern hills—that's where the fae were, on their side. Heading straight there, however, seems unwise at the moment. They'd see us coming, and with Caeo like this...

The sound of him retching draws my gaze back to him. So far, it's only a dry heave, but I tuck his hair behind his ear anyway. His very pointy, very fae, ear.

Even if he glamours himself, we can't risk going to the Order's camp with him like this. Not only is there a chance someone will figure him out, but he'd be completely helpless against even the smallest amount of trouble.

And I'm never incanting again.

"Come on, Caeo. We need to find cover in the forest before someone comes patrolling. Then we'll figure out what to do next."

"Uh huh. Yep." He looks up at me, his face tinged green. "Are you sure I can't just wait for you here, in the fog, while you go talk to your dad? I wasn't really looking forward to meeting him, anyway."

I wrap my hand around his arm and pull him the rest of the way up.

"If you aren't feeling better by tomorrow... maybe. But for now, you're staying. I'm sure you just need time to adjust."

Caeo lets out another groan as I drag him toward the trees.

Chapter 34

Taran

I thought I'd already hit my lowest point—when I failed to stop my mother, my brother and Emlyn both hated me, and the Land tore me away from Ellie, my only spot of happiness. But now, Owena's completely demolished me, and I see how wrong I was.

That torment was alive. Relentlessly writhing within me, with an energy that wouldn't let go. It was exhausting, but no matter how much it strangled me, it never tired, never released me to the hollow depths below.

It's dead down here.

An eternal abyss.

The occasional burst of anger or grief tumbles down from above, screaming as it falls, only to be swallowed by the void before it can pull me out. And through it all, my mother's endless tugs. Slow and unyielding, peeling away my bond with the Land. How much longer until it's hers? Days? Not that it matters anymore.

I don't even feel the sweltering heat of Ystyr anymore. The weight of the air is the same as my body. The soldiers push it along, and it moves where it's supposed to. It walks when they want it to walk, sits when they want it to sit, and drinks when they force water down its throat.

It doesn't eat.

When it's time to sleep, they throw me to the ground, and I fade into nothingness.

On the second day, my captors stop shoving me as much. A guiding hand presses against my arm instead of a forceful strike. Perhaps they've grown tired of testing my silence.

The silence *she* bound me with.

I stumble to the ground, tripping on a root. With my arms tied and unable to catch me, I plow face first into the damp, decaying leaves that layer the forest floor.

They announce a break as someone helps me up, pulling me to a seated position. Yesterday, they would've left me there. Or kicked me.

A strand of curiosity tugs at me. I lift my head.

The landscape is unchanged, still the suffocating jungle that stinks of rotting moisture, the stench that now drips off of me. Outside of a couple nearby guards, most of my captors stand in a group about twenty paces ahead. My gaze lands on Owena, kneeling before a soldier sitting in front of her. She brings her fingers to the sides of his face, the same way she touched mine when she kissed me.

I look away.

Pain.

That's all that reaches me in the abyss. A throbbing pain, reverberating through the nothingness, echoing against my ribcage.

At some point, someone pulls me to my feet, and I'm walking again, my legs somehow still functioning.

The day continues in a daze, with night falling several similar breaks later. Most of the soldiers sit around a campfire, their conversation muffled by the incessant chirring of insects. I could make out their words if I cared, but there's no point. Just like there's no point to the one guard sitting on a fallen log nearby.

From the moment Owena cursed me, I've been helpless against this many trained fighters. Even in Aedys, my shaping wouldn't have been enough—only willbending. Any attempt at escape would end in swift capture and another beating. They didn't even bother to take my sword.

A soft voice breaks through the sounds of the forest.

"You can join the others. I'll watch him."

I look up, catching a glimpse of Owena, then look away. The guard's feet brush against the foliage as he departs.

She lowers herself next to me. "You need to eat, Taran."

I turn further away.

Owena tugs at the wool ropes binding my wrists behind my back. A moment later, my arms fall forward as the sharp pain of my muscles releasing burns through my shoulders. I hiss—except not a sound comes out.

She puts a cloth laden with food onto the dead leaves in front of me. Slices of a dried, unfamiliar fruit, a pile of nuts, and some kind of wafer. I rub at the tightness in my shoulder, if only to give a small part of me relief from the agony chewing me up inside.

I ignore the food. I'm not hungry.

"If you eat, I'll explain everything."

I bring my eyes to hers. I want to see heartless voids within, to make hating her easier. But all that's there are infinite wells of sorrow.

Why?

"Please, Taran." Her voice breaks, and against everything, my heart fractures along with it.

I take a bite of the wafer. It's bland. Soldier's food.

Owena takes a breath, and her eyes drift to the ground.

"I would have explained sooner, but I needed to get Barri's men on my side first. He used to be my guard, so I couldn't have asked for my father to send anyone better. He was willing to trust me and convince his men to do the same."

A silent scoff puffs out of me.

Her eyes come back to mine, harder than before. "My father cursed all of them, Taran. That's what he does. He made half of them deaf, and the other half would die if they succumbed to a willbending. I've spent the entire day breaking their curses."

My stomach knots. I'd heard of Dryfid's cruelty, but this? He doomed half of these men to death to protect himself.

And I would have killed them trying to defend us.

This time, I break her gaze.

"It would have been impossible to get anywhere near my father so long as you were capable of willbending, and if I didn't bring you with me, he'd just as likely throw me in a cell as to speak to me. I had to curse you, to make you unable to speak, so he would let us close to him."

But your curse...

I squeeze my eyes shut when no words come out. In the darkness, it becomes clear. The things she said, always drawing me in before severing the connection.

"You're not a king, Taran." Her voice wavers. "You should be, but you never accepted the title."

She inhales sharply, and I look back at her. Tears pool in her eyes.

"I could curse you so long as you weren't my friend or foe. Something in-between. I wanted to tell you, but your distrust was the only thing that made it work. If I had, it would have ruined everything."

Her eyes are pleading, begging me to understand.

On some level, I do.

She made the hard decisions I couldn't. We're here because I couldn't do what was necessary for the greater good. I couldn't bend my people. Couldn't face my mother.

So she found another solution. All she had to do was use me. Twist me.

Manipulate me.

It hurts so much. A raw, blistering agony searing within.

The same pain bleeds out of her eyes.

She reaches for my hand, and it takes all my strength to pull it away. My weakness is what got me here. Absolving her would only confirm it.

Owena's shoulders slump, her eyes closing. Her voice comes out a jagged whisper. "I'm sorry, Taran. There wasn't any other way. If the price of peace is my heart, then it's my duty to pay it."

The darkness of her eyes pours into mine.

"I hope you can find it within you to forgive me."

She leaves me by myself, taking what's left of my heart with her as she disappears beyond the trees.

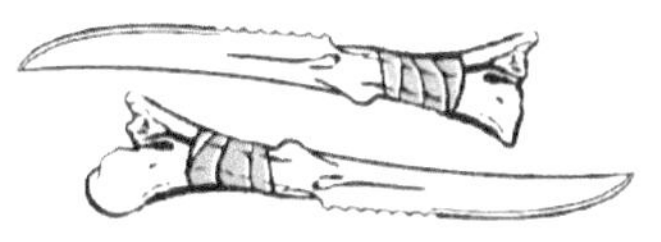

Chapter 35

Emlyn

Jefferies's body falls from my shoulders to the ground with a heavy thump, and I wipe the sweat from my brow with the back of my hand. Hidden in the tall grass at the base of the hill, beyond what I hope the mortals will easily spot from their camp in the morning—it's the best I can do. I've got nothing left.

Lucky for me, Alexis actually cares about Reid and Ellie, so she let me go, realizing that if she murdered me, she'd never find out what happened to them. The watchmen still hadn't filled the gap in their line when I snuck out, and the dregs of my waterskin were just enough for me to distract the closest one with an earth shaping, then glamour myself and the body in darkness as I carried it away.

A nauseous guard disappearing on his way back to camp won't increase patrols the way a corpse will.

My head spins as I drag myself back to the safety of Reid's arms. When I reach the summit, he's sitting a few dozen paces to my right, hugging himself tight as he stares into the valley. I planned it that way; it would've been impossible to sneak up on him if I'd gone straight up.

"Looking for something?" A refreshing breeze gusts through my shirt as I crouch behind him.

He startles, almost falling over. "Ancients' splintery cracks!"

Then he scrambles up, pulling me with him as he throws his arms around me. Before I can sink in, he pushes away, his fingers digging into my shoulders as he scans me all over. "Are you alright? They didn't notice you, did they? I lost track of you once you reached the camp."

"Relax, Reid. I'm..." I want to say 'fine,' but can't. So I tug him back, burying myself in his warmth. "I found her. She's fine. She'll look for us on patrol tomorrow. But..." My breath catches. "I had to kill someone."

Reid stills, then his arms tighten around me. "Em... It's not your fault. If I hadn't let you go—"

I lift my head, meeting his worried eyes. "Don't do that. It was my choice. I did it. Don't blame yourself."

His face softens as he brings his hand up, brushing my cheek with his thumb. "Alright. But you're not alone in this anymore."

With a deep, nutmeg-scented inhale, I nod, then nuzzle back into him, letting the gentle circles he traces on my back draw me into a world where nothing exists but his love.

"THEY'RE COMING," I call down to Reid. I'm perched on one of the higher branches of a large oak tree where I told Alexis we'd be, and we've spent the day sitting around waiting. While I'm partly up here for the view, it's mainly because mortals tend not to look up.

Which is stupid, because they're fighting fae, and we fucking live in trees. Sure, it's usually in some kind of house, not just precariously sleeping on a branch like I've been doing, but still. They apparently haven't realized that.

Reid spent half the night up here with me, until a perilous moment where he almost fell to his death, after which I made him curl up down below. If he gets found, they'll just bring him in for questioning; it'd be a horrible turn of events, but something we can recover from, unlike dying. I'd be lucky if they killed me on sight. Torture and imprisonment are far more likely.

He gets to his feet and moves away from the tree trunk, stretching as he does.

"Wrong way." I love him, but yeesh. He has no sense of direction. "To your right."

He tilts his head up. "Are you coming down?"

"Not until I'm sure they aren't gonna kill me. So pretend I'm somewhere else."

Alexis had told me she'd try to get patrol duty with Sophie, her former roommate. Mainly because she couldn't come alone and Sophie already knows the situation—I guess Alexis somehow persuaded her not to reveal anything—but that girl once set my arm on fire without even speaking. I've gone through so much water that I can't waste any "just in case" I need to defend myself, and with Reid not incanting anymore, I'm not inclined to trust she won't burn me alive the instant she lays eyes on me. I'm sure if she tried, he *would*, but I'd really prefer to avoid that entirely. Otherwise, the Land might see him as an evil mortal again.

Also, fire: bad.

"Reid!" Alexis runs over and throws her arms around him.

Sophie trails behind, her blond hair tied in a tight bun that matches her expression. They're both wearing the boring gray uniforms of rankless soldiers, a simple shirt and trousers. Sabers hang from both their belts, though I doubt they're any better at using them than Reid was.

"Where's the fae?" Sophie asks as Reid and Alexis separate.

Really? They know my name.

"Emlyn's… around. He wasn't sure you wouldn't kill him."

"It depends," Sophie says, glancing between the nearby trees.

"One of last night's watch is missing. Did he have anything to do with that?"

Fuck.

Reid crosses his arms. "Not that I know of. He snuck in with some merchants."

My grip on the branch loosens as a strange stillness overtakes my chest. I hadn't asked him to lie for me. To basically become an accomplice, betraying his people to keep me in his friends' good graces. It's weird to have that kind of support.

I wipe my eyes as Alexis tugs at his hair. "Look at you. You're a mess. What happened? Did you find Ellie and Caeo?"

"It's a long story." He sighs. "We caught up with Ellie, and then found Caeo, but I haven't seen them in weeks."

Sophie and Alexis exchange glances.

"I think you're gonna need to give us the whole story," Alexis says.

"Fine. But then you need to tell me what's been going on here." He sits under my tree, and the girls join him. Then he launches into the tale of everything that happened after we last saw them.

Reid barely mentions me. Like I wasn't even there. It's mostly passive-aggressive commentary on Ellie falling for Taran and how he did everything he could to stop it, only vaguely mentioning how we were trying to overthrow a warmongering, psycho queen. Because that wasn't the important part.

Then he gets to how he rescued Caeo from his wedding and found out his curse was broken by the princess from the southern realm, and that she promised to break Ellie's. But I was injured, so he stayed with me while the others all fled.

"And that was... three weeks ago? Maybe a little longer?" Reid shrugs. "So I have no idea what happened to them."

"Wait. I don't understand," Sophie says, but I can't read her expression from this angle. "Why did you stay with Emlyn instead of Ellie and Caeo?"

I don't have to see Reid to know he's blushing.

"Uh…"

Alexis chuckles, her braids bouncing as she shakes her head. "Oh, honey, you fell for him, didn't you?"

"Maybe?"

MAYBE?

I'm about to jump down there and remind him it's definitely not a *maybe*, but my healthy sense of self-preservation holds me back. Besides—he knows I'm listening, and that's probably enough to make him squirm.

"Look. Emlyn's not bad—he's been trying to stop this war the entire time, and he never meant you any harm. He's never seen humans as his enemy, and he wasn't trying to deceive you. He just thought you'd have fun."

Alexis laughs sharply. "I mean, I *did*. That was probably the most *fun* I've ever had. He certainly knows what he's doing." She pauses, eyeing Reid. It's clear we don't have to worry about her, so I creep through the branches for a better view of Sophie.

Reid sighs. "Yes, he does. Very much."

A beat passes before Alexis takes his hand. "Then I'll *try* to forgive him. For your sake."

"Thank you." He turns to Sophie. "How about you? Do you promise you won't kill him or turn him in?"

Sophie takes her damn time answering, her jaw jutting out before loosening with a long exhale. "Alright. I promise."

Finally. I'd love to know what's going on in her mind, but with Alexis and Reid on my side, I should be safe for now.

I swing to the mossy, fern-speckled ground, landing on my feet next to Reid. All three of them startle back.

"Great!" I plop down, meeting Reid's eyes as I wrap my arm around him. "*Maybe?* Really? After all those 'I love you's?'"

"Not now, Em." Reid makes a show of pulling away, but gives my leg a squeeze and leaves his hand there.

"Whatever." I turn to Alexis and Sophie, both recovering from their shock into annoyed expressions, though Alexis's has a hint of amusement breaking through. "So what's going on with the war, then?"

"Why should we tell you?" Sophie demands. "What will you do with that information?"

Ugh. This woman makes it so hard not to hate mortals. "No idea. My plans ended with getting Alexis to talk to Reid. I'm improvising here, trying not to get killed. Some information would be really helpful in doing that."

Sophie frowns and doesn't offer anything else.

Maybe I shouldn't have come down here. I shoot Alexis a hopeful smile.

"Come on, Lex," Reid says. "Please?"

I meet her gaze. "It's up to Reid, but we could still do that three-way you were hoping for in exchange?" I wasn't planning on trading sex for favors anymore, but since he was briefly into the idea, maybe he still wants to? It's about the same as playing a game of pick-up sticks to me.

Her eyes widen.

"Fuck, Emlyn," Reid mutters, rubbing his face.

"Yeah, that. Exactly. So what do you say?"

Alexis sighs, then rolls her eyes. "Sure, why not?"

An unexpected disappointment tweaks in my chest as she sits back, getting more comfortable. *Maybe she wasn't agreeing to the sex? Maybe just to talk?*

My hand finds Reid's, thumbing his fingers as she rambles about fae attacks starting a couple of weeks ago. At first, the Order squashed them pretty quickly, but then things escalated, stretching them thin. The Academy was ordered to the front, arriving four days ago.

"It's been mostly drills and patrolling for us. The Order's set up right in front of the fog, and there's been some fighting, but the higher-ups think the fae are holding back. Everyone's waiting for the real push."

I take my hand from Reid and chew at my thumb. "Hmm. They're probably trying to acclimate as many of the troops as possible."

"Acclimate?" Sophie asks.

I shoot the unhelpful mortal a glare. "It's really difficult for us to come here, and outside of myself and maybe a few others, no fae have done so in over twenty years. They're probably cycling through soldiers until they get enough who won't be too busy emptying their stomachs to fight. Then they'll push—probably at night. They're hoping to overwhelm you since most of you lack experience."

Alexis raises her brow. "Why at night?"

I shrug. "Outside of the obvious—interrupting your sleep— mortals can't see shit in the dark. We have a significant advantage."

Sophie grabs Alexis's arm. "We have to tell this to someone."

"And say what? That a friendly fae randomly decided to share battle tactics with us?"

Huh. I guess I did do that, didn't I? Probably shouldn't have. But before I can do anything to rectify that mistake, the sound of feet shuffling along the forest floor catches my attention.

I lift my hand, quieting whatever the mortals are arguing about.

Voices. Male and female.

"What's wrong?" Reid asks.

I get to my feet. "Someone's approaching."

"There shouldn't be anyone else on patrol here," Alexis says. "Not for another couple bells."

"They're coming from the other direction," I mutter. *They sound familiar...* "Stay here. I'll be right back."

"Em, wait!"

I don't. Not sure why Reid expected me to. It doesn't matter, because he follows me anyway, with the girls right on his heels.

That's probably fine. Frankly, they can take care of themselves better than I can right now.

It *does* mean that a stealthy approach isn't happening. Oh well. At least I don't have to go very far before I make out what the voices are saying.

"Emlyn's on his way over, and the others are following him." A male voice that sounds on the verge of throwing up.

So... male, fae, and knows me.

It's definitely not Taran, and there's really only one other option that makes any sense. I pick up my pace, and after I round a couple more large trees, I spot them.

Ellie and Caeo. Just strolling through the forest.

Well, maybe not strolling. Caeo has the aura of someone experiencing this realm's death-stench for the first time. Since his land-sense is obviously still working, they must've crossed pretty recently. Less than a bell, I'd guess, by mortal reckoning.

How'd they end up here? It makes sense, since Ellie's dad's probably just south of us. But my skin prickles—this feels too convenient. Could the Land have known they were coming when She encouraged us to head here?

I stumble forward as Reid plows into me from behind.

"Ow. Watch where you're going."

"Sorry." His hand lingers on my arm. "I didn't see you because of the tree. Why are you just standing here?"

"Reid!" Ellie calls, because I wasn't important.

He stops fussing with me and looks toward them. "Ellie? Caeo!" He runs off right as Alexis and Sophie round the tree, and I sidle up against it just in time to avoid a collision.

They don't even look at me, heading straight for their friends.

I sink to the ground, resting my back against the tree trunk. I don't need to be part of their reunion; I barely know them. It's more concerning what it means that Taran isn't with them.

My stomach twists. *It's probably nothing.* Taran doesn't have any reason to be here. They do.

No. He *does* have a reason. If what I heard is still true, and his mother's with the bulk of the army, then she's likely just on the other side of the border.

"Emlyn!"

I look up, and Ellie's waving at me. Fucking Ellie.

I drag myself over to all the relieved mortals and the rather ill-looking half fae.

"Do you know what's wrong with Caeo?" Ellie asks as I approach.

"Of course I do. He's finally realized how disgusting it is here." I kick the revolting dirt for good measure.

Caeo groans. "I've never felt so horrible in my life. It's like I'm walking through a cloud of death."

"Yeah... Do you have any water from Aedys with you? You can drink some of that and you'll feel a little better, but once you run out, you won't be able to glamour yourself, do any shaping, or use your land-sense... so, not the best solution. I should probably just find the horses so you can get something between you and the ground. Unless Reid wants to carry you."

Reid looks at him. "I guess I can?"

"I'm great, by the way, in case you were wondering. Even though

I was practically dead the last time you saw me."

"Good for you," Caeo mutters. "I'll be happier about it when I stop feeling like I'm dying."

Ellie puts her hand on my arm. "I'm very happy to see you, Emlyn, and how much you've recovered. I would love to hear all about it, but I think we *all* have a lot to catch up on." She eyes Sophie warily. Guess she has some sense, at least.

I sigh. As much as I'd like some news about Taran, I do *not* want to sit through another round of mortals playing catch-up. I look back at Caeo. "Your land-sense still working?"

"Yeah."

"Can you pick up a couple horses canoodling somewhere nearby?"

Sophie frowns, because that's her response to everything I say, apparently.

"I can sense them," he says.

"Great." I kneel with my back to him. "Climb on."

"Are you serious?"

"Trust me, you'll feel better once you stop touching the ground."

Caeo wraps his arms around my neck. "Fuck me," he mumbles.

"No! Don't you dare say it." Reid didn't even give me a chance to open my mouth.

"Fine, I won't." I mostly just do it for his reaction at this point, anyway. Though part of me will always be a little disappointed I'll never get to tell Taran I fucked his brother.

I push myself to my feet, securing Caeo's weight with my arms. He's lighter than Reid, but still—hopefully the horses aren't very far. "Which way are we going?"

Caeo gives me directions, and I tell all the mortals we'll see them later—Ellie insists on coming, too, but Sophie, of all people, convinces her not to. I'm certain she just wants to hear Ellie's story without any questionable fae around. Probably hoping for something she can share with her superiors.

Whatever. I'll get the details from Caeo.

"So what are you doing here?" I ask once we're beyond mortal hearing. "Where's Taran?"

"Why don't you tell me about how you kissed Ellie against her wishes, first?"

I tilt my head to glance at him. "Really? That's what you care about right now? You've kissed me, too, in case you forgot."

"Yeah, by choice."

And I'm sure Ellie appreciates your reasoning. "Look. I don't know what she told you. She was wandering around your mom's palace, and I found her before the guards did. There were more than I could fight, so I did the only thing I could think of."

"And that was kiss her?"

"It was a wedding! It's expected for people to sneak off and fuck where they aren't supposed to. And it worked. They just told us to get out of there and moved on."

"Uh huh."

"Hey, I didn't *want* to kiss her. She's basically at the top of my list of people I have zero desire to fuck. So get over it."

"What do you have against Ellie?"

Ancients. Is he serious? I adjust my hold on his legs to keep him from slipping. "Now you're offended I *don't* want to fuck her?"

"You're acting like she's disgusting, so yeah, I am."

"She's not, I just don't like her. She wasn't good for Taran, made my job harder, Reid's life miserable, and she incanted in Aedys, right next to me, TWICE—which, if you don't know, feels like being repeatedly stabbed in the stomach by dozens of arrows. *And* she withheld pain medicine from me."

Caeo doesn't say anything for a moment.

Maybe I could've said that in a nicer way.

"I don't think she realizes you dislike her that much," he eventually says. When I don't respond, he continues. "She'll probably try to make it up to you when she finds out."

"When you tell her, you mean?"

"Yeah, basically."

Great. That's the last thing I need.

I finally spot the horses up ahead. I call out to Daylily, and they both trot over as I kneel to let Caeo get off me. He groans when his feet touch the forest floor.

"How long until this stops feeling so horrible?"

"Took me a few days. You'll probably need to sleep in a tree. It's still pretty terrible, but nowhere near as bad as being on the ground."

"Wonderful."

I turn just in time to catch his grimace. "Is the sarcasm worth the pain?"

"Not really."

I explain the situation to the horses. All their gear is with our stuff, so Caeo will have to ride completely bareback for now. Daylily volunteers.

I help him onto her back, and he immediately breathes a sigh of relief. After I show him where to grip her mane, we start walking back to the mortals.

Now that I've addressed Caeo's ridiculous concerns, I try my question again. "So... Taran. Where is he?"

"Hopefully somewhere in Ystyr by now, but I really don't know."

I frown, glancing up at him. "Ystyr? Why's he going there?"

"To help Owena kill her father, so they can get married and unite the realms."

I stop so fast I nearly trip.

"What?"

Daylily comes to a halt, a concerned eye turning my way.

"It was Owena's plan," Caeo continues, adjusting his position on Daylily's back. "To keep Aedys away from our mother without having to confront her at all."

That's certainly one way to do it. An ingenious way, really.

I bring my hands up to my face, tenting them over my nose. "I'm gonna need a moment." I close my eyes and exhale, but laughter comes out instead. *Ancients, he's serious?*

Of course he is. His face isn't twisting in pain like it normally does when he lies.

"How long ago did you split up?" I ask.

"About a week and a half, I'd guess."

Unless they were really far north, that should've been plenty of time for Taran to get to Ystyr.

"And you got here today?"

"Yep."

"To do what, exactly?"

Caeo sighs, rubbing the strands of Daylily's mane between his fingers. "Ellie plans on telling her father the truth about incanting and convincing him to stop. To get everyone to stop."

"Really? That's a terrible idea, at least as long as we're still attacking them."

"She promised the Land she would."

Fucking Ellie. She just can't stop trying to fix everything. I guess it's admirable, but she's gotta learn to pick her battles better.

I start walking again, clicking my tongue to let the horses know they should follow. "I take it that means she's not keen on waiting?"

"Not really. She was hoping her father was here with the army."

"He almost certainly is, but Alexis and Sophie can probably confirm that."

The conversation dies as various thoughts swirl through my mind. I can barely wrap my head around the idea of Taran marrying Owena. He must be desperate. If he only knew all the shit I've done with her...

Anyway, that definitely hadn't happened before we left Aedys. It would've been a seismic enough of an event that Caeo would've noticed it, too, if it'd happened before he left.

Perhaps not enough time has passed. Perhaps they haven't found Ystyr's king yet. But I also can't imagine how they'd kill the man. I got as close to Dryfid as physically possible—twenty-eight times—and still didn't have a chance. Not without giving my life.

As much as I hate to think it, it doesn't seem wise to assume Taran and Owena will succeed. But even if I left right now, it's incredibly unlikely I'd get to Ywelyn before them. I can only trust that Owena knows what she's doing and won't get Taran killed.

The mortals are sitting in a circle, still chatting, by the time we return. Ellie's face lights up as she sees Caeo, looking significantly less sickly than when we left now that he's been off the ground a while, but she doesn't interrupt the ongoing conversation by greeting us. Instead, she turns to Alexis.

"So how exactly did you explain our disappearance? Do my parents know what happened?"

Alexis glances at Sophie, who averts her gaze. "They know you're missing, but they don't think it's related to fae at all."

"What does that mean?"

Alexis bounces with her shrug. "I told Professor Mallory that you and Caeo had a messy breakup, and in your grief, you and Reid ran off to be together."

Reid and Ellie respond in unison, their eyes popping out of their heads. "WHAT?"

I clap my hands together, laughing. "I'm so glad I made it back for this part."

Reid glowers at me while Ellie keeps pestering Alexis. "Why did you tell them *that*?"

"What else could I have possibly said that'd make any sense? If I told them the truth, they'd have sent the entire Order looking for you, and if they found you, they'd never let you rescue Caeo. And they would've killed Emlyn, which I already knew Reid would never forgive me for."

"Thank you for that," I say, patting Alexis's shoulder as I sit between her and Reid.

She glares at me.

Alright. Still not forgiven, then. Whatever. That's not important right now. What's important is figuring out what to do next, and it'll probably require me to do something rather perilous. It's not like anyone else is gonna step up.

Unless...

I meet Ellie's gaze.

"We need to talk about ending this war."

Chapter 36

Ellie

My stomach clenches as Emlyn fixes his gaze on me, the silence broken only by a snort from Caeo's horse. He clearly expects something from me, but I'm not sure why—it's not as if I'm in charge.

I clear my throat. "Taran and Owena are going to end the war, not me. I'm just supposed to get everyone to stop incanting." *Just. Like it's that easy.*

"Which you can't do until the war ends," he says, cocking his head to the side.

Alexis tosses her braids back. "You're serious about that?"

I take the opening to turn to her. I can hardly believe we found everyone so soon after crossing the border. After what they told me, it makes sense that Alexis is here, but I hadn't expected to see Reid and Emlyn ever again. That we're all together, sitting in a circle— hope sparks within me. Maybe this is fate. Like some higher power intended us to be here.

That can only be a good thing, right?

"Yes. I promised the Land I would, and I meant it. It's awful, Alexis. You've seen what it does here, but it's so much worse where She's actually still alive. As long as people keep incanting, there will always be fae that want to fight us. To stop us."

Sophie raises her brow. "Still alive? What are you talking about?"

My lips press together. I don't know what to make of Sophie's change in behavior. She hated me before all of this started, and it's honestly shocking she didn't reveal everything to Headmaster Gleese the second Reid left the Academy to come after me. I can only assume Alexis somehow talked her out of it, but I haven't had the chance to dig for details. As it is, I need all the support I can get, so confronting her now seems unwise.

"In the fae realms, everything's overflowing with life," I say. "The colors are brighter. Richer. You can *feel* the Land's energy flowing through everything, because She's alive there. Here, She's dead."

I glance around, taking in the truth of my words. Everything looks as if it were painted with watered-down hues. Will our world ever look normal to me again, or am I doomed to spend my life longing for the vibrancy of the faelands?

"So dead," Caeo mutters from atop Emlyn's horse. An ache twists through my heart at how much he's suffering right now.

I turn back to Sophie and Alexis's doubtful faces. "We can't change that, not without letting the fae take over our realm. But we *can* stop incanting."

Alexis's jaw tightens while Sophie looks away, tugging a wrinkle out of her gray shirt.

If I can't convince them, how can I hope to convince my father?

Alexis opens her hands. "Let's say you're right. The only way anyone will agree to stop incanting is if it's guaranteed the fae will never attack us again. We're defenseless without it."

"As I said," Emlyn emphasizes, not even glancing up while playing with Reid's fingers. "The war needs to end first."

"See?" Alexis gestures toward him. "Even the fae agrees."

"I have a name."

I shoot a glare at Emlyn before locking eyes with Alexis. It's his fault everyone's looking to me; he could at least offer something helpful. "Once Taran and Owena unite the realms and become King and Queen, it practically will be. They both want peace, and they're young. They should rule for thousands of years."

"But we only have your word to go by, Ellie." Alexis presses her fingers against my knee. "I want to believe it's that simple, but people won't just believe some girl, no matter who your father is."

My chest constricts in frustration. "In that case, Taran made Caeo his heir, so he should be able to speak for him. Right?" I glance up at Caeo.

His face shifts deeper into green. "Uh... maybe? If no one kills me first."

The words bruise. *Maybe it was silly to feel so hopeful.*

"Wait." Emlyn drops Reid's hand, snapping his head at Caeo. "Taran made you his heir?"

The horse shifts beneath him as Caeo raises his brow warily. "Yes?"

"And you've bonded to the Land? You can shape?"

"Yeah."

"Can you bend?"

"Not as well as Taran, but yeah."

Emlyn runs his hands along his sandy-blond braids. "Well, that changes everything."

My pulse quickens—I don't like where this is going. "What are you talking about?"

Emlyn gestures to Caeo. "As Taran's heir, he should be more powerful than his mother now. She's supposedly with the army, right across the border. We don't have to wait for Taran—we can end the war. Today."

"What?" Caeo sits up so fast the horse startles, taking a few nervous steps back.

I'm on my feet before I realize it. "No. Absolutely not." I promised him I'd keep him away from his mother. Not make him go directly to her.

Emlyn barks something in the Tongue, and the horse whinnies before settling down. "Let him speak for himself."

"Em," Reid warns, squeezing his leg.

Caeo adjusts his grip on the horse's mane before looking at Emlyn. "If Taran couldn't take her out, how can I possibly have a chance?"

Emlyn arches his eyebrow. "Have you met Taran?"

I bite back an outburst at that remark. Emlyn's put down and disrespected Taran every chance he gets. With a best friend like that, it's no wonder Taran feels alone with his burdens. But arguing won't help—I need to think clearly.

"Won't the entire army be protecting her?" I ask. "Caeo can't bend that many people."

Emlyn gets to his feet, brushing off his pants. "He doesn't need to. Taran would, because practically everyone in Aedys knows who he is. Hardly anyone knows Caeo, especially if he's glamoured." He crosses his arms and leans against a tree trunk. "I can probably walk him right in."

"You?" Reid asks, straightening up. At some point, I started wringing my hands. I clamp them tight, lowering them to my waist. Alexis and Sophie keep their mouths shut, their eyes darting between the rest of us.

Emlyn shrugs. "I'm not gonna be so heartless as to suggest he goes by himself."

Caeo looks like he's about to fall off the horse. I rush to his side, my heart racing. After everything we did to get him away from his mother, this sounds beyond reckless.

"You don't have to do this," I say, "and I'll go with you if you do."

Emlyn pushes off the tree. "Uh… no. Caeo and I can walk right in—sort of." He tilts his hand back and forth. "You would give us away almost immediately." He glances at Reid, whose mouth's halfway open. "You too. Sorry. The fae over there are much more familiar with how mortals feel compared to everyone else we've encountered so far. I'm not letting you risk it."

I glare at Emlyn, but Caeo takes my hand. His eyes are softer now, some of the panic dissipating.

"He's right," he says, his voice lighter than I expected. "Besides—I don't think the Land will be happy if you go back without fulfilling your promise."

My throat cinches. *He can't actually want to do this, can he?*

I swallow, tracing the gentle lines of his face. Still crimped in places, but in the same way as before, when it was just the nausea. His breathing's calm, his fingers steady around mine.

As terrifying as it is, maybe it's what he needs. Just like I needed to face the Land. I can't deny him that. I need to support him, like he supported me.

I glance back at Emlyn. "What exactly does Caeo need to do?"

He settles back against the tree. "It's just a matter of bending her before she can bend him. Tell her to keep her mouth shut, then force her to relinquish all claim to the throne. After that, he can summon all the captains, and the Land can confirm he's Taran's heir." He looks to Caeo. "You can order them all to withdraw on his behalf."

"And no one will realize I'm his heir before that?"

"Not through their regular land-sense, no. That'd be rather impractical. The Land typically wants heirs to remain safe."

"But your mother—" My grip on Caeo's hand tightens. "She'll recognize you."

He looks from me to Emlyn.

Emlyn bobs his head in a slow nod. "Yeah, probably. There's no real way to avoid that. But the range of your land-sense should be larger than hers. Once you find her, we'll just have to hurry."

"I'm really not liking this plan," Reid says, standing. He moves closer to Emlyn. "Can't we just wait for Taran and Owena to unite the realms?"

Emlyn rubs Reid's arm before taking his hand. "There's no way of knowing when that'll happen. Or if they'll even succeed. With every passing day, it's more and more likely my people will push for real, and then a lot of people will start dying. On both sides."

The air turns heavy, sinking around us all. That's ultimately what we set out to do all those weeks ago. Stop a war. If we really meant to, we can't turn away now.

"So we're just supposed to sit here while you two risk your lives?" Reid asks.

"You could come with me to talk to my father," I offer. I'd hoped to have Caeo with me, and while we could wait, it'd be better to get it over with rather than sit around worrying. And it'll give my father more time to warm up to the idea of potentially having a half fae son-in-law someday.

Maybe I shouldn't mention that until I'm certain he accepts the truth.

Reid looks between Emlyn and me, his uncertainty clear in the scrunch of his brow.

I force a smile. "I'd really appreciate the support."

He sighs, then rubs his face. "Yeah, fine. I'll go," he says. "So this is it, then? This is what we're doing?"

No one answers, all eyes turning to me. Even Alexis and Sophie, who've been so quiet I'd almost forgotten they were here.

Why are they acting like it's up to me? It makes sense that Caeo would want my reassurances, but Emlyn? This was his idea to begin with.

Yet, the way he's playing with Reid's fingers, averting his gaze when I try to meet it… That doesn't mean he can't be scared, or want an excuse not to do it. Especially after what happened last time he went after the queen. But this time, it's his plan. He gets to make the decisions. And as worried as I am for Caeo, I know he can do this. That he needs to, as much as I wish he didn't.

So I take a deep breath. "Yes. We're doing this."

Alexis claps her hands on her thighs. "Alright then. We can say we found you while on patrol." She gets to her feet, and Sophie follows, looking hesitant.

My heart trips over itself. "You mean right now?"

Alexis shrugs. "There's no reason to wait, is there?"

Caeo, Reid, and Emlyn all start talking at once.

"I'm gonna need a little more time to—"

"They don't need to go right now—"

"I can think of a few reasons—"

Alexis holds her palms up, shaking her head. "Alright, alright. Tomorrow, then?" She glances at Sophie. "We should get back, though, before anyone wonders what's taking us so long."

Sophie rubs her arm, nodding. "I think we're supposed to check in about half a bell from now. We'll be cutting it close."

I exhale, but the knot in my chest barely loosens. Caeo squeezes my hand, and I glance at him, biting my lip. His brow crinkles slightly, but his eyes look calm.

There's more gray in them than there was this morning.

"Alright," I say. "Tomorrow it is."

AFTER ALEXIS AND SOPHIE LEAVE, Emlyn and Reid show us where they've been camping. Emlyn has about two jugs of water from Aedys with him, but he's *very* stingy about sharing with Caeo, despite us only having a couple waterskins that probably won't last till nightfall. According to him, he's already gone through half the water they brought, when he was hoping it would last several weeks. I remind him they're planning on going back tomorrow, but he insists that anything could happen between now and then, so they can't waste it. It seems overly paranoid to me, but Reid and Caeo both agree with him.

The little water Caeo *does* drink makes him feel better, at least for a little while. I end up sharing Reid's supply of local water so Caeo can have as much of ours as possible. The one time Caeo tried it, he immediately spat it out, then threw up everything he drank earlier.

Despite him feeling better while on the horse, she can't, or *won't*, carry him all day. So he ends up spending most of his time slumped on his stomach over a thick tree branch, completely miserable. At least it's low enough that I can rub his back while standing on the ground.

All the optimism I had from surviving the border is gone, with the reality of our future sinking in. Even completely ignoring my worries about tomorrow, how can we possibly end up living happily ever after? If we end the war, it still won't be safe for Caeo or Emlyn to be here. People don't change overnight, and it'll take time for everyone to stop seeing fae as the enemy. Both of them will have to hoard water just to glamour themselves to be here, and every time they go back to resupply, they'll have to suffer like this for days when they return.

While Reid could go live in the faelands with Emlyn, I promised the Land I'd get everyone to stop incanting. I have to be *here* to do that.

So I spend the day spiraling through these thoughts, keeping them to myself as I sit on the branch next to Caeo, brushing my fingers through his hair. He's miserable enough as it is; he doesn't need the burden of my worries, too.

It doesn't help that I'm getting the distinct impression Emlyn doesn't like me. Yes, I was a little short with him, but I tried to keep all my unhelpful thoughts to myself, unlike him. He's probably upset with me for how I treated Reid throughout our journey—I still owe him an apology, but he and Emlyn keep disappearing, so I haven't had a chance.

I can't really blame them. When they are around, the same worry I have for Caeo reflects out of Reid's eyes. If Caeo were feeling better, I'd be trying to cherish every moment with him, too.

I still am, of course, just not as passionately as I imagine they are.

Not that I'm imagining that.

Definitely not.

Now it's stuck in my head. Lovely.

They show up again in the late afternoon, with Emlyn carrying some animal carcasses and Reid with a stack of firewood, so perhaps my imagination was a tad overactive. I turn away as Emlyn starts skinning them, otherwise I'll be as sick as Caeo, looking back only when they have a fire going and the meat's already hanging over it.

Then there's an awkward silence as we all sit around, waiting for it to cook.

"Maybe we should play a game?" I suggest.

Emlyn eyes me from where he lounges next to Reid, and I can't help but smile, remembering a similar moment on our way to rescue Caeo. Back when the two of them were still bickering all the time.

"What were you thinking?" he asks.

"Don't say it," Caeo mumbles without lifting his head from where it hangs over the tree branch.

I give his hair a gentle tug. "We played something called *Never*

Ever with Taran and Owena."

He groans. "That ended horribly, don't you remember?"

A laugh bursts out of Emlyn. "You got Taran to play that? Ancients."

"What is this game?" Reid asks, looking between Emlyn and me.

Since Emlyn's still chuckling to himself, I answer. "You say something you've never done, and anyone who has raises their hand."

"That is not a game you want to play with me," Emlyn says, wiping at his eyes.

I frown. "Why not?"

Reid rubs his brow. "Probably because he's done every fucked-up thing you could possibly think of."

Caeo lifts his head. "Now I kinda want to test that out."

"Please don't," Reid says.

"Alright. Any other suggestions?" I glance at Emlyn and Reid. They both shrug.

Disappointment sinks through me. It seemed like a fun way to connect with everyone. Better than sitting here worrying about tomorrow, at least.

After a few more minutes of silence, occasionally broken by random chuckles from Emlyn, he gets up to check on the meat. He takes some for himself, then splits the rest between me and Reid.

"What about Caeo?" I ask.

"Nope. I don't need any."

I lean closer to him. "You need to eat something."

He turns his head to the other side of the branch. "Not happening. I'm gonna throw up just smelling it."

I look back at Emlyn. "Are you sure this is normal?"

He's in the middle of tearing at the meat with his teeth, so Reid says, "Emlyn was just as bad. Wouldn't eat anything the whole first day, then drank himself into a stupor that night."

Caeo turns his head back to us. "Alcohol does sound good right now."

Emlyn swallows his food. "Sorry, don't have any. But that milk would probably work, if you still have it."

I freeze mid-chew.

That's right. Emlyn's the one who gave it to Caeo to begin with. I force myself to swallow as anger comes to a boil within me.

"Nope. Not gonna do that."

I almost drop the rest of my food as I turn to Caeo. "What? Really?"

"Really. This isn't that bad." He grunts as his face contorts. "It is that bad, but I don't want to." He grimaces again, then presses his face into the branch. "Ugh. This is horrible. I really want to, but I won't. Fuck."

My heart swells. He said no, all by himself, even though it's the one thing that could spare him all this misery. A smile spreads across my face as a steady warmth bubbles beneath my skin, and I lean over, wrapping my arms tightly around him.

Caeo's voice is muffled beneath me. "I love you, but please get that meat as far away from me as possible."

"Sorry!" I slide off the branch, feeling lighter than I have in weeks as I settle next to Reid.

He leans closer to me. "I take it he's been having problems with that stuff?"

My mouth tightens, and I nod.

Reid straightens up and smacks Emlyn on the leg. "I told you that was a bad idea."

"Huh?" Emlyn looks from me to Caeo, then back to me.

I glare at him.

"Oh. Sorry. Though in my defense, I was high as fuck at the time and rather determined to kiss him. I didn't think I'd get another chance."

Caeo laughs, his face still pressed against the tree. "If it was that important, you could've just asked. I probably would've."

What?

No, it's fine. He loves me—he'd never say that so casually if it meant anything. But I hadn't realized he was so comfortable with kissing men; I'd thought it was only from desperation.

Emlyn's brow goes up. "Really? I didn't think you went that way."

"I haven't, but I could probably be convinced." He lifts his head and looks at me. "I mean, if I weren't with Ellie.

Emlyn turns to me and Reid. "Or..."

He draws out the word longer than should be possible.

I throw my hands up, waving them in front of me, at the same time Reid violently shakes his head.

"No! Nope! Not happening!"

Reid grabs Emlyn's hand, pulling him to his feet. "We're leaving. Goodnight. We'll see you in the morning."

Caeo laughs into the tree as Reid drags Emlyn away. As awkward as that was, a smile of my own breaks through. For a moment, it stopped feeling like I was on the outside—like I actually belonged for once.

Chapter 37

Owena

In the dead of night, I weave another curse.

Perhaps my final one.

If the waters favor me, I have no intention of ruling as my father does. I would happily live the rest of my life without ever again cursing another soul.

If not... then I'll likely be dead.

I've curled up on a bed of soft, decaying leaves, away from the others, but sleep eludes me. My guilt, my shame, my sorrow, and my worries fight against one another, each worthy of the entirety of my psyche and unwilling to share. I could seek comfort from the Land, but I don't deserve it.

When morning comes, I'm exhausted.

By the dappled sunlight trickling through the forest canopy, I rebraid my hair, smoothing the kinks away as best as I can. I empty a waterskin, scrubbing the dirt from my hands and face. Today, I'm a lost princess finally returning home. After weeks in the wilderness, there's not much I can do, my clothes stained with mud and sweat and my hair matted and dull, but I need to look as presentable as possible.

I won't ask Barri to glamour me. I would look better than anything I can accomplish on my own, but I refuse to hide today.

The world, and Taran, will see me as I am, and nothing more.

Please don't let him turn away.

My heart rends, but I force it back together. I have to believe. I have to, or I won't be able to take a single step. Even if the worst should happen, my father should be dead by sundown. My plan for a unified realm may fail, but my people will be free of his torments.

As will I.

The soldiers are binding Taran's wrists again when I rejoin our camp. I had them leave him unbound overnight, but we can't risk leaving him free as we approach the capital. If anyone were to sense us before we managed to tie them, they would grow suspicious.

It didn't take much to convince Barri and his men to betray my father. They only served him because they were so entangled in his curses—against their lives, their families, their wills. All I needed to do was assure them of my intentions and break them free. Not to downplay that effort, of course. The thirteen of them were each wrapped in two to four curses apiece, and unraveling them all was a monumental undertaking that mentally exhausted me.

Add that to being physically and emotionally drained, and I really could have used some sleep last night.

The mask I wear, one of poise and regal indifference, is on the verge of crumbling from the flood of tears surging against it. I breathe slowly, forcing them deep down where they can churn and rage and no one will see.

"Is everyone certain they wish to come?" I ask, interrupting Barri's conversation with one of his men, and he straightens to attention as he turns to me. "We can adjust our story to account for any absences."

We were close once, Barri and I. My personal guard, until my father feared his loyalty strayed too far from him to me and took him away. That was years ago, and while any feelings between us have long since cooled, it's a mark of my father's special type of cruelty that he sent Barri to my "rescue" while cursed to die if Taran bent him. I can't bear the thought that he, or any of his men, will suffer because my plan failed.

Barri shakes his head, the ebony ropes of his hair bouncing with the motion. "That's too risky, Your Highness. My men aren't as practiced in twisting their words as you." I barely contain the wince that seizes my insides. "We stick to the truth."

"I appreciate their courage. Hopefully, their faith in me will be rewarded." My gaze wanders over to Taran. Now that his arms are bound again, he sits on a broken log, his head hung low.

"May the waters favor you." Barri's voice pulls me back to him.

"And you."

He turns to leave, then hesitates. "Your Highness, if I may?"

My eyelids sink shut. "No, Barri. You may not."

I don't need words of comfort, and I don't need any more doubts planted in my mind. All I need is to get through today. If I can do that, then not even the combined light of all the stars in the sky could outshine my heart.

From our campsite, it's only a short walk to Anwen's Tears. Ywelyn, our capital and my home, nestles against its banks further south, and at a comfortable pace, we should find ourselves there by late afternoon.

My nerves don't allow for a comfortable pace, and we arrive shortly after midday.

The people in this part of Ystyr don't often live in villages, as they do in Aedys. Small clusters of population, mostly family groups, pepper our central forests. They live in homes built in the canopy, shaped from the strangler figs that twist around the trunks of towering meranti trees. Families will spend part of the year in one set of dwellings, tending to nature's needs until that area can no longer sustain them. Then they move on, finding homes where the forest has recovered enough to support them.

Those living in Ywelyn needn't worry about that ebb and flow. Anwen's Tears provides year-round fishing, but more importantly, a near-constant stream of tribute demanded by my father, delivered by boat. This time of year, the river's banks flood into the capital, but that's hardly an issue when everything's built high in the trees.

Because it's impossible to predict how far the waters will advance, the ramps that lead up to the city begin far beyond its limits. It's here that we wait, as one of Barri's men heads to the palace to deliver news of our return and our prisoner. While my father would have felt Taran's arrival in Ystyr, Taran's strength has diminished enough since then that he'd no longer be aware of our location.

The sky has darkened from the rain that began shortly after our arrival. Taran sits on the muddy ground, a shell of himself, completely surrounded by guards.

I force my gaze away. I can't show any sign of sympathy, any sign of my heart breaking.

Barri's man does not return.

Instead, a dozen new guards march down the ramp toward us. All from my father's most tightly bound men. Soldiers with so many curses on them, it's impossible for them to ignore his command.

Apprehension twists in my chest. This isn't a surprising development, but I would have been far more comfortable with the security of Barri's people around us. Which is exactly why that's not happening.

I step forward, meeting the troops. "Are you to escort us—"

They shove past me, then past the guards surrounding Taran. The first to reach him kicks him hard in the side, knocking him forcefully into the mud.

My mask dissolves in an instant. "Stop it!"

I lunge toward them, but someone grabs my arm, wresting me back.

Another soldier hauls Taran to his feet, twisting his arms behind him. A silent roar contorts his face, and a fist slams into his kidneys.

"What are you doing? Stop it!" I try to yank free, my desperation surging, but their hold tightens. Fingernails bite into my skin.

"His Majesty's orders," says the soldier gripping my arm. "Ensure his silence."

Another strike across Taran's face. The sharp thumps of knuckles colliding with flesh fill the air.

"He's clearly not making a sound! He's bound! He can't speak!" My voice breaks, every blow pounding into my heart. "Stop it, please!"

A fist drives into him, centered right below the ribs. Taran's body spasms, folding in half, inaudible gasps wrenching out of him.

"Stand down." The soldier's voice is deep, expecting compliance.

Taran hangs limply as the men step away.

"Bring him to the king."

Two of the soldiers hook their arms under Taran's and drag him toward the ramp. The one holding me releases his grip, and I wrest myself away, tears burning behind my eyes.

He gestures after them. "Your Highness."

I take a breath, burying my pain behind a new mask. I nod toward Barri, and he steps forward. The other soldiers intercept him.

"Not them. Only you."

I temper my exhale. At least they didn't take Taran's sword from where it hangs uselessly from his hip.

I summon all my poise and head into Ywelyn, surrounded by guards, to face my father for the last time.

THE LARGEST STRUCTURE IN YWELYN is my father's palace, shaped out of colossal banyan and meranti trees. It's too hot, too humid for closed-off dwellings, so it's made mostly of open-air rooms, twisting around the towering trunks. It was never my home—my father had ordered my mother's death shortly after my birth, as she had fulfilled her usefulness. He didn't need her thinking she mattered. I was raised across the city, by my governess and a house full of servants, all bound to ensure my safety.

My chest pounds with my every step, carrying the weight of every decision I made getting here. Every heart-wrenching moment shared, every secret kept hidden. Every tender touch, every cruel word.

I can't dwell on any of it, can't plan my next move. Any such thoughts would make me falter. I know what needs to be done, and all that's left is to do it.

How many heartbeats remain?

The soldiers lead us around a final spiraling staircase, to my father's favored dining space. A large platform in the highest reaches of the forest's canopy, with a thatched roof covering our heads. Raindrops drip down from its edges, plummeting to the levels below.

There waits my father, vainglorious as ever. Sparing not even a glance our way, scooping the pulp from a passion fruit. I anticipated nothing less.

He sits opposite the entrance from us, on the other side of a round wooden table. It's covered with plates full of food, ready to be served, but there's not a single servant in sight.

That gives me pause, my steps halting. Public humiliation has typically been his preferred method of dealing with me. If that's not what's happening... he must already suspect treachery and has moved on to mitigating the damage.

Mats made of woven palm fronds mark the floor where guests are expected to sit. The two soldiers carrying Taran deposit him on the one across from my father, and he collapses against the table. Then they retreat behind me to guard the entrance.

My father's burgundy eyes finally look up.

"So this is Prince Taran? I haven't seen him since he was a boy hiding behind his mother's skirts." His voice booms as he stands, stepping around the table to examine Taran closely. He wears loose silk pants, imported from the east, and an open vest over his bare chest. Compared to the muddy shambles of Taran, he positively glows, his fiery hair adorned with the iridescent pearls of the Ystyrian crown.

He crouches and grabs Taran's chin, tilting his face up to his vicious gaze.

My heart cracks behind my mask.

"Why, Owena, what have you done to him?" He drops Taran's head, and it lolls to the side before settling.

I force indifference into my voice. "I cursed him to be unable to speak. Your men are the ones who abused him."

Father waggles his finger at me as I approach. "Ah, ah, my Owena. This is a man who's suffered more abuses than those of the flesh." I wince at the hint of pride lacing his voice.

He sits at a diagonal from Taran and pats the mat between them. *Surely it'd be more prudent to keep me at a distance?*

He must see that—he's no fool. But whatever he intends, it's no longer important. His curiosity, his overconfidence, has already sealed his fate.

"Sit. Tell me how you ensnared a prince when you're supposed to be unable to curse." He pulls a plate of meat over and begins carving into it with an obsidian blade.

Averting my gaze from Taran, I lower myself to the floor. I can't risk my emotions betraying me now.

I pick an acai berry from a nearby bowl. "I only had to ensure *Prince* Taran saw me as neither friend nor foe." Placing the berry into my mouth, its bitter sweetness floods my tastebuds.

Father's eyes flick wider. "How heartless of you, my Owena. And unexpected." His brow furrows. "Tell me—why bring me such a gift? When you disappeared from your wedding, I assumed you'd fled, and I would never see you alive again."

My pulse quickens. "As you suggested: if I wanted to return alive, I had no choice but to bring you a gift you couldn't resist."

Father's gaze narrows as he sets his knife down on the side opposite me. "Why, Owena? Why did you wish to return after finally being free of me?"

My mouth has gone dry; he's asking more questions than I anticipated. But he'll notice if I swallow, so I eat another berry. "It was my duty. I can't abandon my people."

"And all it cost you was destroying this prince's heart. Have you taken after me more than I thought, or did you wreck your own in the process?"

Perhaps both. Perhaps years of abuse, of lovers being stolen away and violated, has turned me into someone willing to do whatever it takes to destroy him. Does that make us the same?

So long as he dies today, that doesn't matter. And he's given me the opening I need.

My heart pounds as I turn to Taran. During our conversation, he had straightened up, and his malachite eyes flick between us. When I meet them, they stay locked on mine for a moment that longs to last forever, but can't.

"Yes." My voice is barely a whisper. "I did."

Every moment, every day.

My fingers twitch.

I swallow.

Taran's eyes soften, then drift to the floor.

Waters favor me.

With a deep breath, I lunge for Taran's sword, still hanging from his belt.

I never planned to reach it. The weapon is completely impractical, especially at such close range.

But it provides motivation for my father to act.

Before my fingers even brush against it, an obsidian knife rams into my stomach.

Sharp and cold.

I did it.

Pain sears through me as the blade rips out and clatters to the floor.

A loud thump sounds as I fall to the ground, looking up at Taran's horrified face.

Now it's up to you.

Chapter 38

Taran

I can do nothing when Owena reaches for my sword. The instant she moves, her father swipes the knife from the table.

My heart screams. My mouth opens to cry out a warning.

Nothing comes out.

And when Owena's father plunges the blade into her gut, my heart stops.

A heavy beat later, Dryfid retches as his body spasms. Eyes wide, face pale.

A jagged wound appears in his stomach, in the exact same spot as the blood drenching Owena's shirt. As if carved by the same blade. At the same time.

He yanks the knife free.

The weapon slips from his fingers as blood seeps out of him, its tip splintering as obsidian crashes against wood, splattering crimson.

Father and daughter collapse to the floor beside me, a heavy and a light thud.

The guards at the entryway stiffen, but don't move.

Time roars back into motion.

Owena unfolds onto her back, looking up at me as I scramble over on my knees, my insides unraveling.

Owena!

Her dark eyes meet mine.

Voids. I'd called them that, before. Now, as the life drains out of them... how wrong I was.

A fractured groan wheezes out of her father. "What did you do, cursed daughter?"

I can't take my eyes off Owena. Can't see if the king lingers at the edge of his own death, as she does. It doesn't matter. Nothing matters if she dies.

"I cursed myself." Blood paints her lips. She blinks, hazy eyes focusing on my face.

"It was the only way."

No. No, no, no, no, no.

There's nothing I can do. I twist and pull my arms against the coarse ropes that bind them, tearing at my skin, but they're wool. I can't shape them, can't break free.

She's dying, and I can't even hold her.

My heart thunders like it's on its final sprint and will drop dead the moment it stops.

Owena lifts her hand, and I fall closer to her. Her fingers graze my cheek, their touch cold and weak.

"Every curse has a loophole." Her voice drowns in her own blood. "A way out. You have to say the words."

The words.

The curse.

Not a sound, nor utterance,
    will escape your lips,
    Until you speak the words
    that will save me.

My power gathers for a pleading, desperate bending.

Don't die.

My heart beats. Nothing comes out.

There's only the sounds of Owena's ragged breaths against the chirping of insects.

No.

No, no, no.

I scour her body in a panic. A pool of blood spreads beneath her.

What else could it be?

My eyes cease their search when they land on hers. Tears pour out of them, the life within flickering away.

Pain, as my heart splinters into a thousand pieces.

I can't lose her. Even after all she's done, all her manipulations, I still care. Still long for her to let me into her heart.

Please, Owena. Don't die.

The words ring through my mind.

I want you to live.

They scrape out of my throat, heavy with anguish.

To marry me.

To be with me.

My voice breaks.

"I want to love you."

The world shifts, and the darkness in her eyes swallows me.

A twinkle of starlight.

Owena draws a deep breath, and the light of infinite stars swirls within the night sky of her eyes.

"I want you, too."

Her voice is breathy, but alive.

She's alive.

My heart pounds in my ears. Relief, then confusion.

How?

I stare at her, blinking. Fearing I'll open my eyes to a corpse.

But she's still here, life returning to her rosy cheeks.

My throat's dry. "What... what's going on?" I swallow. "What happened, Owena?"

Blood soaks her clothes, but she pushes herself up without a wince. I follow her gaze to her father's body, unmoving, his eyes empty. In a matter of heartbeats, that could have been her.

"Can one of you please untie him?" Owena calls to the guards, who still haven't moved.

They glance nervously at one another, then one comes over, crouching behind me. My arms fall forward, but despite the searing pain in my shoulders, I immediately reach for Owena, pulling her close. I lift her shirt, revealing her blood-stained belly.

My fingers, soaked in crimson, frantically search her flesh for any sign of injury. Nothing. Just soft, smooth, unmarked skin.

"Please send word that my father is dead, and his curses broken. I will speak to the people soon."

The soldier swallows, then nods. "Yes, Your Majesty." He hurries away, past his partner, who eyes Owena hesitantly.

"You as well," she says. "Leave us."

She turns back to me once he's gone. I can barely keep up. Dryfid's dead, she's Queen, and the world's just continuing on.

Tears leak from her eyes as her hand presses against my cheek. It's warm, her thumb brushing against my skin. My heart slows.

"I'm so sorry, Taran. For everything."

I take her hand in mine, both covered in blood and mud, but I couldn't care less.

"Tell me what happened, Owena."

She sighs, but holds her gaze on me. "I cursed you so we could get close to my father, but I knew it would be impossible for me to kill him by myself. I'm not fast enough, nor skilled with a blade. And

I knew he'd be ready for whatever I tried."

The heavy weight of realization descends upon me—the words that bound her.

"You cursed yourself."

Owena nods. "I did. Any harm inflicted upon me would maim my attacker as well. In dealing me a fatal blow, he doomed himself."

I run my fingers along her face. "But you're not dead."

A sad smile forms on her lips. "No. All curses must have a loophole. Something unlikely to occur, but feels like a work of fate if it does. I tied my curse to yours, increasing its strength. If you still wanted me, even after everything I did, then I would live. All you had to do was say the words."

The truth settles into me. My grip on her hand loosens, and my head drops.

I *did* say the words. And I meant them. I still want her, more than I can bear. But I don't know if this twisting pain is a yearning to be with her, or to be free of her torments.

"You manipulated me," I say. "All I wanted was for you to let me in. To let me love you. And you used me." My eyes squeeze shut. "I... I don't know if I can forgive you, Owena."

I look back at her, and her face echoes the same raw ache pulsing in my heart.

Another heavy breath escapes as I take her hand. "I do care. But everything you put me through... I understand why you did it, but it hurt. So much. It still does."

Owena's mouth tightens, her lips curling inward. "If there were any other way... When I set down this path, all I wanted was peace. For my people and yours. Binding myself to someone who hated me... It was a cost I was willing to pay."

Always so headstrong. "I never hated you. You irritated me." My mouth twitches. "You still do."

A smile breaks through her sorrow. "I never expected to love you. I had hoped... but if you didn't, it would have been what I deserved. At least my people would be free." Her fingers squeeze mine. "Please, Taran. If you can't forgive me, I'll still call back Ystyr's forces. I'll help you depose your mother. We don't have to marry."

My heart sinks into darkness, and I look into her eyes.

Starlight glistens in her tears.

"But I want to," she says, her voice cracking. "I don't deserve it, but I want to spend the rest of my life making it up to you."

She couldn't say that if it weren't true.

"Please..." she whispers.

"Just say yes."

The air is heavy between us, her eyes trembling.

The ache in my chest deepens. My pain. My anger. My yearning.

Everything I wanted, and all I have to do is trust her. To trust that she's finally letting me in. That she won't betray me again.

Can I do that?

I want to say yes. To believe that after all this misery, we can find happiness together.

Looking into her starlit eyes, their glow chases the darkness away, drawing me into their infinite cosmos.

I can't say no.

I won't.

It's reckless. Foolhardy. But for once, that's what I want to be.

Our lips meet. Salty from tears, tinged with the sharp tang of her blood. Caked in mud. But we melt into one another nonetheless, the world narrowing to only us. As our kiss deepens, the taste of her seeps through, enveloping me in a steady warmth that builds with every heartbeat, washing everything else away. Like the first time she kissed me, but more. All-consuming, fueled by the hope blazing within.

"Yes," I breathe, as we pull apart. "But only if you promise to never shut me out again. We need to be in this together."

Tears fill Owena's eyes, her smile shining through. "I promise." Bound by the oath, she throws her arms around me, and her lips crash into mine.

I can't hold myself up against the force of her exuberance. A sharp pain slices through my abdomen as we tumble to the wooden floor.

"Ow." My jaw clenches with a grimace. "Maybe... temper your excitement until I've seen a healer."

Owena winces as she pushes herself off of me. "Sorry."

"It's fine." I take her hand and pull her back. "Just be gentle."

A tender glow emanates from her face as she caresses my jaw, her weight on my chest. Then she twists her mouth into her playful grin. "You may have to bend me, as I'm not sure I'm capable."

"I'd rather show you." I pull her closer. These last few heartbeats have already been everything I dreamed of.

Owena's eyes sparkle as she presses her fingers against my lips. "Later. We're both in desperate need of a bath, you need a healer, and I need to deal with the ramifications of all my father's curses unraveling."

Turning to her father's lifeless body, she reaches out and pulls the crown of pearls from his head. It glitters as she sets it atop her golden curls.

She exhales, then smiles. "And, of course, solidify my bond with the Land as Ystyr's new queen."

I yank her back down as warmth floods through me.

I'm marrying a queen. My equal.

"Don't forget about planning our wedding." I trace the curve of her cheek with my thumb.

"I'll have everything ready for tomorrow."

My heart skips a beat. While we *do* need to hurry so my mother can't steal any more of my bond, that completely disregards tradition. "Tomorrow?"

"Of course. We have a war to end, my king." The corner of her mouth curls upward, and for the first time, the title doesn't make my chest constrict—instead, it feels lighter. "You're not having second thoughts, are you?"

I bite my lip, as if deep in thought. Then I pull her close and whisper.

"Not at all."

Chapter 39

Ellie

On the morning of our second day back in Landore, Emlyn wakes us shortly after dawn. He and Caeo have a long hike ahead of them, needing to go the long way around the hills north of the fae army to avoid suspicion. He wanders among the trees while I get up, closing his eyes as he rubs the back of his head. Reid joins him, taking his hand and stepping close, speaking softly.

My chest tightens as I turn to Caeo, sliding to the ground from his branch. He winces as his feet touch the forest floor. Grabbing his waterskin, he tilts his head back as he downs all that remains within it.

I hurry over, taking his hands once he's done. "Are you sure you want to do this? You don't have to. We can keep waiting for Taran and Owena." Even though I agreed to this, and as much as I believe in him, there's so many things that could go wrong, outside of their control. I won't be there to save them this time.

Though, now that I think about it—with a few well-chosen incantations in the faelands, I could completely devastate their army. Not that I ever would, the idea of it already turning my stomach.

Caeo sighs as his eyes meet mine. They're almost completely gray now, no longer glowing with their inner light. If he wore a hat that covered the tips of his ears poking out of his hair, he could pass as human. The thought calms the tension coiling in my chest. If everything goes well today, that will make it easier for him to be here with me.

"I know," he says. "But I think I need to. Not for everyone else, but for me." He traces his fingers along my cheek. "I don't think Emlyn would volunteer to do this if he thought it was too dangerous."

I glance over at him and Reid, wrapped in a tender embrace. While logically, I agree, I can't help the doubts creeping up. Reid clearly thinks it's plenty dangerous.

"Or maybe he has a skewed sense of danger," I mumble, turning back to Caeo.

"I heard that."

And yet, he's not denying it.

The smallest of laughs brightens Caeo's face, but my heart's still twisting in knots. I wrap my arms behind his neck, pulling him close.

"Just come back to me," I whisper as tears threaten to fall.

"As long as I can, I will."

The tears gush out, my chest cracking. It's the most fae thing he's ever said. The best promise he can make without risking a lie.

Caeo pulls back, wiping my tears away.

"You will," I say, because he can't.

His gray eyes glisten as he nods. Then he slides his hands into my hair, bringing his lips to mine.

I pour myself into our kiss, and he does the same. His touch, his taste, his scent... I absorb them all, locking them away in my heart.

This won't be our last.

I pull him closer nonetheless, unwilling to let it end. Unwilling to let him go.

But it does end.

He does have to go.

He presses his forehead against mine. "I love you."

"I love you too. Always and forever."

With my heart aching, we part, as do Emlyn and Reid. Emlyn squeezes Reid's hand one last time before he slings on his pack and pats Caeo's shoulder.

"Come on. Time to go."

Caeo's eyes don't leave mine. "I'm coming." He digs into his pocket, pulling out the small jar of milk. He places it in my hand.

"Hold on to this for me. I don't want to be tempted."

I nod, biting my lip. It means everything that he's trusting me with it, that he's making this choice. But it won't matter at all if he doesn't come back.

He lets go and steps away.

I move to follow.

"Nope." Emlyn holds up his palm, stopping me. "You're staying to wait for Alexis and Sophie."

My heart thumps rapidly. "But they won't be here for a while. We can walk you to the border—it's not far."

He laughs. "You two have a horrible sense of direction. You'd never find your way back." He grabs Caeo's arm and pulls him along. "Don't worry so much. Or, if you must, worry about all the things I could possibly convince him to try during our time together."

Reid groans, and Emlyn winks at him.

Caeo mouths a final "I love you," his eyes locked on mine, before he turns away. Leaves crunch beneath their feet as they depart.

Then it's only Reid and me, standing in silence.

Two humans, hoping our fae haven't just walked out of our lives for good.

W HEN A LEXIS SHOWS UP at our camp around mid-morning, she's by herself. My nerves tighten as I get to my feet.

"Where's Sophie?"

Alexis crosses her arms, sighing. "Off patrolling. She didn't want to be part of this."

"What?" It's not too surprising, since she's never liked me, but my stomach knots. "Do we need to worry about her?"

Alexis scoffs, tucking a braid back behind her ear. "Oh, definitely not. She wanted to spill everything back when Reid first went after you, but I pointed out that reporting your disappearance wouldn't affect her future in the Order as much as making an enemy of the High Marshal's daughter. So now she can't say anything without revealing she knew what happened all along."

I press my hand against my chest, letting out a heavy breath. One less thing to fret about, but it's like stopping a single pebble in an avalanche.

"You're a genius, Lex." Reid stands up, brushing his hands on his pants. "But have we thought about what happens after this conversation?"

My fingers clench around my shirt. "What do you mean?"

"What happens if you tell your dad everything that happened, and he decides we've been seduced and brainwashed by fae?"

Everything coils tight again. "I hadn't thought about that." I've been so focused on getting here, it didn't occur to me what might happen if I fail.

Sinking down to my knees, I hug my arms close. "I guess... he probably won't let us leave? I don't think he'd call us traitors, but..."

He could keep me from ever seeing Caeo again.

And if Caeo came looking for me...

My fingernails dig into my arms.

"Ancients' prickly cones," Reid mumbles.

Alexis cocks her head at him. "What?"

"Nothing." He sighs. "Maybe leave out all the parts about being in love with a fae?"

My voice pitches up. "How do I leave that part out? That's the entire reason we were there! The entire reason we know any of this!"

My heart's racing, and I'm sweating, despite the chilly morning air. *Why did I ever think I could do this? That this would actually work?*

Footsteps brush against leaves, then Alexis kneels in front of me, taking my hands. "Hey. Listen to me, Ellie."

I meet her gaze, and she gives me that easy smile of hers. The one that normally twinkles along with her earrings, but she isn't wearing any today.

"If this were easy, it wouldn't be worth doing. All you have to do is talk to your father. Show him who you are, and how important this is to you. He'll listen."

"He never has before."

He only ever wanted me to be like him. It didn't matter what I wanted.

Alexis's eyes narrow. "Did you ever really *try* before?"

It's a punch to my heart, the thud echoing through my stomach. My entire childhood, listening to what he said, doing what he asked.

Without ever speaking up.

I swallow, then exhale. "No. I didn't."

Alexis's green eyes shine bright, and she offers me her hand.

"Then let's go change that."

REID AND I FOLLOW ALEXIS in silence. Out of the forest, then up and over a hill, where we can see the entire army camped out in the valley below, in front of the thick, purple fog of the border.

My heart stills at the sight of it.

The border radiates the Land's familiar rage, seething through the air, but we're far enough away that it doesn't push against me. Doesn't lock me in place. But it's a grim reminder of the weight of my task, and I struggle to pull my gaze away. My eyes follow its edge as it sweeps along the slope of the hillside.

A massive black curtain hangs between a city of white and gray tents and the fog, blocking the soldiers' view of the border while they're in camp. Beyond it, the valley floor is a large swath of brown, with all the grass completely, utterly dead. Dirt erupts in patches from the ground, and far off incanters send blasts of flame toward figures at the edge of the purple haze.

Some flames bend back at the casters. Others break through. If there are any screams, they're too distant to hear, the wind carrying them away from us.

"Come on." Alexis tugs at my arm as she glances at the fog. "You get used to it. Just keep your eyes on the ground."

I force my eyes shut, turning away. "This is nothing compared to the last time I was in there."

Besides, it's not the only source of dread seeping through me. It's mostly the fighting. The destruction.

What I'm here to stop.

My muscles tense as my heart thumps with resolve.

I pull at Reid's shirt while his gaze wanders over the fog. His stance is surprisingly relaxed, his hands resting against his hips.

"Stop looking at it, Reid. Let's go."

"Hmm?" He glances at me. "Sorry, I was just thinking."

Alexis leads the way down the hill, with me following and Reid trailing behind. When we reach the bottom, she turns to face us.

"They should've noticed us approaching by now. I'll go ahead—

you two stay here and try not to look threatening, alright? I don't know if I'll get to come back for you, or if they'll send someone else."

I nod, wringing my hands. My nerves must be all over my face, because Alexis squeezes my arm and smiles. Then she heads to camp.

Before I can stop myself, my hand reaches out and clutches Reid's. I look up at him, and he glances at me, blinking in surprise.

My throat's dry, but I push the words out. "Thank you for coming with me."

He squeezes my hand. "Yeah, sure. No problem."

"And for everything else, too. I don't think I can apologize enough. You were a better friend to me than I ever was to you. I'm so sorry I didn't listen. I'll do better from now on. I mean it."

Reid pulls his hand out of mine, but then wraps his arm around me. "Don't worry about it. If everything goes well today, then your curse was the best thing to ever happen to me."

"And if not?"

He lets out a deep exhale. "Then at least we'll be miserable together."

I wrap my hands around his arm as I lean into his side.

Then, we wait.

The minutes stretch on, but eventually, Reid pulls his arm away from me as a group of four soldiers approaches.

Alexis isn't with them.

Their uniforms are significantly nicer than her simple one. Dark gray coats, lined with deep purple trim. White cuffs fold up at their wrists, matching the white cravats that tuck into the front of their jackets behind a column of polished silver buttons.

Embroidered on the left side of their chests is the Order of Incanters' insignia: a circle containing a vertical wavy line, intersected near the top by another short wave. A horizontal straight line crosses it about three-quarters of the way down, with another wave beneath it.

The four elements of incanting. Fire, wind, earth, and water.

One of the two in the lead speaks when they arrive, her voice crisp. "Eloise Detura? Reid Vero?"

We both nod.

"Come with us."

The soldiers separate, surrounding us. Two ahead, two behind.

I grab Reid's hand as they escort us to the camp.

If I were to look, I'd guess both our knuckles are white by the time we arrive, our grip on each other that tight. My heart's beating faster than I ever remember it beating before, and I keep forgetting to breathe.

I should've planned this better. I'm moments away from seeing my father for the first time in months, but so much has changed that it feels like a lifetime ago. I have no idea what to say.

Our escorts lead us through a maze of tents, deeper into the camp. We pass countless soldiers—some on break, some rushing past, and others consumed in a task.

Some of them glance up as we pass. Most don't.

It smells horrendous. The stink of bodies that haven't properly bathed in days, of nearby latrines, and smoke.

Somehow, I manage to tighten my grip on Reid's hand even more.

And then we see it: a tent, larger than the rest, in the center of camp.

The soldiers lead us directly there.

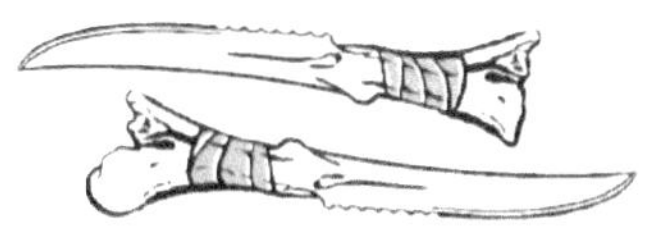

Chapter 40

Emlyn

"**Y**ou'll want both your asshole and her finger completely slathered in oil, and then she has to stick it up there, just a little at first, till you get used to it. Once she feels a lump, she just wiggles it around." I flick my finger like I'm summoning someone, slowing my stride as Caeo and I hike through this stupidly large stretch of windy plains. "Do some tapping, make circles. You'll figure out what you like."

"I don't think Ellie's gonna be interested in doing that."

"Well, maybe someday she'll get bored and want to try something new. Or ask me in eighty years when her and Reid are most likely dead."

Hmm.

That's a downer. Why'd I say that?

And yes, eighty is certainly optimistic, but there is no way I'm saying anything less than that out loud.

Caeo pauses his steps, looking at me. "We don't know for sure I'll outlive her. I'm half mortal."

Oof. He's still in denial.

Whelp. He's gotta accept it someday. Might as well be today.

"It doesn't really matter who your dad was. You have all Her other gifts, so you have our lifespan, too. And the fact that I just said it confirms it." I tug his arm. "We have to keep moving."

Our detour around the army is taking much longer than I intended. From where we crossed over, the army was directly south, in a valley on the other side of the hill we were on. Originally, we would've kept walking east along the hills until we found an inconspicuous place to pass through, or, barring that, gone around the hills entirely.

But all the sheep were on the hills to the north of us, across another valley.

We've been alternating between walking and jogging to make up for having to go so far out of our way, and stopping entirely for a conversation about the transient lives of our loved ones would greatly diminish our progress.

Caeo matches my pace. "If it was that simple, why didn't Owena or Taran say so when I asked them?"

"It's considered taboo to use our relationship with the truth that way. I'll risk it more than most, but still only with things I'm fairly confident about." Which is why I haven't said anything about our odds of success today. The only reason I have any confidence about this at all is because the Land doesn't like the war and wanted us to come here. This has to be why.

"So I'm not gonna age? Like, at all?"

"Think of it as, maybe a decade of aging for mortals will take somewhere between one to five hundred years for you, depending on how well you take care of yourself. But you can always look older or younger with a glamour." I gather the strands of hair whipping across my face and tuck them down the back of my shirt.

"Then when Ellie's old, I'll still look like this?"

I glance over at him. His face matches how I've felt whenever I've gotten lost in these worries, which happens more than I'd like. That's probably why I said it to begin with—to stop being alone with those thoughts.

I sigh. "We can always make ourselves look older to match them. But they'll probably die before us, and we'll have to figure out how to keep living." Not that I have any clue how to do that. Going back to mindlessly fucking whoever has a pulse sounds awful.

Caeo doesn't say anything. When I look his way, he's staring at his feet as we walk.

Guess I have to fix this now.

"Or we might die today. Then we won't have to worry about it at all."

He lifts his head, frowning. "Are you *trying* to make me feel worse?"

"No, I'm saying that even for us, moments are fleeting. Some people die, others outlive them. Even if you were both fae, there's no guarantee you'd grow old with her. So we just have to cherish the time we have with them."

His eyes soften. "You're trying to convince yourself just as much as you're trying to convince me, aren't you?"

"Yeah, I guess." The weight of my hair around my neck's growing uncomfortable, so I pull it free, even though the wind will just make it go crazy again. "Look, I'm sorry I brought it up. It's just... it's nice not being the only fae who loves a mortal, you know? Even if I don't agree with your taste."

Caeo glares at me before letting out a heavy exhale. "At least once Ellie's dead, I can look forward to having a man's finger up my butt."

I clap him on the shoulder. "That's the spirit! Though for your sake, I really hope you can convince her to try it sooner than that. I think I'd kill myself if I had to go eighty years without someone poking around up there."

He groans. "You're so weird. And stop touching me." He smacks my hand. "How does Reid even stand you, let alone love you?"

I take my hand off him. "I honestly have no idea."

My heart wraps me up in a warm blanket as I think about it. After today, everything should be dandy. The war should be over, and I can find somewhere over here for Reid to hide until Taran makes it official that he can stay and no one's allowed to kill him. He owes me that, at the very least.

Assuming, of course, that he doesn't get himself killed trying to assassinate King Dryfid. But that hasn't happened yet—otherwise, Caeo would be King. And if it does, then Caeo can do it instead. He likes Reid. He'd want him around if he ends up stuck here.

We just have to not die today.

I'm not gonna think about the odds. For now, we just need to get to those sheep.

Or, specifically, to the people tending the sheep.

They started out as tiny dots when we first spotted them, but we finally get close enough to speak around mid-morning.

"Let me do the talking," I mutter to Caeo as we approach.

"That sounds like a terrible idea."

I give him a side-eye glare before focusing on the shepherd ahead of us.

His long, reddish-brown hair is tied in a knot to keep it from blowing in the chilly breeze, and he wears a rough poncho of undyed wool. He eyes us warily, moving between us and the sheep. "Who are you? What do you want?"

"Not very friendly, are you? Is that because of the army back there?" I point over my shoulder with my thumb.

The shepherd's eyes narrow.

Not giving me much to go with here.

I explain how Caeo's Taran's heir, and we're planning to get rid of the false queen and order everyone to leave. I squeeze Caeo's shoulder as I glance at his bewildered face, then look back at the shepherd.

It's like he's Caeo's twin, both their mouths just hanging open.

"You can test his bond, if you'd like," I add.

The shepherd's eyebrows knit together. He's probably looking for any deceitful holes in what I said. I don't think there were.

"Now, I could be wrong," I continue, "but I'm assuming you've been begrudgingly trading with them since they got here? We just need some goods so we have a reason to be there that doesn't get us detained. I'll make sure you're reimbursed by the real king for your troubles."

I smile brightly. "So what do you say?"

It takes a little more persuading and assurances nothing will get traced back to him if we fail, but soon enough, Caeo's pushing a poorly shaped wheelbarrow full of bundles of wool while I try to keep a couple stubborn ewes following us. It's like he purposely gave us his most annoying sheep in case we didn't return them.

I'm debating whether the disguise is good enough to merit taking a more obvious path through the hills, or if we should go the long way around, when Caeo speaks up between heavy breaths.

"I've never ever fucked a sheep."

I stop in my tracks. "Seriously? That's what you think of me?"

He raises his brow.

Ancients. "No, I haven't fucked a sheep. Or any living thing outside of mortals and fae. Or fruit, if you consider those alive, but I don't. A carrot might count, but it was arguably fucking me."

Caeo lets go of the wheelbarrow to raise his hands in defense. "Hey, Reid's the one who said 'the most fucked up thing you can possibly think of.'"

"You clearly lack imagination." I smack at one of the ewes as I start walking again. "Try something like, 'I've never ever been gagged and bound while getting fucked in the armpits.' Then I'd be enthusiastically raising my hand."

"The armpits?"

"It was a weird night. Didn't really do anything for me. Never saw those two again." I snap at the ewes to keep them following. "You can stop to eat when we get there."

"I've never ever—"

"No." I swing my hand out to stop Caeo. "You don't get two turns in a row. I thought you played this before."

"Fine, it's your turn, then."

I pinch the bridge of my nose. "I'm gonna have to think about this for a while."

That's really why no one enjoys playing this with me. Racking my brain, trying to come up with embarrassing things other people may have done that I haven't—it really slows the game down. And I have more pressing things I should be considering right now.

"I think we need to go around all the hills. It'll take longer, but that's what actual shepherds would do."

"Sure. Can you take a turn pushing now?"

I sigh. "Fine, but we have to switch before anyone notices us."

Caeo releases the wheelbarrow and steps aside. "Why?"

"Because." I hoist it up. Fuck, it's unwieldy. "We want them to talk to me, not you. You can't wrangle the sheep because you don't speak the Tongue, but if I'm doing that *and* pushing this thing, they'll think you're in charge."

"So what's the plan exactly?"

"We show up, offering to trade. If they try to send us away, we insist on seeing the quartermaster, saying we want to establish a long-term arrangement. If that's not working, you bend them into taking us to see him."

"To the quartermaster?"

"We'll ditch them partway there."

"How?"

I grunt as I adjust my grip on the handles. "That depends on you. The easiest thing is, once we're somewhere that isn't too conspicuous, I signal you and you bend them to go away and forget about us. But if you're gonna be like Taran, I'll probably have to knock them out or kill them before they cause a commotion, which is considerably more risky."

"You're still mad at him, aren't you?"

I drop the wheelbarrow. I can't talk about Taran while pushing this thing.

"Did he tell you what he did?"

"I... overheard something. But it's obviously been tearing him up for weeks."

"Good. It should be." The words refuse to carry all the anger I intended, turning it back into me instead.

I press my fingers against my eyes, rubbing in slow circles. Then take a breath and meet Caeo's gaze. "He made everything so much harder than it needed to be, all because he wouldn't bend anyone until it came time to panic, when it was too late."

Caeo opens his mouth, but I cut him off.

"Do you know what it feels like to be bent into not dying? To not have enough blood in your body to continue functioning, yet be forced to not only keep living, but keep walking? I guarantee that whatever you're imagining, it's not enough. Nowhere close."

I look away as my insides go tight, then grab the wheelbarrow's handles and start pushing. "We don't have time for this. We need to focus on what we're doing."

"He's getting better about it," Caeo huffs as he catches up to me. "He refused to teach me to bend at first. But then he bent two platoons into going back home."

I freeze. "What?" I can't have heard that right.

"Yeah. He told them to go home instead of coming here. Then he taught me how."

My mind is spinning.

How did that happen? What'd I miss? Did what he did to me finally break him out of his paralyzing fear?

No, that should've only made him worse.

I turn to Caeo, lowering the wheelbarrow. "You're leaving something out. There's no way he just finally got over himself and started doing shit like that on his own. What happened?"

Caeo's cheeks puff as he holds back a laugh.

Not the reaction I was expecting.

It bursts free. "Owena happened. She was lecturing him about how he needs to be willing to bend people if he wants to be a good king, and a few minutes later, he was bending her while they dry-humped under a tree."

My brain goes silent.

"I'm...

"... I'm gonna need a moment."

I hold my finger up as I turn away, trailing it behind me.

WHAT THE ACTUAL FUCK?

I rake my fingers along my face as my eyes water.

"Are you alright?" Caeo asks from behind me.

My head nods. "Uh huh. Yep."

The back of my hand presses into the bridge of my nose as laughter starts falling out.

Shit. I did not see that one coming.

I should've, when Caeo said they were getting married, but I just figured Taran was so fucked up by his mom that he'd rather be forced into a political marriage than deal with her himself. Not that he might actually be into her.

"I mean, it makes sense. Owena's totally into being dominated." Though it'll take him a while to catch up to the number of times I've fucked her—it was a busy three days.

I wipe the moisture from my eyes.

Ancients.

"It's so weird that you know that about the woman your best friend's marrying."

Is he still that? I guess if I compartmentalize my relationships, he is.

I turn back to Caeo. "And now you know it about the woman your brother's marrying. Who's the weird one now?"

"You are. Still." He walks ahead of me.

The wheelbarrow catches on a tuft of grass as I push it after him, shouting at the sheep to keep up.

"She also enjoys being tickled behind the knees."

"Please stop talking."

"I can tell you how big Taran's cock is, too, while I'm at it."

"Stop talking."

I lose my words. I open my mouth, trying to force something out, but it's like my brain forgot how to form any.

The bastard bent me.

I let out a sigh. So much for Caeo being fun. But at least he's more willing to bend than Taran. That makes me feel slightly better about our plan.

Chapter 41

Ellie

One of the two soldiers leading our escort lifts the tent flap as the other guides Reid and me inside.

"High Marshal." The soldier snaps to attention with a salute.

My eyes adjust to the shift in the light as he announces us. It's darker in here—while some sunlight permeates the white canvas of the tent, much of it comes from beeswax candles on small tables and closed trunks scattered around the space.

And on a large mahogany desk, right in the center. Behind it stands my father.

He looks older than he did. It's only been a few months since I last saw him, not even half a year. But the skin of his face looks thinner, with more white peppering his dark hair and mustache.

His gray eyes light up when they see me. My clammy fingers squeeze Reid's, my knees wobbling.

The next thing I know, Reid's dropped my hand and I'm wrapped in my father's arms. The other soldiers have left. It's just the three of us.

I don't recall my father ever hugging me like this in my life.

My hands finally find his back, returning the embrace. His comforting warmth presses into me, calming me. I let out a shaky breath.

"Hi, Papa." What I called him when I was little. It feels appropriate.

He releases me, but keeps his hands gripping my arms. Like I might disappear if he let go.

"Eloise. Where have you been? Your mother's been beside herself with worry. I've—when Gleese informed us you went missing... The Order's been looking everywhere for you. Until the cursed fae attacked and I had to call them all back."

His eyes search my face as my thoughts swirl. *Where to even begin?*

"I... It's a long story."

Father's gaze shifts over to Reid, and he straightens, his face turning hard. "Is this him? The boy you ran off with?"

Reid goes white as he throws his hands up in front of his chest, stepping back. "No! No, sir—that's not—"

I step between them, grabbing my father's arm. "No, Father. That's not what happened. That was a lie. Reid was with me some of the time, but he's just a friend. He came to rescue me."

His gaze shoots back to me. "Rescue you? From what?"

Here it goes.

"I was kidnapped. By the King of Aedys."

An oversimplification, yes, but I'll probably have to do a lot of that, at least for now.

My father's eyes slowly close, and his hold on me releases. He walks back to his desk and sits down, rubbing his brow.

I glance at Reid, unsure. *That wasn't the reaction I expected.*

He shrugs.

I hesitantly move closer to my father, padding softly on fabric over matted grass, and Reid follows a few steps behind.

Father glances up at me. "You don't need to make up stories, Eloise. I was young once. I know what it's like to get caught up with romance and want to abandon all your responsibilities."

Do you?

I shake my head, refocusing. This was never going to be that easy. "I'm telling you the truth." Pulling out the simple wooden chair opposite him, I sit down. "I did—" Deep breath. "I *did* fall in love, but not with Reid. With Caeo."

My father frowns. "The boy who broke your heart?"

Curse Alexis.

"That was also a lie. Let me—I'll start at the beginning. Just listen and try to keep an open mind. Please?"

He looks at me for a moment, then gestures with his fingers to continue.

I start by explaining how the Border Wars ended thanks to the queen of Aedys being exiled. That she settled in Haven with her half human son, Caeo.

"But he didn't know any of that," Reid interjects. Still looking out for him, even after everything.

I nod. "Caeo and I were together." My palms are sweating, but I force myself to keep looking at my father's eyes. "*Are* together. Still."

He says nothing, his expression unreadable. So I press on, describing how the queen took Caeo back to Aedys while attempting to steal Taran's throne. That he kidnapped me, hoping I'd convince Caeo to turn on their mom. I find myself drifting from oversimplification into total fabrication, but the details probably aren't helpful.

My father taps his fingers on his desk. "Our investigation did say this Caeo and his mother disappeared a few days before you two did."

With a spark of hope, I sit up straighter. "We rescued him, but weren't able to take out the queen, so now Taran's attempting something else. We came here to do what we could. To stop the war.

For peace."

I wait for my father to say something. He needs to accept this part for there to be any chance he'll believe the rest.

After a few seconds of his eyes darting across my face, he waves his finger back and forth, gesturing at me and Reid. "How does your being here stop the war? *We're* the ones being attacked."

I take a deep breath. That was probably the best response I could've hoped for.

"The two of *us* aren't stopping it. But Caeo's on the other side of the border, right now, trying to depose the queen. His mother." My chest tightens—he could be facing her as we speak. "And should that fail, Taran's attempting something that should hopefully end the wars for as long as he lives."

"And that is?"

"Killing the King of Ystyr and marrying the new queen to form a new realm whose leaders have no desire to fight with us." For some reason, that came out sounding like a question. I take another breath.

My father presses his hands to his face and slowly rubs circles into his brows.

"I couldn't make all this up, Father. I have no reason to."

An excruciating moment of silence later, he sighs, lowering his hands. "I suppose we'll find out if the fae ever withdraw."

My shoulders relax.

That's true. Once they do, he'll have to believe me. Hopefully, later today. The tension comes back, my throat tightening, but I swallow it down—I have to believe in Caeo.

Father presses his hand against his desk and stands up. "I'm going to have someone escort you back to Durnam. Your mother deserves to see you."

My stomach drops. He can't just send me away.

I shoot to my feet. "Wait! There's more. There's so much you don't understand. The reason the fae keep attacking us. There won't truly be peace until everyone knows. Until they understand."

"You said the wars would end if this Taran makes a new realm."

"Yes, but... the wars are actually *our* fault. *We're* instigating them. And until we stop, there will always be fae that want to attack us."

Father slams his fist onto the desk, and I jump back. His gaze sharpens as he looks at me.

"That's enough, Eloise. I've entertained your story. If the fae end up withdrawing, then perhaps I'll even believe it's true. But we have *never* attacked the fae. Not once. Don't you dare suggest otherwise."

My pulse races, now face-to-face with the anger I never experienced but always feared. What kept me in line, doing as he expected. *How can I pull him back from this?*

I try to think of a response, but every thought comes up blank.

"We were fae once."

Reid's voice. Shaky, but clear. A light to hold on to.

My father and I turn to where he stands behind me. I hadn't anticipated him speaking up. He didn't need to—he could've disappeared into the background, slipping away while my father dealt with me. But he's once again risking his future to help me, despite how I treated him.

The knots within me loosen slightly.

He rubs his hand against his pants. "We were fae, thousands of years ago. Before we went out of balance with the Land. We took more than we gave. So the Land denied us Her gifts and shut us away from the rest of the fae realms."

Father scoffs. "That's ridiculous. How could we possibly not know that?"

Everything tightens again, and I resist the urge to wring my hands, clasping them tight. "Fae don't write. They live for centuries. Millennia. They have people dedicated to remembering the past. Ours all died when we became mortal—human. By the time we developed writing and started recording history, the knowledge was lost."

Still standing, Father shakes his head, then shuffles a stack of papers on his desk. "This is nonsense. The fae have clearly warped both of your minds."

I'm seconds away from losing him for good. I need to think of something. How can I—

"I can prove it," Reid says, stepping right up next to me.

I snap to him, my eyes wide. "What? How?" *And why didn't you tell me this?*

My father glances between the two of us before settling on Reid.

His weight shifts under my father's gaze. "The Land doesn't consider me mortal anymore. I can cross the border as easily as any fae."

What? "How did that happen?"

Reid's jaw tightens. "There's a theory that I'd rather not get into right now." His fingers clench as he meets my father's eyes. "But I can do it. I can show you right now. Preferably further away from a battle."

I can see the cogs ticking in Father's expression. My breath catches—what if he takes this the wrong way? He could easily see it as a boon to the fight. Reid may have just doomed himself to being a tool. An experiment. Why did he take that risk for me?

Father rubs his chin. "We will certainly test that claim."

Reid swallows, glancing at me. I reach over, taking his hand and giving it a squeeze. I'll do everything in my power to make sure he doesn't regret this.

He squeezes back as my father continues.

"*If* what you say is true..." His head shakes with an exhale. "...we can't be held accountable for something our ancestors did thousands of years ago." His face hardens, muscles constricting around his jaw and forehead as he meets my eyes. "It's still the fae attacking us. We've only ever defended ourselves."

A cautious glimmer flickers in my heart. *We might actually be getting through to him.*

"Yes." I lean forward against the desk. "The fae started the war, and they were wrong. Most of them see that now. The Land had already punished us, and it wasn't their place to keep doing so. But then we started incanting.

"They recognize they drove us to it, but even after twenty years of peace, we're still doing it. It hurts the Land, so as long as we continue, the fae will keep having a reason to hate us. There will never be real peace."

My father frowns. "We've always known incanting was hard on the land. That's why it's limited to the Order. But it's *our* land. Why do they care?"

"It's not just land. It's *the* Land. The spirit that the fae worship within it. We're forcing fae magic out of Her, against Her wishes."

He has to see the truth. He's witnessed its cost more than anyone.

Other than Reid and me.

I move to the other side of the desk, next to my father. "I've done it, over there, where the Land is still alive. It's so much worse. If you saw what it did... if *anyone* saw what it did, they would never want to incant again."

I can see it, darkening his eyes. The price he's carried for decades, dampening his resolve.

He sighs. "So that's why you're here. To convince us all to stop incanting?"

I take his hand. "I know it's not possible until they stop attacking us. But once they do, you can help me make that happen. You can help me make everything right."

His eyes linger on mine for a moment, darting in thought. Then the corner of his mouth twitches, almost into a smile. "And here I always thought you'd be helping me defend our home."

"I am, just in a different way. My own. One that can bring about lasting peace." I search his face—his gray eyes that, according to my mother, were once a brilliant blue.

Before a lifetime of incanting.

"Please. You have to believe me. We can fix everything."

He looks down at our hands and rubs mine with his fingers. His gaze drifts to the tent flap, to all his soldiers beyond, waiting for the fae to strike in earnest.

With a heavy exhale, he meets my eyes. "Then you'd better hope they withdraw."

They will. They have to.

But all I can do now is believe in Caeo and wait.

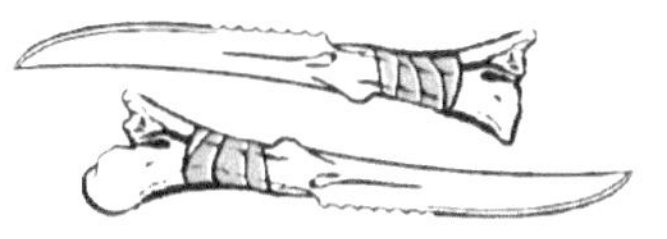

Chapter 42

Emlyn

I'll admit we make much better time with me being unable to speak. It's also amusing to watch Caeo corral the sheep by himself, herding them like a mortal's dog.

If anything happens to Taran, we'll have a king that can't even speak the Tongue.

He better not get himself killed for that reason alone.

Thankfully, Caeo got the brains in the family—which isn't saying much—and lets me know when he senses the army's lookouts. I drop the wheelbarrow so he can take it back.

Which he does, but ignores one other important thing.

I step in front of him and draw circles around my mouth with my finger.

Caeo sighs. "You can speak."

"Thank you. I've never ever stuck my tongue in a mouth that a blood relative has also had their tongue in."

"Oh, fuck you."

"You have to raise your hand."

He does. To give me the finger.

"Later, if we live and Reid approves. From this point on, keep your mouth shut unless I signal you, in which case, bend someone."

"What's the signal?"

I tap my thumb and middle finger together twice.

"What if I can't see your hand?"

I slap my palm against my face and groan. "Use your land-sense, man."

"Oh. Right. I knew that." His face twitches.

Sure.

"And don't forget to look for your mom. With your land-sense, not your eyes."

Caeo gives me an annoyed look. "How do I let you know when I find her?"

"You don't have to. Your body will react, and I'll notice. Now be quiet and keep up." I switch to the Tongue. "Come on, sheep."

I count my steps as we go. It's not perfect, since we aren't going directly in a straight line, having to follow the curve of the hill, but I'm at eighty-three paces when I pick up the closest lookouts. Then I start again, back at one.

I'm at a hundred and fourteen when they spot us. One of them holds up their arm, gesturing for us to stay put. The other jogs toward us.

Shit. That's gonna mess up my count.

"State your business," he says when he arrives.

Unlike mortals, our army doesn't wear uniforms. We don't have the means to mass produce anything, but we also don't need them; no one's gonna confuse who's mortal and who's fae in a fight, even with our eyes closed. So the lookout's wearing regular clothes, a wool shirt and some leather pants, just like us. The only difference is a beige strip of fabric tied around his upper arm to signify his role. And the fairly large knife tied to his waist, along with the bow and quiver on his back.

I hid all my blades on the underside of the sheep.

"Trading? We figured there's interest here."

The lookout pokes through the wheelbarrow, checking for anything other than the obvious bundles of wool. Then he eyes the sheep.

"Follow me."

Perfect. Now where was I? A hundred and fifteen...

I'm at two hundred and forty-seven when we reach his partner, an imposing woman taller than the rest of us.

I go through all the math as they talk back and forth. The queen's land-sense should be stronger than mine, but less than Caeo's. So it's probably safe to assume that within about thirty to forty paces of Caeo sensing her, she'll sense us. Then maybe another forty until I can sense her.

Adding it all together, she'll be somewhere around two hundred and eighty paces away from us when she senses Caeo.

I can probably run that in about a mortal minute, halving the time if I sprint. But that's in a straight line, with no obstacles. Caeo should be able to bend her before we cover that entire distance, but she can bend us, too.

The outline of a plan begins to form in my mind, slowly taking on a familiar shape.

It's Taran's plan, of all things. *Ancients.* Hopefully, it goes better this time.

The tall lookout decides she'll escort us to the camp. We follow her in silence, outside of me having to badger the sheep into coming along.

The only similarities between the fae camp and the mortal one are the smell and how crowded it is. We may glamour ourselves to look clean, but you can't glamour away the stink of living outside and not bathing since Ancients know when, and the odor of a thousand such fae hangs over the entire valley. Plus all the shit and piss.

There are hardly any tents, with everyone set up to sleep somewhere on the ground. In that way, it looks significantly more disorganized than the mortal camp. There's maybe a dozen large yurts scattered throughout that I assume are for the captains, and one likely belongs to the queen. Other than that, there's some simple structures set up to provide shade—just fabric stretched over wooden posts—and large groups gather under them and the scattered trees to escape the sun's rays.

We come to a stop shortly after entering the sea of soldiers lazing about, many napping, as the lookout explains us to her superiors. They must be bored, recovering from the mortal realm, or preparing to attack tonight.

Our escort departs as her boss sizes me up. Though he's shorter than me, he's much heavier. Not someone I'd want to fight.

"I can make you a deal for the wool and the sheep," he says.

"I was really hoping to speak with the quartermaster? See if he's interested in arranging something long-term? Seems like you'll be here a while."

"We're not doing that. We'll take what you have, and you can come back again to offer more."

I tap my fingers together.

Nothing.

I look at Caeo. He's not looking at me, his gaze drifting across the camp.

Great.

I tap his arm, and he startles, turning to me. "You wanna give this a try?"

He blinks, then his eyes widen. "Oh. Sure."

He turns to our current obstacle, keeping his voice quiet, though it still hits heavy in the air. "Please take us to the quartermaster."

Oh good, he said please. He's not a total idiot.

The man stiffens, then turns around without saying anything. He starts walking, and we follow him.

I lean into Caeo as he pushes the cart and whisper, "Pay attention."

"Sorry," he mutters back. It'd be nice to be stuck with someone competent for once.

He tenses as I wrap my arm around him, nuzzling my face into his.

"What are you—"

I speak as quietly as I can and pray nobody decides to listen. "Once you sense her, stop him. I'm gonna leave, and you count to five hundred. Then you go straight to her as fast as you can and bend her as soon as you're able."

"What?" he hisses. "Why—"

Ancients, he's even worse at this than Reid.

I boop his nose with feigned affection. "She's gonna focus everything on you. It'll be chaos. If you can't bend her, I can help you better if I'm not with you." I pat his cheek and give him a quick kiss on the other. "Don't forget to look for her."

Caeo glares at me when I pull away. He's already tense as fuck, so I give him a playful poke to help people assume it's only from unwanted advances.

Unfortunately, we reach the quartermaster before Caeo finds his mom.

Fortunately, he's inside one of those yurts.

And even better, Caeo picks up on my signal and puts both him and our escort to sleep without me having to say anything.

I pull the band off our escort's arm and wrap it around my own, then dig my knives out of the sheep's woolly coat.

"I'm not—"

I hold my hand up, cutting Caeo off. "People can hear, dear. I don't think you want me embarrassing you again."

Caeo's jaw clenches, then he stomps over to me while I strap my blades around my legs. He leans close to my ear and whispers.

"I don't like this plan."

"It's the same as it always was, except I won't be with you. Which is better, because if you fail, I'll still be alive to do something. Now come on."

We leave the wheelbarrow, sheep, and sleeping fae behind as we go back outside. After a quick glance around, I lead Caeo toward the largest tents, weaving through napping soldiers and clusters of awake ones, passing the time with various conversations, games, and exploits.

If Caeo was tense before, he suddenly goes stiff as a pine tree.

I move close, as if to kiss him. But I don't.

"Where?"

"The tent behind your left shoulder." He swallows, his eyes full of panic. There's nothing I can really do about that, other than reconsider the entire plan.

Yeah… Nope. This is still the best option.

"Sit down. Count to five hundred. Then move as fast as you can. Bend whoever you have to and bend her as soon as you're close enough."

I squeeze his arm before I leave.

One.

Two.

Three.

My heart pounds with my counting as I take a roundabout path to the specified yurt, speeding up as I go. That's probably alright— Caeo's likely counting faster than me, anyway. The goal is to get behind her, since she'll be directing everything toward him. I just have to get there nonchalantly enough that none of her guards pay attention to me.

A hundred and seventy six.

I sense her.

My heart rate spikes.

This will work.

I'm not gonna die today.

I'll see Reid again.

Caeo's far enough away that I can't sense him anymore. I fight the instinct to pick up my pace, knowing he'll probably start counting faster once I get out of his range.

I'm behind her yurt now, but far off to the side. Crouching down between two soldiers having a snoring competition, I futz with my boots. Hopefully for long enough that people forget what direction I was traveling, but not as long as I normally would. I'm already at three hundred, so I can't dally.

I make my way there.

The first shout happens before I hit four hundred.

Shit.

Caeo counted too fast. As expected, but still annoying.

I pick up my pace as the people around me start moving, drawn by the commotion. Not enough to stand out, but to pass as someone extremely curious.

The queen's voice breaks through.

I run.

People are scattering in every direction, and I fly between them, narrowly avoiding collisions with those unsure if they want to flee the queen's wrath or see what's happening.

My pulse pounds as I rush by.

There's the queen, her back to me. In front of her stands Caeo, his arms held behind his back by one of the guards.

Fuck. She got him first.

Reid's face flashes through my mind, and my heart drops. I could leave. Go back to him. Let Caeo fall and Taran handle his mother on his own.

But that's not me. I do what they can't.

I draw my knives.

Chapter 43

Caeo

One. Two. Three.

I can't believe Emlyn left me—just sitting here, staring at my mother's tent, my skin itching as murmuring voices press in around me.

As annoying as he is, his presence was comforting, even if he kept feeling me up. I think he was only doing it to hide all his whispering, but we wouldn't have had to whisper so much if he'd explained everything ahead of time.

What number was I on?

Shit.

I pick up again at sixty, because I think I've been sitting here that long. Maybe?

I count slower just in case.

Sixty three.

Sixty four.

My heart's pounding three times between numbers. Maybe that's too slow? Or is my heart beating too fast?

I speed up my count.

Emlyn made it sound like this would be easy. Just walk in, bend her, and be done. I should've known it wouldn't be.

All I have to do is tell her to be quiet. But she'll be trying to do the same to me. And she'll have the advantage of being able to send people to attack me.

Which I guess is why I'm supposed to run.

I close my eyes.

This is impossible.

Think.

I can tell anyone who comes near me to stop. That's easy. I can do that.

I'm fairly confident that despite everything, she won't tell anyone to kill me. Probably. She enjoys controlling me too much. Hopefully, that means no arrows.

My hand comes up to my arm, rubbing the bandage where the arrow grazed me at the bridge. Maybe they only let loose because Ellie was with me, and they didn't know who I was? That makes sense, right?

They could shape the ground to trip me up. I can tell them to stop that, too.

But the closer I get, the more people I'll have to bend. I can't bend more than two or three at once, but I don't know how it works going back to back. Will the ones I bent earlier on break free as I bend more? And how will I know when I'm close enough for my mother to hear me?

How long has it been since I stopped counting?

Five hundred is... what? A little over eight minutes? I don't think I've been sitting here that long, but I couldn't begin to guess how much time it's actually been. And I've lost track of Emlyn.

It's probably better to be late than early. But my heart's pounding, sweat dripping down my back. I don't know how long I can sit here before I fall into a full-out panic.

If I fail... Failure is her bending me first.

Then she'll never let me free.

My throat tightens against a void that opens in my stomach and sucks everything down.

I can't. Can't think about failing. Not now. But I can't run away, either. I chose to do this.

I'm here, and I need to see it through.

I meant what I said to Ellie. It's the only way we have a future. One where we stop everyone from incanting, then settle down in a place of our own near Taran or Reid. Have a real family. Maybe tending sheep.

I take a deep breath and look at all the soldiers around me. The ones who might be attacking as soon as I start running.

How many are here by choice? How many will try to stop me of their own free will? They're all so peaceful right now, sleeping, making jokes, staring up at the sky.

How many of them will die if I fail? Or don't even try? That'd be worse, right? For all those deaths to weigh on my conscience if I turn away?

I can tell myself that, but I don't really know. Not unless I let myself go back to how it felt to be trapped under my mother's will. Which I can't do. If I do, I won't be able to take a single step.

Stop thinking.

I take a breath.

If I sit here any longer, I'll go crazy. Hopefully Emlyn's wherever he needs to be.

Another deep breath.

I push to my feet and start running, straight to my mother's tent.

She's standing within seconds—much sooner than Emlyn predicted. How? She's not supposed to be that strong. Did something happen to Taran?

My steps falter, but it's too late to pull back. Nearby soldiers turn their heads, startled by my passing, but I'm gone before they do anything.

Guards burst out of her tent, charging forward.

I focus on the two in front as they draw close, summoning the power like Taran taught me.

"Stop."

They stumble to a halt, those behind plowing into them.

Some run around as others recover.

The ground shifts under my feet. I stumble.

"Stop!" I yelp.

I can't see who did it as I struggle to regain balance, but the shaking stops and I sense his hands freeze against the ground.

The earth pushes up beneath me. I fall forward.

Shit.

Someone's arms grab mine, yanking me up.

"Let go."

They do.

My heart's on fire, a blaze searing inside my muscles.

I lift my head. Two more, rushing at me.

My hands are already on the ground, so I push through it.

The earth blasts up, knocking them aside.

I scramble to my feet as hands grasp for me again, and I barely slip free.

"Stop!"

I stagger away, colliding with the wall of dirt I made, tripping over the soldier next to it. Lurching past him, I spin around, my heart thundering in my ears.

"Quiet."

Mother's voice rings out from behind me, echoing through my veins. Ice douses the fire within me, freezing it over as it plummets into my stomach.

I open my mouth, but nothing comes out.

I failed.

The cold seeps through my entire body as the soldiers around me get to their feet.

"No more speaking."

The pylon of dirt returns to the ground as someone grabs my arm.

No!

I pull free, pushing myself away—

"Stop resisting."

—and I fall into the soldier standing next to me. He pulls my arms behind me, and I just let him do it, the weight of compliance settling into my bones. My mind is so, so tired of fighting, my eyes drifting shut.

"You came back. I didn't think you would."

My head droops down.

This can't be it. Where's Emlyn? Did I go too early?

Did I ruin everything?

I never should've come here. Never should've thought I could do this.

Now I'll never see Ellie again.

"Turn him around."

The soldier spins, and I go along with it. No resisting. That'll be my life from now on. All hope of a nice home with Ellie and sheep flickers away.

No.

Owena overcame my willbending. That means it's possible. And I did not get Ellie across the border just to lose her now, because I wasn't strong enough.

I lift my head and open my eyes. My mother stands before me, unchanged from the last time I saw her. The sharp tips of her golden crown press into her dark hair, cascading past her cruel face. The face I once loved, that was once my entire world, but now haunts my nightmares. Her green eyes pierce into me, full of disdain.

I pull together everything I have, forcing my mouth open.

"No." Barely a whisper, but it's there.

Mother's eyes widen.

And behind her, Emlyn rushes forward, blades drawn, as the ground begins to shake.

Chapter 44

Owena

Warm, sultry air clings to my skin as I stand before my wedding gown, completely nude, surrounded by my handmaidens. I haven't seen Taran since yesterday, when I left him with the healers while I spoke with my people as their new queen.

It's done. I actually did it.

I'm alive, and Taran still wants me, despite everything. It's as if I'm walking through a dream, hoping I never wake up.

But I won't. This is real.

I suppose he has until the ceremony itself to change his mind. While the thought sends nerves spiraling through me, I doubt he will. Not after how he looked at me, his eyes glowing with devotion.

From the moment I announced our intentions to marry—to end all the wars for good—preparations began, my father's former servants springing into action. I promised each and every one of them that they needn't worry about being cursed into servitude again, and I would speak with them all individually to ensure their needs were met.

After the wedding.

Everyone in Ystyr should have felt my father's death and my ascension to power. There's a high likelihood our armies have fallen into disarray, with their leadership no longer bound by curses.

While some might abandon their posts, most should continue following their last orders. I sent word to stand down, but even the fastest messengers will take days to arrive at the border. It won't take nearly as long for the armies of Aedys to hear about my coup, and I can't imagine anything good will come of that.

As such, everyone agrees that the wedding is our highest priority. The unification of Aedys and Ystyr should hopefully disrupt the chaos, forcing everyone to pause until they understand what's happened.

And hopefully, anyone who decided to turn on me will question that decision when they realize I've married an immensely powerful willbender. Not that I have any desire for Taran to bend anyone into submission, other than me, but they don't need to know that.

My wedding gown was compact enough that I kept it this entire time, buried at the bottom of our pack. I knew I'd need one, and crafting something new would have delayed the ceremony. My servants spent the morning smoothing out the wrinkles and are now wrapping me up in its delicate silks.

They're preparing me in what once were my father's chambers, now mine. Soon, mine and Taran's, at least when we're here. Which likely won't be for long, as I imagine he's desperate to escape this heat. But I still had most of the furniture replaced, not needing any reminders of my father or his cruelties. The bed, I had burned.

Taran spent the night in my home, on the other side of Ywelyn. He's still there, at the edge of my land-sense, going through similar preparations. Warmth spreads through me as I imagine him having slept on my pillow, surrounded by my things.

We've eschewed many of the traditional preparations for our wedding as they simply aren't practical. I spent a decent amount of yesterday evening solidifying my bond with the Land as Ystyr's new ruler, but outside of that, too many things required my attention for me to dedicate myself to isolated meditation. While I've kept my meals light, Taran was in no shape to force into fasting.

I'm a little concerned about how much the healers will have been able to help him in less than a day. When I lifted his shirt to inspect the damage, horrific splotches of deep red and purple covered his torso. He'll likely be on a low dose of milk of midnight star to help manage the pain, but it won't be much since he needs to be able to move.

My face burns as heat rushes to my core, imagining *all* the motions we'll be making together. It doesn't help that fingers keep brushing against all my most sensitive areas, pressing silk into the contours of my curves, adhering it to my skin with a sticky sweet tree sap.

After they finish with my dress, they sit me in front of a large, obsidian mirror to do my hair while I glamour myself for the first time since I was a child.

I've long grown accustomed to using powders and the like to highlight my natural beauty, but it's so much easier, and there's so much more I can do, with a simple glamour. I have to rein myself in to keep from going completely out of control. A rosy flush to my cheeks, a deepening of the peachy pink of my lips, a sparkling shadow above my eyes.

My eyes. I can barely hold back the tears stinging behind them as the light within reflects back at me. The light I haven't seen since my father stole my magic, but now shines brightly from the dark depths of my irises. They match Ellie's drawing, resting against the black stone's base. There's nothing to enhance there.

A handmaiden weaves the last of the delicate blossoms into my hair, and then I'm ready. I take a deep breath and a last look at myself in the mirror, and then they lead me out of the room, to my wedding.

Where Taran waits for me.

One of the first things I did as Queen was elevate Barri and his men to be my personal guards. He stands at the entrance of my chambers, offering his arm to escort me to the river.

We walk along the twisting, curving catwalks of Ywelyn to the steady beat of gentle drums. While our path has been kept clear, my people crowd every other surface that could possibly provide them with a glimpse of me, chanting blessings in the Tongue as I pass. Some even hang from the trees. Despite not everyone agreeing with our actions, no one wants to miss such a historic event—the birth of a new realm.

Sweat drips down my neck, even though the heavy afternoon heat's a familiar comfort to me. My nerves tighten, anxiety building with every step. All eyes are on me, all the expectations.

But none of that matters now. All that matters is Taran's eyes when he looks at me.

The catwalk finally slopes downward, spiraling around the trunk of a majestic meranti tree to the flooded forest floor where a small boat awaits. Barri offers his hand, and I lower myself into the shallow vessel. Once settled, I glance up to meet his eyes.

"May the waters favor you, Your Majesty."

I nod, my nerves strong enough, for once, to limit my speech. I force the damp, floral air into my lungs, then dip my hand into the water, shaping it to move the boat forward, into the river. So simple, a child could do it.

The royal shapers, as well as everyone who wished to help, spent all of last night and this morning pulling a small island up from the depths of Anwen's Tears to its surface. It was far more than I ever imagined anyone doing, but they insisted; there was no better place to unite the realms than in the river that flows between them.

My people stand in the knee-deep water as I pass, with more and more arriving by the moment. Once it becomes deep enough to swallow them up to their waists, I finally break free of the mass of fae and trees, into the pull of the river's current.

Into the sunlight.

Toward the island where Taran stands, his hands tucked behind his back, waiting for me.

His eyes sparkle in the golden light when they meet mine.

He's not wearing much more than I am. A dark green loincloth hangs down to his knees, with strips of peach-colored silk flowing over it that match mine, stopping right before they brush the water that comes up to his ankles. A rainbow of flowers blankets the river's surface surrounding his feet.

My gaze trails up his bare chest, glistening in the sunlight from his sweat—not a bruise in sight. More green and peach silk wraps in a skirt around each of his biceps, the fabric twirling in the light breeze.

By the time my boat arrives, my gaze is back on his face. His beautiful face, his malachite eyes piercing into me as he offers his hand. I take it, and his fingers wrap firmly around mine as he helps me up. A refreshing chill flows around my toes as they enter the water.

"You took your time. I've been burning up out here." Taran's fingers drift gently down my sides, coming to rest on my waist. A loose, grazing touch that tickles against the heat.

"Then we should get this over with, shouldn't we?" I bring my hands to his chest, resting them tenderly against the contours of his muscles. "How are you feeling? Does it still hurt?"

"Not as much as you'd think, if you could see the bruises behind my glamour. But I've taken more tonics and elixirs today than in the rest of my life combined."

"Then I'll try to be gentle."

Taran raises an eyebrow. "Before or after you slice my arm open?"

I glance at the wooden pedestal at the center of our island, the only thing here other than us and the flowers. An obsidian dagger sits upon it.

"Both."

My heart pounds as I pick up the cool, heavy blade and offer it to Taran. I have no qualms about the ceremony itself, but our lives are about to change forever.

"Last chance to back out," I say, unable to keep a tremble out of my voice.

Taran's eyes flick to the knife. Instead of taking it, he wraps his fingers around my hand, then guides the tip to the soft skin of his inner forearm. It slices through with hardly a graze, and his blood pours out, dripping down his arm.

"I take you, Taran Evermoor, as my husband, and my King."

Bringing my lips to his skin, the sharp tang of his blood fills my mouth. I trace the crimson path along his arm with my tongue until I meet the puncture in his flesh.

I wince as Taran pierces my arm, a sting drowned in warmth as my blood seeps out.

"I take you, Owena Briarwood, as my wife, and my Queen."

Wrapping my mouth around his arm, he bleeds into me, and I into him, his tongue lapping against me. When the flow finally stems, we pull our blood-stained lips free.

I lift my arm between us, hand up and open, waiting for his.

"Forever one."

Taran clasps my hand, entwining our fingers.

"Forever one."

And when our lips meet, an earthshaking pulse resonates through me with an intensity that nearly shatters my bones.

Our fingers clench, digging into our skin.

Our kiss deepens, lips and tongues and teeth pressing together in passion and pain. Pressure builds, throbbing in my veins until we finally burst, gasping for air.

A pulse ripples out of us, reverberating through the air. Through the water.

Through the Land Herself.

Then we melt into one another's arms, holding each other up. Our eyes meet. A distant roar of applause and cheering fades away, unimportant.

"Was that it? Are the realms united?" *They must be.*

A deep breath. Lips curl into a smile that ignites a tranquil heat within. *Those eyes. So beautiful.*

"I think so."

We sink down until we're sitting in the cool, shallow waters of our island of flowers.

"There's only one thing left."

Fingertips trace along gentle curves, soft and firm. A tug against silk, sliding smoothly off skin.

"Only one? I can think of several." Images flash by of every sultry position possible.

The space between us dissolves as we press together for yet another kiss. There will never be too many. Our hearts pound in time, fingers straining against flesh.

A grimace. *Ancients.*

"Maybe just the one. At least until the bruises heal."

"For now. No promises about later."

A trickle of laughter. One more tender kiss.

"I love you, Taran," I whisper, gazing into the evergreen eyes that hold my entire world.

His fingers graze the side of my face, weaving into my hair. "I love you, Owena." *More than anything.*

He pulls me to his lips, his tongue slipping into my mouth—delicate at first, then building in passion, in hunger, fanning the flames that burn through my core. I feel his body ignite, as if it were my own.

Our marriage bond. Thoughts and feelings, now shared.

I trace my hands gently down his chest, and he tenses beneath my touch, kissing me deeper. I shift aside the water-soaked fabric of his loincloth, and my fingers land on the silky-smooth skin of his substantial length, already hard. Waiting. A tingle runs through me at my own touch.

He groans into me, and I breathe it in before tugging off the remaining silk clinging to me. His hands cup my breasts as I lift myself up, my eyes locked on his, and then I slowly lower down.

A sigh drifts out of me as he enters, bit by bit, stretching me, filling every need, every want within. My own tight heat, engulfing him. What we did before... that was nothing. This is how we belong.

A distant whoop carries through the air.

Of course. We have an audience. I had forgotten.

Might as well give them a show.

I lean back, my hands splashing into the cool water as I prop myself up, arms locked, presenting myself to the sky. I roll my hips slowly, taking my time building up our entwined pleasure into something greater than I've ever experienced before.

Taran's lips meet my breast, pulling my nipple into his mouth, sucking it, teasing it. Moans roll out of me in time with the motion of my hips, and then a sharp tug with his teeth sends a cry rippling out of me.

"Louder, so they can hear."

The bending itself sends a spike of arousal through me, and my muscles clench around him as my voice carries through the air.

I push back up, wrapping my hands behind Taran's neck, pulling myself close.

"As my King demands."

My Queen. Taran winds his arms tightly around me as I rock my hips, keeping him fully inside as I grind against him. My eyes never leave his, with all his love, all his being pouring into me as our foreheads press together. Our breathing picks up. Once I find the perfect angle, I pick up the pace, bucking my hips faster as our passion builds, coiling tighter and tighter. It's impossible to tell where his pleasure ends and mine begins.

I tilt my head back, cries of ecstasy pouring out of me, loud enough for all to hear. Taran's fingers dig into my skin as his breath smolders against my neck. I'm nearing release, my voice pitching higher and higher, I'm ready to burst—

"Not yet." His voice echoes, low and tight.

Oh fuck. Amusement bursts through our bond.

My motion stalls, my eyes dropping to Taran's piercing gaze.

"Keep going, but you won't release until I allow it."

My hips roll again all on their own. A whimper falls out of me as our pleasure tweaks to an unbearable level.

"You tormented me for weeks." His eyes flutter shut as a moan interrupts his words. "I won't torture you nearly as long."

His arms release me, moving behind him to hold up his weight. Then he thrusts upwards, deeper into me.

A wail quivers out.

Again and again, each one a spike of pleasure that should send us over the edge to blessed release but doesn't. I collapse into him, clawing desperately at his skin.

"Don't stop," I beg.

Taran thrusts harder, faster, and my hips pick up their pace to match.

My cries escalate, interrupted by my ragged breaths, until I can't breathe at all anymore. Everything coils tight—clenching, twisting, burning.

Completely overwhelming.

Begging for deliverance.

Until a single word breaks through.

"Release."

It shatters my mind.

Taran cries out, his body jerking as he empties into me. My back arches, throwing my head up to the sky as a sob of pure relief flies out. Our climaxes ripple through me—unraveling me, ruining me.

He catches himself on his elbows as he falls back into the water, and I sink into him, heavy and unmoving, save for my lungs forcing deep, slow breaths. A stabbing sensation builds throughout my torso.

"I'm in a lot of pain right now," Taran groans after a sharp inhale. *That must be what I'm feeling.*

He huffs, then grits his teeth. *No more bearing things alone.*

"Can you get off me?" he asks.

"You should've thought of that before you ruined me," I mumble, my face buried in his shoulder. "I don't think I can move."

"Of course you can." He rolls over, sending me splashing into the brisk river water, full of significantly more flowers than before.

I yelp as my muscles shock into motion.

"Is that any way to treat your wife?" I splash water back at him as I push myself up. Despite the shallow depth, my hair is completely soaked, and I'm dripping wet.

"No. This is." He wraps me in his arms, engulfing me in a kiss to end all kisses.

No. To *begin* all kisses. And our new life together.

As King and Queen of a united realm.

Chapter 45

Caeo

Mother's face twists as a pulse vibrates through the Land. It plows through me, my body shuddering as aftershocks come trembling behind.

Through the soldier gripping my arms.

Through my mother.

Through everyone except Emlyn, who's moving too fast to be stopped.

His twin blades pierce my mother's sides.

Her scream echoes through the air, and by the time the Land quiets and I stop shaking, Emlyn yanks his knives out of her, and she collapses to the ground.

Is that it?

It's over?

Emlyn exhales with a whistle. "Hooray, we did it."

He wipes his forehead with the back of his arm, bloody blade still in hand. "Though it seems Taran's married now, so perhaps if you'd counted properly, this would've been a lot easier. And I might not have had to murder anyone."

After a deep breath, his voice wavers. "I'm gonna need a moment." He glances at the soldier holding my arms. "Maybe let go of him? You have a new king and queen, and he's their heir, so…"

The soldier releases me.

My brain finally catches up, and my gaze drops to my mother, crumpled on the grass with blood oozing out of her sides. Absorbing into the ground as if the Land's already claiming her corpse.

She still breathes.

I fall to my knees beside her. She looks up at me, her eyes dimming, breath ragged.

"Caeo?" She grasps my hand.

My throat tightens. "Mother."

That's what she was, once. The one who kissed every hurt, who tucked me in every night, who chased away my nightmares.

Until she became one herself.

"Why?" She coughs out blood with the word. "Why did you betray me?"

My brain buckles.

What?

It takes a few tries for my mouth to form words.

"I-I didn't. You hid the truth from me my entire life. You took everything that mattered to me. You made me your puppet. All I did was leave."

The smallest of smiles turns her lips. "Have you finally learned to lie?"

My heart stops. The truth sinks in, cold and heavy. *She doesn't think she did anything wrong. She believes it so much that it's become her truth.*

She's breathing slower. Tears leak from her eyes, blood from her lips. There's not much time left.

It's now or never.

"Did you ever love me? Or Taran? Did you love either of us?"

Her fingers tighten around mine, her voice a hoarse whisper.

"You loved me. That was enough."

My lungs catch, my voice tripping before it breaks out. "So that's it? The whole reason you had me? For your own sake?"

She doesn't answer, her eyes slowly closing as a tear falls down her cheek.

And just like that, the last ache in my heart fades away. The mother I loved was a lie.

Her eyes open as I pull my hand free of hers.

"I don't anymore."

I turn my back, leaving, so she can die how she deserves.

Alone.

I WANDER, unsure what to do in the cloud of chaos swirling around me. Panicked soldiers. Officers shouting, trying to maintain order. Eventually, I find Emlyn, sitting in the shade of an oak tree with his arms behind him, propping him up. The grass is all matted between splotches of dirt from all the soldiers who camped here earlier, but now everyone's gathered in groups throughout the valley, their murmurs filling the air.

His eyes are closed, his head tilted slightly to the sky as a light breeze flutters through his hair. His bloody knives rest on the ground next to him.

Opting to sit on his opposite side, I keep my voice low. "I've never ever killed someone."

A soft laugh falls out of him. "Lucky you."

He tilts his head toward me, opening his eyes. "Don't worry, it's not my first. I haven't killed anywhere near as many people as I've fucked, but the number's still quite high." He sighs. "It doesn't get easier, though."

"But you do it anyway."

Emlyn shrugs. "That's my job. I do the things no one else will."

He shifts his weight, then runs his hand through his hair. "I didn't think it was worth the cost anymore, but this time… maybe it is. It may not have been necessary to end the war, but it seems like it was for you. So I'll carry it."

"Thanks." I press my hands against the ground to shift my position. "You're still weird, but I guess I can see why Reid loves you."

A smile stretches across Emlyn's face. "Thank you. Now, I'm sure he's worried sick about me, so if you could go order everyone to withdraw so we can go back—"

He cringes.

I sit up straighter. "What?"

"Ancients. We'll have to adjust all over again." His face pales with disgust. "Maybe you should order the withdrawal, and we can wait on this side of the border until they send Reid to look for us."

"Why would they send him?"

"The border doesn't bother him—he can cross without me."

Wait. What? But before I open my mouth, he slaps his hand on my back. "Come on, Prince Caeo. Time to send everyone home."

He ignores my questions as he pulls me to my feet, leaving his daggers behind. How could that possibly have happened? Does that mean Ellie might be able to someday, too?

All those thoughts die as we pass my mother's corpse. I avert my eyes, following Emlyn in silence. A group of fae gathered nearby turn to face us as we approach, and while many look at me with judgmental eyes, a few approach Emlyn.

I guess they know him? Hopefully only professionally.

Emlyn quickly explains that Taran and Owena are married, and we're now living in a new realm. He grabs my arm and introduces me as Taran's heir, here to give them orders on his behalf.

Unlike the shepherd, the captains—at least that's who I assume these guys are—don't just take his word for it. Which makes no sense, because he can't lie, so maybe it's some kind of formality? Whatever the case, I have to sit down and bond with the Land while they do the same, somehow feeling something different about my connection with Her.

They *do* all mumble words in the Tongue, so maybe they're just asking Her? I really need to learn that language someday. But that's the least of my worries. It looks like I'll actually have to take being Taran's heir seriously now, at least until he gets here.

Before that can overwhelm me, I take the opportunity to lose myself in Her steady pulse. If anything, it feels more... serene? than ever before. Slower. Softer. Yet at the same time, stronger. A twirl of happiness chases each thud, echoing through me.

It washes away the lingering aches hiding in the deepest parts of my heart. My mother's gone, and she'll never torment me, or anyone else, ever again. Everyone can finally move on.

Humans. Fae. The Land.

Everyone.

Emlyn tugs me out of my trance once the captains have all confirmed I'm the heir. I open my eyes to them kneeling before me, awaiting my orders.

"Um... the war's over. Send everyone home?"

Emlyn clears his throat. "Maybe not everyone. You're a prince. You need *some* protection."

"Can't you do that?"

His palm hits his face. "Ancients, I can't catch a break." He points to one of the captains. "You. Leave a company behind. Everyone else, go home." Then he looks at me, raising his eyebrows.

"Yeah—what he said."

With a slight nod of their heads, the captains get to their feet and follow my command.

By nightfall, about half of the soldiers have begun their long trek home. Those who remain settle in to sleep, planning to head out in the morning.

Emlyn and I camp right in front of the border.

It's highly unlikely Reid will come through tonight. Even assuming everything went well with Ellie and her dad, only a crazy person would think the fae completely withdrew after just a few bells of not fighting. It'll probably take them days to believe this isn't some kind of trick.

I'm inclined to go back to where we crossed over originally and return to our campsite to look for them, but Emlyn thinks that's too risky; if Ellie didn't convince her father, they won't be there, and we'll still be the enemy. Ones who can barely function from nausea.

It's only the knowledge that he's as desperate to see Reid as I am to see Ellie, and still thinks it's a bad idea, that keeps me from going.

So we wait.

The whole first night, and the whole second day. We pass the time by continuing the world's slowest game of *Never Ever*.

By sunset, I know more about Emlyn's sexual history than any sane person should ever want to, and the rest of the army's gone, except the company that stayed behind to protect me. It's overkill, but I guess there's a chance some of Ystyr's army may have gone rogue when their king died, so they could randomly decide to attack.

By the next morning, the two of us are ready to risk a crossing.

"We can't both go," Emlyn says. "Someone needs to stay here in case Reid shows up."

"Then that should be you. If he's at the campsite, I'll tell him you're waiting and that it's safe for him to go through." I start walking toward the hill. At least we can just hike over it this time—no need to go around.

Emlyn grabs my arm, stopping me. "And what if they're not there? What if there's soldiers waiting for you?"

"Then they'll kill me, just like they'd kill you if you went." I pull my arm free.

He slides in front of me before I take two steps. "But if they kill me, I'm just dead. If they kill you, then I'm the one who let Taran's brother and heir get himself killed."

"And that's worse than being dead?"

"In some ways, yes."

I rub my temples. "Why do either of us need to wait for Reid? If he comes through and we aren't here, he can just go back. We can even leave a message with the soldiers for him."

"Because I was really hoping to see you guys, not some random soldier."

Emlyn and I spin around.

Reid's standing there, right at the edge of the fog, scratching the back of his neck.

How did we miss him?

Alright, I wasn't paying attention to my land-sense at all, but that's not surprising for me—I was distracted. It *is* surprising for Emlyn, but I guess that's just a sign of how worried he actually was.

He confirms it by flying to Reid in a matter of seconds. Emlyn throws his arms around him, wrapping him in a kiss with enough force that they stumble back into the fog. Now that I'm paying attention, I can sense them through the purple haze as Emlyn repeatedly plants kisses all over Reid's face.

When Reid finally grabs hold of Emlyn and brings their lips together, I turn my land-sense away, giving them some privacy.

I force myself to be patient, knowing they deserve this moment, but anxiety creeps in as the seconds crawl by. I'm nervously tapping my fingers against my hand by the time they pop out of the fog, probably less than a minute later, but it felt so much longer.

"Hey, Caeo," Reid calls, his arms still wrapped around Emlyn. "Ellie's waiting for you."

That's all I need.

I rush into the fog, past the both of them. My feet can't keep up with my heart, pounding faster and faster the deeper I go.

Then I'm bursting out of the purple cloud, into muted colors and the stench of death.

Shit.

I double over as my head spins, and nausea rolls through me from my feet, up to my stomach, and into my throat.

Not again.

But warm, soft arms catch me. A familiar lavender scent.

I lift my face and find hers.

"Ellie."

She lights up with a smile, her eyes full of tears, streaming down her cheeks.

"Caeo."

My heart's on the verge of bursting, pressing against the walls of my chest and into my throat.

No. That's my stomach.

I turn away right before it empties itself all over the ground.

Chapter 46

Taran

I've woken up every morning of the last two weeks wrapped in Owena's arms, blanketed in the mingling scents of citrus and pine.

Our time together hasn't been completely perfect; I've spent most of my life avoiding my responsibilities and the politics of court, so being thrust into ruling a forcefully united realm is frustrating, to say the least. I thought all I'd have to do was support Owena, but she's determined to have us rule as equals, sharing our duties and refusing to make important pronouncements without coming to an agreement with me first. It's led to many arguments, the most ongoing of which being what to call our new realm, but the heat of those moments fuels the passion of our nights, tangled up in one another.

We may not agree on much, but the bond we now share between our hearts and minds... it's everything I never knew I wanted. Everything I need. I'll never have to carry anything alone again.

We left Ywelyn as soon as possible to head to the border, but it still took four days of preparation after our wedding. Owena spent the time meeting with as many of our people as she could, determining reparations for the curses her father put on them, while

I sent messengers across the continent, explaining what we'd done.

When Aedys and Ystyr united, everyone felt it. A shudder through the Land, pulsing out of Owena and me. Significant portions of what were once eastern Aedys and Ystyr shifted into Llynos as the Land rebalanced our borders. We don't expect Llynos's queen to complain about her new territory, but she *did* get a sudden influx of very confused people because of the change. We'll be heading there soon to figure out a solution.

But first: Lyndir.

Gone are the carefree days of traveling the wilderness by myself. Now, we need an entire entourage worthy of the monarchy—it's maddening. Worse, it takes over a week by boat on Anwen's Tears to finally escape the sweltering heat of the southern half of the realm. Hopefully, I'll never return. I don't care how cold Owena is up here—I can keep her warm, but it's impossible to feel cool down there.

Along the way, some of the messengers she sent to Ystyr's armies find us and provide an update on the state of the war. As predicted, when Dryfid died, the reaction varied across his forces. Those fighting in the south mostly split between following their previous orders or holding while they awaited direction. For the most part, they all withdrew when they received Owena's new commands.

A few battalions went rogue, including one led by a cousin of hers. Owena sent messengers back, informing them that their new king is capable of bending an entire company of soldiers, so she expects them to stand down and swear fealty at once. Not my first choice of a response, but a rebellion's the last thing I want to add to our plate right now. With luck, they'll fall in line, and we won't have to deal with them anymore.

Those who'd joined Aedys's forces continued serving under my mother while they awaited new orders. According to our latest messenger, the next day, the queen was dead.

My heart stops as he tells me, only starting up again when Owena takes my hand. *I'm here, my love.*

My mother? Dead?

I don't hear anything he says after those words, and I cut him off mid-sentence.

"She's dead? How?"

The messenger blinks at the interruption, then recovers. "The details are unclear. Stabbed, by two blades, but I'm unsure by who. It happened while she was speaking to your heir, Prince Caeo, right as the realms united. He ordered a withdrawal on your behalf shortly after. One company stayed behind for his protection."

Owena thanks the messenger and sends him away as I sit against the low wall lining the side of the boat, my head spinning with the gentle sway of the river. She winds her arm around mine as she joins me, the softness of her touch pulling me back into the moment.

"That was certainly unexpected." Starlight swirls in her eyes, calming my heart. "Are you alright?"

There are so many thoughts, so many emotions, circling the steady calm of Owena's presence in my mind. She keeps quiet, adding nothing but her warmth. My mouth sticks as I stutter through where to begin.

"It's hard to believe she's dead." I scratch my brow before dropping my hand with a sigh. "I always thought I'd speak with her again someday. To ask her why." I meet Owena's eyes. "Maybe it's best that I didn't. I doubt the answer would have changed anything."

She squeezes my arm, then caresses it gently with her fingertips. "Caeo was there. Perhaps he asked her. But I think she's simply what happens when people get swallowed up by their trauma. They pass it on to others."

Perhaps. I was five years old the last time I spoke with her. All I know is that she hated the mortals for killing her father. Anything else... did she blame him—blame herself—for not being strong enough?

Hopefully my brother found enough closure for the both of us.

Letting out a slow exhale, I take Owena's hand. "I hope Caeo and Ellie are alright. They shouldn't have been there."

Her head sinks into my shoulder.

"I hope so too. We'll find out in a couple of days."

IT'S STRANGE TO NO LONGER have the most powerful bond with the Land. I still do, but Owena now matches it. So she senses the camp the same moment I do. But she hasn't spent enough time with the two people mixed in among the soldiers to recognize them right away. At least not recently.

I kick my horse into a gallop and fly toward them, my heart pounding along with her hooves. Owena calls after me, her irritation surging through my chest—she's probably never galloped on a horse in her life—but she can catch up later.

The lookouts sense me coming first, falling to their knees as I pass, charging into the valley. The soldiers relaxing in their camp are next, jumping to their feet, then immediately dropping to the ground, lowering their heads in respect.

Another thing to add to my never-ending list: get people to stop doing that.

Only two people remain as they were, though one of them startles and glances nervously at everyone else.

I'm off my horse before she comes to a complete stop.

"Emlyn."

He looks up from where he sits with Reid, polishing one of his bone knives. His amber eyes meet mine, no longer dim like the last time I saw them, but radiant with their golden glow. My hand reaches for him, but I catch myself, my mind racing as I struggle to find the right words to say.

"Taran." He pushes himself up, sliding his blade into the strap around his right leg that matches the one on his left.

Two blades.

"You killed my mother, didn't you?"

Emlyn crosses his arms before meeting my gaze. "That's what you care about? No 'glad to see you're alive,' or 'I'm sorry for'"—his mouth quirks as he tilts his head, thinking—"well, let's just say all the things. You know what they are."

I suppose I deserve that.

Reid gets to his feet and moves closer to Emlyn, looking between us.

I step right in front of Emlyn. "I'm not sorry I bent you. I never will be, because you would be dead if I hadn't. But I am sorry for everything I put you through."

Emlyn narrows his eyes as he searches my face. I stare back, waiting.

He breaks first, his familiar grin tugging at the corner of his mouth. "I guess I'll forgive you, mostly because I rather enjoy being alive. And because I need you to make it so Reid can stay." He wraps his arm around Reid, who smiles nervously.

I clap my hands on both of their shoulders. "Done. You're under my protection. I'll make it known that any action taken against you is an action against me."

Reid breathes a sigh of relief, and Emlyn lets go of him, keeping his gaze fixed on me as I drop my hands.

"Thank you." Emlyn tucks a wisp of hair behind his ear. "And yes, I did kill your mother. I hope you're alright with that."

"I am." I'll never be able to repay Emlyn for everything he's done for me. The weights he's carried while I was too caught up with my own to notice.

I hesitate, then pull him into a hug.

"Ancients, we're hugging? You haven't hugged me in like, ten years." But he relaxes into it, bringing his hands to my back.

"I thought you'd take it the wrong way."

"Probably." He gives me a quick pat. "But maybe let go of me before Reid gets jealous?"

"Why would I be jealous? Hug him all you like."

I give Emlyn another squeeze just as Owena's bright voice rings out behind me.

"Waters, Taran, this is no way for a king to present himself. Where's your dignity?" Her feet hit the ground as she dismounts, sending a trill through my land-sense.

"Oh shit." Emlyn releases me, jumping back.

I fold my arms, glancing back at my wife. *This was bound to happen eventually.*

Her eyes widen as she trails her fingers along my shoulder, her gaze locked on Emlyn.

"Griff?"

I almost jump as her shock bursts through our bond.

"Nice to see you again, Owena." Emlyn tugs Reid closer and mumbles in his ear, "Now would be a good time for you to go get Caeo and Ellie."

Reid rolls his eyes, shaking his head. "Yeah, you're dealing with this on your own." He pulls free of Emlyn's grasp and strolls toward the border.

"You're Emlyn?" Owena demands, staring him down. She looks at me. "This is Emlyn?"

I exhale, then take her hand. "Yes. Emlyn, this is my wife and your new queen, Owena."

Emlyn's lips curl inward as he nods. "Mmhmm. Yep, I know."

I look down at Owena. "And I already know he slept with you. I've known that for years."

I didn't think her eyes could go any wider, but they do. I hold back a smirk. Perhaps with enough time, tormenting her will lose its fun, but for now, my wounds are still fresh.

"For years? Did you—is he a spy? Did you send him to spy on me?" Her shock gives way to annoyance, burning through me as she tears her hand out of mine.

"Your father, specifically. But I didn't tell him to get in your bed—he did that on his own."

"You kind of knew it would happen, though. It's me. What else was I gonna do?"

I shoot Emlyn a glare.

Owena folds her arms, shaking her head. "And he'll be sticking around now, I assume?"

We both look at him, waiting.

He chews at his nails for an exaggerated moment, then shrugs. "I'm sure Reid will want us to visit Lyndir from time to time, but that was my plan. Someone has to keep you from making stupid decisions. I mean, I'm gone a few weeks, and you end up married? You're lucky you're not completely miserable."

"How do you know I'm not?"

Owena gently smacks my arm. I grab her hand, meeting the stars in her eyes. Despite our disagreements, I'll never tire of getting lost in them.

A smile presses across her face. *I love your eyes too.*

"Well," Emlyn says, "outside of the obvious signs of affection... Caeo told me everything. I'm kind of jealous, really. Willbending is just about the only thing I haven't tried, sexually. Maybe that's another thing I can talk Caeo into in eighty years.”

I rake my palm down my face, groaning into it; I don’t want to hear about whatever he has planned with my brother. “Emlyn, just go away.”

His legs start walking. “You really just bent me again, after all that? Hey—don’t forget to tickle behind her knees!”

Ancients. I lower my hand and glance at Owena. “Behind your knees?”

Her mouth twists. “Later, my love. We’ve already put on enough of an undignified showing.” She nods to all the surrounding soldiers, still kneeling.

I’m never going to get used to this.

Yes, you will.

“Can you handle it?” I ask, glancing at the border. “I’d rather go wait for Caeo.”

Owena’s eyes soften. “Of course.” She lifts herself onto her toes to kiss my lips. Light, but quick. “I’ll join you soon.”

I linger for a moment, watching her tell the troops to rise. A warm serenity fills the air as she walks among them, taking the time to greet some individually on her way to the captain. She’ll likely explain that we won’t need them to remain here any longer but won’t know for sure until we’ve spoken with Caeo.

My chest tightens as I turn toward the border. Emlyn’s there, staring at the fog with his arms crossed. As I approach, his tension becomes palpable. I’ll never understand how he became so attached to Reid. Out of all the people he’s been with, why him? There were plenty of others who’d be significantly less bothersome.

I come to a stop beside him. “You sent Reid through by himself?”

He stops chewing his thumb to answer. “Yep. He’s fine with it now—doesn’t bother him. But it doesn’t stop me from worrying that every time he goes through, he won’t come back.”

Reid can cross the border on his own? That's something we'll have to take seriously. The potential ramifications… Is it possible mortals could become fae again?

I don't want to think about that right now. We've already shattered what's normal enough for one lifetime.

"Do you know what's going on over there?" I ask.

Emlyn sighs. "Caeo went back two days after we sent the troops home. He hasn't returned because he doesn't want to deal with reacclimating, but he said he would if you showed up. From my understanding, he's under the protection of Ellie's father, and outside of some trusted officers and Ellie's roommates, no one knows he's fae. Reid has free rein to go back and forth as a messenger, but I'd still get attacked on sight."

That's better than I'd hoped. "So Ellie spoke with her father? Did she convince him to stop incanting?"

"She convinced him it's 'a problem,' but the only thing he's done so far, other than protect Caeo, is send all the Academy students home indefinitely 'to recover.' The Order's still posted all along the border, waiting to see if this is some kind of trick."

I cross my arms. "It was never going to happen quickly, but that sounds like a decent start." And I know Ellie won't give up until it's done.

Owena's on her way over, her steps pulsing through my land-sense. While we only share thoughts when we touch, I feel her wherever she is now. We haven't yet traveled outside of one another's land-sense, but I think I still would, even then. I already can't imagine going a single moment without feeling her presence. It'd be like a part of me went missing.

She slides her arm around my waist as she settles next to me, watching the fog along with us. I unfold my arms to wrap one around her.

"Are you sure this is dignified enough?" I ask.

Owena chuckles. "We're waiting for your brother, not their king. The most important thing for him to see is that you're happy."

"And you're certain I am?"

Her beautiful smile graces her lips. "Try telling me you aren't."

"I have plenty of things I'm not happy about. Would you like the list? We'll likely add a few more items before sunset."

She wraps her other arm around my waist, turning me to face her. "And after sunset? Will you be happy then?"

"You know I will."

I bring my lips to hers and surrender to our kiss. We've already made it through the darkness, through our worst moments. No matter what comes at us, from this point on, we're facing it together. No more secrets.

In the back of my mind, I pick up Caeo stepping into the fog. Owena does, too, as we both pull apart at the same time.

He carries Ellie in his arms, and I breathe a sigh of relief. There's no anger, no rage, boiling through me.

"Looks like the Land forgave her," Owena says.

"Seems that way." I give her another quick kiss before we face the fog, waiting for Ellie and Caeo to emerge.

Then two more people step across the border.

One is Reid, as unaffected as Caeo, but he's supporting a mortal who's being crushed by the Land's fury. Someone much heavier than Ellie, too much for him to carry.

"Shit." Emlyn rushes forward to help.

I consider joining him, but at that moment, Caeo appears, breathing heavily as Ellie clings tightly to him. He lowers her feet to the ground, then collapses next to her.

I squeeze Owena's hand as my brother's eyes find me. The cloud of gray washes out of them, glowing a bright sky blue.

Chapter 47

Ellie

"We really need to figure out how Reid does it," Caeo huffs from the grass next to me.

I'm still where he set me down, on my feet, doing my best not to fall over. To not be jealous of Reid. It should be enough that I could come back at all.

Taran offers Caeo his hand, pulling him straight into a hug. "You made it."

"We did. And you got married." Caeo pulls away from Taran and embraces Owena. "I guess you're my sister now. So glad I never kissed you."

What? Was that actually a possibility? He never mentioned it before, but I suppose I don't have any standing to complain.

Owena laughs as I straighten up. I wipe away the tears that pooled in my eyes during the crossing and look over her and Taran. They appear relaxed, with no sign of the tension that gripped Taran every time he saw me before we parted.

He actually looks happy now. It fills his eyes, his smile, and his entire being in such a way that every moment I previously thought he was happy now feels like a lie.

It's a bittersweet tang in my heart.

His gaze drifts over to me, the tranquil swirls of his emerald eyes no longer crackling with the Land's rage.

I grab my own hand, twisting my fingers together as my nerves get the best of me. "Taran, Owena. I'm so happy to see you."

Why can't this be as easy for me as it is for Caeo?

Owena frees herself from him and pushes toward me, pulling my hands apart as she takes one in each of hers. There's a sparkle in her eyes now that wasn't there before, like stars speckling the night sky. It's similar to the drawing I did—is that why she seemed so moved by it? "We're delighted to see you, too, Ellie. And there's no anger from the Land, in case you were wondering."

Taran wraps his arm around my shoulder and gives a tight squeeze. "I'm glad you made it."

Tears fill my eyes again, but happy ones this time. I rip my hands free of Owena's and throw my arms around her and Taran. They both startle back.

"You and your surprise hugs," Owena says, patting me gently.

I let go and step away. "You hugged Caeo."

"He's my brother now. You're not my sister"—she glances to Caeo—"yet."

Caeo's face tightens, and he glances at the border fog. "Maybe don't say things like that right now."

The two fae follow his gaze to where Reid and Emlyn finally stumble out of the haze, my father supported between them.

Keeping my eyes off the fog, I rush over as they indelicately drop him to the ground, then stagger to the side to sit and catch their breath.

"Father? Are you alright?" I kneel next to him, my chest tightening with a tangle of relief that he made it, pride that he came at all, and concern for what he'll think.

He tugs at his purple and gray uniform, straightening it out before he looks up at me, panting. "You could have prepared me better, Eloise."

"I told you it'd be difficult. That you'd feel all the anger the Land has for us. That's the anger that drives the fae to attack."

Taran clears his throat.

I wince. They probably don't appreciate the oversimplification. I need to start weaving in the nuances.

My father lets go of me immediately after I help him to his feet, his eyes widening as he takes in our surroundings.

For the faelands, this valley's rather lackluster. Far-off trees speckle the space between grassy hills, and the distant smell of waste wafts through the air. But the grass is greener and more brilliant than any in Landore, its blades varying between a multitude of shades as they roll like waves in the breeze, in time with the barely perceptible pulse that thrums through everything.

"Father, I'd like to introduce you to King Taran and Queen Owena, of...?" I look questioningly at them.

"We haven't decided on a name yet." Taran slides his hand around Owena's waist.

"Typically, one bows or kneels before royalty," Owena says as my father takes turns staring at them.

My face warms as my breath hitches. I should've anticipated this but didn't—they've never made me recognize their royalty before.

Father stiffens, then jerks slightly at the waist for a barely noticeable bow. I drop into a curtsy worthy of an audience with our own king to make up for his lack of effort.

Several seconds pass with no one saying anything, then Owena's gaze shifts to me. "Is that all?"

Why are they making this so hard? We're supposed to be friends, almost family... right?

I inhale deeply, and the rhythm of my heart settles. We are, but they need to be monarchs now.

"Of course not. Caeo and I—we explained everything. About the war, and how our ancestors were fae, and incanting. My father wished to see proof with his own eyes before we went to the king. And to get assurances of peace."

Taran's eyes narrow. "What kind of proof? I will not allow you to incant here, and should you ignore that, the Land would likely kill you as you attempt to return home."

Really, Taran? Not helpful.

"I think just seeing the difference between here and home is enough. Right, Father?"

"I think so." My father's voice comes out gruff and stiff. His gaze keeps wandering, his eyes alight with wonder as they absorb the sights. A large group of fae, I assume the leftover soldiers, gather further along the valley near a collection of tents.

"Come on, Taran." Caeo elbows his brother in the side. "Just give some assurances of peace so we can get on with this."

Taran gives him a side-eye before looking at Owena. Neither of them says anything, but seconds later, she smiles, and they both look back at the rest of us.

"Emlyn, would you show Ellie's father around for a bit?" Taran says.

Prickles run along the back of my neck as Father straightens up even more, his shoulders tensing.

"Show him around where?" Emlyn asks from the ground. "There's nothing here."

Taran responds with a glare.

Emlyn lets out an exaggerated groan, then drags himself to his feet. He looks at Reid, still lying on the grass. "Are you coming?"

"Ancients, no. Have fun."

"Whatever." Emlyn wraps his arm around my father's shoulders, pulling him along as he starts walking, completely ignoring Father's panicked expression. "So you're Ellie's dad? Fair warning, you probably won't like any of the stories I have about her. Or Caeo, for that matter."

Every nerve in my body knots up. "Maybe I should—"

Owena cuts me off. "No, we have matters to discuss with you two."

About what? Have I already messed this up that much?

Caeo looks to Reid. "Can you *please* go keep Emlyn from saying anything that'll result in me murdering him?"

Reid sighs. "Fine. But you owe me." He lazily pushes himself up, then starts after them, pulling Emlyn's arm off my father when he gets there.

A sigh of relief falls out of me. While Father's been treating Reid respectfully, I know Reid's still a little nervous around him. It's understandable—Reid's the only person who can comfortably pass between realms. If I were him, I'd be worried Father might decide that's something that needs to be controlled, too.

I glance back at Taran. "What did you want to discuss?"

He unwraps his arm from Owena and looks between Caeo and me. "It seems you're not planning on staying here?"

My eyebrows flick up in surprise. "No. I wish we could, but I promised the Land I'd get my people to stop incanting. I can't do that from here."

A cloud passes over the sun, shrouding us in shadow. Taran's gaze lands on Caeo.

He avoids Taran's eyes, scratching the back of his head. "I'm staying with Ellie. We'll come back to visit, but until she's fulfilled her promise, we can't stick around."

Taran nods slowly as a heavy exhale escapes him, and my heart twists. It should've occurred to us he wouldn't want to say goodbye again so soon. I take Caeo's hand, and he gives me a squeeze.

"I'm sorry," I say. "I'll do my best to get it done as soon as possible."

Owena wraps her hands around Taran's arm. "It will go as it goes. As Caeo said, you'll visit." She turns to him. "Besides, we have a job for you."

Caeo takes a slight step back, his brow furrowing. "For me?"

"We'd like you to be our official representative in Lyndir. To speak for us, should an occasion arise that necessitates it. Should any harm come to you, it would be considered an act of war."

"You don't need to add threats to everything, Owena," Taran mumbles.

"I'm simply trying to keep your brother safe."

My stomach tightens at the reminder. So far, we'd been keeping Caeo's heritage a secret. That won't be possible if he accepts this role.

Taran rubs her hand before leveling his gaze at Caeo. "What's your answer, then?"

"Um..." Caeo looks at me.

I press my lips together, then tell him exactly what I think. "You should. You'll be good at it, and I think it will help."

He takes a deep breath. Seconds later, a smile tugs at the corners of his mouth. "Alright. I guess I will."

"Then that will be our truce," Owena declares. "So long as the mortals allow you free passage between realms and treat you with respect, then we will have peace. But should anyone harm or imprison you, they will face our wrath."

"Feel free to remind them what I'm capable of," Taran adds. "Another war would be quite different from what they're used to."

I hadn't even considered that. *That's probably something we should ease people into.*

Otherwise, those terms seem reasonable. "You should probably repeat all that for my father before we go, but maybe leave out the last part? Caeo can let them know that later."

"I'm gonna need to bring a lot of water with me," Caeo mutters.

Owena smiles. "Then let's get started on that."

CAEO SPENDS THE REST of the afternoon with Taran and Owena while I take my father back from Emlyn and Reid. Despite our fears, Emlyn actually did a good job leading him around; not only did he show off some shaping with the earth and trees, but he even bonded with the Land through my father so he could feel Her pulse. The only stories he told were about when he taught me to ride a horse, and how he killed the queen.

It stings a little how much fulfilling my promise depends on my father. I wish it were something I could do entirely on my own, but Alexis was right—without him, I'm just a girl no one will listen to. In time, hopefully I'll have put in enough effort and changed enough minds that I can lead the push myself, but for now, I need him.

I've spent more time with Father in the last two weeks than I have in the rest of my life combined. Perhaps that's an exaggeration—I spent a lot of time sitting quietly in his presence during my childhood. Now, we're talking. He's finally seeing me for who I am, and I don't think he's disappointed. If I'd had the courage to stand up for myself earlier, my life might have been completely different. But then none of this would've happened, so I suppose it's good I didn't.

He even seems to like Caeo, despite Caeo being absolutely terrified in his presence. Hopefully Owena's decree will ease his worries that he'll be killed if he gives my father any reason to dislike him.

Though he hides it well, Caeo's been struggling with his new place in the world. He misses his land-sense and keeps trying to shape before remembering he can't. We'll be staying here for another day while Taran and Owena's entourage gather a sufficiently large supply of water we can bring with us, which should help. Once he gets past the first few days of nausea, he shouldn't need much on a regular basis since his human half seems to make his eyes fade to gray, and he can always style his hair or wear a hat to hide his ears. Willbending, as a bloodline ability, seems unaffected so far, but we haven't revealed he can do that and don't plan to anytime soon.

I've caught him eyeing the milk of midnight star more than once, but as far as I know, he hasn't used any since before his mother's death. I'm optimistic that being free of her will finally allow him a chance to heal.

Just before sunset, Reid and Emlyn escort Father back across the border. Caeo and I set up a campfire far away from all the remaining soldiers and Taran and Owena's escorts. Far enough to give me the illusion of privacy, though from everything Caeo's told me, I know I'm lying to myself.

As proven when, right as Caeo's hand slips under my blouse, Reid and Emlyn show up, plopping down next to the fire.

Lovely.

Caeo pulls his lips away from mine, and I quickly sit up, running my hand along my hair to make sure it's flat.

"Really?" He glares at them. "Don't you have anywhere else you can be?"

"Hey, you two have all the time in the world to be together now, whereas I have no idea when I'll see you again," Reid says, sending a bittersweet warmth through my chest. While the two of us spent a fair amount of time catching up in the few days after the fae withdrew, he's mostly been here. It's disappointing that after finally connecting, we now have to go our separate ways.

"Between days of crippling nausea and practically living with Ellie's father—no, we don't have 'all the time in the world,'" Caeo says.

I pat my hand on his knee. "He's right, though. We shouldn't waste this time with them."

Caeo sighs, then tucks his arm behind me. "Fine. So why don't you tell us how to get Ellie passing through the border as easily as you do? Maybe then we can come back more."

Reid shrugs. "Just get the Land to stop seeing you as a mortal."

"How?" I ask.

"You can try absorbing more of Caeo's fluids," Emlyn suggests. "Though he's only half fae, so it'd probably take twice as many."

Reid nudges Emlyn in the side with his elbow. "I'm fairly certain that's not it."

"I know, I'm just joking."

My fingers clench against Caeo's knee as excitement surges through me. "So you do know how?"

Reid scratches his head and sighs. "Like I said, I have a theory, but I don't think it'd help if I told you—you wouldn't be sincere. You'll just have to figure it out yourself."

"Sincere? What do you mean?" I look to Caeo, and he shrugs, so I turn back to Reid with a frown. "Did you ask the Land?"

"No, I didn't. Trying to figure it out will only send you in the wrong direction, so stop. If it happens, it happens, and then I can explain it to you if you still haven't figured it out."

"But you'll explain it to us, right?" Owena's voice.

I glance toward the source to find Taran holding Owena's hand as she gracefully lowers herself to the ground, so smoothly it's as if her legs melted away beneath her rose-colored gown. Taran drops down next to her like a box of rocks.

We're all here now.

For the first time, really, as hard as that is to believe. And who knows when it will ever happen again?

"Yeah, of course," Reid says. "After they leave."

The fire crackles with a burst of sparks, briefly illuminating everyone in the darkening night. Burning tears collect behind my eyes, and Caeo takes my hand.

"It's alright, Ellie. We've got plenty of time to figure it out."

"No, it's not that." I wipe my eyes. "I'm just realizing how much I'll miss everyone."

"Even me?" Emlyn asks.

I chuckle. "Yes, even you. Why wouldn't I?"

He shrugs. "Because I don't—"

Reid covers his mouth with his hand. "Not an appropriate time, Em."

My brow furrows, then I sniff back some of my tears. *What was he going to say?*

Owena leans forward, the firelight dancing warmly across her face. "I will certainly miss you. We wouldn't have been able to do any of this without you."

I shake my head. "That's not true. I hardly did anything."

"You saved mine and Emlyn's lives," Taran says.

Owena nods. "And while you may not realize it, you lent each of us your strength when we needed it most. I, for one, would not have made it this far without it."

Caeo wraps his arm around me. "Me neither, Ellie. You're the strongest of all of us."

My heart could burst out of my chest right now. I can't say anything, because if I did, I'd start crying. All I can do is smile as I meet Caeo's beautiful blue eyes, full of devotion.

"If that's the case, she was only here because I did all the hard work of keeping her and Caeo together, so technically, I stopped the war."

Reid's comment makes me laugh, pulling me from my dalliance in Caeo's gaze.

"You could only do that because I pointed the curse out to you," Emlyn says, stretching his legs out as he leans into Reid. "And if I hadn't told Taran about it, he never would've come up with his stupid plan."

"Stupid plan?" Taran asks.

"It was a stupid plan. The worst. It got me killed, remember?"

"Didn't you use a similar plan to kill my mother?"

"The circumstances were very different. Details are important, Taran."

I snuggle into Caeo's side as the argument about who stopped the war continues, with Owena joining in, making points both for and against Taran. By the end, Emlyn seems to have made the best case for himself, though that may only be because everyone else grew tired of debating it.

It's clear that we all played a part, and despite the awful, tangled mess of it, we came out for the better. There's still so much to do before balance can truly be restored, so much healing that still needs to be done. But even if we're apart, we'll all be working toward it.

Together.

Epilogue

Ceirios

I haven't seen my son in three years.

It's disappointing, but not surprising. Before he showed up nearly dead at my door, it'd been four since his last visit.

At least this time I knew he had someone, even if that someone's a mortal. In some ways, it makes sense—my son, who's never shown any interest in committing to anyone, latching on to someone who won't even last a century. It's as if he decided to test out a devoted relationship while being guaranteed he could someday return to his promiscuous ways.

Then a messenger arrived, inviting me to his wedding. I thought they were confusing me with some other Emlyn's mother.

So here I am, in Aedallan, as a guest of honor. It's no longer the capital, but will always be Taran's home, so he and his queen spend a significant amount of time here. It's a slow process to make their more centralized capital anywhere near as grand, so for now, most of the court resides either here or in Ywelyn.

As I wait to announce myself to the guard at the gate, I spot Aerona heading over, her lively, auburn curls impossible to miss.

"You shouldn't be waiting," she says, wrapping her arms around me in a hug. She's taller than me now, no longer the child always finding trouble with Taran and Emlyn. "You're the mother of the groom."

"Tell that to him."

She laughs, then pulls me past the guard and into the palace grounds. They're surprisingly empty, lacking the merriment typically found at weddings.

"Where are all the other guests?" I ask.

Aerona's jaw tightens. "There aren't many. While no one openly contests Reid's place at court, few support a union between mortal and fae." She glances my way, her lips twisting into a smirk. "Besides, it'd probably be awkward to have a wedding where the groom's slept with two-thirds of the attendees."

She leads me to the throne room, excusing herself before I enter. Despite living in the palace for several years, my breath still catches at its beauty. Sunlight pours in from hundreds of tiny windows, reflecting off the golden antlers inlaid on the walls and floor. The last time I was here, probably sixteen years ago, only one throne sat upon the dais.

Now there's two. Queen Owena sits in one, as majestic as always—except for the first time I met her, sitting in the grass outside my house, desperate for food. She's deep in conversation with the occupant of the other: the mortal woman I met briefly that same day, years ago.

Rumors abound that our king and queen's marriage is tumultuous, but unlike Emlyn, Taran does escape to visit on occasion. While he's certainly stressed, whenever I ask about Owena, his love for her rinses the tension from his face, his eyes warming with a tender glow.

She glances up at my approach, alight with a smile. I drop into a curtsy.

"No need for that, Ceirios." Owena walks toward me, taking my hands. "You're family." She glances back at the young woman. "You remember Ellie, don't you? She's visiting from Lyndir, and is my sister now—at least by mortal laws."

"It'll be that way for a while," Ellie says, standing. While the moments our paths crossed years ago were during an arduous time, to put it mildly, she looks more worn-down than she did then, her pale skin shadowed beneath her eyes. "Caeo still isn't keen on fae weddings. We'll be skipping the ceremony itself."

"Are you certain?" Owena asks. "You may not get another chance to witness one."

Ellie's face flushes pink. "I'm sure. I don't really want to watch Reid and Emlyn... doing that."

I hold back a chuckle. Mortals and their modesty. Emlyn always made sure I was well out of his land-sense for Reid's sake.

"Speaking of my son, I'd like to see him before. I doubt he'll make any time for me after." I wish things were different, but that's just who he is. His father was the same—indifferent to most people's feelings but completely devoted to me. In that respect, perhaps this marriage will last.

Owena smiles. "Of course. He's in Taran's old room, getting ready. Reid's in the one you used to share with Emlyn, if you'd like to visit him, too."

That's not a bad idea.

It's strange to be back in the palace after all these years. Memories echo along the stairs and through the halls of rowdy children, now long grown. I couldn't be prouder of Emlyn and Taran, or happier for them.

I almost walk straight into my old room, remembering to knock at the last moment. The door opens to an adolescent Taran standing before me.

I blink in surprise.

No. This is Taran's brother, Caeo. I saw even less of him than I did Ellie three years ago, but it's striking how similar they look.

His mouth quirks. "Emlyn's mom, right?"

"Yes. I came to see Reid."

"Yep, he's here." Caeo steps aside, letting me in.

He closes the door behind me, then plops on the bed next to the groom's wedding attire, laid out upon it. Reid paces through the room, his face full of nerves as he glances at me.

"Ceirios," he says, pausing. "Hi." His brown hair's longer than when I last saw him, hanging past his chin.

"I just wanted to say hello before the ceremony." I move closer, taking his hands. "You look nervous."

"I am. But not about marrying Emlyn. Just the process." He averts his gaze. "The..."

"The drinking his blood and public fucking?" Caeo offers.

Reid glares at him. "Not helping."

I squeeze his fingers tightly. "Don't think about that. Ignore everyone else, just focus on him. It should be easy, since..."

My words trail off as I find myself unable to complete the sentence.

"Since what?" Reid asks.

My eyebrows knit together. I was going to say, since he doesn't have any land-sense. But he must, or I would've been able to finish.

How is that possible?

I press my face into a smile. "Never mind. Just pretend it's only the two of you, and everything will be fine."

He nods, letting out a heavy exhale.

"I should go check on him," I say, releasing his hands. "Will you be alright?"

Caeo comes over, wrapping his arm around Reid's shoulders. "Don't worry, I'll make sure he shows up."

Reid elbows him in the side. "I will be. Thanks for coming."

I let myself out, then make my way to my son. It's only a few doors down, since I needed to be close to Taran when I lived here as his governess.

"Three years, and you didn't even invite me to your wedding?" I ask upon entering the room, crossing my arms.

Emlyn's eyes flick over to me from where he lies on the bed, tossing an apple into the air. "What are you talking about? You're here, you were invited."

"By Taran. Not you." As much as I try to match his levity, to not pressure him into being someone he's not, it still hurts.

"So you're a guest of the king. Isn't that better?"

I glance at Taran, leaning against the wall. He rolls his eyes, then crosses the room to give me a hug.

"It's nice to see you," he says, kissing my cheek.

"What happened to his fasting and isolation?" I ask. It's understandable for Reid not to follow tradition, but Emlyn has no excuse.

Taran sighs. "You know him."

"Hey, if our king didn't do any of that, then I shouldn't have to, either." Emlyn takes a bite of the apple, then sets it aside. "Did you come here just to give me a hard time? Maybe that's why I didn't invite you."

"I wouldn't be giving you a hard time if you had." I approach the bed and stare at him expectantly.

He closes his eyes, then exhales before dragging himself up. "Thanks for coming, Ma." He wraps his arm around me in a lazy half-hug.

I squeeze him before he can escape. "You're sure about this?" I ask, keeping my voice low. If Reid truly does have land-sense, this marriage could be a longer commitment than he thought.

Emlyn pulls away, pointing his finger at me. "There. That's why

I didn't invite you."

I search my son's eyes. Behind his flippancy, the truth flickers.

He knows.

"You're right, I'm sorry," I say, patting his shoulders. "That was out of place."

He glances at Taran. "You heard that, right? I'm not going crazy?"

I lean in to kiss his cheek. "You're not. And I am happy for you. I just hope the two of you will visit more often."

Emlyn sighs. "Maybe. But no promises."

We're cut off by Taran clapping him on the back. "Sorry to interrupt, but you have a wedding to get to."

Emlyn blinks a few times, then bounces on his toes. "Yes. Mine. So if you don't mind, I'll be going now." He rushes out the door before I can respond.

Taran rests his hand on my arm before he follows. "I'll see you there."

With them both gone, I sit on the edge of the bed, taking a moment to calm my heart. My son is getting married today, and despite my worries, both of my boys are happy.

I couldn't ask for anything more.

Acknowledgments

SOMEHOW, I wrote two books in a year. Crazy, right? But the only reason it happened was because my friend Meredith complimented some writing of mine she'd read years ago, which gave me the confidence to write the story you just finished.

I once again have to thank Marley for your unwavering support as this story consumed my life during the last year, and Rae—my first reader, first fan, and biggest cheerleader. While this book didn't go through as much critique as the first one, I only became the writer I am today through the help of everyone on Critique Circle who provided feedback on both.

I'm forever blessed to have found my editor, Lindsey, who helped me get all the character development to the state you've all enjoyed, and suggested other improvements that I grumbled about until finally agreeing they were the right call.

Thank you to all my beta readers who helped make the book better with your feedback. Two in particular gave me some late-stage notes that hopefully improved the experience for all of you: Chris Redd and Victoria Szalay.

Finally, thanks to everyone in my author's group who helped support my journey into self-publishing.

More from Briella Brezzo

Their Tangled Fates: Tangled and True Duology Book 1

For free bonus content, the latest information on release dates, and opportunities to join ARC and beta reading teams, subscribe to my mailing list at www.briellabrezzo.com

If you enjoyed *Their Tattered Truths*, reviews can help other readers find it! Thank you for supporting indie authors!